Praise for *Rebel Seoul*

"Oh deftly weaves a high tech world contrasted with the old and traditional. *Rebel Seoul*'s nonstop action is underscored by deeper themes of loyalty, love in all its forms, and the family we have and the family we choose. A thrilling and wonderfully layered debut."
—**CINDY PON**, author of *WANT* and *Serpentine*

"Warning! Don't start this book unless you have time to finish it in one sitting because you will not want to put it down! I read this book as fast as I could just so I could read it all over again! This is a heart pounding, wild action packed adventure with characters that you will fall in love with and that stay with you long after you've finished the book. It is one of the most vivid books I've read in a long time— it literally played like a movie in my head. Stunning."
—**ELLEN OH**, author of *Spirit Hunters*, founder and president of We Need Diverse Books

"*Rebel Seoul* is a stunning debut and a haunting read. Axie Oh will steal your heart with her deft prose and unforgettable characters. I couldn't put this book down. Don't miss it."
—**ANN AGUIRRE**, *New York Times*-bestselling author of *Enclave*

"Open the cover of *Rebel Seoul* and you'll enter the thrilling worlds of Old Seoul and Neo Seoul, where the lines between humanity and technology blur, oppression and treachery are ever-present, and battles are fought in the coolest giant robots in YA literature today. I was mesmerized from start to finish. Look alive, world, here comes Axie Oh."
—**MIKE JUNG**, author of *Unidentified Suburban Object*

REBEL

SEOUL

AXIE OH

TU BOOKS
AN IMPRINT OF LEE & LOW BOOKS INC.
NEW YORK

Copyright © 2017 by Axie Oh
Jacket illustration copyright © 2017 by Sebastien Hue

TU BOOKS, an imprint of LEE & LOW BOOKS Inc., 95 Madison Avenue, New York, NY 10016
leeandlow.com

Manufactured in the United States of America by Worzalla Publishing Company, September 2017

Book design by Elizabeth Casal
Book production by The Kids at Our House
The text is set in Granjon

10 9 8 7 6 5 4 3 2 1
First Edition

Cataloging-in-Publication Data is on file with the Library of Congress

FOR JASON

REBEL SEOUL

NEO SEOUL

The Tower's searchlight circles the Gangnam district of Neo Seoul at a uniform rate. At the center of the district, a band calling itself C'est La Vie gives a regulated concert: four guys on lead guitar, bass, keyboard, and drums; one girl on voice.

The light is yellow as it searches the grassy park where the concert's being held, yellow as it searches the food and promotion carts forming a broken wall between the park and the blue-lit streets of the Grid. It rests for a moment at the front of the stage, fake sunlight in the night, illuminating pale faces in the crowd.

Suddenly, the searchlight turns from yellow to red, a jarring, hitch-in-the-breath switch. It's a warning.

Twenty minutes until midnight. Twenty minutes until the

trains stop in the sky, until the magnet of the Grid shuts down, until the Dome closes. Twenty minutes until curfew.

Red. The color of fear. It makes everyone look harsh and inhuman, bloody and faceless. And then it's gone. The light passes. It moves on to the rest of the district.

Nobody at the concert seems to notice its arrival and departure.

Nobody but me.

I reach into my pocket and pull out a couple of square pills, popping them quick. Bright lights give me headaches, loud noises irritate me, but I have only myself to blame. I've been to concerts before.

There's a momentary lull after the last set, enough time for the Tower light to sweep over the crowd. The lead singer of C'est La Vie, her heart-shaped face enlarged on the holo-screens behind her, lifts her microphone to her pink-stained mouth. I can see the puffs of breath that fall from her lips. No instruments accompany her, not for these first words, spoken as if they're her last.

"Please tell me," she sings, "Please tell me why people hurt one another."

A bitterness creeps through me, familiar and irritating. "Such is life," I mutter.

I lean my shoulder against a nearby food cart, feeling the coldness of the steel through the thin fabric of my shirt. I had a coat tonight, but lost it sometime between the beginning of the first set and this last one, to a girl with soft lips. She traded a kiss for warmth. I can't say the same for me.

My phone chirps in my pocket, and I take it out. The number fifteen flashes red across the screen.

Fifteen minutes until midnight. Fifteen minutes until curfew.

I haven't forgotten. I wouldn't forget something like that.

I glance to my right. Civilian cars are lined up on the back streets of the Grid, waiting to zip concertgoers safely away to the residential areas of Neo Seoul, to the skyscrapers full of the loving parents who will welcome them home.

Open doors.

Open arms.

Fourteen minutes, forty-two seconds until curfew.

It takes a little less than ten minutes to reach the nearest bridge, which means I have four minutes, forty-two seconds before I have to leave.

My sneakers squish against the wet grass as I step away from the cart. Something sticky attaches to the sole of my shoe—a discarded piece of gum. I sigh and lean down to pluck it off.

I hear another squelch. The toes of two studded boots enter my line of vision. I straighten and pocket the gum. Trash receptacles get taken away every night at 2200, and fines for littering go up fifteen percent after they're gone.

"Ay, Lee Jaewon, that's disgusting," Bora says, her voice light and cheerful. She checks beneath her high-heeled boots to see if she's suffered the same fate.

She hasn't.

"I just saw a girl in the crowd wearing your coat. Daebak!

You work fast. I'd say color me impressed, 'cept you'll probably die from a chill."

Tonight Bora wears a heavy coat entirely of blue feathers that puff out, making her small torso appear larger. The coat falls to mid-thigh, accentuating her long legs, poorly protected from the cold by a pair of black tights. She adjusts her wig—one that I haven't seen before, black with dark blue streaks. Shiny stars pasted over the rims of her cheeks flash silver as she smiles.

Bora's last accessory is Minwoo, his own ruddy cheeks pasted with stickers of hearts and diamonds. His mop of curly hair falls across eyes hidden behind dark sunglasses. Bora's got a strong hold on Minwoo's sleeve, and I can see the seams of his sweater breaking at the shoulder.

"She's so cute!" Minwoo yells, trying to make himself heard over the music. It's been gradually picking up instruments as it gains momentum.

I nod at Minwoo's compliment, thinking he's speaking about Bora.

"Really," he continues, "if Sela were my girlfriend, I'd just die from happiness." Minwoo grabs a handful of fabric at the front of his sweater and rubs the area in a circular motion, as if pained. "And her name. It's the prettiest thing I've ever heard."

Bora releases him in disgust. Minwoo stumbles, clearly intoxicated, and falls to the grass.

"It's her stage name," Bora says, rolling her eyes. "Her band is called C'est La Vie. It's, like, French or whatever. She's just called Sela 'cause she's the lead singer and it rolls off the tongue."

"Don't belittle my goddess!" Minwoo shouts from the ground.

I listen as the instruments drop, one by one. Now it's only the singer, her voice somehow quiet even with the microphone pressed against her lips. "Please tell me. Why do people hurt one another? Why do people kill one another?"

"This song is depressing," I say.

"No, it's not!" Minwoo jumps off the ground, surprisingly nimble, and grabs me by the front of my shirt. "It's goddamn poetry!"

I shrug him off, along with his alcohol- and cigarette-tinged breath. I gave up smoking two years ago. They don't tolerate the stuff at the academy, not for scholarship students. The pungent tobacco wafting from Minwoo makes me infinitely aware that I'm better off without it.

"Jaewon-ah . . ." Bora takes me by the arm. I glance at her hands circled around my shirt. If she tears it, I really will die from the cold. "You nervous about the new school year? Minwoo says he bribed the members of the school board. We're for sure going to be in the same class again this year."

I nod slowly, somewhat amused. Bribing a group of corrupt old men to get into the same class as your friends. It's a different kind of bribery than that conducted in Old Seoul. In Old Seoul, bribery isn't just about money.

C'est La Vie's song heads into the second chorus, gearing up for its grand finale. Some of the lights in the stage-rafters shatter in a coordinated explosion of pink-and-blue pixie dust. Heavy fans blow the dust into the crowd, and the way people are gulping in the air, I wouldn't be surprised if the band added stimulants to the glitter.

"Song Bora," Minwoo squeals in excitement, "hurry up! We don't want to miss the finale." He rushes back into the crowd, swallowed up on either side as he pushes his way through.

Bora hesitates, glancing back at me. "You coming?"

I shake my head.

She watches me another second. "Okay," she says. "I'll see you tomorrow." She follows Minwoo into the crowd.

I resume leaning against the abandoned food cart. I have about one minute and forty-nine seconds in the park before I'll be forced to leave. Cars registered to the Grid are allowed out later than curfew, but taxis aren't, especially taxis heading for one of the few bridges leading out of the city. I need to be gone before I'm taken in, accused of and convicted for something illogical.

I imagine how it'd go down. They'd ask me why I was out so late—inside the Dome, when my Citizen ID says I should be outside it. I'd say, "I got caught out." I'd say, "I'll call a friend." They'd tell me I was out late planning something treasonous against the state. I'd say, "Bullshit." They'd put me in prison.

When I walk away from the cart, I watch where I step. The grass, coated with a combination of rainfall, melted sugar, and glitter, sticks to my shoe.

I check the time once more: one minute, twenty-seven seconds.

I'm heading out to the main streets when I see someone.

A girl.

The lights of the stage only reach so far across the grass until it blends to darkness, and that's where she stands, completely still, her eyes riveted on the stage.

I don't know what stops me; maybe it's her stillness. Maybe it's the fact that we're the only ones not packed in front of the stage. We're a couple meters out, nothing around us but abandoned food carts and grass, and the blue-lit streets of the Grid behind her.

I've seen girls like her before, middling height with long black hair, some falling over her shoulders. She wears a loose, long-sleeved gray shirt and pants of the same color. And yet there's something arresting about her—the way she stands, as if she'd run across the city and just arrived, her chest moving slightly as she breathes; the way she hasn't blinked since I first laid eyes on her.

She takes one step and she's in the light.

The look in her eyes is fierce and warm and full of longing.

I inhale sharply and feel the cold sweep through my mouth.

I have exactly one minute left before I have to leave. I can talk to a girl in a minute.

I take another step, smoothing my shirt over my stomach, and a shattering of wind blows me back. A police droid descends from overhead, a shaft of light issuing from its projectors and exposing the girl. She doesn't even glance up. Nor does she blink when airborne police trucks slide onto the grass, leaving the organized streets of the Grid, their sirens raging red like the searchlight of the Tower. Each truck releases four soldiers carrying standard-issue electro-guns, their sighting-lights trained on the girl. She's covered with a dozen neon red dots all focused on fatal parts of the body—her long neck, her pale forehead, her beating heart.

Her eyes never leave the stage as the soldiers drag her away, and when they jolt her with the electro-gun, her eyes remain open, only the fluttering of her lashes showing she felt it at all.

Through the whirring noises of the droid's engines and the wailing sirens of the police trucks, Sela breathes the last words of her song.

"Even if I've never heard you, I hear you. Even if I've never seen you, I see you. Even if I've never known you, I miss you. I wait for you, my love, my land of the morning calm."

Something about the words makes me flinch.

I watch as the soldiers drag the girl's limp body off the grass and into one of the trucks.

They're gone in under a minute.

A cheer goes up behind me, and I quickly turn around. The members of C'est La Vie are bowing on the stage. The small figure of the lead singer blows kisses into the crowd with a bubble blower. Blue and pink roses fall at her feet, and a chant rises up out of the tumult.

"Sela! Sela! Sela!"

Nobody seems to have seen the police take the girl. And if they had, they wouldn't care.

She's just another lost soul in the city of Neo Seoul.

The city of tomorrow's dreams.

I have zero minutes and zero seconds until I have to leave.

There's a feeling in my chest that feels something like disgust, but whether for the police or the crowd or myself, I can't tell.

I walk onto the street and call over a cab. I open the back door, then slide into the soft interior. It smells faintly of smoke. "Can you take me across the nearest bridge?" I ask the driver.

I wait, expecting him to charge me extra—it's almost midnight, after all—but he just nods.

I cross the Han River from Neo Seoul into Old Seoul with three minutes, thirty-eight seconds to spare. I don't wait to see the Dome solidifying as it closes behind me.

Midnight shuts the old from the new.

02
OLD SEOUL

"Ajeossi," I say, looking at the cab meter and pulling out what I owe, "I'm getting off here."

The driver stops the cab and stares at me in the rearview mirror. "In the middle of Banpo Bridge?" he asks. "I can take you the whole way."

I give the old man the money, my right hand already against the handle of the cab door. "I want to get off here."

"I won't charge you," he says.

I meet his eyes in the mirror. "Thank you, but I'm going to walk."

Seconds pass before the old man nods, turning to take the money from my hand. I open the door.

"This bridge is famous," he says softly, his voice gravelly with age.

I fight the urge to leave the cab, but only a punk skips out when an ajeossi is speaking to him. "It is," I agree. "It connects North and South Seoul, Old and Neo Seoul."

Everyone knows this.

"That's right. It's a connector," he says, "but it's also a divider. You could think of it as a symbol, of how our world is divided. North of the Hangang and South of the Hangang. Old and New."

I wait for him to finish speaking.

"I've only had one person ask me to stop in the middle of this bridge. A young woman. Right after the Second Act of the Great War. She'd asked me to stop here. She said she was going to walk the rest of the way. I told her what I'd told you, that I'd take her to the end, but she insisted. Her last words to me: 'I want to see the river.' I left her here, and in the morning, I saw the news."

I tighten my hand on the door handle. "I'm not going to jump."

"You wouldn't, would you? How badly I want to believe you."

I sigh and lean back against the seat. "It's four minutes past midnight," I say. "You have a place to stay?"

The Dome, non-corporeal during the day, solidifies at midnight, allowing entry only at certain military checkpoints.

The ajeossi looks to the digital clock on his dashboard. "Ah, so it is. I guess I'll have to stay in Old Seoul tonight."

"I'm sorry," I say. I'm the reason he's been caught out.

"No, no. This has been good for my state of mind. But thank you for your concern. You're a good kid. Let's just say tonight I'm full of irrational worries, and you're full of rational ones."

I nod, stepping out of the cab. It takes the ajeossi a few

minutes, but finally he drives the rest of the way down the bridge.

I watch until he's disappeared from sight before I approach the railing.

I want to see the river. The last words of a dead girl.

I can understand the feeling. I hadn't been thinking of jumping, but now it's all I can think about. How cold would the water be? The air brims with moisture from the river. In the middle of the bridge, it's silent. What would stop a person from jumping?

Family? I have none.

Friends? A face comes to mind, and I shake my head, dispelling the image.

What did that girl think before she jumped? She'd have looked out at the river and seen to the right, modernized, Neo Seoul—high on Tech. To the left, Old Seoul. Which did she call home? Both halves of the city cast trails of colored lights along the river's edges—orange, purple, white. From the distance, they look like miniature waterfalls. The colors sink into the river, disappearing into the darkness.

I curl my hands around the banister. "Ay," I mutter to the night, "I wouldn't have thought of jumping if you hadn't said anything."

■ ■ ■

I'm almost at the end of the bridge when my phone vibrates in my pocket.

INCOMING CALL → ALEX KIM flashes green across the screen.

I slide my thumb along the arrow, lifting the phone to my ear.

"You forgot." Alex's deep voice resonates through the speaker. Not accusative, just bored. I imagine him calling me from his penthouse in Neo Seoul, a wealth of Tech and modern furniture surrounding him.

I reach the end of the bridge, the smooth cement turning to a broken, unkempt road. I scuff my sneaker against the gravel, dislodging a rock that skitters across the ground. "I haven't."

I've put off his request until the night before the tests, but I haven't forgotten. Seniors in Neo Seoul are required to take tests to determine where they'll serve their mandatory military quotas, whether as officers in the armed forces or as engineers or in safer, cushier jobs in the realm of politics. Alex Kim had approached me at the end of last year with a request for a special kind of Enhancer, something that would give him an edge in the tests, but also keep it from detection in case of a blood analysis. He figured I'm from Old Seoul; if anyone could get him the illegal drug, it would be me.

"Can you get through the gates with the Enhancer," Alex asks, "or do you need me to meet you before school?"

"I can get through."

Alex is quiet for a moment, and I wonder if he's hung up, but then he says, "I still want you on my team for the senior tests. Think about it. You won't have a better offer."

"I'm hanging up," I say, and hang up.

He's right. I won't have a better offer. But I know any test he's taking will be at a high level with more risks, and it's just not worth it. Maybe if I had more ambition than getting out of Old Seoul . . .

But I don't.

I pocket my phone and approach the end of the bridge. I smell the food cart before I see it. Every week, I pay the ajumma manning the cart five thousand won for watching my motorbike. It's beat-up, but it gets me to my part-time jobs—grocery delivery and late-night Tech support.

Tonight, only a metalworker stands beneath the tarp roof of the food cart, one hand in his pocket, the other holding a stick of steaming odeng. He bites the fish cake off the stick and reaches for another, the pile of sticks kept warm in a shallow vat of hot broth. Two pots of ramyeon boil on a makeshift stove behind the cart, their lids rattling against the metal rims of their bowls.

"Ye-ya!" the ajumma yells from behind the cart, ducking beneath the tarp to stand in front of me. She's half my height. I lean forward, trying to level our eyes. It's almost like a bow, which seems to please her. "You owe me for the week," she chides.

I nod.

"And even a little extra for the copper pot."

I frown. "What copper pot?"

She pulls a pot out from behind her back, holding it by the handle. A huge dent mars the metal. "I stopped a thief," she says, lifting her chin.

Food cart pots are flimsy and cheap, used mainly for boiling and serving ramyeon, but . . .

"That must have hurt."

A wicked smile plays along her lips. "He won't be coming back."

I grin and straighten my back. I pull my wallet out of my pocket, my grin turning into a grimace at the low count of browns and blues. I take out what I do have and place it all onto her rough palms.

A wave of guilt passes over her lined face, and the ajumma tries to give me back half of what I gave her. I take the bills from her hands and sweep around her, stuffing them deep in the pocket of her ratty coat. She protests, then stops when she catches my grin.

"Jaewon-ah," she says, patting my back. "Good kid." She grabs some sticks of odeng out of one of the vats of boiling water, wraps them up in paper towels, and hands them to me.

I bow and take them with both hands. I'm a fast eater, and they're tucked away quick—warmth in my stomach. But by the time I'm done, the ajumma's left and returned. She holds the keys to my motorbike along with a black fleece-lined jacket.

"For my future son-in-law," she says.

I smile, taking the keys and turn to let her help me shrug into the jacket. It's warm. I zip it all the way up. "But you have only one daughter, and she's married."

The ajumma scowls. "Don't remind me. You're much prettier than the man she married."

I shake my head, retrieving my helmet and antipollution mask from the back of my motorbike. "Every time you mention your daughter, you make me depressed. I can't have her as a wife. I can't have you as a wife . . ."

"Ay," she says, swatting playfully at my head.

I duck away and get onto my motorbike, revving the engine. I don the mask, clip the helmet beneath my chin, and give the ajumma a thumbs-up before sliding the bike onto the streets of Old Seoul.

YOUNG

There are a few motorbikes and cabs out at this late hour, none following the color-coded rules of the traffic lights. I pass buildings with boarded-up doors and shuttered windows seeping broken light onto the battered sidewalk. Neon signs missing the fluorescence in most of their lettering flicker, ghostlike, down the empty streets. I pull my mask higher over my nose to block out the smell of smoke.

It's a quarter to one by the time I reach the main road outside Hongdae, the area surrounding the old Hongik University. The Kings, the local gang, have built a barricade to bar trespassers—a haphazard pileup of trucks, furniture, motorbikes, and even a tank, the barrel of its gun facing outward. There's a wooden plank that runs over the barricade, probably placed there and forgotten by a group of rabble-rousers.

Lining up my wheels for the jump, I rev my engine. I accelerate up the ramp and hit the air. A shattering of wind blasts my face. The bike comes down hard in the middle of a packed street, skidding to a halt before a stalled car.

Across the barricade, it's like entering sinsegye, a whole new world filled with people laughing, flirting, yelling.

Mostly at me. My entrance pissed off a good number of them.

I move my motorbike through the traffic, edging around a raucous crowd surrounding an impromptu b-boy battle near the Playground. Farther down the street, neon-lit stairs descend into colored darkness, smoke billowing out like exhaust from an engine.

I find a space for my motorbike beside a NO PARKING sign and drop the kickstand. The low building beside the sign is a noraebang. Its patrons' out-of-tune, drunken singing spills out onto the street. I recognize the butchered song from the concert, one of C'est La Vie's less depressing numbers.

I walk through the alley next to the noraebang, grimacing at the strong smells of sewage and garbage. I keep to the shadows, stopping when I reach the end.

Beyond the alley, there's a street lined with brightly lit buildings. One building takes up the most space, a bar and restaurant with a line extending out the door. Loud music issues from the bar in a language I don't recognize. Girls and boys sit at the curb, sharing cigarettes.

A side door of the restaurant opens, and a man steps through. Park Taesung.

He has a red moon stitched to the lapel of his suit, the

symbol of the most influential gang in Old Seoul. Deep crow's-feet branch out from the corners of his eyes. It's a trick. If he's ever smiled, it's never been for anything pleasant.

As if sensing my gaze, he swings his head in my direction. Quickly I step back, letting the shadows in the alley shield me in darkness.

The last time I'd seen Park Taesung, he'd been breaking me, the steel of his shoes finding the same place beneath my ribs over and over again. Hours after the incident, I'd had to wrap my chest and wash the dirt from the open wounds on my face in the silence of my apartment.

And the whole time, I'd had to remember the moment when Young had chosen obedience to Park Taesung over his friendship with me.

That was two years ago.

The familiar burn of resentment rushes through me, and I try to control it, my vision filtering in and out, tunneled on Red Moon's boss. Whether he sees me or not, the corners of his lips lift in a cruel smile. With a short, biting laugh that travels across the street, he enters a black car parked along the curb.

I don't watch him leave.

Leaning back against the wall, I breathe in the rotten sewage of the alleyway. The vapor forming in every breath I exhale is a reminder. It's cold outside. It's always cold.

Memories flood my mind. The memories are not in the shape of moments, but colors. Red, for a memory of pain. Red, for a memory of betrayal.

Blue, for a memory of lightness.

This last—it hurts the most.

"Lee Jaewon?"

I open my eyes.

Two guys stand on the street outside the alley, watching me intently. Jeon Daeho and Ro Jinwoon.

"Ah, it is you." The hood of Daeho's sweatshirt is up. He has his fist against his mouth as he speaks, muffling his words. "You look different. Taller."

Jinwoon presses his shoulder against the opposite wall—a comfortable stance, nonthreatening. Like Daeho, Jinwoon is dressed casually, in an old leather jacket.

"Lee Jaewon," Jinwoon says, his voice deeper than Daeho's. "You here to see Park Young?"

"Yeah, is he in?"

"Mhm," Jinwoon says in the affirmative.

I wait.

Neither of them moves.

"Lee Jaewon," Daeho says, taking his fist away from his mouth, "Young said you were never coming back."

I flinch. "I'm not coming back to the gang. I've left for good. I just came to speak with Young. I don't want trouble. Just tell him I'm here."

"He knows you're here," Jinwoon says. "He was told the moment you'd entered Hongdae."

"He's waiting for you on the roof," Daeho adds, gesturing with his thumb over his shoulder toward the restaurant. Having apparently delivered his message, Daeho stuffs his hands into the pockets of his pants and shuffles away.

Jinwoon remains near, kicking his shoe against a loose rock. When he doesn't say anything, I move to pass him.

"Jaewon-ah," he says, just as our shoulders brush, "don't be cruel. Young isn't strong, not like you are."

My response is quiet. "Park Young's a boss. He's stronger than he looks. And I've come to ask him for a favor. I'm not going to hurt him."

Jinwoon meets my gaze. "You're the only person who's ever hurt him."

Reaching out, I grab Jinwoon by the collar and jam him against the wall. "Don't you dare say that to me," I growl. "He was the bastard who betrayed me!"

My voice cracks on my words, and I drop Jinwoon, hands trembling. I stumble backward, wondering if I should leave, take my motorbike, and never look back. I could be gone from here. Screw Alex and his Enhancer. I'll get the money for my academy tuition some other way—take up more after-school jobs. Or just quit school entirely.

I press my palms against my temples until all I feel is the pressure.

How did it become like this? I joined Red Moon when I was eight after my parents abandoned me to the streets. I was forced out at sixteen by the gang brothers I trusted the most. Old Seoul has only brought me heartbreak—I want to leave it all behind. If I can just hold onto my academy scholarship, Neo Seoul will give me a future.

I push past Jinwoon, cross the street, and enter through the same door Park Taesung had exited.

Inside is a red-lit hallway, the subdued noises of the restaurant issuing from double doors to the right. I walk past the lowTech elevators on the left, heading through a door at the back with a blue EXIT sign glowing above it.

There are five flights of stairs to the roof, and I take them fast, hand sliding against the banister as I round each corner. The door at the top is already open, the cold wind pushing against me as I step through.

Young stands at the edge of the rooftop.

He's grown since middle school—the first thing I notice. If he were to stand beside me, he'd be as tall as me. Not like when we were young. Then, he'd been half a head shorter. I'd always teased him about it, saying that the girls he liked in school always liked me better because I was taller.

"Young-ah, don't you know that in our society height equals attractiveness?"

"You saying I'm not attractive? Look at this face. I'm beautiful like a flower."

"Saekki. Are you kidding me?"

"I'm always kidding you. I'll be kidding you till the day I die, and a day after, too."

"Lee Jaewon." Young's voice pulls me out of my memories. "It's been awhile."

He wears a thick black sweater, a gold crown pinned crooked at the collar. He removes the cap he's wearing and places it on the ledge behind him. Without its shadow covering his eyes, he looks younger, his black hair sticking out in all directions.

22

He looks familiar.

I turn from him, studying the graffiti on the roof walls. An artist has drawn a garden along the whole interior, giving brightness to the otherwise dull gray cement. Alongside the flowers are messages from Young's gang brothers: *Hyeong, I love you! Hyeongnim, you're the best! Hyeong, I believe in you. Take care of me until the very end!*

I linger on this last message.

I remind myself why this pain is bearable.

I may be alone in this world, but Young isn't. He has Daeho and Jinwoon. He's the seventh of the Seven Kings, a new position, only six months old, but gaining recognition among the smaller gangs outside Red Moon. People surround him. It'd be better to think they're forced to love him—he's their boss—but I know it's not like that, not for him. It'd be natural for them to want to follow a guy like Young. He's hot-headed and brave, smart and . . .

Loyal.

"What did you need?" Young asks, his voice tired. "Tell me what you need, and I'll get it for you."

I turn from the wall. "I need an Enhancer. One that won't be identified on a blood analysis."

He squints, his hand whitening as he grips the pavement of the ledge. "Why?"

"Alex wants it for our senior placement test tomorrow."

He nods slowly. "Alex wants it . . ."

"Alex Kim. The Director's son."

"I know who he is." Young rubs his jaw. He watches me

carefully, his frustration evident in the way his eyes narrow. "I just . . ." He takes his hand away from the pavement and runs it messily through his hair. "It's not for you, is it?"

"I said it was for Alex."

I wouldn't use an Enhancer. The effects are unpredictable, temporary, and the side effects are painful—headaches, vomiting, hallucinations. Even if it makes you stronger, smarter in the moment, it makes you weak for days afterward, your body rejecting the enhancements.

Young takes his phone out of his pocket, speaking low.

Several minutes of silence pass before a voice calls from the doorway. "Hyeongnim?" It's a kid, a silver crown pinned to his shirt. He holds the Enhancer—a plastic tube shaped like an L.

"Thanks, Dongwoo-yah," Young says, waving the kid over and taking the Enhancer from him.

Once Dongwoo leaves, Young holds the Enhancer out to me. "If you get caught with this, you'll get expelled, maybe even imprisoned."

I take the drug from him and put it in my pocket. "I won't get caught."

"You've done well in your school. Don't mess it up now."

I raise an eyebrow. I've done awful at school. Years of accumulated street knowledge don't add up to years of academic excellence. Only my high simTech ranking keeps me enrolled. But to Young, I guess staying in school would be considered doing well.

"I won't."

"Do you trust Alex?"

"I don't trust anyone."

Young scowls, crossing his arms. "That's not healthy."

"Are we done?" I turn my back to him and head toward the stairway.

"Your father's ten-year memorial is in three weeks."

I stop, my heart pounding. *Park Young, we'd been doing so well. Talking about safe things.*

"Your father was like a father to me. He was a good man. He deserves a proper ceremony. At least once. From you."

My voice comes out quiet, distant. "Do you go to the site of his death every year?"

"I do."

"Do you perform the rites of a son to a father who isn't your own?"

Young doesn't respond.

An image comes to my mind of Young standing on the ashen grounds of the old medTech buildings in Incheon, bowing to the ground in memory of my father—like a dutiful son.

"You can have him," I whisper. "You can have my father. You can have your father. You can have it all. There's nothing in the world you can't have. Just know that I don't care. About him or about you."

"Geojinmal," Young breathes.

Whether I agree or not—whether I'm a liar or not—I'll never admit it. I *have* to say I don't care; otherwise, I'm the most pathetic bastard that has ever lived.

I move blindly toward the doorway, stumbling down the stairs. I cross the street outside and fumble for my keys in the alley. I drop them in a puddle and pick them up again with shaking fingers.

Everything will be okay.

I speed through the blurring streets, heading toward the south side of the Mapo district.

I trudge up the six flights of stairs to my apartment and sink onto my bed, fully dressed. It's cold, but I don't put on the heater, and I don't pull the blankets around me. I do lift my hands and place my palms over my eyes.

It's dark.

But I'll be okay.

04

ALEX

"Wake up, Sleeping Beauty. I'm freezing my ass off out here."

Lifting my arm from my eyes, I blink up at Alex Kim's face. The sunlight behind him casts his features in shadow. He leans over me, two cups of coffee in his hands.

I groan and sit up, grimacing as the icy wind over the rooftop blows against my skin. After an early morning making deliveries for my part-time job, I'd headed over to school earlier to catch some sleep before the welcome assembly. The walls of the roof block out some of the wind, but it's still cold enough that I can't *forget* it's cold.

"Here," Alex says. He hands me one of the steaming paper cups of coffee, probably bought off one of the mobile vending machines on the first floor.

Alex puts his cup down on the concrete slab and takes a

packet of cigarettes from inside his blue uniform jacket. He taps the packet against the center of his palm, and a cigarette slides out. He lights it. Minutes pass as he drags out the smoke. When he's finished, he flicks the carcass to the ground, picks up his coffee cup, and gulps the rest of the liquid down.

I watch as the still-smoking cigarette rolls across the cement, looking like a used bullet shell. The fine for littering outside school property is eighty-eight thousand won; inside, it's one hundred thousand won, four penalty points, and ten laps around the athletics field.

I point to the cigarette. "Are you going to pick that up?"

"Probably not. Have you got the Enhancer?"

I reach into my coat and pull out the Enhancer. There's no one in the courtyard to witness our exchange—we're an hour early—and the drug is wrapped tightly in a paper towel.

Alex takes the Enhancer in one hand and reaches into his jacket with the other. He hands over an envelope full of banknotes. "I'll triple the amount if you join my team for the tests."

I shake my head. "I doubt you're going to take one of the easier simTech tests. Why should I risk my chances at getting a secure placement through an easier test? Even if *you* were to fail a high-level test, you'd still have a second chance at another. I wouldn't."

Alex nods, absently agreeing. He might be a rich, privileged bastard, but at least he knows he is.

"For glory?" he asks, then laughs when he sees my frown. "I have no idea why you'd risk it. I wouldn't, not if I were you.

I'm not going to try to convince you, either, with whatever one uses to convince another, beyond cold cash. I failed debate, much to the chagrin of my politician father."

"You hate pretense."

Alex shrugs. "I know I'll pass the test. It'll just be easier for me to pass it with you as my Runner. You might suck at academics, I'll grant you that, but you're damn good at simulations. What's your record? Five hundred wins, ninety losses?"

"Ninety-five." I lean down to pick his dead cigarette off the floor and drop it into my empty coffee cup. Getting up, I deposit everything into the nearest trash receptacle. "I don't take your offer lightly. I'll think about it."

If anyone were to pass an impossible test, it'd be Alex, whether by his own skills or those purchased from others. He's had two years to determine which of us are good enough to make the cut, who scored highest in our end-of-year exams— in piloting, firearms, infiltration tactics, engineering, and martial arts. I've no doubt he's gathered a formidable team, with or without me.

"You'll think about it," Alex repeats, laughing softly, his voice moving away. I turn to see he's taken my spot on the jut of concrete, his fingers already playing with another cigarette. "You think about it, Lee Jaewon. Nice and slow. Be sure to tell me before the placement tests start in about . . ." He looks at his bare wrist. "One hour, thirty minutes. Or whenever you feel like it."

"Sarcasm doesn't suit you."

"Eh," he says, the cigarette between his lips muffling his words, "something in this world shouldn't."

"Jjajeungna," I mutter, and Alex laughs, amused at my annoyance.

The doors from the rooftop ripple open as I approach them, their sensors catching my body warmth and weight.

The Apgujeong Academy is built like a box in four levels, outdoor courtyards on every level, each ringed with classrooms. I push the door at the nearest corner and head down the stairs.

■ ■ ■

Bora tackles me from behind in the main hall of the academy. "Ya, Lee Jaewon, have you heard?"

I turn to look at her. Bora's usual short hair is no longer hidden beneath a long-haired wig. I ruffle the mop of her hair, and she bats me away.

"Don't you dare," she shouts. "I still need to look presentable for the welcome assembly. I hear there's gonna be some kind of show afterward, like a singer or a band, maybe."

"Did you eat breakfast already?" I place a hand on my stomach. "I'm so hungry."

"Are you even listening to me?" Bora yells. "The assembly's been moved to the outer courtyard to make more room for the performers. *Outside.* In the cold. We're going to all be passively murdered on our first day back."

That sounds . . . unfortunate.

Bora cocks her head to the side, snapping her fingers. "Do you still have your PE clothes in your old locker?"

Before I can answer, she runs off toward our second-year classroom at the back of the school, where we kept our personal effects in assigned lockers. I never bothered to take my PE clothes home before winter break. I grimace at the memory of last year's physical tests, which grew more intense as the year rounded out, obstacle courses in the rain, schoolwide showcases pitting students against one another.

With how much time we spend in simulations, the school puts us through a grueling physical-training regime to keep us in shape. After all, real fighting doesn't take place in virtual reality, but on the battlefield. Our bodies need to be as sharp as our minds.

As the Proselytizer—that masked enemy of the NSK—often says, "Students are the future, and the future needs more weapons."

I check my phone for the time. I have fifteen minutes before we have to be seated for the assembly.

I cut across the hall and make my way to the small snack bar situated beside the closed cafeteria doors, where second- and third-years are crowding the bar. Shelves of packaged foods are situated outside the cashier counter—stacks of packaged ramyeon and assorted snacks, refrigerated shelves of beverages, and a variety of to-go items. I grab a wrapped sandwich and a bottle of water.

There's a line forming directly outside the bar. I wait at the back of the crowd, wondering if I should pick up anything else. Is it too early in the morning for ramyeon? It takes about a minute to boil hot water in the boiler beside the snack bar.

"Jaewon-ah," Bora says, reappearing beside me, "look what I've brought."

She carries a pile of clothing in her arms—two gym shirts and a thick black sweater—items pilfered from my locker. Underneath her uniform skirt, she wears her yellow gym pants. "Put these shirts on," she commands. "It'll be bulkier, but at least you'll be warm. And I'm going to wear your sweater, okay? 'Cause I'm a genius and deserve a reward."

"You are a genius," I acknowledge, shrugging out of my blazer and unbuttoning the top buttons of my dress shirt. I pull it over my head. Underneath, I wear a T-shirt. I'm freezing as I put on the two gym shirts over it. Lastly, I struggle into my long-sleeved button-down. Four shirts in all, plus the school blazer. I'm almost warm.

"Ai—shhh!" Bora whines, pouting. "Even with all those layers, you still look thin."

She pats me on the stomach, then catches sight of a bobbing head ahead of us in the crowd, yelling, "Chang Minwoo, how'd you get up there?"

Minwoo turns toward the sound of her voice. Like the night before, he's wearing sunglasses. He must see her through the dark tint, because he yells, "Sorry, Bora-yah! I love you, but no cutting!"

She moves to push through the crowd, but gets shoved back. Mumbling profanities to herself, Bora pulls a bag off one of the shelves and opens it, stuffing crackers into her mouth.

A loud clash startles the students in the crowd—short

screams, and then silence. I turn to see a trio of underclassmen standing beside an overturned rack, packets of crackers scattered over the floor. Their sneakers crunch on the packets as they brush through the crowd. Kids back away as they approach. I lift my arm to block Bora when she moves to intercept the leader. "It's not worth it."

She ignores me, picking up a fallen packet off the floor and throwing it at the leader. It glances off the back of his head. "Ya! Who do you think you are?" she yells, approaching him. "Are you kkangpae or something? Get in line like the rest of us."

The leader scowls, grabbing Bora's wrist. The fact that she's a senior, older than him, doesn't seem to matter. She tries to break away, flinging her wrist downward, but he holds fast.

"If you don't have the strength to stop me," he growls, his hand twisting her wrist, "then don't even try."

I place all the items I'd been holding onto the nearest shelf, then walk over to Bora and the thugs. The leader of the group watches my approach with narrowed eyes. Reaching out, I extract his fingers from her wrist. He lets go—not in shock, but in anticipation.

He anticipates a fight.

I insert my body between hers and theirs, my back to the leader. "You need to be careful," I tell her. "You're a designer. Don't designers need their wrists?"

Her eyes widen when she realizes what I've done—put myself as their target over her. She shakes her head in denial. "Damn it. I shouldn't have said anything."

"It's fine." I look up to see Minwoo has moved back down the line toward us. He places a hand on Bora's shoulder.

"Don't do this." She struggles against Minwoo's hold. "There are three of them and only one of you."

"What?" I turn away. I don't expect Minwoo to join me—he's not a fighter. "You're not going to be my second?"

"You can joke at a time like this? You'll get expelled if you fight!"

I grimace. *I know.* Little misdemeanors—leaving school early, not wearing my uniform correctly—result in community service, cleaning the school bathrooms for a week. A brawl on school property would not be a little misdemeanor. There's only one way to get out of this.

Throw away your pride, Jaewon.

I turn to the leader. "Let's go somewhere else." The crowd grows larger the longer we stay here, forming a thick circle around us. Students have their phones out, many of them on hover mode, already set to record. Others are texting and calling their friends, telling them to hurry to the snack bar or they'll miss the fight.

"Why?" the leader asks, his lips curling. "You afraid you'll lose? You embarrassed?"

"That's right," I say. "Let's go somewhere else."

"Are you mocking me?" He pushes my shoulder. I let it give, stumbling backward away from him.

"No." I keep my voice steady. "It's too crowded here. A teacher will come."

"You afraid of a teacher?"

"Yes." When the leader's eyes narrow in suspicion, I realize I've answered too quickly.

"Saekki," he curses. "You think I'm a fool?" Again, he pushes me in the shoulder. I stumble, this time in a curve, the circle of people too closely crowded against me.

No, he isn't the fool. I'm the fool for getting involved.

The thugs take my silence as an insult, rushing me one at a time. I block the first punch, take a kick to the stomach, and manage to avoid a second punch by veering to the side. If we were out in the open, on the rooftop or on the sports field at the back of the school, I could easily escape, but the wall of students keeps me in this fight—to either take the beating or fight back.

One of the lackeys throws a fist at my face, and I duck and jab him with an elbow. He topples to the floor. The other thug kicks me in the side, and that's when the leader gets me in the face, right below the eye. He's wearing a ring, and it tears a cut across my cheek. Blood flows—hot compared to the cold halls of the school. The leader pulls his fist back again, and this time it hits me on the mouth, knocking my head sharply to the side. I fall into one of the food stacks, sending packages of chips and crackers tumbling to the floor. My hand lands on the handle of a broom, and I recognize the hard plastic for what it is—a weapon, a bludgeon. I curl my fingers around the smooth plastic for a moment, feel the strength beneath my grip, before letting it drop to the ground. I turn to face the leader.

His gaze darts from me to the broom. "Why won't you fight me? You're not afraid of me, so why won't you fight me?"

His fist connects with the side of my head, his ring slicing my ear. My vision blurs, and I grab the counter to keep from falling to the floor.

When the buzzing in my head clears, I realize it's silent again in the snack room. For whatever reason, the crowd's gone quiet. I right my body and turn around, sighing when I see who's broken up the fight.

Alex holds the thug's wrist. "We've got our placement tests today," he says, quietly addressing me.

"I know." I gingerly take off my blazer and dress shirt, throwing them to the ground. Then I pull the first of the T-shirts over my head and use the cloth to clean the blood dripping down my cheek and clotting at my lips. Gritting my teeth against a sharp stab of pain in my jaw, I lift my fingers to feel along the bruised skin.

"Didn't I tell you I want you on my team? I can't use you if you're expelled."

I shrug.

Alex releases the leader. "Kim Jobi?"

The thug scowls, rubbing his wrist. "How do you know my name?"

"You know mine, don't you?"

Kim Jobi doesn't answer. Of course he knows Alex's name. On the Internet search rankings of Neo Seoul, Alex consistently ranks number one. Netizens search the words "Alex Kim" more than the "Great War"—what his height is, what middle school he attended overseas, who he's currently dating.

For someone who does absolutely nothing for the state, he's the most famous person in it.

"Apologize to him," Alex says, tilting his head in my direction. "He wasn't in the wrong, but more than that, he's your senior. You never raise a hand to a senior. Didn't your father teach you that?"

It's a taunt, intended to bait Jobi.

Jobi doesn't take it. He swallows his pride, choosing silence over a fight with Alex.

"If not, your father has failed you," Alex says, dismissing Jobi with a casual turn of his head.

"What about him?" Jobi spits. He points at me. "Shouldn't his father have taught him to have some self-respect?"

They both look at me, watching for my reaction. Do they expect me to answer? Maybe I took the beating because I'd rather not get expelled. I only have one year of school left. Maybe I took the beating because I didn't have an incentive to fight. Or maybe I took the beating because I deserve it.

Maybe my father never taught me to have self-respect.

"When I die, I'll be sure to ask him." I grab my shirt and blazer off the floor, and get the hell out of there.

ASSASSINATION

Bora hurries after me, but I lose her once I walk into the restroom, running my hands beneath the hot water of the sink. The evidence of the fight isn't showing too thickly on my face yet—just a scratch across my cheek and a purpling along the corner of my bottom lip. I lift up my shirts to see the skin underneath. It's already bruising. Still, it's nothing I won't recover from in a day or two. MediTape would heal the ache quicker, but I won't waste money on it.

I walk out of the bathroom to see Alex and Bora waiting.

"Jaewon-ah," Bora begins, "I'm so sorry, I—"

I reach over to ruffle her hair, cutting her off.

"Ya!" she yells, batting my hand away.

Alex watches us, not amused. "Let's go," he says. "The assembly's about to start."

We follow him out the academy's front entrance and down the short set of stairs. Like all military academies, the school has an entrance courtyard situated between the gates and the main building of the school. It's an open space meant for conducting drills and gathering for assemblies like this one.

Seats for the assembly are positioned facing a stage set up at the west side of the courtyard. Technicians are on the stage making last adjustments to the holo-screens suspended overhead. Each holo-screen holds an image of the Neo State of Korea's black-and-white flag whipping in an imaginary wind.

While I've been in the restroom, the seats have filled out, underclassmen to the back and upperclassmen at the front. The chairs are divided by an aisle, and the principal, the head teacher, and the rest of the faculty are already seated in the first row. The principal shoots me a hard look as I approach with Alex and Bora. I duck my head in a bow, Alex and Bora following suit. We take seats on the other side of the aisle. As student president, Alex is required to sit at the front. I plop down beside him and stretch my legs out. Bora takes a seat to my left and pulls out her phone.

A girl taps Alex on the shoulder, and he turns to speak with her.

"Where's Minwoo?" Bora asks, looking down at her phone and scrolling through a list of flashing messages.

One message reads: I heard Lee Jaewon got in a fight. What was it about? Was it over you?

Bora furiously types her answer: Of course.

"Seonbae?" A small voice breaks my attention away from

Bora's screen. A girl, her low fringe brushing the tops of her eyelids, stands in front of me. I don't recognize her. She addressed me as "seonbae," so she must be a first- or second-year. "I bought these for you," she whispers, pushing a cloth package into my hands. "Eat them and get better quickly." She pivots and hurries away down the aisle, disappearing into one of the back rows.

I look down at the bundle. I can feel an assortment of items through the cloth, some of them hot enough to heat my palms. When I untie the knot at the top of the package, the folds fall apart, revealing three warm milk buns, a hot bottled-tea drink, a roll of MediTape, and four heat patches.

"Daebak!" Bora yells, eyeing the package's contents.

Alex turns back around in his seat. He holds a satin box.

"What?" Bora shouts, her volume making Alex and me flinch. "She gave you cookies? What the hell? Is this how you live your lives?"

Ignoring her, Alex holds up a brown, flower-shaped cookie. "I'll trade you for a heat patch."

I nod.

We make the trade.

"I can't believe this is happening. I can't believe I'm witnessing this." Bora scratches furiously at her hair. "Life must be so easy for you two."

I pop the cookie in my mouth and open a heat patch, peeling the filmy paper away from the sticky side. Gritting my teeth, I lift the layers of my shirts—the shock of cold air against my skin causing me to tense—and ease the heat patch underneath, sticking it directly onto my stomach. Instantly, the rich heat of the patch spreads to the rest of my body.

I sigh in contentment, sinking into my chair.

"That girl should have more pride," Bora mutters to herself. "What's the point in giving *you* a gift? It's not like you'd date her. I bet you don't even know her name."

I hold up a heat patch. "Do you want one? I'll give you one if you help me with the MediTape."

Bora smiles, immediately placated.

I stand, lifting my shirts as she unrolls the tape, circling around me as she wraps it. The effect of the MediTape isn't instant, not like the heat patch. Knowing that it's healing the bruises helps, though.

"She's watching us," Bora says. "You should see the expression on her face." She slaps her own heat patch onto her stomach, then peels the last one and sticks it to my back. "She looks about to kill me."

"Who's about to kill you?" Minwoo asks, coming up from behind and putting his hands on her shoulders. "I could offer some good tips. It's a subject I've thought about a lot."

"Ai—shhh!" Bora curses, swinging a hand at his head. "Where have you been? The assembly's about to start."

"I've been gathering important information. I've already put my bet in on who's performing at the assembly. If it's not CODA, I'll be down five million won. I could go to ten concerts with that kind of money."

A clamor of voices erupts from the back of the courtyard. Reporters amass outside the school's steel-plated gates, the lowTech cameras in their hands flashing. HighTech cameras hover in the air above, angling for a shot. The school guards keep most of the reporters back, only letting through a select few individuals.

A small entourage of black-suited men and women enter through the gates, surrounding the slight figure of a girl.

Alex pops another cookie into his mouth. "So much for your five million."

Minwoo doesn't respond, speechless. His eyes are on the girl. The moment the rest of the students recognize her is palpable. Whispers of C'est La Vie spread through the crowd. One boy tries to reach out and touch her as she passes, and is immediately pushed back by one of her bodyguards. She turns to blow him a kiss, easing his wounded pride.

Another group of people enter the courtyard behind them.

Beside me, Alex tenses.

The Director of the NSK strides forward, backed by a platoon of heavily armed soldiers. His chest is lined with medals—all earned from five decades of war.

My eyes focus on the soldier who follows directly behind the Director, dressed all in black. He's around fifteen years old, slight and small in body. He wears a gun holster beneath his military long coat. He lifts his head, and I immediately recognize him from the *Herald*'s coverage of the war.

General Tsuko, the NSK's greatest hero-soldier. In two years, he has risen to one of the highest positions in the state, much to the resentment of older, more experienced soldiers. Though no one can deny his accomplishments—he's won more battles than most senior military leaders in their lifetimes.

"Attention!"

It's the principal, shouting from the stage. His harsh voice silences the whispers.

My body automatically responds to the command. Along with the rest of the students, I stand and turn to face the aisle.

"Salute!"

In unison, every student bows toward the Director, bending at the waist with our eyes downcast.

We hold our positions for a minute as the Director strides down the aisle, taking a seat with the rest of the faculty—and Sela—in the front row before the stage. Our heads are still bowed to the ground as the principal announces the Director of the Neo State of Korea.

I wonder what we look like to the people watching the televised assembly from home. If we all look the same, a sea of bowed heads without faces.

Even though I can't see the Director, I can hear the *click* of his metal-heeled dress shoes ascending the short few steps to the stage. Another minute passes before his powerful voice, amplified by a mike, issues through the speakers. "Be at ease."

We collectively ease out of the salute, straightening our backs. Everyone but the guards—now spread out amidst the crowd—takes their seats, Alex at the extreme edge of his.

I glance from Alex to the Director. They don't look alike. Then again, the Director is in his late sixties. If they'd shared features once, the Director's age has wizened them past recognizable. I've never seen Alex's mother, a Korean American citizen of the American Neo States. Whether he looks like her, I wouldn't know.

Overhead, a flight of clouds drift by, throwing the stage and the Director into shadows. For a moment, we're in the light, and he's in the dark. And then the clouds pass.

"Citizens of the NSK," he begins, his image repeated on the large holo-screens behind him, "the new year marks a change in the wind. The forces of the Neo Alliance have quelled the latest rebellion in South China. Our own soldiers at the war front have represented our neo state with pride and glory."

The holo-screens switch to an edited feed of the war front. General Tsuko's famous God Machine, the Shi, stands on a field of a battle, the flag of the NSK protruding from behind its left shoulder. It's an impressive image, if a little contrived.

I know what comes next—the usual spiel we get whenever anyone discusses the history of the Great War of the Pacific: "The First Act, fought between the East Asian nations over territory and pride, resulted in the creation of the Neo Council, a governing body to make decisions for all East Asian states, humbling and unifying us. The Second Act, fought between the East and the West, resulted in a victory for the Neo states in the Alliance, and a cementing of our governing body. We are nearing the end of the Third Act, and the rebels who seek to destroy our way of life will be defeated.

"Soon," the Director continues, his voice dropping, "the war will be behind us, and peace will finally reign throughout Asia. Let us take a moment to pray for this long-awaited day."

He closes his eyes, letting the silence ring out loudly.

I raise my head and look around at the crowd. Everyone's eyes are closed except for mine. And General Tsuko's. I wonder what this says about us; maybe it shows a poor upbringing, or a coldness of heart.

"When we will have nothing to fear," the Director says, opening his eyes, his teeth glinting in a smile, "except for whether or not Sela will grace us with her lovely presence. Sela-ssi, would you indulge us with a song?"

Sela stands, mike already in hand. "Of course, Director."

She makes her way up the steps, bowing to the Director as she passes him. Two dancers wearing bright pink trench coats hurry to the stage, positioning themselves on either side of her.

It's a strange transition, from the solemnity of the Director's address to the heightened anticipation of a performance.

The Director reclaims his seat beside the principal and Tsuko. The music starts. Sela lifts the microphone and begins to sing.

I lean back in my chair, my gaze traveling to Sela's projected image on the holo-screen.

"I only ever saw you in my dreams," Sela sings. "What am I supposed to do? Now that you stand here in front of me."

It's a love song, I think.

Two minutes into the song, it breaks into a dance number. Sela's two backup dancers hurry away, giving her space for a solo. Her movements are graceful. She's obviously as skilled a dancer as she is a singer, which makes sense. Being a pop star is her job, whether she's in a band or performing solo.

The screens only show Sela, so my attention wanders to the backup dancers waiting at the edge of the stage. One girl watches Sela carefully, readying to rejoin her. I look to the other dancer.

Her eyes aren't on Sela, but on the Director.

It all happens in the breath of a second. The dancer reaches inside her long trench coat, fingers wrapping around something within.

I stand up, knocking back the chair.

The dancer whips around, a long, black-edged knife in her hand.

A gasp runs through the crowd.

The dancer turns, springing off the stage and into the air—her agility arresting in the moment of the jump—the knife in her hand raised high above her head. She lets out a harrowing scream, full of fury.

Tsuko slides a long-barreled gun from his uniform jacket, lifting it level with his shoulders.

He shoots her out of the sky.

THE TEST

The dancer plummets to the ground, her legs splayed awkwardly beneath her, a short distance away from the Director's polished boots.

Tsuko shot her in the chest.

Quickly guards circle around the Director and the dancer, forming an impenetrable wall, their guns trained outward upon the chaotic crowd of students rushing from their seats.

Alex strides to the circle, attempting to shove through the guards. When they block him, he punches the nearest guard in the face. Turning, the guard jams Alex's shoulder with the butt of his gun. Alex stumbles backward from the blow, twisting to fall on his hands.

My wounds still smart from earlier, but it's better to repay a debt sooner rather than later. I rush the nearest guard and tackle him to the ground. Alex grabs a chair and brings it down on the head of another.

We break the circle.

Beyond it stands General Tsuko, the barrel of his gun aimed at Alex's chest.

Alex ignores the gun. "You need to move my father. Now. There might be a bomb on her."

"There is no bomb, son."

Tsuko lowers his gun and steps to the side, revealing the Director. He sits in the same chair he'd occupied during Sela's performance, one leg casually crossed over the other. His face is calm, holding only the slightest frown.

Alex and I bow.

"General Tsuko searched the young woman," the Director explains. He waves to the dancer on the ground, whose shirt is torn open from Tsuko's examination.

"Why wasn't she searched before the performance?" Alex glares at the general.

I'm wondering the same thing. On the ground, the assassin holds still, but barely. Her lips are pressed tight to keep from trembling. Her eyes are closed. She can't be much older than me.

"Her body was scanned," General Tsuko says calmly, "but the knife is made of non-metallic components. It didn't register."

The circle opens again, letting in Sela and an older man. Sela approaches the Director and immediately drops her head in a low bow. The older man, most likely her manager, falls to the ground in a deep genuflection. I flinch as his forehead hits the cement.

"My sincerest apologies," Sela says, her voice small.

"The girl was a last-minute hire," the manager explains, his words stifled from his position. "Our primary dancer became ill. Please forgive us."

"I'll need the name of the group you hired her from," Tsuko says, "and the name of the dancer who became ill. And both of you will have to have your brains scanned."

The Director stands, bringing his fingers to Sela's chin. "For precautionary reasons," he adds, his voice placating as he lifts Sela out of her bow. "It's not that I suspect you, my dear. You are the victim here. The scan will only take a moment of your time."

Sela nods, her eyes downcast. "Of course, Director."

One of the guards leaves the circle, and Sela and her manager follow behind him. For a brief second, Sela looks up at me, her gaze traveling from the cut below my eyes to the bruising along my lips. Her eyes narrow in confusion before her manager tucks his hand against her back, pushing her out of the circle.

I bring my attention back to the Director, who's now leaning over the body of the dancer.

"Father," Alex cautions, "be careful."

"Careful?" The Director laughs without a trace of humor. "I'm always careful. With this state and its people. It's when individuals go through such unfathomable lengths to become martyrs that it proves hard to be careful." He brushes the hair above the dancer's closed eyes. The act is almost gentle, father-like. Her eyelids quiver at the touch, and wetness forms at the corners, slowly seeping beneath the lids. "Who are you," the Director croons, "young woman with broken legs? It's hard, isn't it? To live after you've chosen to die."

The dancer opens her eyes, and although she's crying, her tears are just the body's form of rebellion, a reaction to the pain. She hocks and spits directly at the Director's face, some of the phlegm reddened by the blood in her mouth.

"Traitor," she cries, her voice heated with wrath.

Alex curses and moves to drive a kick into the dancer's splayed legs, but the Director holds up a hand.

"No, anger will only make her willpower stronger. She's already decided to die. Let us finish what she's started."

Standing, the Director takes Tsuko's gun in one hand and a linen handkerchief in the other, wiping the dancer's spit from his face.

"I'll do it," Alex says, reaching for the gun.

Again his father refuses. "I think I owe the girl this much." He hands the handkerchief to one of his guards and lowers the gun. "You see, I've failed her. I've allowed her to build hatred in her soul. And on such a hopeful occasion as this, the final push to end the war once and for all. I should have known there would be discontent. Luckily, this day's events won't spread past the courtyard."

The dancer sputters, "You're wrong. A picture will get out, and then they'll . . ."

"Even so," the Director says, cutting her off. "It really does pain me to say this, my dear girl, but nobody knows who you are. Who are you? You are nobody. You are nothing. Did you think that your death would be noted because of the life you have lived? What life have you lived? How old are you? What is your name? I know none of these things. And you will die with no one knowing any of these things."

For a moment, the girl looks stricken, her breath coming in short gasps, but then she swallows. A calmness seems to take hold of her, her whole body going still. She looks past the Director and into the sky. "You're wrong," she whispers. "You could never be more wrong. My death is my own. The light of the sky reaches me. It passes through my soul, and I am made of light."

"Be at peace, daughter," the Director says, his finger on the trigger.

She closes her eyes. "Even in heaven," she says, her voice clear, triumphant. "Even in heaven will I love my country."

I look away and quickly move out of the circle.

The sound of a gunshot always gives me a headache.

■ ■ ■

I head up to the infirmary to rest. This morning I had to wake up early for my part-time job making deliveries. A lot of the Old Seoul veterans of the war refuse to leave their homes due to physical or psychological trauma. They hire me to bring them their groceries. It doesn't pay much, but I don't need a lot, and it's a reminder of what happens when you're an Old Seoul foot soldier. No compensation for your efforts, no honor in your sacrifices. My ambitions aren't grand, but they do include not ending up like these veterans.

The infirmary is empty when I arrive.

I manage to get in fifteen minutes of sleep before my phone chirps in my pocket. The screen lights up green. It takes me a bleary-eyed moment to read the message.

Report to Room T4 at 1600 for your
simTech test; instructions upon arrival.

Alex must have signed me up for his team for the senior tests despite my nonanswer.

"Arrogant bastard," I mutter. My voice sounds loud in the quiet sleeping cell of the infirmary.

"Well, it's nice to know what you think of me." Alex stands silhouetted in the doorway. He walks over and kicks the legs of the cot. "Get up. Simulations are like sleeping. Ours starts in fifteen."

Cursing under my breath, I get to my feet. Alex heads back to the door, looks out to check the hallway, then closes it. Reaching into his pocket, he takes out the Enhancer. He rolls it in his hand before holding it up to the scant light filtering in from the cell's lone window.

"Here goes nothing," he says.

"Geonbae," I say in dry celebration.

He sticks the nozzle of the Enhancer into his mouth and presses the round gray button, ejecting the gas as he inhales. Fumes of it slip from between his lips, and I wave my hand in the air, dispersing the drug. He holds his forearm against his mouth. "It tastes awful." He coughs. "How long does it last?"

"I have no idea."

He slumps against the wall, his fingers digging against the steel. After a moment, he rights himself, shaking his head to dispel the nausea. "Let's go."

We head out of the infirmary, taking the lift to the fourth floor, where an oval of eight simulation rooms sit at the top of the school. Seniors mingle in the center waiting area, trading tips and placing bets on whose teams will come out with top placements.

No one is talking about the botched assassination attempt. Either the school sent out a warning, or people just don't care.

Alex takes a cigarette from his pocket and lights it while walking. I raise a brow at his blatant disregard of the rules. We pass several teachers, but none of them spare him a second glance.

We arrive at our testing room, and Alex keys in the code to open the door.

I follow him inside, immediately recognizing two of his recruits, No Seungri and No Seungpyo. Twin brothers—thin, fast-talking guys. Their father owns simTech companies in Neo Seoul and Neo Beijing, specializing in programming simulations.

They'll be strong allies in the test.

Jessica Lim, a tall Korean American girl, is the other person in the room. She was a late transfer last year, her parents having moved to Neo Seoul from the American Neo States, but she's already made a name for herself as the academy's top sharpshooter. And Alex's current girlfriend. She stands when she sees him and runs across the short distance, then throws her arms around his neck and draws him to her for a long kiss.

When she releases him, licking her lips, I can tell she's speculating if he's smoked more than a cigarette. I wonder if she can taste the Enhancer on him.

At this moment, the Enhancer should be telling Alex what the probabilities are of him getting caught—50 percent without the cigarette, 48.976 percent with the cigarette dulling the smell of it.

"What happened to your face?" Jessica asks, turning from Alex to look at me.

"Jobi happened to his face," Alex answers, lightly wiping his mouth with his fingers.

"Ay," Seungri says. "I don't know if I want to entrust my future to a kid who got his ass handed to him by Jobi and the boys."

"Boys," Seungpyo says, laughing. "Jobi and the Boys. Sounds like a rap group."

"Jaewon is the best Runner in the school," Alex says—not defending me, just stating rank. He collapses into one of the chairs at the regulators' square table, set up in the middle of the room. The metal table has monitors on its surface, screens from which the regulators will watch our every action during the simulation test.

Six simTech pods ring the table against the walls—two at the back of the room and two to the right and left. Our team will hibernate in these pods during the simulation.

Six pods, but only five of us in the room. We're missing a person.

The doors behind me slide open, letting in a loud racket—yelling from the common space. C'est La Vie's Sela glides in. She's changed out of her stage outfit and into a cream-colored suit.

I guess the brain scan went well. After all, she's alive.

She blushes a little at the silence that follows her entrance, her gaze darting from me, closest to the door, to the brothers leaning against the wall to the right.

Seungri elbows Seungpyo, but neither of them comments.

Her eerie gray-blue eyes settle on me. "Hello," she says, clearing her throat. She places her hands on her lower stomach and bows.

Immediately I bow in response.

"My name is Sela. What is your name?"

I blink, surprised she's introducing herself with her stage name. Does she even *have* a real name? "Lee Jaewon."

"It is nice to meet you, Jaewon-ssi. Please take care of me in our upcoming test."

There's a beat of silence.

"*Our* test?" I ask.

Seungpyo and Seungri snicker, amused.

"I forgot to mention," Alex says, still seated in the regulator's chair, "Sela is the sixth member of our team."

Sela bites her lip, nodding. "It's a requirement of the state that all citizens participate in two to four years of mandatory military service." She's parroting Conscription Law, the laws of the state. "I was born in Neo Seoul. I am a citizen of the Neo State of Korea."

"Even though she's not a student at the academy," Alex explains, "she still has to take a test in order to receive a placement in the military. To fulfill her service requirements."

Everyone looks at me, waiting for my reaction.

I frown. "She shouldn't be on our team."

"Ya!" Jessica hits me in the arm. "What is wrong with you?"

"No," I say, scratching the back of my head. "I mean, why doesn't she join a different team? The test we're taking is at the highest level of difficulty. Since she's not trained in combat simulations, she won't be prepared for what we'll face inside the test."

It seems logical to my mind. Without a justifiable reason, it's foolish to burden ourselves with a disadvantage in an already difficult simulation. Not to mention Sela could get a satisfactory placement without taking a gamble on a more challenging test.

"I asked her to join us," Alex says, getting out of the regulator's chair to stand beside me. "I found out she needed to take a test for her service requirement, so I invited her onto our team. We don't need a sixth member to win, but it's a requirement for the test. More importantly, we'll get a lot of publicity with Sela on our team. If we win, the positive exposure will bring in more offers of high-level positions. For us, it could mean getting a placement as an officer at the war front. For Sela, it could mean getting a safe yet prestigious placement in one of the war offices."

Seungri nods, serious for once. "For Seungpyo and me, it could mean getting positions with all the rewards and none of the risks. Sorry, Sela, you're a burden, but we can carry you through it. Alex is right. If we win—which we will—then we'll be famous *and* recognized for our skill. We'll be the team that defeated a high-level test *with* an international pop star."

Seungpyo pumps his fist in the air—his form of agreeing.

Alex and Sela are already famous, but I don't point that out. I guess it makes sense—the more high-profile the test and its players, the more opportunities for outstanding placements.

Behind me, the doors to T4 open again.

General Tsuko steps through, trailed by three regulators. I catch a glimpse of flashing cameras before the doors shut behind him. The information about Sela's participation in the test must have gotten out.

I thought General Tsuko had left with the Director, but he still wears his black uniform from the assembly.

Without preamble, he waves the regulators forward. "Test them for Enhancers."

This is standard procedure before the commencement of any high-level test, but my heart still misses a beat. I don't look at Alex, focusing on the gray-haired regulator jabbing a needle into my arm. The syringe fills with blood, and he deposits several drops onto a tray that turns green. "All clear," he says, pressing a bandage to my wrist.

Seungri and Seungpyo also come up green.

Sela, surprisingly, comes up blue. She smiles at the frowning regulator.

"General . . . ," the regulator says hesitantly.

Tsuko looks over briefly before turning away. "Blue is not an illegal Enhancer."

Which means blue is a *legal* Enhancer. I wonder what kind of drugs Sela's been taking. There are a variety of legal ones on the market. As a pop star, it's likely she's taken mild Enhancers for sleep deprivation, softening of the vocal chords, even cosmetic Enhancers. Maybe her gray-blue eyes are only gray-blue for the day, at least until the Enhancer wears off. Now that I think about it, Alex could have taken a legal Enhancer to trick the test, as long as he had more of the blue in his system than the green. It would be a risk, but it could work.

Jessica's tray of blood comes up green, and then it's Alex's turn.

Tsuko personally sees to Alex, pressing the needle through the skin into his vein. The blood drops on the tray swirl red, then orange, before changing to green. He's clear.

Tsuko drops Alex's wrist and turns away. "Line up beside the pods you'll be hibernating in during the test."

The brothers move to the pods located on the left, and Alex and Jessica take the pods at the back of the room. I move to the pods on the right, Sela following to stand before the pod beside mine.

The regulators begin to fiddle with the monitors at the table. One sticks a port drive into the system, uploading the test.

The doors open once more. This time a camera crew enters. They bow to Tsuko before setting up, releasing highTech cameras to hover mode. I look over at Alex and the others, but none of them seem surprised. Either that, or they don't care, used to their lives being documented for millions of viewers. For Alex and Sela, the Director's son and the NSK's most famous pop star, it's not surprising. And Jessica has been on the news lately as Alex's girlfriend. Even the twins are famous gamers.

I shift in place when one of the highTech floating cameras zooms in on me. With a scratched cheek and bruised lip, the audience will think I look more like a gangster than a celebrity.

It now makes sense why the Director sent General Tsuko to oversee this test. Give the people what they want. Their hero-general. Their stars. Their war games. And reap their sponsorship and loyalty. It's the oldest strategy in the book— create a distraction so that people forget the harsh realities of war, and thank you for it.

One of the camerawomen gives Tsuko a signal. The broadcast must have gone live. Tsuko bows. "Good afternoon, citizens of the NSK. My name is General Tsuko. As you might know, the war effort has gained ground lately in a string of decisive victories in South China, but that won't be enough. We need more soldiers. More leaders. Today I'm here at Neo Seoul's Apgujeong Military Academy to oversee a simulation test, the results of which we will use to place some of the academy's brightest and most exemplary students into positions that will benefit the NSK."

A hover camera closes in, panning over each of our faces. Beside me, Sela flashes a wide smile and holds up two fingers in a peace sign.

Tsuko walks the perimeter of the room. "Simulation tests

run the gamut in terms of thematic relevance—some are battles between two teams from different schools; some are levels designed by programmers with goals to complete. Simulations are the highTech training ground of soldiers, where Tech mimics reality. If it's snowing in your simulation setting, you will feel the wet coldness of every snowflake. You will smell the tangy copper of blood spilled. You will slip on it if you step in it. SimTech battles allow soldiers to build experiences, yet death in an artificial reality cannot take that soldier away from their ability to serve their state. The Tech's artificial reality trains you for the reality of living as a citizen of the NSK."

Tsuko now stands by the doorway. "A change has been made to your test," he says, for the first time directly addressing the six of us instead of the cameras, "with the Director's approval. It had been made known to your team leader beforehand, so this shouldn't come as a surprise."

Five heads swerve toward Alex. It is a surprise, it seems. To all of us.

"As I said, simulations mimic reality, but they aren't real, because you cannot perish in a computerized setting. In my personal opinion, I prefer this form of testing; a soldier's life should not be wasted. However, the Director thinks it necessary to mimic reality as closely as possible . . ."

Tsuko scans the room, noting our confused looks with a raised eyebrow. I guess he expected us to be more informed before we agreed to take this test, or at the least, not lied to. My heart kicks up in speed, and I don't know whether it's from fear or adrenaline.

"Hence the new stipulation: if you die in the simulation test conducted here in this room"—he looks down at the metallic watch circling his wrist—"beginning, now, February fourth, 2199 AF at 1600 on the hour, you will forfeit your life in reality."

Jessica gasps. "What the hell?"

Seungpyo and Seungri shoot murderous looks at Alex.

I think about withdrawing, then realize we can't. We're being watched not just by Tsuko, but also by the whole city. The Director would never let us walk out. Bad publicity. It would carry the stench of dishonor. Morover, Tsuko had already begun the test when he'd announced the rule change. There's a possibility that forfeiting could lead to our immediate deaths.

Sela, surprisingly, remains calm. I expect tears, but all she does is frown, watching as Jessica berates Alex with harsh whispers. Does Sela think she's above the new rule? That they wouldn't televise her death? One of the cameramen fiddles with the regulators' controls—whatever happens in the simulation will be broadcasted to the city. Or does she have confidence in our team's abilities? We'll try our hardest to keep her alive, but there are countless things that could go wrong—detonations hidden beneath piles of debris or a stray missile getting past our line of defense.

I take a deep breath. Calmness settles over me. I recognize the feeling. I always get this way before a battle, whether it's a simulation or an Old Seoul street fight. It's the only time I ever feel safe. I know that only I can save myself. No one else can be blamed for how much effort I put into it.

Plus, Alex took an Enhancer. I might have absolutely no faith in him as a leader, considering he's sold us out, but it's in his best interest to see his team through to the end. Casualties would lose him points on the test.

"But there's no kill-switch on these pods," Jessica says, still trying to figure out a way to nullify the rule.

"We've programmed your pods to release a sleeping gas, should the need arise."

Tsuko says this in a flat voice, as if the manner of our deaths is of little consequence. He then shifts his attention back to Alex. "Name your team."

Alex nods and turns to face Jessica. "Jessica Lim. Defense Tactician and Markswoman."

Jessica, fuming, gets into her pod, its glass shield closing her in.

Next are the twins. "No Seungpyo, Melee Combat and Left Guard. No Seungri, Melee Combat and Right Guard." The brothers clasp hands briefly before falling backward into their respective pods.

Finally it's Sela's and my turn. "Sela," Alex says. "Rear Guard."

Sela has trouble getting into her pod, so I hold out my hand, and she takes it, balancing herself.

Once she's seated, I move back in front of my own pod.

"Lee Jaewon. Melee Combat and Mid Guard."

I don't wait for Alex to state his positions—Team Leader and Front Guard—before stepping into my pod. The roles are just for the record, anyway, for the regulators to get a sense of what we should be doing, where we should be positioned on the field of battle. Other than that, the titles don't matter. During a simulation, a player needs to be able to fulfill all positions in order to survive.

Half-lying, half-sitting on the white cushioned seat of the pod, I watch the familiar glass of the shields come down around me.

The glass of the pod fogs over, cracks of black ice creeping out of the corners. Soon all is black.

A sexless voice issues forth from the speakers inside the darkened pod. "State your name, please."

"Lee Jaewon."

"Welcome, Lee Jaewon. Your standing in your battle ranking is currently at one."

I sit still as a needle in the pod is inserted into my neck, connecting with the small chip installed there and allowing the computer access to my brain. I feel myself black out, only to come awake a second later, a little addled from the transition.

I'm no longer in a pod. I'm sitting in the piloting seat of a mobile landcraft. I won't know what kind of craft until the test begins. I hope it's highTech, some sort of advanced fighter plane or a God Machine.

"You're programmed to conduct Test 5061: The Tower. Commencing in five, four, three, two . . ."

07

GOD MACHINE

The screen lights up, and I gaze around at the terrain pro-grammed for the simulation test. I'm inside a building with gray-blue walls. The landcraft I pilot faces a set of wide, floor-to-ceiling windows. I look out to see fair skies and a paved strip of land. Two or three planes—gutted of their parts—lit-ter the field.

An airport.

The upper right corner of my screen shows a full green bar with a percentage to the left of it, recording my damage count. It's currently full at 100 percent. The left bottom corner of the screen holds a circular map of the area. Six blinking green lights at the center of the map indicate the locations of my team members. There aren't any red dots, which suggests hostiles haven't arrived on the scene.

I turn my landcraft's position from the window to see the rest of Alex's assembled team spread out behind me.

Immediately I recognize the type of weapons we've been given to pilot. The massive, human-piloted machines of modern warfare.

God Machines.

This particular model of GM is type TK-009. Shaped like squat humans, weighing in at seven tons, and standing twelve and a half meters tall, TK-GMs were used during the early years of the wars in the Pacific as foot soldiers and scavengers. They have slow reaction times, but are highly defensive and resistant to the most powerful GM firearms.

Inside the cockpit, I tap a small symbol of a firearm at the bottom of the screen. A list of weapons in my inventory scrolls across the surface, complete with an image and description. My particular GM comes equipped with two massive knives, a power rifle with an extra magazine full of clips, and a pointed shield. Unless GM weapons can be found amongst the debris of the stage, these few weapons are all I'll have to get through the test.

On the left panel of my screen, Seungri's face pops up.

"I guess they want to test our knowledge of history as well as our aptitude. These GMs are from the First Act of the War. And mostly lowTech, by the look of it." His voice is a little muted by a low murmur of static. Seungri's GM moves its arms up and down, then rotates its torso sideways 180 degrees. Of the brothers, Seungri's the younger. Even in the simulation, he wears his yellow beanie, the bright color differentiating him from Seungpyo.

He disappears from the screen, replaced by Jessica, her eyes smarting red at the corners. "Are we seriously going to ignore the fact that Alex just betrayed us? I'm sorry, I can't—"

She's cut off as Alex's face appears, his image canceling hers out. "We've already entered the test, Jessica. We can fight about this after. Concentrate on the matter at hand." His words are clipped; his eyes are cold. I guess in some ways, Alex is like his father.

Jessica doesn't respond.

Alex continues. "Everyone, listen closely. If the layout of the airport's any indication, there's a high chance we're in Busan before the war."

"Busan?" Seungpyo repeats. He moves his face closer to the camera, raising an eyebrow studded through with a metal bar. "What the hell you guys doin'?" His voice is low, laying on a thick Busan saturi.

"What the hell?" Seungri shouts, laughing.

I move my hand to the GM's keyboard, downloading a map of prewar Busan. On the Korean peninsula, Busan is the second-largest city after Seoul, located the farthest south. I've never been to Busan in the Real, but I've gone through enough simulations that feature the port city as a setting to know what to expect.

"Since Busan borders the Strait," Alex says, "there's a high probability we'll have enemies coming at us from the water. Our GMs are so old they lack air mobility, and if you get pushed or dragged into the water, the thrusters won't ignite. You'll sink straight to the bottom of any deep water. That'd be game over. In here and in real life."

"Gah," Seungpyo yells. His face doesn't show up on my screen.

Alex resumes speaking. "Our objectives are about to arrive, and there's a high probability they'll involve not only rooting out all enemies and destroying them, but also getting to some announced goal that will force one of us to leave our GMs and enter a building. This will be your moment, Jaewon. You're plugged into body movement as well as piloting. You'll be able to leave your GM during the simulation in order to achieve whatever final goal they'll set up."

"Eh." As I speak, I know my face is showing up on all their screens, due to the voice-activated video system. "Tell me again why I have to put my life on the line, and not you?"

"You're ranked first in battle rankings," Alex says, "and you're our Runner." I can see his smirk through the pixelated screen. "Suck it."

"Oh, Lee Jaewon," Seungri says, "you're my goddamn hero!"

"Jaewon-ssi," Sela says, for the first time adding to the conversation. Her pink hair and pink-tipped eyelashes contrast with the bluish light given off by the screen.

"Holy crap!" Seungri shouts. "It's like watching a music video!"

Seungpyo laughs so hard that his face actually appears on my screen, flickering in and out.

"Jaewon-ssi," Sela repeats, insistent. "Be careful."

I nod, which she can't see. The simulation only picks up voice messages. "Alex," I say, "give us some more probabilities. What's the probability that we'll all survive?"

"Thirty-eight point nine-eight-three percent."

That shuts us up.

Our screens light up with words and the sound of the standard computerized voice.

> Objective 1: Defeat all hostiles.
> Objective 2: Find the Tower.
> Objective 3: Defuse the explosive.
> Objective 4: Rescue the hostage.

Seungpyo pops up on my screen. "What the hell?"

"But there's no friggin' Tower in Busan." Seungri shows up on my screen with a frown. "It got destroyed during the first battle of the Great War."

Seungpyo adds, "Four. Four. Four. Four objectives. Bad luck. Bad luck. Bad luck. Bad luck."

"Ya!" Jessica yells. "Do not make me kill all of you for being hostile to this mission!"

Alex's face appears again, glowering through the screen. "There's a high probability that Objective Two will be evident once we leave the airport. The Tower will be a tall building in the city, presumably. The bomb and hostages will be inside. No Seungpyo, No Seungri, block for Lee Jaewon. When we're out, Jessica, position yourself in a concealed spot with the best view of the city. Snipe for offense. Sela, stay with Jessica. Let's move out."

I slowly tip the lever of my control forward. My GM rolls toward the exit of the airport, leaving overturned luggage and smashed carts in its wake. I'm glad there aren't any simulated bodies on the floor. Even in a simulation, the cracking of bones beneath wheels isn't a heartwarming sound.

Outside, I can smell the odor of Busan's old fish markets. Seungpyo's and Seungri's TKs clunk over cars beside mine, the boys obviously enjoying the way their massive God Machines crush all obstacles in their path. They better be careful not to ruin the link that keeps their wheels balanced. Unlike the more highTech GMs used by elite soldiers at the war front, ones with mobile legs or powered thrusters for air mobility, TK-GMs have wheels with tracks like tanks—slow-moving and more easily disassembled.

We head southeast from the airport, over a highway riddled with the shells of cars. It seems to be the best direction to take, as the highway leads into a denser part of the city. I can see the red lights of Seungri's and Seungpyo's scanners honing in on suspicious elements in the debris of Busan's broken buildings. We're heading downhill, scanning the terrain for any tall buildings that could be the Tower.

I'm in the front with Alex.

"There's a parking structure," Jessica says, her face visible on my screen. "It looks intact. Sela and I will get positioned up top." The girls break away from our group.

I check the left-corner map again to see if any red dots

have appeared, but it's still just the six of us, our green dots blinking in the black.

As for the streets of Busan, I'm impressed with whoever designed this simulation. The details of the city are extraordinary, the many signs in both Hangeul and English. Glancing through the windows of apartments, I can see low tables, cabinets, and beds, sheets twisted as if slept in. There's even legible graffiti on some of the walls. I stop to read the nearest slanting words.

In the beginning, God created the heavens and the earth.

The first shot comes out of nowhere, clipping my GM in the shoulder. My damage count bar blinks red for a moment before recalculating itself at 97 percent working capacity.

"Watch out!" Alex shouts. "Snipers on the rooftops up ahead and incoming hostiles down the street."

Loud gunshots ring out from behind—Jessica picking off the enemy snipers. Several GMs fall from their perched positions atop the low rooftops. They shatter into pixelation as they hit the ground, this particular simulation programmed not to burden the ground with metal carcasses.

Red dots emerge on the circle map at the bottom of the screen, where there hadn't been any before.

I count thirty of them total.

Seungri groans. "Why do they give us a map if it doesn't even work?"

Alex's face appears. "The enemy is here. All GMs. Type RL-003s. Second Act models. I'm forwarding you their stats."

At the left of my screen, a message icon pops up.

I tap it, revealing an array of technical diagrams—the front, back, and side of a standard RL-003. Numbered extensions branching off the diagram pinpoint the RL's strengths and weaknesses.

Alex's voice accompanies the images. "Each GM comes equipped with machine guns on both arms and homing missiles at the shoulders. Some might have an additional knife hidden beneath the left gun."

I tap on the knife to enlarge it. It's a standard GM army knife, a long, wicked-looking blade.

"No Seungpyo," Alex says, addressing the older twin, "you and Seungri need to get Lee Jaewon in close. The enemy won't be able to defend against melee attacks."

"Roger that," Seungpyo and Seungri say together, saluting the cam.

"Jessica," Alex says, "snipe to kill. Through the chest, if you can."

"I can," Jessica responds. "And I will." She cuts off her transmission.

"Lee Jaewon." Alex's face hardens when addressing me. Or maybe it's a carryover; maybe he actually feels bad about betraying Jessica.

I sweep the diagrams off my screen, clearing my view of the imminent battlefield.

"Concentrate on the cluster of GMs up ahead. Leave the rest to Jessica and me."

I'm too focused to respond, my mind calculating the best way to proceed—only to disregard thought altogether. There is no best way. A fight is a fight. We'll just have to break through.

Flanked by the brothers, I move forward down the narrow street, leaving Alex to pick up the rear. Both Seungpyo's and Seungri's GMs come equipped with massive tower shields, almost the full length of their GMs. They lift their shields on either side of me, blocking the three of us from the bullets barraging down the street.

I measure the distance between the sounds of the shots and our GMs rolling forward at high speeds. The louder the gunshots, the closer we are to the enemy.

Eight hundred meters.

I move my GM's shield to its back.

Five hundred meters.

I flip out the blades attached beneath its forearms. The blades are thick, made of a metal alloy stronger than steel, each the length of my GM's arm.

Two hundred meters.

The shots are at their loudest, bullets slicing through the gap between the brothers' shields.

One hundred meters.

I propel my GM free from its position in the middle, lifting the blades, arcing them high above my head.

We crash into the front line of hostiles.

Seungpyo and Seungri use the strength of their GMs to push me through the crush, bashing the hostile GMs with their shields. I ram my blade into the helm of an RL to my left. The helm explodes and careens backward.

A long-bladed knife slips through the barrier, trying to gut me in the side. I swerve my GM at the last moment, and the knife misses. I twist and grab the arm holding the blade, ripping it off.

"We'll funnel 'em," Seungri shouts, making a wall with his and Seungpyo's shields. They let through one, then two GMs at a time, controlling the flow of the battle so they're not all on me at once. I decapitate the first GM through the gap, pushing my sword into the chest of the next. Pilots of GMs are located in the chest. Significant damage to that area would effectively cut off the GM's movements. You don't stop a God Machine by tearing off its head, but by ripping out its heart.

The brothers move ahead, their shields pushing back the RLs. Once they've broken up the enemy's positioning, they open up, letting more GMs through for me to destroy.

It's slow progress, but it's a working strategy.

Alex dispatches the GMs that get by our line of defense, crushing each in the chest with his sword, yelling out orders to the team as we progress down the alley. "Take a right at the bend. Incoming missile, east side. Seungri, watch your left. Your bot's sparking."

"Ah, I see it." Seungri pops up on the screen chewing a piece of gum. "Hyeong," he says, addressing his brother, "let's switch sides in the next bout. You take the left."

Seungpyo answers, "How the hell are you chewing gum? We're in a friggin' simulation."

Seungri bursts into laughter. He's laughing so hard he doesn't see the hostile GM behind him. I move to block it, stabbing downward into its neck with my blade. It falls over, sparking against the cement. "Stay focused," I say into my comm. "We're almost at the end of the road."

Seungri's response: "Was that a metaphor? I believe we just turned a corner, literally and figuratively."

Gritting my teeth, I break away from behind the brothers' defense, swerving my GM through the staggered enemies. I dispatch machine after machine, keeping close watch on my damage count. When I finally break through the line, I'm at 89 percent.

Behind me, Jessica takes out the rest of the GMs in our vicinity, shooting through the central cockpits of the GMs' armored chests where the virtual pilot sits.

Seungri rolls to a stop alongside me. "Way to blast us with your bot dust," he says, spitting his gum out at the camera. It hits the lens, sticking.

Seungpyo rolls to my other side. "Stop showing off. We get it; you're good at simulations."

"Lee Jaewon," Alex growls from behind us, "don't rush ahead like that again. Stay with Seungpyo and Seungri. They're there to block for you." He pushes through our GMs, taking the lead.

We follow him, leaving the congested area of the main city and coming out onto a short ledge overlooking the rest of Busan's lower city. Shielded as we were between the tall build-ings, we hadn't seen the city's waterfront.

"Ai—shhh," Seungpyo curses. "Who said it was gonna be easy?"

The entire oceanfront is lined with GMs. Not just any type, but Third Act GMs—type H-100s, better known as Hydros. The Neo Alliance currently uses Hydros at the war front. It's the NSK's main offensive naval weapon. A platoon of them took down the entire South Chinese fleet last month in one of the most decisive battles of the war.

Seungri scowls. "Why can't we avoid the water?"

I look past the beach to a small island positioned several hundred meters out—the only way to get there a long stone bridge. There's a tall structure on the island.

"The lighthouse," I say, resigned. "The lighthouse is the Tower."

The realization of what we'll have to accomplish hits everyone at the same time.

Seungri laughs shakily. "There go my future wife and kids."

I grimace. I don't like giving up before the end, but Seungri's words have some truth to them. At this point, surviving this test seems close to impossible. We're piloting out-of-date lowTech GMs against a horde of state-of-the-art highTech GMs.

Alex's face shows up on our screens, his eyes flashing. "Your life is your own until it's not." He propels his GM forward, making his way down the sloping road toward the lower city.

There's a pause.

"Wait," Seungpyo says. "What did he just say? When did Alex become Tsuko? Spouting words of wisdom like he's freaking Confucius."

Shaking my head, I turn my GM. The sound of Seungri's laughter follows me down into the lower city.

■ ■ ■

Jessica and Sela join us at the bottom of the slope, their GMs mostly undamaged. We're still several hundred meters away from the GMs we saw, out of their line of sight for now.

"Nice sharpshooting," Seungri says as Jessica rolls by, raising his GM's hand for a high five.

She ignores him. "Alex, what's the plan?"

"We're heading to the lighthouse," Alex says, his eyes averted from the camera. He wipes sweat off his forehead.

I frown, noticing the slight trembling of his hand. Is the Enhancer finally showing its infamous side effects?

"Alex?" Jessica repeats.

"Something's not right," he says. "The lower city. It's too quiet."

I check my GM's visuals, but nothing seems out of place. The map on my screen shows an empty lower city leading to the Hydro-filled beach.

"There's nothing on the map," Jessica says.

"Yeah, well, our map is the shittiest map in the history of maps," Seungri says.

"Shut up," Alex gasps. "All of you. I need to concentrate. There's a high probability that there's—" He breaks off.

We see his mouth move, but we don't hear his words, drowned out as they are by a wall of sound.

A blast from a high-power beam cannon pierces through

our group. Most of us are quick enough to get out of the way. Sela isn't. Her GM takes a brutal hit to the back, her bot sparking dangerously.

"Sela!" Seungpyo shouts, grabbing her GM with his own. He chucks her to the side as another beams blasts through.

It's an overhead ambush, a line of RL-005s on the rooftops. Like the ones in the upper city, but with advanced upgrades, including beam cannons and increased mobility. Third Act war machines.

I retract my blades, detaching my power rifle and shield from my back. With my shield angled horizontally to block my chest, I steady my rifle on the shield rim, the barrel aimed skyward. I'm a decent shot; one out of every three bullets finds its mark. Jessica's much better, but there's only one of her.

Seungpyo grabs Sela's unused rifle, twisting around to shoot two-handed.

Defenseless, Sela backs up. An enemy RL bursts through a building behind her. It wraps its arms around her GM's chest and squeezes.

I rush forward, taking a close-range shot to my shoulder. I jam one of my blades into the helm of the RL holding her. It lets go, reeling back, and I blast it in the chest multiple times with my rifle.

Inside my GM, the cockpit flashes red in warning.

Damage count: 47%

My GM lists, going haywire. The shots from above have stopped, giving me time to check my status. Sela's face pops up on my screen. "Jaewon-ssi, are you all right?"

"I'm fine," I say, gritting my teeth.

I am pissed, though. If this were a real battle, I could get out of my GM and quickly fix some of its more damaged parts, but the program won't allow me to leave until I've reached the Tower. Yes, we can die in real life, but we can also fix ourselves when we're broken.

"None of this makes any sense," I growl into my comm. Alex flickers in to watch my rant. "You can't simulate real life in a simulation. It's impossible." I point the red light of my rifle on the nearest building. "That building is shaking with pixelation. If I had a can of spray paint, I couldn't draw on the wall. Tsuko says he wants us to experience real-life combat, but simulations can never replicate real life."

Alex shakes his head. "This isn't the time for debating the morality of the test. Not to mention we're being monitored by Tsuko. Try not to piss him off and get a default death. I still need you in order to win."

I close my eyes and take a steadying breath. I open them. "All right, let's finish this."

Alex follows me out of the city streets and onto the cement roads curbing the beachfronts of Busan. The bay that lines the stone bridge leading to the lighthouse is packed with Hydros— their massive rocket launchers already primed for firing. The bridge itself is deserted, but it's without cover, and narrow enough that one shot could fling us into the water.

"The game's rigged," Seungri says. "There's no way we can get across that bridge."

"We can," Alex says. "We just have to force our way." His face doesn't show up on my screen. He must have disengaged the ability of his GM to transfer his visual. We can only hear him, the calm cadence of his voice issuing out of the speakers. "It'll be risky, but it's the only way. As a bulk unit, we'll have a better chance of making it across the bridge."

"What are you talking about?" Seungri asks, maneuvering his GM onto the sand.

"I'm saying we're going to have attach our GMs to one another, front to back, and move as quickly as we can across the bridge. We'll be bombarded with shots on both sides, but as a bulk unit, we'll be too heavy to knock into the water. Jessica will snipe from the beach. If we can make it across the bridge in less than a minute, the armor of our GMs should be able to withstand the assault."

Seungpyo's face looks almost blue in the image projected across my screen. "And if we can't?"

"Then we die," Alex says simply. Again, his face fails to show on our screens.

"Alex," I say, looking directly into my camera. Even if I can't see his face, he can see mine. "What are the statistics of a plan like this succeeding?"

Alex's response is immediate. "Seventy-five point-eight-seven percent."

Seungpyo whistles. "Not bad."

I ask my last question. "What's the percentage of all of us surviving?"

"Eighty-nine point-three-two percent."

"I'd high-five that high percentage," Seungri shouts in English.

I shut off my own cam and close my eyes.

The twins might be fooled, but I'm not. I don't trust those numbers. They're not just high. They're too high.

"Jaewon-ssi," Sela says, her singsong voice cutting through my troubled thoughts. "Are you all right?"

I roll my shoulders and press my comm back on. "I'm fine." I jerk my GM forward. "I'll take the front."

"No," Alex says. "You take the middle. Your GM's too damaged."

"I'll take the front," Seungpyo says, positioning his GM in front of mine. "Leave it to me. I got you kids covered."

Seungri sputters. "Kids?"

"Yeah, kids. I was born eighty-eight point-five-six seconds before you, remember? I got you, my cute little brother."

"Little?" Seungri falls over in his seat with laughter. "Cute?"

"You heard me," Seungpyo says, engaging the back of his GM with the front of mine. He grins into the camera. "Now shut up. Let's end this simulation in time for dinner."

"Dad's making dumplings!" Seungri shouts.

I shake my head. Brothers. I extend the arms of my GM outward, the right holding my power rifle, the left holding my shield. The front of my GM presses against the back of Seungpyo's, the back against the front of Seungri's. Alex takes up the rear, both of his guns aimed wide. The girls position themselves on the beach to snipe.

"On the count of three," Alex says, his face reappearing on our screens, expression blank. His calmness settles my nerves. Almost. "Three."

We jet forward. My gears are in neutral, propelled by Alex's speed and Seungpyo's direction. I pivot the head of my GM so that I can see the ocean to my right, aiming at Hydros in the water and blasting them with my power rifle. On my left, I can feel the bombardment of bullets hammering against the thick metal shield.

Halfway down the bridge, the gears in Seungri's wheels give out. His GM jerks to a stop, almost knocking all of us off the bridge.

"Ai—shhh. I'm disengaging," he shouts. He gives my GM, still attached to the back of Seungpyo, a powerful push, propelling me forward.

It happens in a second.

One moment, Seungpyo and I are speeding down the bridge, faster without the added weight of Seungri and Alex. The next moment, there's a blast. I'm thrown violently to the side. My machine staggers, but somehow remains upright. Ears ringing, I look up to see an empty space where Seungpyo's bot once stood. Frantically I zoom my camera in on his GM. It's in the water, sinking. Half of it is blown away, cockpit included.

Damage count: 23%.

My screen is static. Pieces of sharp metal fall from the

ceiling. The cockpit flashes red in warning. I grab the straight horizontal bar-shift and jam it forward into full throttle. My GM flies across the last remaining meters of the bridge, plunging through the shoddy gates surrounding the lighthouse. It smashes into the belly of the Tower, the walls crumbling down on either side of me.

"Seungpyo's down!" Jessica cries into the silence and smoke.

I watch on my circle map as the green dot labeled N.S.1, for No Seungpyo, peters out into nothing.

My eyes immediately focus on the still green dot labeled N.S.2, for No Seungri. It remains unmoving, still stuck on the bridge.

My eyes are glued to the dot, my throat swallowing dry air.

"Lee Jaewon!" Alex shouts.

They're brothers.

"Lee Jaewon!"

How can one live without the other?

"Jaewon-ah, listen to me. This isn't how it ends."

"Seungpyo's . . ."

"I know. *I know.* But you need to bring the rest of us home."

I take a breath.

Home.

I have no home.

I unclip the belt holding me down, and it retracts with an audible *zip.* "Here goes nothing," I murmur, turning the handlebar that opens into the lighthouse.

THE GIRL

It's cold in the lighthouse. A breeze whistles through the cracks in the mortar like a thin scream. I've never been near the ocean in reality, but the clinging salt of the air stings as it hits my skin.

Leaning forward out of the cockpit, I see my GM has burst through the rubble wall of the lighthouse, the front half of its body jammed against the crumbling spiral staircase.

Gripping the metal handlebar situated right outside the cockpit—placed on the GM to help the pilot maneuver in and out of the machine—I jump, feetfirst, onto the nearest staircase landing. A few chunks of cement fall from the stairs, crashing to the floor below.

Inside the GM, I'd been wearing my school uniform, but sometime between leaving the cockpit and landing on the stairs—maybe in the air as I jumped—the simulation changed my outfit into a standard soldier's uniform, black with one red armband. I also have a handgun tucked away in a holster attached to a gun belt worn across my chest.

I take the stairs three steps at a time, feeling winded by the eighth landing, even if this is a simulation. I'm surprised I haven't yet run into any enemy soldiers protecting the perimeter. The thirteenth landing ends at a door, the shadowed light of the lantern room seeping through the cracks.

I slowly turn the doorknob, press the toe of my boot against the wood, and ease it open. I raise my gun. I'm here to defuse a bomb, but it's likely guarded within the room.

The room is dark, the only source of light the lighthouse's lantern beam that slowly sweeps the gray-blue ocean waters, searching for imaginary ships in the night.

I wonder how many hours we've spent in this simulation. Time moves differently here. What could seem like hours in here could be minutes in the Real. It's how soldiers get trained so quickly and at such a young age. We spend so much fake time training in simulations to die in a moment in the Real.

Something flickers to my right.

"Sela?"

She stands behind the bars of a holographic cage, watching me, her eyes wide and dull. "Save me," she says, her voice sounding electronic and hollow. "Save me."

I flick on the mike at my ear, attached to my comm. "I found the hostage," I say dryly.

"Good," Alex responds. "What about the explosive?"

I peer around the room. It's hard to see anything. There are deep shadows in the corners, where the beam of the lighthouse fails to reach.

"It's not here."

"It has to be. The mission hasn't ended yet. Are you sure you checked all the rooms?"

I look around. There *are* no other rooms other than this one and the empty main chamber my GM crashed into. But maybe there's something hidden with Sela in the cage.

"No," I say, "one sec—"

I'm jarred to the side as a body hurtles into mine, a fist connecting beneath my rib cage and knocking the breath out of me. My gun slides across the floor, hitting the side of Sela's holographic prison.

My assailant, his face hidden beneath the shield of a pilot's helmet, is smaller than me, the top of his head reaching a little past my shoulders. Still, he's got a powerful punch. It takes all my strength, bolstered by adrenaline, to push him off. He veers into a wall, his helmeted head banging against the hard cement. He stumbles backward, raising his gloved hands to the base of his helmet.

I rush to Sela's static cage, grabbing my gun from the floor and twisting to shoot.

The globe of the helmet rocks upon the floor, revealing the face of my attacker.

I lower my gun.

"Lee Jaewon!" Alex shouts from the comm. "What's happening?"

I watch as the girl cocks her head to the side, as if listening to Alex's voice. There's no possible way she can hear him.

"It's you," I say.

I've seen her before. Last night at the concert. She'd been staring at the stage as Sela sang the last words of her song. Even if this moment in the lighthouse is simulated, yesterday night was real. I remember the way the police droids tumbled off the Grid and took her away. Who is she?

"Lee Jaewon!" Alex shouts again, and I squint at the pain of it in my ear. "Did you find the bomb?"

"There's a girl."

"That's nice," he growls. "Is she hostile?"

I'm about to answer when the girl lifts her hands to her collar. She wears a black jumpsuit that zips to her throat. Her face remains expressionless as she lowers the metal zipper. I swallow, my hand tightening on the gun. Why is she . . . ? Blue-and-red wire peeps out of the collar of her suit.

"It's on her," I say into my comm. "The bomb. She's wearing it."

There's a pause on Alex's end. "She attacked you, didn't she? Then she's hostile. Shoot her and defuse the bomb."

"This isn't the first time I've seen her. I think she's real."

"What the hell are you talking about?"

To my right, fake Sela flickers in her cage, a poorly constructed hologram wearing a pale pink dress that washes out her vacillating face.

The programmers of the simulation have Tech to make Sela appear real. Why would they choose to project a weak, almost blurred image of Sela, yet put small, unnecessary details on the image of the girl I'm facing? Even with the dim lighting of the lantern room, I *see* her. She has a light brown beauty mark at the bridge of her nose, thin lips, and empty eyes. Is it a trick? Is *she* the hostage?

"Lee Jaewon!" Alex yells from the comm. "I'm coming up. If you're still alive, I'm going to kill you."

I can't concentrate with Alex shouting in my ear, so I take out my earpiece. It's attached to a cord that wraps around my neck, and I have to duck my head to take it off. When I lift my head, the girl is no longer empty-handed. She holds a gun aimed at my chest.

Well, then.

She releases the gun's safety with an audible *click*.

We stare at each other. When she doesn't immediately shoot, I wonder if she's as curious about me as I am about her

"I've seen you before," I say.

"You couldn't have."

Her voice is clear like a wind chime.

Simulations can't respond without prewritten dialogue, so I decide to test her. "It was last night, a little before midnight."

She blinks, a first sign of emotion. "You were at the concert?"

"I was. The music could have been better."

The girl steps forward, eyes flashing. "You're wrong. It was beautiful."

Of course she would think that. I'd never seen someone so captivated by a song before.

A flash of surprise crosses her features, and then she scowls. "It doesn't matter if I was there or not. It doesn't matter if you were there or not."

"It matters to me." I step forward. "Who are you? Are you like me, taking a test at a different academy?"

She doesn't answer, pursing her lips.

I bend my knees and place my gun on the floor, then kick it away out of reach. I won't kill her, even to beat the simulation. If she's under the same test rules we are, killing her in the simulation would mean she could actually die in the Real. She watches me, a frown on her lips.

"I'm not going to shoot you," I say.

I watch as she slowly lowers her gun. "I—" she begins.

I never get to hear the end of that thought. The doors behind us bang open, and Alex explodes into the room, his comm already pulled off and hanging around his neck. He throws it to the floor, where it slides through fake Sela's cage.

"Shit, Jaewon," Alex says, breathing heavily. I can see the slight tremors in his hands, the onset of the Enhancer's withdrawal symptoms. His gaze moves from the girl's gun, raised again when Alex barreled into the room, to mine, clearly dropped on the floor. "Couldn't you have chosen a better time to lose it?"

"Alex, I think she's a student at another academy, taking a senior test just like us. If she dies in the simulation, she dies in real life."

Alex shakes his head, frowning. "That can't be right. I know for a fact that we're the only team taking this high-level test in the state. It broke regulations, but my father told me beforehand. To my knowledge, she's just a sim."

"If she's only part of the program, why hasn't she shot both of us already?"

This truth grabs Alex's sense of logic. We face the girl, seeing that she's lowered her gun.

"Kill me," she says.

I blink, thinking I've misheard her. "What?"

Alex picks up the gun from the floor. "If I kill you, will you die?"

"Alex . . . ," I warn.

"I'm already dead," she answers.

I pause, not understanding. I can't detect a lie in the blunt tone of her voice.

Alex's eyes narrow. "Are you taking a test somewhere else?"

"I am not."

"Do you want me to kill you? If you respond in the affirmative, I will shoot you."

"Yes."

He lifts the gun.

"Alex!" I shout, rushing him in the side. I hear the deafening sound of a gunshot.

Alex stumbles into the holographic cage. I whip around, scramble to the body of the girl, who is falling. Before I can reach her, she flickers with static, suspended centimeters above the ground.

I stop and look down at the erratic, pulsating image of her, the slow process of a simulated person canceling out of the program.

"You're not real," I say slowly. "You haven't died."

Alex crouches beside me. He has a regulation knife in one hand. He reaches for her chest, takes the red cord, and cuts it.

Immediately I feel myself being sucked out of the simulation, back to reality. Soon the shadows will creep close enough to pull me into unconsciousness.

Whether the girl's simulation feels pity for me (a strange thought) or whether I make up her response as my conscious dims, a few last words brighten my mind before I black out completely.

A person who doesn't exist can't die.

RAIN

I wake to the sound of shouting. Jessica slaps Alex hard across the face. He doesn't try to dodge it. He takes the bite of the slap with his eyes open.

"How could you?" she screams. "You lied about the test, and you lied about the percentages, and now Seungpyo's dead."

I look across the room. Seungpyo's body now rests on the hard floor of the simulation room. Seungri is on his knees beside him, his back turned from us.

His shoulders are shaking.

Tsuko has followed through with the rules. He sits at the regulators' table, calm, dictating some last notes to his mobile tablet.

I climb out of the pod. One of the cameramen corners me, talking into my ear. I ignore him and make my way to the door.

"Alex Kim and Lee Jaewon," Tsuko says, not looking up from his notes. "Report to the Tower in Gangnam for your official placement, Monday, February eleventh, 2199 at 12:30:00 KTC."

I don't wait to hear Jessica's or Seungri's assignments. I exit the room.

Sela waits outside in the circular common area, alone. Our test got out an hour later than the others, and the rest of the students have gone home.

"I thought you were very brave," Sela says. She bends at the stomach, bowing. "Thank you for taking care of me in the simulation. If it wasn't for you, I wouldn't be alive."

I shake my head, not sure what to say. An anguished cry issues from inside the room. Seungri.

I turn away from Sela's gaze. "I have to go," I say. I can't be here right now. Everything's so messed up. This school. This world.

Me, too, I think.

■ ■ ■

It's dark when I exit the gates of the academy. Storm clouds loom over the horizon, and the harsh winter winds sweep through the city. I stuff my hands deep into the pockets of my slacks. I just spent hours in an unreality, only to wake up to this one—a far cry from welcome. If there are stars out, I can't see them through the black clouds.

When the rain finally decides to drop, I want to be out of

this city and in my own. I'm tired of being in places where I don't belong.

"Lee Jaewon?"

A thickset man leans against the outer wall of the academy, his sunglasses already wet with the first droplets of rain.

When I don't answer, the man pulls his phone out of his pocket, holding the screen up in front of his face. He must have a photo of me, because he looks from the screen to me several times before placing it back in his pocket. "I have something for you."

"I don't want it," I say, brushing past him.

He reaches inside his coat and pulls out an envelope. "Come on, kid." The man holds the envelope out in the air between us. There's a scent to the envelope's paper—pomegranate blossoms. "You don't even know what's in it."

"Have you looked?" I ask.

He nods slowly, giving nothing away. I can't read his eyes behind his dark lenses.

I think briefly of leaving, but there's a betrayal of hope that creeps into my heart. I reach for the flap of the envelope, tipping it open slightly. Maybe it's a letter. Maybe it's an address. Maybe it's anything but what's actually there.

A wad of cold cash.

I swallow my disappointment, put my hand back in its pocket. "Tell her I don't need it."

"She'll worry," the man says.

It takes me awhile to respond. What he's said, it's just not true. "You're more persistent than others she's hired."

He shrugs. "Your mother pays well."

I nod, understanding. "You pocket the money and say you gave it to me."

"What if she—"

"She won't ask."

The man sighs, and then slides the envelope back inside his coat. "Is there anything you'd like me to say to her?"

I grimace. He must be feeling generous. Rich in money. Rich in thoughts.

"There's nothing."

I cross the street, trying to put distance between us. A traitorous thought gnaws at the back of my mind—if my mother gave him the money from her own hands, then he'd have seen her. He could describe her to me. Does she still have the small mole beneath her right eye? Or did she get it removed, like she said she always wanted? Does her smile still take up her whole face, like the moon at its brightest? Or does she never smile anymore?

I stop halfway down the opposite sidewalk. My hands are fists by my sides. Maybe I should ask him. It wouldn't hurt to ask him. It'll help make clear the image I have of her—an old image, a memory of her. I look, but the hired man is gone. He's called over a cab and fled.

At least he didn't stay long enough to see me turn around.

■ ■ ■

I'm not surprised when I step off the bridge and see Young

standing beneath the bridge cart ajumma's tarp roof. He's downing odeng and making the ajumma giggle like a schoolgirl.

"You've been cheating on me," I say to her as I approach, taking a place next to Young beneath the tarp. She holds out a stick of odeng over the vats of steaming broth, and I accept it with both hands.

"He says he's a friend of yours. You didn't tell me you had such a handsome friend. You've been stingy with me."

She's too taken with Young to see the marks on my face, the evidence of my earlier fight with Kim Jobi. I'm grateful for this. I don't want her to worry.

Young laughs at the ajumma's words. "Ajumeoni," he says, pouting, "Jaewon's a bad kid, isn't he? He's been selfish. If I'd known there was such a beautiful ajumeoni here, who cooks like an *angel*, I'd have visited every chance I could get."

I choke on the odeng, coughing into my fist. "You leave a bad taste in my mouth with lines like that. No wonder you don't have a girl."

"You don't know that I don't have a girl," Young says, turning his cap backward and crossing his arms.

"Do you?" the ajumma asks, chuckling at his exaggerated frown.

Young drops his shoulders with a dramatic sigh. "Girls just don't understand me." He pauses. I can see the moment a new thought comes to him, his mock-frown turning into a wicked grin. "Then again," he says, his teeth glinting, "you're not a girl. You're a woman."

"Ya!" the ajumma shouts, swatting a hand at his head. He ducks to avoid it.

I shake my head. "Stop fooling around." We bow to the ajumma. I left my motorbike at my apartment, so I head home on foot. Young follows me out.

Neither of us speaks as we walk away from the food cart, our hands in our pockets, our eyes on the broken ground. As we pass beneath a lit lamp, I hear Young suck in a breath. "Shit, Jaewon. Did you get in a fight?"

I don't say anything. I didn't actually do any fighting.

"Please tell me the other guy got it worse."

"I didn't touch him."

Young shakes his head. "I don't believe it. There's no way you let some punk get the best of you. That's not the Lee Jaewon I know."

I flinch.

"I mean," he says quickly, "that's not like you. You've too much pride."

"People change."

Young quiets, and I let out a breath, the warmth of it visible in the air. I'm being an asshole, I know. Why am I like this? Who am I trying to hurt? I look at Young.

His eyes are on the deserted street stretching ahead of us, most of the buildings lightless but for one or two doorways seeping out warmth. He looks tired. There are dark shadows under his eyes, a fresh wound on the side of his cheek. Has he been fighting? Who has he been fighting? How could Ro Jinwoon and Jeon Daeho let someone close enough to hurt him?

I turn away.

"Lee Jaewon?"

"I'm listening."

"The assassination attempt on the Director, it's all over the Net. NSK soldiers have already interrogated the other dancers in the assassin's troupe. They were all UKL agents and sympathizers."

The UKL. The United Korean League.

So it got out, the news. The Director must be furious. A rash independence group gaining attention in Neo Seoul won't look good for the NSK. It'll look like the government doesn't have full control.

"The girl herself was a new recruit. She'd found out last week that two of her sisters had been killed in combat overseas. Her attempt on the Director's life was more reactive than anything."

I remember how the girl had looked on the floor of the courtyard—young and afraid.

I force away the image. "What about Sela from C'est La Vie? She could be implicated for hiring her."

Young shakes his head. "I doubt it. The Director was seen tonight having dinner with the CEO of her entertainment company. It pays to be rich."

I grimace at Young's turn of phrase. It pays both figuratively and literally.

"Are you sure it's okay for you to go to that school?" Young asks. "Won't they recheck your papers? With the UKL making trouble in the city, there are bound to be more crackdowns in Neo Seoul. If you need new papers, I know a guy."

"I'm fine," I say. "I had a good forger the first time around."

"Yeah, but . . ." Young trails off. He takes his cap off, punching the inside of it. He puts it back on his head. "What about your mother? With the news of the UKL—"

"Worry about your own family," I say, my voice thick, the run-in with the man my mother hired still a fresh wound. She'd said she was leaving to help give me a new life. But I didn't *want* a new life, not at eight years old. I wanted her.

Young shakes his head. "I don't have a family."

I open my mouth to contradict him—only yesterday, I'd seen the last member of his family—but he speaks before I can get a word out. "My father died when your father died. My mother left when your mother left."

I hold his gaze. "You've experienced a lot of loss in your life."

"I have."

A drizzle of rain hits my shoulder.

"Stop this." My voice comes out tired, ragged. I begin to walk away, but he grabs my arm.

"Jaewon-ah . . ."

"Let me go."

He doesn't.

Let me go, Young.

I'll never tell him this, but today, when Seungpyo died, what upset me most wasn't that he died. It's that he'd died in front of his brother. And I'd thought, in the moment of his death, how it'd be hard to go on if Park Young had died in front of me. And then I thought of how Park Taesung could have killed me that night, two years ago. And how Young was the one who would have let it happen.

Young lets go.

He stays on the street corner, his gaze turned east toward Hongdae, the low glow of the neon signs lighting his face in eerie fluorescence.

I walk most of the way to my apartment, only running the last few minutes when the rain begins to pour from the sky.

10

THE TOWER

Our assignments don't start for another week. There's a funeral service for Seungpyo in Jamsil that I don't attend. Neither does Alex. Seungri's father pulls him from school and sends him abroad to study at a military academy in Neo Tokyo.

I continue my normal school and part-time job schedule that week. As I go through the motions, I think of Seungri, wondering if I'll ever meet him on the battlefield. The Neo States of Japan and Korea are allied in the war, but I wouldn't blame Seungri if he should look upon my face one day and see an enemy, someone who won a placement on a test while he lost his brother.

Jessica passes Alex and me in the hall. We don't speak.

Later I find out she's received a placement in the NSK's

defense cabinet, one of the more lucrative positions available. I'm glad for her. Even if she's lost a boyfriend in Alex, at least she's gained something more permanent.

Bora gets a placement working in supply inventory for the navy fleet, which satisfies her mother because Minwoo also gets placed in the adjoining navy training corps as a junior officer.

After school on Friday, Bora pulls me into one of the physical education supply storage rooms that she's converted into a private design studio. After she's completed her military service, she hopes to pursue fashion design. She bribed one of the janitors with cash to overlook her use of the storage room. And she's bribed me with food to be her fitting model.

I take a bite of a ham-and-cheese sandwich, standing shirtless on a pile of gym mats with half a jacket dangling from my shoulder. She waves a large pin in the air, and I eye it nervously.

"My mother keeps on goading me to 'secure' Minwoo, whatever that means. Does she want me to get pregnant or something?"

I refrain from commenting.

"I mean," Bora continues, "I get that he's, like, super rich or whatever, and that if I married him I'd be set for life, but God, let me count the ways my life would suck. I'd have to schmooze with the elites of society, all those stuck-up, judgmental old men and women, and I'd have to be *nice* about it. I couldn't have a career that his family didn't approve of, and I couldn't do anything to besmirch *his* family name."

"You couldn't," I say loyally. "You could only increase their status."

Bora lights up, and in her excitement, jabs me with the pin. "What if Minwoo finds a mistress?" she groans. "The new pop star after Sela, or maybe even Sela herself. I'd feel so pathetic."

"He wouldn't. And we're talking about Minwoo." I don't think Minwoo has ever spoken to a girl besides Bora.

"I know," Bora agrees. "All of what I've been saying is conjecture, and it doesn't even really matter in the long run. I couldn't marry him because I'd destroy him. I just feel like I'd walk all over him, you know?"

"Well," I say, "at least you're aware."

I get another jab, this time on purpose.

■ ■ ■

Monday is the start of our senior assignments. After class, I meet up with Alex outside the school gates. One of the incentives to join his team was his promise that he'd cover any assignment or transportation fees that might arise, and Alex, for all his many faults, never goes back on his word.

The courtyard buzzes with seniors waiting to move off to their assignments. The majority of them are taking cabs or the Skyway, a network of bullet trains in the sky.

I wave to Bora and Minwoo as they hop into a cab outside school. They'll head out to Incheon, where a naval port sits on the Yellow Sea.

Behind me, there's a chorus of oohs and aahs as a sleek imported car swerves up the streets outside the academy. Its doors lift open to reveal an empty leather-cushioned seating area. Alex walks over, signaling me to follow. I slide behind him into a car worth more than I could make in several lifetimes. The doors shut, and Alex plugs his phone into the jack.

"Athena, wake up," he says aloud in English. I raise an eyebrow. Sometimes I forget that Alex was born in the American Neo States. English is his first language.

"Good afternoon, Alex," says a distinctly female computerized voice from the speakers.

"Take us to the Tower."

"Confirming destination: the Neo State of Korea's Tower of Operations in Yeoksam-dong, Gangnam-gu, Neo Seoul. Arrival time is 12:24:47 KST."

The car moves smoothly onto the main streets of the Grid, picking up speed as we head deeper into the city.

In Old Seoul, roads are paved with prewar cement, and a driver determines the speed and direction of a vehicle.

In Neo Seoul, vehicles on the Grid are electro-magnetized, allowing for self-driving vehicles. Cars are programmed with a destination and given an optimal speed in which there is a less-than-.001-percent chance of collision or accident. The only cases of accidents occur when a foreign object disrupts the Grid—a drunk accidentally wandering off the sidewalk—but even then, the Grid corrects itself, compensating for unforeseen incidents.

Of course, not all cars are self-driving. The majority of

socialites prefer to have a driver, and cabs, like the ones I usually take, serve Old Seoul citizens—who, although they cannot own property in the city, are allowed transient visas to work low-level jobs in the service industry. Cabs with drivers are also cheaper than the self-driving cabs, owned by big Neo Seoul tech conglomerates, which charge exorbitant rates.

The Grid rumbles with the sound of the magnet working beneath it, a low grinding offset by the zooming of the cars. At midnight, the magnet shuts down, slowing speeds significantly. Cars can still move on the Grid, but the max speed lowers from one hundred twenty kilometers per hour to sixty.

The interior of the car is L-shaped, and Alex sits on the two-seater, while I sprawl out on the longer bench. The walls of the car double as windows to the outside and display screens. At present, the windows are set to the news of the day, live from City Hall.

A woman stands outside on the black marbled steps of the government building, speaking into a bouquet of floating mikes. Her voice is low and monotone, relating news she couldn't care less about. "The trial for the UKL traitors who were behind the attempted assassination of our city's Director concludes today."

So they're blaming the attack on all the dancers, not just the girl. Perhaps to make an example of anyone tied to the UKL.

"After four days of intense deliberation, the High Court of Neo Seoul has sentenced these five men and women to death by firing squad, which will be carried out in two weeks' time on the military base at Incheon."

The screen switches from the reporter to the Director, presiding over a large chamber inside City Hall's municipal building.

His voice booms through the speakers of the car where Alex and I sit, silently watching. "Their deaths will not be recorded, nor will their bodies be buried, but burned, their ashes scattered in separate places from one another, far away from the NSK. It is ironic that their greatest punishment will not be that they have died, but that their restless souls will never be cradled in the bosom of the homeland they say they will have died for. We will not be haunted by these worthless shades of men and women."

The screen pans out to show the full room. Below the Director kneel the members of the dance troupe, three women and two men, their hands locked together with electro-braces, their heads bent toward the floor. One dancer, a boy who couldn't be older than fourteen, sheds tears on the marble.

Alex slides his hand over a panel, and the windows of the car clear into a view of the city. We're passing through a university center, where the car slows due to traffic.

On either side of us are cafés, two per city block, alongside colossal tiered restaurants, crowded interiors visible through clear windows. SimTech bars top almost every building, where a person can pay an hourly fee to use the simulation rooms, experiencing any kind of unreality.

Moving walkways on the street take shoppers from block

to block, slanting upward to bridge over the Grid. Advertisements line the walkways, flashing with colors—ads for makeup brands; cosmetic surgery physicians; brands of coffee, tea, and alcohol, all produced and shipped from factories in southern Korea. Sela of C'est La Vie appears on floating billboards and on the sides of Skyway trains overhead, endorsing a variety of multicolored products.

Alex sweeps his hand on the panel again, and the windows darken. He lights a cigarette, the spark of the lighter temporarily dispersing the darkness inside the car, revealing his face for a moment, his eyes downcast and focused on the cigarette.

"They're not telecasting the news of the execution on the billboards," I say. Usually important bits of news make it in between the commercials and music videos.

Alex presses a switch on his armrest, which opens a window that sucks out the smoke. Like all pollutive gases, it'll eventually get swept up through one of the large purification pillars that rise up from the city and released into the atmosphere outside the Dome. They say you can see the halo of smoke over Neo Seoul for three hundred kilometers. You can definitely feel it in Old Seoul. In Old Seoul, it's in your skin.

"No one wants to watch something so depressing," Alex says.

With the window of the car open, I can hear the noises of the city streets—the humming rush of the Grid cars and the indistinguishable sounds of thousands of voices merging together, all set to the backdrop of booming techno music.

A group of middle school kids, their blue-and-white uniforms placing them at an academy in Nonhyeon, walk down a side street. I watch as one girl throws an arm around another. One of the boys jumps on the back of his friend, who carries him halfway down the street.

To think that in a few years, these kids will be conscripted to join the war effort, a two-year requirement for all Neo Seoul citizens eighteen years and older. The senior placements give students the opportunity to start their military quotas in higher-level positions, and many students choose careers in the military even after their quotas are fulfilled, but one of the consequences of living a privileged life beneath the Dome is a two-year sacrifice outside it, defending the Neo State. Of course you hear the stories of rich kids paying their way out of service, but to many, a life of such dishonor is a fate worse than death.

Old Seoul citizens are not required to serve, although many young men and women join with the hope to better their situations, for themselves and for their families. It's also the most common way aside from marriage for an Old Seoul citizen to become a Neo Seoul citizen. However, they face disadvantages from the outset. All Old Seoul citizens start off as foot soldiers, who have the highest rate of casualties in the war, and unless they prove themselves exemplary soldiers, it's very difficult to raise their initial rankings.

Still, the hope of a better life is a dream most Old Seoul citizens share.

I know I do.

Alex closes the window, and we don't speak the rest of the way to the Tower.

■ ■ ■

We arrive at the Tower at 12:24:47 KST, the exact time Athena had calculated for us.

The Tower is the tallest structure in the city, a giant monolith hundreds of meters thick and over a kilometer in height, constructed of reinforced concrete and steel. It was completed between the end of the First Act of the War and the beginning of the Second, a building to symbolize the power and prosperity of the NSK. It's rumored that an elevator ride to the top of the Tower takes twelve minutes—five minutes in a high-speed elevator.

As I think this, an observation car at the side of the building ascends from one of the lower floors into the Spire, the highest point of the Tower. The car travels higher and higher, the vague figure of a person standing inside. Squinting against the sunlight, I watch it disappear as if sucked straight up into heaven.

Alex's vehicle comes to a halt at the front of the Tower, and the doors lift open. We follow the representative waiting outside into the lobby.

An enormous replica of the Tower's most famous weapon from the First Act of the Great War, the infamous God Machine called the Marionette, dominates the middle of the floor. It's a huge machine, around sixteen meters tall, built for air mobility with jet thrusters, a machine gun attached to its right arm, and a titanium blade in place of its left.

In the war, the computer-operated Marionette was a

killing machine. Without a pilot, it could carry out ceaseless attacks, unable to feel pain or fatigue, the common weaknesses of human pilots.

Marionette production ended after the Second Act of the War, though, due to the high expense of producing even one of them, as well as the reality that, as a machine, it couldn't account for human ingenuity, or even human error. On the battlefield, well-placed or forgotten detonations from its own side could destroy a mindless Marionette, and a skilled pilot could break through the Marionette's programmed maneuvers, evidenced by "ace pilots" throughout the end years of the war.

"She's a beauty, isn't she?"

We turn to see a small, skinny man with round glasses approach us across the lobby, the representative having disappeared during our examination of the machine.

"I cried at her funeral," the man continues jovially, "but I've come to accept that all great inventions will be replaced by even greater ones."

The man blinks at us, his eyes magnified behind his glasses. He's about half my height.

"You must be Alex Kim and Lee Jaewon." We bow to him, and he smiles. "My name is Koga Hiroshi, but you can call me Dr. Koga. I'm one of the directors of weapons development here at the Tower. If you'll please follow me, I'll show you around."

Dr. Koga walks away without waiting for a response. For a man who looks like a turtle in a white coat, he moves fast.

"The first three floors of the Tower are public and act as our state's premier military museum," he informs us. "Floors five through fifty are private and function as headquarters for our Department of Defense. Fifty and above comprise the Spire of the Tower, which holds offices, a few private living quarters, and of course, at the very top, the Skyroom, where we host sponsor-related events."

The Spire also has the searchlight, but he doesn't mention it.

We follow the doctor through security—a wide, metal-detecting gateway—and into the main interior of the building, a construct of leveled floors. Dr. Koga leads us to a receptionist, who scans our eyes and records the cadences of our voices before issuing us Tower IDs, complete with a photo she takes on the spot—I attempt a smile in mine; Alex doesn't—and our employee numbers.

Lee Jaewon. T1103.

She injects the ID, programmed into a chip, into my wrist. The wound left by the injection smarts only for a moment before the receptionist places a square of MediTape over it, dulling the pain. I don't ask how I'll get it out later.

"Now that's taken care of," Dr. Koga says, "we'll go to the conference room and debrief you on where you'll be placed in the Tower."

I hope I'm not placed anywhere above floor ten. I'm not afraid of heights, but I'd prefer to be closer to the ground. Actually, a placement in the museum would be great.

Dr. Koga leads us toward the elevator bank at the back end of the lobby. Before we can reach it, though, a man stumbles out. He's wild-eyed, one hand pressed to his head. He stares dazedly around the hall before his eyes land on Koga. The man swallows an agonized breath of air before gasping, "She's escaped."

The loud wail of a siren pierces the air.

11

THIRD MEETING

Koga grabs his comm, shouting, "Shut it down!" As abruptly as the sirens started, they stop. It was a short enough amount of time that most workers remained in their stations.

Koga helps the wounded man to the floor. "How did this happen?"

"I went into the room to check on her. We got into a fight, and she threw me against the wall. I blacked out." The man is in his late thirties, powerfully muscled. Whoever he fought with must be pretty tough.

"How long ago was this?" Koga retrieves a small mobile tablet from his coat. It displays a map of the Tower. He presses a button, and a flashing red light appears against a 3-D floor plan.

"About fifteen minutes," the man says. "After I woke and realized what happened, I came here directly."

"That was the right thing to do," Koga says. He checks the man's head wound. "You'll be fine." He motions to the receptionist, who summons a medic with a gurney. They lift the man onto the bed and wheel him away.

Koga stands. "According to the beacon of her tracker, she hasn't left the Tower. But she must have jammed the signal. It shows her location to be here in the lobby."

We survey the large room. Since he's using the pronoun "she," I look for identifiable women in the lobby. There's the receptionist behind her desk, who's currently fielding phone calls, and the rest of the women are either guards or scientists.

"Is it possible she could have taken out her tracker?" This from Alex, who, for all I know, is as in the dark with all this as I am.

"Possible, but unlikely," Koga says. "The tracker is located inside her chest."

And I thought the ID chip inserted in my wrist was invasive.

"It's more likely the jammed signal is confusing the depth of the Tower." He points on the tablet screen to the flashing red dot, which hasn't moved for the past several minutes we've been standing here. He moves his finger in a line upward, dotting in green the different levels of the Tower. "She could be on any of these floors, and as we just discussed, there are over a hundred levels in the Tower, not including the basements." Although Koga was friendly before, his voice is hard now, faced with a difficult situation. It changes slightly my initial impression of him as a hapless scientist. "If we don't find her soon, we'll have to notify security. They'll evacuate the Tower, which will lead to questions from the media. I want to avoid that if at all possible."

As he speaks, I have a thought. "Can I see that?" I point to the tablet, and Koga hands it over. "On the way here," I say, thinking out loud, "I noticed the Tower is mostly comprised of steel-reinforced glass, which would make an escape from the windows impossible. There are exits, but at different points with varying accessibility." I tap the exits, which are high-lighted in red. They're not anywhere close to the beacon. "If she's attempting to escape, then she'd either be here"—I point to the lobby, which has the obvious public exit—"or here." I point to the roof of the Tower, which, from my limited knowledge of the Tower's infrastructure, has escape capsules in case those on the upper floors need to evacuate.

Koga gives me an approving nod. "That's a good lead." He takes back the tablet. "I think we'll follow it."

He heads over to the receptionist desk and scans his wrist to open a panel in the wall beside it, out of which he removes two electro-guns and a set of electro-braces. He hands Alex and me the guns. We follow him to a different bank of elevators across the lobby, the high-speed ones with access to the upper floors.

I'm surprised he's not bringing more guards with us. Alex and I placed second and fifth in marksmanship at the academy, but he doesn't know that. Then again, he must have reviewed our records, since he's in charge of our placements.

Before the elevator closes, a voice calls out, "Dr. K!", and a hand reaches between the doors, causing them to reopen. A girl around our age stumbles into the elevator.

"I just heard the alarm!" she pants, obviously having run a distance. "I want to help."

Koga seems shocked to see her. "How did you—?" He cuts off, glancing at Alex and me. He takes off his glasses and begins to wipe the right lens with the hem of his lab coat.

I wonder if this newcomer is Koga's daughter, but I don't see a resemblance. Her features—large, light brown eyes, and sun-burnished skin—place her parentage in China, possibly the South, while Koga is a Japanese surname. She also hadn't called him "Father."

"Dr. K," she says, her voice higher in exasperation, "I think *I*, of all people, should be able to handle this situation. I mean, I'll just logically explain to her, in graphic detail, why jumping off the roof would be in bad form."

She pauses. "Pancakes!" she yells, causing Alex to jump a little.

"Oh, sorry," she says. "My mind just went there, you know; first I was thinking of Tera jumping off the building, and then I pictured her flat, like a pancake, and then I was thinking how I'd love pancakes right about now."

She grins, revealing two dimples. She's cute.

Alex doesn't say a word, just stares at her, his expression guarded.

"It's past noon," I say. "You've missed breakfast."

"I know," she groans.

I think of what I ate for breakfast this morning. Hard-boiled eggs off the bridge ajumma's food cart. Six of them.

"Oh," the girl whines, "You're making me hungry."

I hadn't said anything aloud.

"Ama!" Koga says worriedly, "You always say you dislike heights, my dear. They give you . . . headaches."

"They pop my ears!" Ama says. "I might even swoon." She glances back up at Alex, smiling shyly. "But you'd catch me, wouldn't you? You're the kind of boy who catches girls, aren't you? Do you have lots of girlfriends?"

"No."

"No to everything or no to just to the last?"

"No."

"That wasn't a yes or no question."

"I don't have a girlfriend."

"Ama!" Koga says, exasperated. "This isn't the time! Can you hear Tera?"

Ama rolls her eyes. "Please, Dr. K. Not even *my* hearing is that good."

I ignore their conversation and check the electro-gun's chamber. It's fully charged.

A couple more minutes pass before we reach the top of the Tower and the doors open.

We face a marble platform with staircases that drop to the left and right, descending into a massive ballroom lined with round tables and high-backed chairs. The walls of the room are all floor-to-ceiling windows. Clouds outside obscure the sunlight and cast patches of shadows across the mosaic floors.

"We have to take the stairs," Ama says, moving away from

the glass elevator to a side door. She wrenches it open to reveal four flights of cement steps, leading up. Ama, in her haste, takes them too fast, and trips. Alex catches her arm before she can fall on her face.

I take the lead. I'm first through the heavy metal door at the top of the stairs. It opens onto the flat roof of the Tower.

A girl stands at the ledge of the roof. Her hair whips wildly out from behind her like a kite caught in the wind. She's barefoot, and her back is to us, but I recognize her immediately.

A person who doesn't exist can't die.

"Tera!" Ama shouts from behind me. "Don't be a pancake!"

The girl—Tera—doesn't seem to hear.

"Jaewon," Alex says, "go grab her. I'll cover you."

I check the safety of my gun and tuck it into the waistband of my pants. "Try not to shoot me."

I leave them and make my way slowly across the roof, scuffing my shoes against the cement so that Tera can hear my approach. When I'm standing behind her, I cough to signal my presence. I don't try to grab her; instead, I move to her left and look over the ledge, whistling at the far drop. Even the tallest buildings beneath the Tower are hundreds of meters away.

The Skyway is in motion, its trains zooming throughout the city. The Tower is located next to a main terminal, and I can see the colored pathways of the Skyway branch off into colored lines, one yellow line leading to Bundang, one orange line leading to Apgujeong.

I plot the trajectory of the girl if she were to jump. There's a chance she'd hit one of the colored lines.

"I'd wait until night if I were you," I say. "The Skyway shuts down then, and the lines disappear. You'd have an unimpeded fall. Much less messy."

A tightening around the corner of her mouth is all she gives me as an answer. Apparently, she's not amused. I switch from sarcasm and try Alex's usual tactic. Cold intimidation. "Step down before the wind knocks you over, and it's no longer your choice." I reach out, thinking I'll grab her arm, but hesitate when she turns to look at me. Her eyes follow my outstretched hand to my face, and I realize she's waiting for me to touch her. But not in kindness, not in concern. She's waiting for me to touch her with force. I can see it in the way she watches me, her dark eyes expectant.

I drop my hand.

Her voice, when she speaks, is just as I remember it from the lighthouse, soft and clear. "I want to feel free." I have to strain to hear her words in the whistling wind. "If only for a moment."

"Death isn't freedom." I try to sound like I believe my own words.

She raises an eyebrow. "Who says I want to die?"

"You're standing at the edge of a building a kilometer in height."

"One kilometer and two hundred and fifty meters," she corrects.

"It's that extra fifty that will do it."

She scowls, and I grin—why do I feel this urge to annoy her?

"Well, you're wrong." She closes her eyes and spreads her arms wide. "I don't want to die." She inhales and breathes out, "I want to live."

For half a second, I think she'll jump. I move to reach out and catch her. But she remains still, holding that position. She breathes deeply the cold winter air. I can see her eddying breaths; they escape past her lips like whispered ghosts. Her chest moves and up and down, slow and rhythmic. I've never seen someone so in the moment, as if this was the first time she's ever breathed, or the last.

The gun feels like a weight at my back.

"Are you a prisoner here?" I ask. Maybe she's a rebel. One of the assassins from the dance troupe. Then again, what do rebels even look like? She's wearing what she wore at the concert, a loose shirt and pants. And even if she were a rebel, it doesn't explain *why* she was at the concert or in the simulation.

She opens her eyes again to look at me. "You don't know?"

"Let's assume I know nothing right now." These are the things I know: I saw her at the concert, where she was taken away by the police. I saw her in the simulation, in which I thought she was a student taking a test at another academy. And now I see her here, standing on the rooftop, breathing in the air as if she can absorb the wind. Who is she?

"You'll know soon," she says, her eyes moving across my face. "And then you won't look at me the way you're looking at me now."

"And what way is that?"

Like she's unlike anyone I've ever met before. Like she's mysterious and strange and easily annoyed.

"Like I'm human."

I feel a presence at my back, and I look to see Alex standing close behind us, with Ama and Dr. Koga. I'm grateful to see Alex has put away his gun. In its place, though, he holds the electro-braces.

Tera looks at the braces.

Koga shrugs helplessly. "The others will be nervous if you're not . . . secure, my dear. Jaewon-ssi, would you do the honors?"

It's strange how he's so polite about it. Tera steps down from the ledge and turns her back to me. I take the braces from Alex.

Electro-braces are the highTech counterpart of Old Seoul handcuffs. When powered on, an unbreakable electro-chain forms between the two links. I carefully close the cuffs around her wrists and switch on the link. The spark of electricity ignites in a white-gold chain, and a light buzz fills the air. It looks wrong, seeing her cuffed.

I peer down at my own wrists, the jut of my veins the only color beneath the skin. I wear a ring on my left middle finger—a platinum band, cheap, meaningless. It's just a ring. It doesn't hurt, because I can take it off.

Ama throws me a curious glance before approaching Tera. I notice for the first time that they're wearing the same outfit. Their appearances, though, are markedly different. Tera is average height, pale and slim, while Ama is short and rosy-cheeked. She puts her arms around Tera's shoulders and leans in to whisper something.

Who are they? How do they know each other? I'm bursting with questions. If Tera isn't a prisoner, then what—*who*—is she? Alex appears just as curious, watching Ama with an unnerving intensity.

We follow Dr. Koga back to the elevator. All of us crowd inside, Koga at the front, the girls in the middle, and Alex and I pressed against the back.

The only sound to break the silence is the buzz of Tera's cuffs. Ama moves Tera's long, unbound hair over her shoulder so it won't get caught in the electric chain.

When we reach the lobby, the elevator doors open to reveal a contingent of waiting guards. They're in riot gear, helmeted and carrying thick shields. Tera walks out, and they ring her. Alex and I exchange a glance. What's going on? She's unarmed. What do they think she can do to them? It's an eerie sight: a ring of faceless men and women dressed in black surrounding Tera, defenseless, her hands hooked behind her.

They walk across the lobby, round a corner, and disappear from view.

12

WHITE FLOWER

With a promise to get us some answers soon, Dr. Koga directs Alex and me to a conference room on the thirtieth floor, and then tugs Ama away with him in the direction Tera and the soldiers had taken. I have to call Alex's name several times to get his attention. He shakes his head. "Sorry." We take one of the steel elevators off the lobby and approach the conference room. The door has a biometric lock, so I hold my bandaged wrist to the scanner. It reads my ID through the MediTape and whirs open.

It's a standard room, with windows at the back. The main feature is a long glass table that stretches down the middle of the room.

Alex heads over to the table and collapses into a chair. I take the seat opposite him, farthest from the window and closest to the door. The table is bare except for a bowl of water at the center, atop which floats a single white flower.

My phone buzzes in my pocket. I pull it out to see that I have three messages. The first is from Bora. She left early from her assignment and is now getting a haircut. It comes with a small video of her in a swivel chair, making peace signs. I mute it and watch the minute-long video. The second is from Min-woo, who says he's bored and heard about some sort of breach at the Tower. He asks if I know anything, and I text back, No. The last is from the food cart ajumma who asks if I can man the cart tonight for a few hours. This I text back with an affirmative.

I put my phone back into my pocket and glance over at Alex to see he's watching coverage of what they've titled the "Tower Incident." News travels fast. I lean back in my chair and look around the room. The far wall features a display screen that currently depicts the symbol of the NSK, a black circle over a white background. The words issued by the Neo Council after the Great War are printed in Chinese above the screen. I can't read the characters, but I remember what they say.

Only countries destroy other countries. Only selfishness breeds selfish actions. Without nationhood, there is no war. Without nationhood, there is only peace. Unity in all things; humanity above monstrous division.

This was the basic ideology of the Neo Council after the First Act of the Great War—that if countries were disman-tled, lasting peace would be attainable. Each country became a state—China, considered too powerful, had been separated into North China and South China—and each state elected a representative to sit on the Council. The first test came when Western powers, fearing a united East Asian sphere, declared war on the Neo Alliance. This was the Second Act of the Great War. It ended in a decisive victory for the Neo Alliance, which cemented its sovereignty over East Asia. For several years, the Neo Council ruled without dissent, until a charismatic ruler arose in South China, calling for independence. Under his influence, South China seceded from the Council. After months of guerilla attacks by the rebels, North China declared war on South China, pulling the whole alliance into war. The Third Act of the Great War had begun.

Five decades of war—hundreds of millions of deaths. And for what?

Alex, having finished watching the news, sprawls across the table. His fingers extend out to graze the petals of the white flower. "I don't see the use of flowers," he says absently. He pulls a petal from the flower in the bowl and drops it into the water.

I'm about to respond, probably to say something as inane, when the doors whir open. Dr. Koga walks in, accompanied by a middle-aged woman with Eurasian features. Immediately Alex and I stand and bow. When I look up, I'm surprised to see the next person to walk through the door.

"Jaewon-ssi!" Sela cries happily. The pop star rushes to my side and takes my arm. The last time I saw her—besides on the billboards on the way over here—was a week ago at the test. Maybe her enthusiasm is a carryover from when I saved her life during the simulation.

I wonder if she knows I would have saved anyone in that specific situation. It would have been shitty not to.

"Take a seat," the woman who walked in with Dr. Koga says, and Sela takes a seat to the left of me. Koga and the woman approach the display screen, and it syncs to Koga's tablet, transitioning from the NSK flag to a blue background. "My name is Dr. Natalie Chung," the woman begins, her Korean accented and clipped. She's tall and lean, a contrast to Koga's short and squat. "I'm the lead machinist here at the Tower. I work in weapon design and the development of God Machines.

"You were all specifically chosen for this project by our board of directors, which includes me and my esteemed colleague, Dr. Koga Hiroshi." She pauses for Koga to give a little bow. "Together we went over the results of your tests and chose each of you as candidates for our project."

She keeps saying "project." I wonder if she'll ever get around to telling us what it is.

"Before we move forward with our presentation, I would like you all to sign this nondisclosure agreement, which prohibits you from speaking about your time here in the Tower without Dr. Koga's or my express authorization. Just press your thumb to the signature at the bottom."

Sela emails the NDA to her lawyer, who gives her the go-ahead to sign a few minutes later, and I think Alex actually reads the whole seven or eight pages before pressing his thumb down.

Since everyone else signs it, I sign it. I don't have a lawyer or a fast-processing mind. I don't even have a real identity. The one programmed with my thumbprint is for another Lee Jae-won whose mother is dead (false), whose father is dead (true), and has no ties to the United Korean League (true/false).

"Now," Koga says, "onto the main reason we brought you here today." He clears his throat and clicks the tablet. The words THE AMATERASU PROJECT display across the screen. "In the year 2152 at the end of the First Act of the Great War, the Board of the NSK constructed the Tower as a special center to build the world's greatest weapon. A scientist by the name of Sato Jun was the head of the project. He named it the Amaterasu Project, after the sun goddess of Japan. The Director at the time gave his team the go-ahead, and they began production."

The Amaterasu Project. I've never heard of it before. I glance at Alex to read his reaction, but his face remains blank.

Dr. Koga scrapes his hand against his stubbled chin. "During the First Act of the Great War, Enhancers made war a mad bloodbath that ended in more deaths than lives saved. With the drug-addled Enhanced of that war, scientists began conducting tests to see why humans reacted so negatively to the drugs, why they couldn't retain the Enhancements in their body without succumbing to addiction and psychosis."

No wonder they asked us to sign an NDA. After the First Act of the War, performance Enhancers were illegalized, in Korea and in every single state in the Neo Alliance.

"Of those scientists, Sato's team was able to weave some of

the Enhancements into the genome of a human child, altering a select set of genes in their DNA and allowing for the drugs to enhance the child before the onset of puberty. In fact, they deduced that the drugs are ineffectual after *puberty*, which accounts for their misuse by adults prior to their studies. The drugs also work exclusively within the genetic makeup of a female rather than a male, due to the unique expression profile of females during puberty. There were some setbacks along the way, but now, almost fifty years after it first began, we have two test subjects who've made it past childhood and into adolescence who've shown stability in skill levels. They are our prototypes. Our goddesses, if you will."

THE AMATERASU PROJECT flashes bold on the screen.

The pieces click into place.

A person who doesn't exist can't die.

Amaterasu.

Ama. Tera. Su.

Ama . . .

. . . Tera

They're code names.

13

THE AMATERASU PROJECT

"Ama," Dr. Koga says, tapping a button on his tablet to display an image on the screen of the girl from the elevator, smiling and lovely, dressed in a blue jumpsuit, "or Weapon 3016, is sixteen years of age, the first prototype of her category." Koga swipes across the tablet screen, and Ama's stats appear in vertical script alongside her image—her weight, height, place of birth, and a short description of her skills and temperament.

"In her inherited genetic code, Ama already had an inclination toward the psychic; her parents and grandparents were shamans in China—all of whom were casualties in the war. The Enhancers mutated this natural inclination into an ability."

"She's . . . psychic," Alex says slowly.

"Correct. She can pick up thoughts as well as dreams and memories. She, however, suffers some minor side effects of the drugs, including a weakness of the body and an inability to fully control the use of her Enhancements."

Dr. Koga gives his tablet another tap.

The screen switches from depicting an image of Ama to an image of Tera. Unlike Ama, Tera isn't smiling in her photo. Her straight brown hair falls loosely around her shoulders. Her dark eyes are focused on the camera.

"Tera," Dr. Koga says, "or Weapon 3017, is seventeen years of age. She differs from Ama in that her Enhanced abilities are mostly physical."

Another swipe and this time, Tera's stats roll vertically down the screen. Like Ama, it shows her weight and height. Her place of birth is recorded as Neo Seoul in the Neo State of Korea, a year after my own. Her list of abilities is long, including the distance she can jump, the rate of her cell regeneration, and her strata of knowledge on a variety of subjects, namely battle strategies. Her temperament is left blank.

Sela raises her hand, and Dr. Koga nods at her. "You said the other weapon, Ama, suffers side effects. Does Weapon 3017 manifest side effects?"

"Yes, although Tera isn't weak of body—quite the opposite—she does suffer occasional headaches, and of course, difficulties in controlling her Enhancements."

He exchanges a quick glance with Dr. Chung. I have a feeling they're not telling us everything.

Alex asks, "Did this project pass an ethics board?"

I glance at him, surprised he'd care.

Dr. Chung answers. "The project hasn't gone public yet. And those are issues that perhaps Sela can help us with, as we've decided to bring her onto the project to help with public relations." The machinist has neatly avoided answering Alex's actual question of whether an ethics board looked at this project before it began nearly fifty years ago.

"Yes!" Dr. Koga says jovially. "Which brings us to the last item on today's agenda."

He clicks his tablet, and Alex's stats appear on the screen.

"Alex, we believe you are the perfect candidate to lead the team. You've been student president every year at your academy, you've received stellar grades in all your classes, especially leadership and diplomacy, and you've led your team to victory on one of the hardest tests ever administered to seniors."

"And as the Director's only child," Dr. Chung adds, "doors will be open to you that wouldn't be open to anyone else, which can only help the project long term."

If Alex is bothered by this blatant admission of his familial ties and advantages, he doesn't show it.

"Although you will be the point person on the project, making sure all the members of the team are informed, you will spend the majority of your time working closely with Weapon 3016."

Alex sits forward in his chair. "Ama," he says.

"Correct. As I said, although we haven't gone public yet, we will soon. We need to, in order to gain sponsors and further the program. In light of this, we're working closely with our prototypes to prepare them. You are assigned as Ama's primary supervisor."

Before I have time to absorb this information, Koga moves on. "And lastly, Lee Jaewon."

They skip over Sela, but she doesn't seem to mind, sitting quietly in her chair with a content expression. I wonder if they briefed her earlier.

Koga pulls up my record. Born in Old Seoul. 186 centimeters. I have above-average scores on all my subjects, nothing too impressive. The most outstanding part of my résumé is perhaps my battle count, the sheer number of simulations I've run, and the ratio of wins to losses. Students are required to run a minimum amount of battle simulations, around ten to twenty a semester. I ran more for credits—which can be used at school to purchase supplies and food—but also because they kept me sharp, and they're fun.

"You're a well-rounded student," Dr. Koga says, nodding to me, "but more than that, you're a good soldier. The board was in mutual agreement that someone with your strength of character and soldierly aptitude would be best suited as Weapon 3017's primary supervisor. You will oversee her afternoon schedule, which includes daily blood work, a variety of skill tests, and anything else required of her. You will write up reports that will be issued to the Board and the rest of your team. But your main responsibility is to monitor Tera."

I wonder if this was the job of the man who came out of the elevator with a head wound. Still, it would be a lie to say I'm not intrigued about the project, and about Tera.

"Well, that completes our presentation for today. We'll reconvene tomorrow."

We all stand.

"Jaewon-ssi." Dr. Koga stops me. "Can I have a word with you?"

I bow to Dr. Chung and Sela as they pass. Alex gives me a questioning look, and I shrug. I have no idea what the good doctor wants.

When the room empties, Koga signals for me to join him at a window at the back of the room, where it looks out on the city. Sometime in the past hour, it began to rain, and a deep fog coats the air.

Dr. Koga coughs into his fist. "I pulled you aside because I wanted you to know that it won't be easy," he says. "Tera has had several supervisors over the years, all of whom have quit. She has . . . episodes, a result of the Enhancer. It's not a matter of intent. Tera's a good girl. She can't help herself."

I don't say anything. The rain begins to fall harder. The Dome might cover the city, but it's permeable, allowing aircraft and weather to pass through. It takes an unearthly amount of electricity for the Dome to solidify, which is why it only occurs at night or when the city is under attack.

Koga continues, "I just wanted to be up-front with you. Out of everyone, your job will be the most difficult and the most dangerous. In fact, the fine print of the NDA contract says that even if you were to suffer an injury during the interim of your assignment, you can't press charges. Even if you were to die, your family can't seek recompense. This clause doesn't really apply to the others, but it will in your case."

Ah, so that's the real reason I was chosen. My life is expendable.

I turn to Dr. Koga. "You said it yourself. I'm a soldier. Soldiers follow orders. I'll do what I need to do." To complete this assignment. To graduate. To take my exorbitant stipend and leave.

Koga holds my gaze, scrutinizing me through the glare of his lenses. "Very good. Until tomorrow, Lee Jaewon."

I bow and walk from the room.

■ ■ ■

I find Alex in the lobby, looking out into a downpour.

"Shit," he says in greeting. He grabs two umbrellas off a rack next to the doors, umbrellas provided for Tower employees on occasions such as this.

I come up alongside him, taking the umbrella he hands me. "'Shit, it's raining,' or 'shit, what did we sign up for'?"

"The second," Alex answers. "It's always raining."

We stand there in silence, watching the droplets hit the pavement. Maybe Alex is thinking of Ama. I wonder briefly if we'll have a conversation about what we'd seen in the Tower, but Alex doesn't disappoint.

"See you later." He steps outside, opening up his black umbrella to shield himself from the rain. In only a few steps, he's disappeared from sight.

I'm about to step out into the downpour myself when I hear footsteps behind me. I'm not alone in the lobby.

The presence of another person wouldn't normally put me on edge, but whoever this is waited until Alex left before emerging from the shadows beneath the Marionette.

"Of all the places I'd think to find you," a familiar voice drawls, "the Tower would have been the very last. You're playing with fire, Lee Hyunwoo's son. It's almost as if you had a death wish."

Memories flash in my mind.

I don't want to die. The thoughts of an eight-year-old boy.

I want to live. At sixteen years, my thoughts had been the same.

I turn to face Park Taesung, the red moon pin on the lapel of his jacket a reminder of the scarred circle burned over my heart. The scarring was part of the initiation process into the Red Moon gang. I've had it for ten long years, even if for the last two it hasn't had any significance beyond a bad memory.

"No greeting for your old boss?"

Slowly, as if there's a gun pressed to the hollow of my back, I bow.

"Ah, that's better." He takes a step forward, and I have to will myself not to take one back.

Don't show fear.

I don't know why he's here in the Tower. Park Taesung is an Old Seoul criminal. He's a thug and a murderer, and he's hurt me more times than I can remember, but that's not why I fear him.

He knows the name of my father.

"Lee Hyunwoo's son," Park Taesung calls, laughing. "Lee Hyunwoo's beloved son." I look around sharply. There's only a receptionist in the lobby, and he's seated far enough away that he wouldn't be able to hear our conversation. "What would the Director say if he heard that name? What would he say, Lee Jaewon?"

Park Taesung steps close, and I grit my teeth. His hot breath rakes across my skin, our cheeks almost touching as he whispers close to my ear. "He'd say, 'Tell me the name of the traitor's son. Tell me, so that I may kill him.'"

I squeeze my eyes shut. *I won't die for my father's mistakes.*

I feel Park Taesung step away, a lightening in the air around me.

"Jaewon-ah, you haven't said a word to me. Aren't you going to ask me why I'm here?"

You're here because you're a shark in the water, and you smell blood.

"I've become a sponsor on a project. They call it the Amaterasu Project. Have you heard of it?"

I open my eyes. He's moved to the base of the Marionette, his hand held out to knock against the God Machine's foot. It makes a hollow, ringing sound.

"I want to know every detail about the project. I already know the main players. Ama . . . and Tera . . . but I want to know more."

He must have a death wish, asking me to spy on the government for him while we're inside the Tower. I look up at the nearest security cam, which more than likely records audio as well as visual.

He chuckles at my uneasiness. "No one will know we've spoken. You'd be surprised how many people actually work for me at the Tower. It'll be like old times. You in my gang, reporting to me. What do you think?"

"Do I have a choice?"

Park Taesung walks toward the doors of the lobby, his back facing me. "You always have a choice, Lee Jaewon. That's the one thing you can be sure of."

Live or die. I guess those are choices.

"The Amaterasu Project is the future," Park Taesung says, "and I want a part of that future. Don't you?"

He doesn't give me time to answer. He steps through the doors and into the rain.

I'm alone in the dark lobby, with only the Marionette for company. It doesn't surprise me that Park Taesung knows what's going on behind the Tower's high walls and steel-locked doors. Red Moon is the largest crime syndicate in Asia, and he's its boss. He has the funds, the connections, the spies, and the Tech.

My father once said that if only Park Taesung used his influence for good, then he could achieve something truly great in this world. Then again, "good" is relative. As is "greatness." Maybe Park Taesung thinks the Amaterasu Project is greatness. Maybe he thinks a finely honed weapon is good.

I exit the lobby and call over a cab on the Grid.

The cab driver watches me slide into the backseat. "Where to?"

"The Banpo Bridge."

As we cross the Han River from Neo Seoul into Old Seoul, I allow myself to remember the reason my father rejoined the resistance in the first place.

It was for a rumor. There'd been a rumor of young girls being snatched off the city streets, turning up dead in the Han River months later.

Their cause of death: Enhancer overdose.

My father had wanted to know who was taking the girls and why they were injecting them with Enhancers. When cross-city officials performed the autopsies on the bodies, they'd found enough drugs in the blood to kill a grown man twice over. Nobody could figure it out—the why or what of it. Or at least, nobody who knew the truth lived long enough to spread the truth.

After my father died, the rumors gradually stopped.

Young and I had been eight at the time. I remember him asking me, right after the third body showed up, what I thought would happen to a person if they were pumped with Enhancers.

"They'd die," I'd said.

Young had nodded, his bottom lip bleeding as he chewed on it. "And if they lived?"

"They'd be immortal. But they wouldn't be human."

14

EXTENSION

The next day at school, I break up a fight in the cafeteria.

"Bora," I say as I pull her away from a second-year, "relax."

Bora struggles in my grip. "Nobody talks to me like that!"

I release her. "She messed up your hair."

Bora's fierce scowl turns quickly to a look of horror. I grin as she pulls out her phone to check her appearance. She has several strands sticking out, but other than that, she's fine. The second-year she'd been fighting with hasn't fared so well. The girl crouches on the floor, holding her head between her hands and wailing in apparent torment.

"Liar." Bora laughs. "My hair's perfect." She tucks the strands back into place. "Well, now it is."

School goes by slowly. We have lectures all morning, PE after lunch, and then simulation runs in the early afternoon.

Bora and Minwoo both seem to like their assignments out at the naval yard. Minwoo thinks he'll work there permanently after graduation. "It's easy," he says with a shrug. When they ask about mine, I cite my NDA.

Outside the gates after school, the same thug my mother hired before approaches me with an envelope of cash.

"She let you come again," I say. "You must be a good actor."

He peers at me from beneath a bushy eyebrow. "Sure, kid. Same old, same old?"

"Yeah." I wave him off and get into Alex's car. The screens are blacked out inside, and he's leaning his head back against the seat. He's not sleeping—I can tell because his fingers are tapping against his thigh. His other hand is wrapped in a brace, and I wonder if he injured himself during a PE drill. We don't speak, and he has the presence of mind not to ask about the thug.

With the blacked-out windows, the only proof that the car moves is the slight vibrations beneath my feet. Is this how Alex usually travels, in darkness?

At the Tower lobby, we pass through security and scan our ID badges. The receptionist gives us new uniforms, black pants and a white shirt with a red patch on the shoulder. We change in the bathroom and return to receive the rest of our uniform—a shoulder holster complete with an electro-gun. "It's locked to your biometrics," the receptionist tells us. "Only you should be able to shoot that gun."

"Right," Alex says. He checks the safety and secures it in

the holster at the side of his chest. I follow suit.

The receptionist then informs Alex that Dr. Koga waits for him in the basement. As for me, I'm to report to Dr. Chung in the GM hangar. It's a large building attached to the Tower through a Skybridge on the twenty-third floor. We head toward the bank of steel elevators at the back of the lobby and part ways.

I press the button for the floor. As the lift ascends, I receive a message from Koga on my phone. "Good afternoon, Lee Jaewon," it relays in his cheerful voice. "Every day you'll receive instructions upon arrival at the Tower. You have a meeting with Dr. Chung now in the hangar. After your assignments have concluded, please write up a report and send it to this number."

The elevator doors open to a bridge, walled on four sides by glass. Far below I can see the water gardens that trail between the Tower and the hangar. There's a group of people moving through the area. To the left and right is the greater Gangnam area with all its colorful lights, and above me, the sky.

The bridge ends at another security checkpoint beyond which are huge metal doors. It takes both guards' clearance on a biometrics pad before they open. Stepping into a cavernous room, I'm met with the sounds of low hum of machinery at work, the cling and clang of moving parts, raised voices above it all. The hangar smells of oil and fuel. I walk to the railing to get a better look. Below is a huge room filled with God Machines. They're lined up in rows, I estimate fifty or so total.

Industrial walkways are built around the hangar at the level of the GMs' torsos.

Two lie horizontal on the ground floor. Masked machinists weld large pieces onto a GM's body, while engineers stand to the side, pointing to holographic diagrams. I take a long escalator down to the ground level. I'm not into GMs the way Minwoo is into cars or Bora is into fashion, but even I can appreciate the awe-inspiring sight of so many different models in one space. There are the standards TKs with wheels, like the ones from the test, as well as the RLs and their upgraded counterparts. But there are also infantry GMs, with powerful legs and jet packs to skim across short distances, and suits with air mobility. These last I have an itching to try.

"Lee Jaewon!" I turn at the sound of the muffled voice. One of the welders lifts his mask, revealing a guy a little older than me with a goatee. "I was told to look out for you." He points to the back of the hangar where there's a small door. "Dr. Chung is through there." I nod in thanks and head in the direction he indicated.

At the door, there's another security lock. Only a red line marks the spot where they injected my ID. I hold my wrist up, and the door opens to another room off the main hangar, smaller and quieter. The room is dim when I enter, filled with shadows. There's no one here but Dr. Chung, who stands at the center of the room behind a large control panel. I approach her, wondering if I should yell out that I've arrived. She should be able to hear my approach, the loud tap of my shoes against the metal floor. It's eerie, the silence and the darkness. And then there's a sharp *click* as a spotlight turns on, illuminating the space beyond.

An incomplete God Machine hangs suspended by cable wires at the center of the room. It has no weapons, and it's missing a left arm, but there's no denying it's an advanced model. It has long, distended legs, a thin torso, a narrow head, and black eyes. Its one arm looks to have retractable claws.

I reach Dr. Chung. "What is it?" I ask.

The machinist glances up from the control panel. "We're calling it an Extension," she answers, "due to its unique capabilities. It's built to be an extension of the pilot. Unlike a normal GM, in which the pilot sits inside the cockpit and controls the exterior unit, like a ship, the Extension acts like a suit of armor. The pilot in a way merges with the suit so that her movements inside are directly mirrored by the God Machine."

"Sounds like an Enhancer," I say.

"It is exactly like an Enhancer. In fact, the cerebral connection between the pilot and the machine would be the equivalent of taking five hundred Enhancers at once. For a normal human, it would be too much for the brain to process."

Normal human.

"Tera will be the pilot," I say, and she nods. I turn away so the machinist won't see my expression. Five hundred Enhancers at once? I saw Alex take one the day of our placement test, and he'd looked ready to pass out. I swallow. "Won't it . . . harm her?"

"It's possible," Dr. Chung says, without emotion. "But she's already shown great aptitude in connecting with the machine.

We've been increasing her minutes incrementally. Today she managed to complete a simulation without any visible side effects."

I whip my head around. "She's inside right now?"

Dr. Chung raises a brow. "Tera isn't an ordinary pilot. You would do well to remember that."

I nod, chastised. "Of course, doctor."

"We've finished her tests for the day. There's a GM lift." Dr. Chung points to a metal platform that pilots use to board upright GMs. "You can take it up to retrieve her. She should be coming out of the connection, but she might be a little disoriented. You have your gun?"

"Yes." I wonder if I'm about to witness one of Tera's "episodes" that Dr. Koga had warned me about.

I step onto the lift, where there's a panel with a green button and a red button. I press the green button, and the lift ascends. Simulations can be run most anywhere as long as there's sim technology, but the most accurate readings for pilots are measured through simulation tests run *inside* GMs. The GM is deactivated and put into sim mode, and the pilot can use the GM's controls while completing missions in a simulation.

The Extension is tall for a GM. I press the red button when the lift is level with its torso. The chest cover is closed, so I have to pull to manually open the hatch.

Inside, Tera slumps on the seat with her eyes closed.

"Tera!" I say, immediately concerned. Her breaths come out shallow, her face pale. I reach out to touch her shoulder.

Before I can make contact, Tera's eyes open, shining a brilliant, unnatural blue, like stars. She blinks, and they begin to fade to her natural brown.

I wait for her to, I don't know, attack me—but she just lifts her hand to her head, rubbing her temple. "My head hurts."

Instinctively, I reach to my chest, as if I've medicine or a cold pack on me. But all I have is a gun.

"It'll go away," she says. "It doesn't last long."

I nod and lean back from the cockpit to give her more air. Soon her breaths lengthen and slow. Whatever connection she had with the Extension wears off, and the color returns to her cheeks. Like in the simulation, her lips are thin but pretty. Her bottom lip is thicker than the top.

I realize I'm staring. I cough and step away from the opening. I lean back against the outside of the GM and wait for her.

She emerges, stretching her arms above her head.

"We haven't officially met," I say. "I'm Lee Jaewon."

"I know who you are," she says. "You're my new partner."

That sounds better than *supervisor*. "I am."

"The last one didn't last long."

She sweeps past me. I turn in time to see her jump off the boarding lift. She does a graceful somersault in the sky and lands on her feet. She stands and looks back at me. Our gazes meet. "Show-off," I mutter.

It takes me a lot longer to reach the ground via the lift. She's waiting for me at the bottom with Dr. Chung. "Try not to lose her on your first day," the machinist says. The woman doesn't necessarily smile at Tera, but there's a camaraderie that's unexpected. I wonder what the dynamic is between the doctors—Koga and Chung—and Tera and Ama. If Tera and Ama began the project as young girls, then Koga and Chung have known them for over a decade. Can you stay objective toward a person you've known over a decade?

"Escort Tera to the labs, Jaewon-ssi," Chung says. She nods at two guards, who stand waiting at the back door. "And take these." At first I think she means the guards, but she holds out a pair of electro-braces. "It's more for appearance's sake than anything else. After what happened yesterday, we don't want any complaints from the staff."

Tera wiggles her nose but doesn't protest.

Dr. Chung chides Tera, "Until you've earned back our trust, you'll have to wear them outside confined areas."

I take the braces.

Outside in the main hangar, the guards wait for me to cuff Tera. I place them around her wrists, but then I hesitate over the switch that powers the link. "Dr. Chung said it was for appearances. If you keep your hands behind your back, no one will notice the difference."

Tera shrugs and we head back through the hangar, the guards giving us a wide berth.

I keep a close watch on Tera because I'm supposed to—but also because I'm curious to know what she's thinking. She gives no signs that she's aware of my presence, keeping her eyes focused straight ahead. She's so remote and standoffish, it makes me want to annoy her just to get a reaction. Or maybe I want her attention.

"That's how my grandfather used to walk," I say, referring to the way her hands are placed at the small of her back. We're moving up the escalator. Since I stand two steps above her, she involuntarily makes eye contact.

"Your grandfather was a prisoner?"

"No, he just had bad posture."

Her eyes narrow. "Your jokes get worse."

As we move across the glass bridge, she says, "You do know I'm dangerous, don't you?"

The thing is, I do. I can't ignore the warnings. The armed guards. Koga himself told me that all her previous supervisors had quit. The Proselytizer once said that if you put two men in a room, give the first man a gun, and tell him the other is dangerous, the first man will find a reason to shoot the second.

I've been told she's a super soldier. I've been told she's dangerous. But I have a mind of my own, and I'm not looking for reasons to shoot her. "I know."

"I hurt him," she says, and I know she's speaking about the man yesterday, the one who told us she'd escaped.

"Did he deserve it?"

She looks at me sharply. "No one deserves to be hurt."

I hold back from saying this reveals she has at least a sense of morality.

We step off the Skybridge and head toward the elevator. "Are you going to hurt me?"

The doors open, and she steps in. "One day I will."

15

THE PROMISE

The rest of the afternoon is spent in the lab. I watch as a team of scientists takes samples of Tera's blood. Then we move to another room, and I watch as they make her run on a treadmill to monitor her heart rate. She has a nutritionist, a physical trainer, and a psychologist, a foreign woman with short gray hair and silver eyes who introduces herself as Dr. Trumbull. I spend my time against the wall of whichever room we're in, taking notes to send to Dr. Koga.

Curious about Tera's life in the Tower, I observe the way the scientists treat her. The answer is pretty clear after about an hour: with indifference. No one speaks to her except to give her instructions. She's the center of their attention, and yet they never ask her questions unless it pertains to the actual examination.

When Tera finishes with her tests, it's already 2100 at night. We head to level B8. The elevator doors open on a narrow, blue-lit hallway. One guard leads the way, and the other follows. Since late afternoon, they've been rotating in and out, and I've given up learning their names, relegating them to Guard One and Guard Two.

I walk beside Tera. We haven't spoken much. She's been busy with her tests, and the few times I thought about engaging her in conversation, I noticed she looked less standoffish and more tired.

"It's 2100," I say. "I'll drop you off, finish up my report, and send it to Dr. Koga. I think tomorrow will be more of the same." More tests. More waiting. We're on standby until a sponsor event is scheduled.

Tera nods.

We enter a room at the end of the hall. It's occupied by two scientists seated behind a set of monitors. The room is split in two by a glass wall. The larger half functions as a monitoring room while the second half behind the glass appears to be a holding chamber. It's entirely white with one piece of furniture—a bed. The generated lights in the ceiling give the room a sterile glow.

The monitors show different parts of the room. All four corners. The bed at eight different angles. How does she sleep with that many cameras on her?

"Soldier," one of the scientists addresses me, "your duties for the evening are complete." It's a dismissal. I turn to Tera to say good-bye. Her eyes are on her room behind the glass.

Unlike the way she'd looked at the sky on the roof, or the stage of the concert, her eyes are empty.

A person who doesn't exist can't die.

"Dr. Koga wants me to check the room," I hear myself say aloud. It's a lie, and a poor one. A quick call to Koga would reveal the truth.

"Check the room for what?" This from one of the guards. He doesn't look convinced.

"For ways to escape." It's the first thing that pops into my head. I distract from the poor excuse by pointing to a metal tray on a table. "Is that her dinner?" It contains standard cafeteria fare, rice and a variety of vegetables in the tray's individual slots. There's also a red apple on a napkin, blunt chopsticks, and a spoon. "I'll bring it in."

I pick up the tray. There's a door in the far corner that separates the two rooms, and I head toward it. I think for a second the scientists won't indulge me, but the door opens, so I step inside.

The space is small. I'd guess twelve square meters—four meters in width, three in length. I usually don't mind confined spaces. My one-room apartment is the size of this room. I walk a little farther into the space and turn to see the glass window from the opposite side is a mirror.

"Whatever this is, it's not going to work." Tera stands by the door, having followed me through.

"This?" I ask. There's an alcove in the wall, and I place the tray into it.

"Being kind to me. It won't make me trust you."

I raise a brow. "Have I been kind to you?"

"You haven't been cruel."

I think of that moment on the rooftop, when I held out my hand to her and she'd looked at me with cool resignation. What must it feel like to *expect* cruelty from a stranger?

I move farther along the wall. I have to at least appear to the guards outside that I'm checking the perimeter for flaws. The walls have built-in panels like those in the lobby. These must open up to amenities like a closet, a toilet, a shower.

"Well," Tera asks, "what do you think? Can I escape?"

"How'd you do it the last few times?"

"I overwhelmed my incompetent guard and gave him the slip."

"Ah." I turn a corner and make my way along the far wall. "All guards are incompetent with you as their charge."

"But you're not my guard, are you? You're supposed to be my partner. You're supposed to get me to trust you, so that when we're in public, I'll listen to you, to the orders *you've* received from Koga or whoever. Cogs in the machine, that's all we are. And you, you're just the same as them, no matter your feigned empathy."

So this is how she sees me. And although it pisses me off, I don't blame her. What she's said is true. One of the Proselytizer's slogans: *We are at war, and war is a machine.* But she's also revealed something of herself. If this is a machine, *she's* not satisfied with its moving parts. It makes me wonder.

"Why did you go to the concert that night? You'd escaped

from the Tower. Why not leave the city, the country? You're smart, resourceful. You could have found a way to stay free if you really wanted to."

"You wouldn't understand."

"Try me."

She opens her mouth as if to answer, but then she looks away. Moving to the bed, she sits down, pulling her legs to her chest and wrapping her arms around them. "You're annoying," she mumbles into her kneecaps.

I decide not to push her.

I lean my back against the wall. "It's not so bad," I say. "You get food. You get me."

She lifts her head. "Are you mine?"

"For six hours a day. Not including weekends."

"And I can do anything I want with you?"

"Within reason." I nod at the one-sided mirror. "We're being watched."

"I don't know why they gave you to me," she says. "You're not like the others. Did they think I wouldn't break you just because you're young and attractive?"

"Do you watch a lot of films?"

She narrows her eyes. "Why?"

"You sound like a villain in a bad film."

"Bring me my food."

I retrieve her meal from the alcove and approach the bed. "Is there a table?"

"There was. But they took it away after I threw it at my last guard and knocked him unconscious."

I sit down on the bed and place the tray between us. "Whatever this is, it's not going to work."

She scowls at my use of her words. "This?"

"Threatening me, telling me you're dangerous so that I'll be wary of you."

"You don't believe me when I say I'll hurt you?"

"Oh, I believe you."

"You think you're the exception to the rule?"

"I think," I say slowly, "that I got pretty far in taekwondo."

"Are you joking?"

I shrug. "I did manage to defend myself pretty well in the simulation."

"Simulations aren't real life."

"I know." They just mimic real life. Real life is sitting in a cold room a hundred meters beneath the Tower talking to a girl on a bed while two scientists monitor our conversation.

Tera brushes her fingers over the bedspread. "People who get close to me wind up getting hurt or worse. I'm not lying to you. You should be on your guard. I *will* hurt you one day."

She keeps on saying that. I wonder if it's a self-fulfilling prophecy. "My father always said intent is what matters in all things."

"Said?"

"He died when I was eight."

"How sad for you."

"Can I eat this?" I pick up the apple.

"You're asking if you can eat from my highly prescribed rations I'm allowed twice a day?"

"What are partners for if not to eat each other's food?" I take a bite of the apple. It's crisp and flavorful, but there's a metallic quality to the aftertaste. It must have been preserved and shipped from somewhere overseas.

"We won't really be partners. I'll be the gun, and you'll be the hand holding the gun."

"That's an apt metaphor."

"The only reason I went along with any of this was the surety that I would be a weapon and nothing more. And like a weapon, I can be stopped."

I watch her carefully. A super soldier without a will to fight. "Dr. Koga said you have difficulties controlling your powers."

She nods. "The Enhancers have left lasting effects, and most of them aren't good."

"Can you feel them coming? The episodes."

"Sometimes. Other times, they're triggered. By memories. By dreams. It's why I spend most of my time in this room. At least if I were to have an episode, I'd be confined." She picks up the tray, food uneaten, and places it on the floor, returning to curl even farther away from me on the bed. "I know you're a decent person. I know you mean well, coming in here and talking to me. Pitying me. But you shouldn't. You need to stop."

I start to object, but she shakes her head. "Don't deny it. I saw your expression when you looked at the room for the first time. You saw—you *see* how bare it is, how empty my life is. How this room is a cage. But there's something you don't understand. Yes, it is a cage, but it is one that I *choose*."

"Are you sure about that?" I think of the concert, and just yesterday, the roof.

"There's a reason I never went far."

Why? Because she's afraid she'll hurt people? "If I'm not supposed to pity you, what am I supposed to feel for you?"

"You shouldn't feel anything for me."

"But I do."

It sounds like a confession.

She looks up, her eyes stricken. "Don't. Please don't."

"Tera . . ."

There's a hollow knock on the window from the outside.

"Dammit." I stand. "I should go."

As I leave, she reaches out and grabs my hand. Her hand is cool and light. "Tomorrow, be a soldier to me, Lee Jaewon. Don't be anything more."

A soldier. A stranger.

"Promise me," she begs.

"I promise."

She lets go.

As I walk out of the room, I look back through the glass to see Tera lying on the bed, her long black hair spilling out behind her like ink on paper.

16

THE PROSELYTIZER

The rest of the week is more of the same. I escort Tera to her appointments. When she doesn't attempt another escape, Dr. Koga authorizes her to walk around without electro-braces. We keep our interactions brief, impersonal. I don't make any more bad jokes. She's right. We should keep our distance from each other, at least emotionally. This assignment isn't forever, and the feelings I have for her—pity for her situation, shame for benefitting from the system that entraps her, empathy for her sadness—they don't help her. They don't help me.

First- and second-year students have physical examinations on Friday, so seniors are given the day off. Bora drags Minwoo and me to a new hot dog joint that opened in the Gangnam Station area. The doors open on a packed narrow space filled with seniors from schools in the surrounding districts. I recognize some of the uniforms as schools we've competed against in athletics and simulations.

Like most Neo Seoul establishments, the place is self-service with automated food dispensers and one attendant present in case of malfunctions. Bora goes up to the counter to pick up our hot dogs, while Minwoo and I grab seats in one of the booths along the walls. A cleaning droid promptly arrives to wipe the table down.

I check my phone to see I have two messages—one from Alex, who informs me I should arrive fifteen minutes earlier to the Tower for a sponsor event—our first, and one from my landlady, reminding me rent is due in two weeks. I get paid my stipend from the Tower every two weeks, so I should be able to pay her on time for once.

There's a loud bang as Bora drops a tray onto our table. I count eight hot dogs, all covered with a variety of toppings.

"Song Bora!" Minwoo shouts, wide-eyed. "Are you going to eat all of those yourself?"

"No. What do you take me for?" She play smacks him on the head. "One is for you and two are for Jaewon."

"So," Minwoo says slowly, "you're going to eat *five* hot dogs?"

"Wow," Bora drawls, "your high school education has really done wonders for you." We share a large soda between us. Minwoo inhales his hot dog. He then slides down the booth to talk to two seniors from a different school.

I finish off my first hot dog, one with the least amount of

toppings, and then pick up another covered with a suspicious-looking pink dressing.

"How's your partner?" Bora asks. She takes a large bite of her cheese hot dog.

I'd told her and Minwoo a simplified version of my role in the Tower, which may or may not break the NDA I didn't read. They know I've been assigned a "partner," and our role in the Tower is to test new weapons in the field. It's more or less the truth.

"We don't speak," I say. That *is* the truth.

"Hmm." Bora picks up to the drink to see that it's all gone. She scowls at the back of Minwoo's head, the last person to drink, then turns to me. "Refill, please?"

I take the bottle from her and slide out of the booth. The restaurant is narrow but long. I make my way down to the fountain and condiment stand. A girl in a navy blue skirt and jacket is covering her hot dog with red beans. I step around her and reach for the drink pump.

"You're Lee Jaewon."

I turn to see the girl staring at me.

"Uh, yes." I check to see if I'm wearing my school name tag, but I'm not.

"I saw your promotional footage for the senior tests. You were on a team with Alex Kim."

I'd forgotten they'd aired the test. "Did they show all of it?"

"Only highlights."

"Right." It makes sense for them to edit out parts to

present an ideal image. I finish filling Bora's drink and cap the bottle.

"Did that boy . . . did he come back to school? The one whose brother died?"

I turn to face the girl. Her head is turned down.

"That was awful," she continues in a low voice. "How could they? I know it was in the rules that if you were to die in the simulation, you'd die in real life, but is it so hard not to pull the trigger just because you've been given a gun?"

The girl looks up, and her eyes widen. "Oh, sorry, you don't want to hear this. Sorry . . ." She backs away.

"Wait."

What she'd said is treasonous, as is any criticism of the state. She must be extremely distraught to speak of it in so public a space. There's terror in her gaze; she must have realized her mistake.

"It's—" I say. "It's not hard." It should never be harder to save a life than it is to take one.

The girl holds my gaze, then nods. She makes her escape.

When I get back, Minwoo's sprawled in the booth and Bora's on her phone. "What did that girl want," Bora asks, "your autograph?"

I think about telling them, but decide it's better for them, and safer for the girl, if I don't say anything. "Yeah." I hand over the drink.

"I'd be such a fabulous famous person," Minwoo says.

"Please." Bora rolls her eyes. "I'm trying to eat."

Even after we've finished our hot dogs, we hang out in the

booth. We have three more hours to kill before we have to leave for our assignments.

Bora holds court from our booth. She belongs to several after-school clubs and charities as well as four different cram schools. Kids stop in to greet her and catch up. At one point, Kim Jobi comes in with his cronies, apparently skipping class. They stay away from our table.

Bora sticks her tongue out at their retreating backs. "Who'd ever have thought knowing Alex Kim would be useful?"

"Who is Alex's partner at the Tower?" Minwoo asks.

"Another student," I say. It's not technically a lie. Tera and Ama are students in a way. They take simulated classes during the day while Alex and I are at the academy.

Bora leans forward. "What's Tower protocol on hookups?"

Minwoo laughs, pulling out his phone to play a game. "I like how thinking of Alex Kim immediately makes you think of hooking up."

Bora shrugs. "That boy is sex incarnate."

"Mhm," Minwoo agrees.

Bora turns to me. "What about your partner? Are you attracted to her?"

I cough. "I've known her for less than week." Not including the concert and simulation.

Minwoo looks up from his game. "Is she hot? Or is that part of your NDA?" He snickers.

I take a sip from the drink.

"Well, is she?" Bora repeats.

I think about Tera.

"She's not . . . hot. She's cold."

"Harsh."

"Not in a bad way."

"How can she be cold in a good way?" Minwoo asks, not looking up from his phone.

"Her skin is cool to the touch. She has thin lips and a long nose. There's a beauty mark at the edge of her nose, and her eyes are dark. Everything about her is cold except for her eyes. The way she looks at things, I've never seen anyone look like that, as if she's seeing the world for the first time." I blink to see Bora staring at me intently. "What?"

"Close your eyes." Bora leans in.

"Why?"

"Just do it."

I indulge her.

"Describe me," Bora says.

I picture the way Bora had looked sitting across from me. "You have short hair and brown eyes. You're friendly and cute."

"That also describes me." Minwoo laughs.

"Open your eyes."

Bora's staring at me, elbow on the table, hand cupping her chin. "I think you like her," she croons, grinning.

"Why do you say that?"

"You remember specific details about her."

"I don't know if that's true," Minwoo says. "I mean, I

probably can't describe *your* face, Bora-yah, even though we've grown up together.

Bora looks at Minwoo, then at me. "My point exactly."

We leave the hot dog joint at a quarter to four and say our good-byes.

"How are you getting to the Tower?" Bora asks. "Want to share a cab?"

"You're going in the opposite direction," I say. "I'll take the Skytrain."

I part ways with Bora and Minwoo and head toward the station. I'm wearing a new overcoat that keeps out most of the chill air. Winters are long in both cities, long and cold and wet. Snowflakes start to fall from the sky. I hurry and take the escalator up to the Skytrain platform. I contemplate purchasing a hot drink off one of the vending machines, but the speaker overhead announces the arrival of my train.

The tracks light up green as the train pulls into the station. The doors slide open, releasing passengers. I wait to the side until they pass before entering and moving to stand by the opposite doors.

I only have one stop to go. I could have walked, but it's a lot warmer and faster in the train.

Halfway to my stop, the holo-screens in the train go static, the colorful commercials replaced by a man in a white hanbok wearing a wooden mask carved to look like a grandfather. The Proselytizer. I look over the shoulder of a girl sitting in a seat to my left who'd been playing games earlier on her phone. The masked figure appears on her screen as well.

"In war, you are a commodity." The voice blasts through the Skytrain speakers and through every electronic device in the train car, possibly the whole city. "How much are you worth?" The phrase and the question are repeated four times before the message ends. The commercial resumes playing its cheerful melody through the speakers.

"This is still going on?" a man farther down the train car growls. "I can't believe they haven't caught him yet."

"Honestly," a woman in a business suit answers, "I don't think he's one person."

"Me, neither," the girl in the seat beside me mumbles. She's shut down her game, instead checking into various social media portals to discuss the Proselytizer's latest slogan.

The businesswoman explains her theory. "Masked man, synthesized, unidentifiable voice, purposefully inflammatory messages. Most likely a marketing team at work."

That's a strange way to look at it: marketing a revolution.

"Well, whatever he or she or they are," the man grumbles, "it's damn annoying. I was watching Sela's new music video."

The Skytrain reaches my stop, and I exit. Outside, people linger on the train platform, peering at their mobile devices. There's usually an upsurge on the portals after one of the Proselytizer's media blitzes.

The masked figure appeared for the first time about three months ago, broadcasting over every electronic device in Neo Seoul. He hasn't directly admitted ties to the United Korean League, but everyone knows he's their unofficial spokesperson. His slogans always have to do with war or some policy of the

NSK. At first the government and the people didn't think too much about the blitzes, beyond them being an extreme case of cyber hacking.

However, that girl in the hot dog shop today is evidence that not everyone is content with the current order. Maybe the Proselytizer's words are reaching more people every day.

17

THE BURDEN OF WAR

I run into Alex in the lobby of the Tower. As he walks toward the elevators, something's off. He's limping.

This is the second time I've seen him visibly hurt, and I've never heard of Alex getting into a fight inside or outside school. He's a model student.

"Hey." I grab his shoulder after we've passed through security. "Are you all right?"

He brushes me off. "I'm fine." We continue toward the back elevators.

"Did you fall?"

"Leave it, Jaewon. I said I'm fine."

We enter the elevator, and Alex presses the button for B25. The elevator car begins to descend. I don't know much about Alex's life outside school and our assignments at the Tower.

The news used to run bits about him, but not lately. Either he's keeping a low profile, or he hasn't done anything to interest the tabloids.

He pulls out his phone. "Today's a last-minute addition to our schedule. Did you hear the latest news from the war front?"

"Yeah." I'd watched a short video while at the shop. The NSK suffered a major loss in the Guangdong Province late last night, with hundreds of casualties. The official number hasn't arrived yet, but it's rumored to be in the upper eight hundreds.

"The Director is putting pressure on the project because of it."

The Director, Alex's father.

The elevator slows, and Alex and I look up at the numbered floor. B12. Someone else is getting on the elevator.

Alex puts away his phone and steps back to make room. The doors open. Tsuko stands outside, dressed in full military regalia. Behind him stretches a dark hall. Only the light of the elevator illuminates him, his pale skin and the heavy bags beneath his eyes.

"General," Alex says. We bow.

Tsuko steps inside, and the lift once again begins to descend.

What is Tsuko doing here instead of where he must have been hours earlier, at the battlefront? There's only a small body of water between the Neo State of Korea and South China, but it's still a fraught distance to travel during wartime, with multiple naval blockades up and down the coastline. There's blood spatter on Tsuko's left epaulet.

In front of me, he shifts his stance as if he's uncomfortable. He has a severe haircut, shorn at the base of his skull. I can see nicks in his skin and places where old scars have healed over.

Like Alex, Tsuko's life is well documented for the consumption of the public, although many believe his history is a fabrication, including his name. According to every news outlet, he graduated from an academy in Taipei at the age of twelve, a prodigy, an orphan who saved the Director's life on one of his ambassadorial trips. Tsuko went on to become the Director's bodyguard for a year before he was recommended for a lieutenancy. With the Director's sponsorship, Tsuko rose to prominence, with a stellar record of wins in the war, and was promoted to second general only three months ago at the age of sixteen.

In fact, it's odd that the Director would elevate Tsuko yet give none of that attention or precedence to his own son. But if Alex resents Tsuko, he doesn't show it. He leans against the wall, his attention focused on the descending numbers of the elevator.

Again, Tsuko shifts in front of me, and then suddenly he pivots. Alex and I both straighten away from the wall.

He looks us both up and down, a sneer curling his upper lip.

There's a short, tense pause. "General?" Alex asks.

"The Board voted on whether to bring in outsiders for the project. On whether it would be wise to give responsibility to untested academy seniors who have yet to prove themselves on a battlefield."

I refrain from pointing out that both Alex and I are older than him.

"It was a seven-to-one vote."

It's not hard to guess who had the dissenting opinion.

"Why?" Alex asks.

At first I don't think Tsuko will answer. He drops his gaze. But then he says, his voice low, "I wanted the Board to give *me* control of the project."

"That's arrogant of you," Alex says. "You're already general of the armed forces in the Pacific. You can't be in two places at once. Although," he adds dryly, "maybe you can."

"They needed someone *responsible* to make sure the project yields *results*. The *war* is at stake."

"The responsibility of this war doesn't belong to you."

Tsuko lifts his eyes, a dark glimmer in their depths like silver. Or steel. "Who does it belong to, then? You?" He laughs without humor. "A privileged, spoiled prince of the NSK. War isn't a game, nor is it a pastime."

Alex growls. "You don't know me."

"No," Tsuko say scathingly, "I don't."

I look between Alex and Tsuko. I take back my previous opinion. There's resentment here, on both sides.

B25. Finally.

"This is a warning," Tsuko says. "If either of you should do anything to screw up the success of this project, I *will* kill you myself."

The doors to the lift open. Tsuko pivots and strides through them, his military coat whipping out behind him like a goddamn cape.

Silence.

"He has great timing," I say.

"God, I hate him." Alex limps out, and I follow.

We're in a small waiting room. A man at a desk buzzes us into a larger viewing chamber. Cushioned seats and lounge chairs circle a platform at the center of the room. Men and women in civilian clothes mingle around the space, holding flutes of champagne. These must be the sponsors.

There's no sign of Tsuko. He most likely went through the door at the back of the chamber. Alex catches sight of Dr. Chung and makes his way over to the machinist. He's doing a good job hiding his limp, but some of the sponsors shoot him curious looks.

"Jaewon-ssi?"

I start, not realizing someone stands so close beside me.

"Sela," I say, turning to face the pop star. "How are you?" She wears a black suit, her name printed on a card clipped to her jacket. Her hair is dyed red and falls to just below her shoulders.

"Fine, thank you. And you?"

"Good."

We stare at each other. I'm not one for small talk, and neither is she, apparently, because we both turn to survey the crowd of richly clad strangers. The men and women here must be representatives of chaebol groups, conglomerates that hold most of the wealth and property in Neo Seoul. Minwoo and Bora both belong to chaebol families, although Bora is one of many grandchildren while Minwoo is the sole heir to his family's fortune.

A prickle of awareness shoots down my neck. I quickly trace the source to a man standing in the shadows by the far wall, watching me.

Park Taesung. What is he doing here? He'd said he had spies in the Tower, but I didn't think he himself would be directly involved. None of the sponsors seem to care that an Old Seoul gangster lurks in their midst. They ignore him, nibbling on their hors d'oeuvres and drinking from their flutes. He meets my gaze, and I flinch.

"Jaewon-ssi," Sela asks, "are you certain you're 'good'?"

"Sorry." I shake my head. "I thought I saw someone I knew."

It's the wrong thing to say. Immediately Sela's eyes move in the direction of Park Taesung. I doubt she'd recognize the Old Seoul boss, but I want to avoid any connection between us.

"Wait." I grab her by the shoulder.

She blinks in surprise, her attention drawn back to me. "Jaewon-ssi?"

I rack my brain for an excuse. "I heard you have a new music video."

I sound ridiculous, but she smiles brightly. "You saw it?"

"Yes," I lie.

"I was worried it would depart too drastically from my image. I'm marketed as a pop rocker, not a pop singer."

I'm unsure how to respond. Is there a difference?

The doors to the other side of the chamber open. Tera walks in, accompanied by Dr. Koga. She's wearing a GM flight suit, a uniform that pilots wear inside God Machines to keep their body temperature stable at high altitudes. Hers is outfitted differently than the standard. It's skintight and black, with a red design that zigzags up across her upper thighs and torso.

"Jaewon-ssi?" Sela asks.

I realize I'm still holding onto her shoulder. Quickly I drop my hand. "Excuse me."

"Lee Jaewon!" Sela grabs my arm. I look back at her in surprise. She lets go and blushes. "I thought we were speaking . . . about my music video."

"Ah, right." I scratch the back of my head. "Can we talk about it another time?" That'll give me an opportunity to actually look up the video and research the difference between rock and pop music.

"Of course," she says softly.

I bow and turn to make my way toward Tera.

Tera watches my approach with a frown. Her gaze flits over my shoulder.

I remember the way I described her to Bora. Cold and distant. The closer I get, the further away she seems. Until I'm right next to her, and she's as far away as the stars.

"Ah, you're here," Dr. Koga says. At least he has a smile for me. "I'll leave Tera with you. She's been suffering headaches for the past hour. Earlier today there was a demonstration with the Extension. I wanted her to rest, but she insisted on coming. Ama's half of the demonstration is in a few minutes."

Across the room, Dr. Chung calls Koga's name. He moves away, leaving me alone with Tera. This close, I notice the sickly pallor of her skin. There's sweat on her brow, and her breaths are shallow. If she's just run a simulation in the Extension, she's coming off a high equivalent to five hundred Enhancers.

"Are you sure you're all right?" I ask.

"I will be. For Ama."

I don't question her motivations. The two girls must be good friends. I wonder if they grew up together in the Tower.

"Is the Extension complete?" The last I'd seen the machine, it was missing an arm.

"Not yet. They had me run a simulation, but the sponsors weren't impressed. They want to see it in action."

"Are you ready for that?"

She grimaces. "I'll have to be."

Koga and Chung gather up the sponsors, who take seats around the platform, where I now notice there is a single chair.

The back doors to the chamber open once again, and this time Ama walks in with Tsuko. He leads her to the platform, whispering fiercely in her ear. Tera's expression darkens. Alex is no better. He circles the room, his eyes never leaving the two of them. After the third revolution, he comes to stand by me.

"She's afraid," he says, nodding at Ama.

Tera scowls. "You don't know her."

"I know that she hates being the center of attention, and that she's shaking."

He's right. Ama is visibly distressed. Tsuko sits her down in the chair, hard, and snaps at a scientist who brings him what looks like a large helmet. It looks like a piloting helmet, except that it's made of metal instead of plastic. He places it over her head and latches it closed.

Dr. Koga approaches the dais, nervously bowing to Tsuko, who gives him a cursory acknowledgement before stepping off the platform.

"Just as the Extension extends the reach of Tera's strengths," Koga explains to the sponsors, "the Helm augments Ama's psychic abilities. Today's demonstration will showcase how the Prototype Weapon Ama can manifest images in the mind. This, we hope, will prove useful in stealth operations."

A sponsor raises his hand. "Does she have precognitive abilities?"

"Unfortunately, no." Dr. Koga fields several more questions before Dr. Chung holds up her phone to indicate the time. "Yes, well," he blusters, "let us continue with the demonstration." He turns back to Ama and makes adjustments on the Helm.

Alex's gaze flits to the clock on the wall. "They need to hurry."

"Why?" I ask.

"She's—"

"Claustrophobic," Tera finishes.

Alex nods. "The longer she's inside the Helm, the more panicked she'll become."

"Now," Koga continues, "you can choose to close your eyes or leave them open. Although I warn you, it can be jarring to transition your mind if your eyes are open."

I leave my eyes open, as do Alex, Tera, Tsuko, and Park Taesung. The rest of the people in the room close theirs.

The helmet on Ama's head begins to glow an iridescent blue.

"Let's begin," Koga says, "in five, four, three, two . . ."

18

MEMORIES

I blink, and I'm in a meadow. Grass stretches into the distance, infinite in all directions, and the sky is light blue, although there isn't a sun. It feels like a simulation, except there is no interface to interact with the world, and no mode of escape. This *should* be disturbing, but somehow it's not. The part of my brain telling me that none of this is real is at war with the part of my brain that's currently hijacked and telling me it is real.

"Now," says Dr. Koga, his voice booming across the sky like the voice of God, "we will slowly introduce more senses and details into the world."

A bird appears out of the air, a magpie with blue-tipped wings. It warbles a greeting before flitting away across the meadow. The wind picks up, and the grasses rush with sound.

I can *feel* the wind against my skin, warm and sweet-smelling. Maybe my mind isn't very strong, because I could easily give in to this unreality. To stay here, in a complete state of contentment. It's a dangerous dream. An actual problem with simulation technology. When your unreality becomes your haven, or your heaven, it's hard to wake up to the real world. It's an actual sickness they call the Long Sleep.

An apple tree appears, and in my hand, an apple. I take a bite. The skin is crisp, the flavor sweet. There's no metallic aftertaste, unlike the apple I stole from Tera.

Tera.

The world pulses. For a heartbeat, I see the chamber juxtaposed over the meadow—two worlds at once—before the vision stabilizes. I drop the apple and it disappears into the tall grass. What just happened?

"Lastly," says Koga, "the difference between Ama's abilities and a simulation is that she can trick your mind into *feeling* emotions. You can imagine how useful this would be for interrogations. Of course, seeing as this is *not* an interrogation, we will stick with a much more benign emotion."

Forced emotions. That's interesting. Simulations can't force people to feel emotions, although they can put you into situations that may elicit them.

I don't have time to guess what type of emotion Koga hopes to send through before it hits me, starting in my chest and blazing outward.

Joy.

Irrepressible joy.

Instinctively, I fight the feeling, which is probably a strange reaction to have, but happiness like this is so unnatural to me, it's almost painful. It *is* painful. Because although my mind tells me that this warmth in my chest is joy, my memory tells me I haven't felt like this in a long time. All the people who used to bring me this feeling are gone.

After an agonizing few minutes, Koga's voice invades my mind. "The demonstration is coming to an end. Everyone please remain seated as we transition you back into your bodies."

It's over. My heart beats erratically from joy and pain, my mind a mixture of happiness and despair.

Suddenly there's a scream, loud, deafening. I lift my hands to my ears, but the scream is in my *mind*.

The world shifts and blurs, turning nightmarish colors. Then the scream cuts off, and instead a searing pain invades my skull. I double over. I hear Alex shout Ama's name. Although I don't see him, I can sense him by my side, pushing off the wall and stumbling toward her.

And then, abruptly, the pain stops. In its place, I'm hit with a barrage of moving images, like clips from a movie, but more vivid and imbued with sound and smell and feelings that don't belong to me. They're images of places I've never been to, people I've never met, one right after the other—a misty city at dawn with boats drifting down its watery avenues, a beautiful woman kneeling before a child. "I will come back for you," she says. "Be strong for me."

Are these . . . memories? A girl stands on one side of a

window and places her hand to the glass. On the other side is another girl. She can't be more than six years old. Tera? The memory abruptly switches, and this time it's viewed from the other side of the glass. Six-year-old Tera reaches up to place her palm against six-year-old Ama's. Is this the moment they met? I'm pulled away into another memory, a little boy, crying, alone in a basement, his face to his knees.

Memories, on and on, one right after the other. Some sad, some happy.

A memory of my own plays back to me. Young and I are in the makeshift basketball court behind our apartment building. I feel the sweat on my back, the ache in my muscles, and the joy in my heart. Young has the ball. He's running. We've constructed a basket out of an old laundry hamper and ropes. Young leaps and dunks the ball through the hole in the basket, but his weight causes the whole contraption to collapse on top of him.

"Young-ah!" I rush over. "Are you all right? Are you hurt?"

He's landed on his butt, making "ah, ah," noises, but then he looks up at me, a big grin on his face. "Yeah, but did you see that? I think I deserve double points for bringing down the whole hoop!"

I laugh along with him and hold out my hand. He takes it.

Memory after memory. One ends as another begins, for however many people are in the chamber.

After a while, the memories begin to ebb, and there's a lull. It seems to be over, but then a last memory creeps out of the darkness, heavy with a feeling of loss. The feeling mutes the memory, blurring its edges. Yet when the memory begins to shape itself, I immediately recognize where we are.

The old simTech buildings at Incheon. But they're intact, as they were before they were destroyed ten years ago. Sunlight glints off the mirrored surfaces of the low buildings.

A man stands with his back to me. My heartbeat picks up speed. No. This can't be. Why is he here? Whose memory is this? I can't see the man's face, but I know who he is.

My father.

"It's not over," he's saying, and *his voice*, his voice. I haven't heard it since I was eight years old. How could I have forgotten the sound of his voice? My chest throbs, and I can't tell if it's the pain of the memory, or if it's my own pain of the moment.

Whose memory is this?

"Wait here," my father says, and even though it's not my memory, I shout, "No!"

A hand reaches out. Is it my hand?

"No!" screams a voice, and the sound of it is a punch to the gut.

Park Taesung. This is Park Taesung's memory. There's a tremendous boom as the buildings explode, a roaring inferno rushes forth to engulf my father in flames, and I'm scream-ing . . . or is it Park Taesung who's screaming?

No. No. No.

I'm dropped out of the memory.

I'm on the ground of the chamber, my throat sore. The

room is in chaos, sponsors sobbing and yelling, all of us stripped bare of our memories, our secrets.

"Jaewon-ah." I realize Tera's beside me, her hand on my forehead. My face is hot, but her hand is cool. She helps me to a sitting position. I look up past her shoulder and search the room for Park Taesung, but he's nowhere to be seen.

"She's not a weapon," one of the sponsors shouts, pointing at Ama. "She's a monster." He follows a tight group of men and women hurrying out of the room.

At room's center, Alex crouches beside Ama, helping her out of the Helm. He finds a bar at the back of the helmet that detaches from the contraption. The helmet breaks into halves. Released, Ama throws her arms around Alex, burying her face against his neck.

Tsuko strides onto the platform. He yanks Ama out of Alex's arms. "Did you do it on purpose?" he shouts.

The sponsors have fled the chamber to the outer waiting room. Dr. Koga, Dr. Chung, and Sela are out there as well, most likely to attempt damage control, leaving only the four of us and Tsuko.

"Are you sabotaging the project on purpose?"

I push back the pain of seeing my father to focus. Why is Tsuko so pissed?

The sponsors might be angry and hurt, but in due time they'll realize that the project *was*—*is* a success in its delivery of a human with manifest psychic abilities. The glitch at the end was . . . unfortunate, but it was a glitch, most likely Ama's inability to control her powers amplified through the Helm.

It's a fixable problem.

No, it seems Tsuko's anger is more of an emotional reaction. Which makes me wonder which memory was his.

"Let her go," Alex growls. He pushes Tsuko's shoulder.

Tsuko tenses. Before Alex can step away, Tsuko shoves his palm against Alex's chest. Alex's stomach arcs inward, and his body flies across the chamber.

"Alex!" Ama screams.

He hits the far wall and slides to the floor.

What the hell? A light push like that shouldn't have had that kind of force. *What's with this guy?* No one in the outer chamber seems to have noticed, everyone still caught up in their own upset feelings.

Ama wriggles out of Tsuko's grip and rushes over to Alex's side. Tsuko makes a move to follow.

I wouldn't call Alex a friend, but I've fought by his side twice already. Apparently it's become a habit. I get to my feet and full-body ram Tsuko. It's like running into a wall, which doesn't make sense. Tsuko can't weigh more than fifty kilos. I stumble away, rolling my aching shoulder. All I've done is piss him off.

It happens in a moment. Tsuko moves to punch me. I won't be able to dodge it—he's too quick. But then Tera's between us. She grabs Tsuko's wrist in midair and forces it down.

Tsuko's eyes widen and then narrow. "Tera."

"He's my partner," Tera says. "I won't let you hurt him." A spark of pleasure burns in my stomach at her defense of me.

Regardless of Tsuko's unnatural strength, he's not a match

for Tera. She releases him, and he rubs his wrist. She's left bruises in the shape of her fingers on his skin.

"It's not Ama's fault," Tera says. "You know her. You know she was never meant for this."

"She's a weapon! *This* is her purpose."

"She's not like you. She's not like me."

This seems to placate Tsuko, because he says, "You and I are the same." There's a tinge of desperation in his voice.

"We are. But can you deny that Ama was born with a pure heart? Giving and accepting pain is unnatural to her. She's joyful and good. Would you really force her to be what she's not?"

Tsuko looks from Tera to Ama. "Ai—shhh." He pivots and strides out of the chamber.

Before I can dwell on what just happened, a low moan reminds me of Alex. I turn to see him slumped against the wall, Ama hovering at his side. I jog over to his prone body and kneel down beside him. "Are you alive?"

He answers with something unintelligible, most likely a curse.

Ama looks at me, tears in her eyes. "Is he going to be all right? His thoughts are all jumbled."

"He'll be fine," I say. Alex lets out another curse, more distinct this time. "More than fine."

Tera joins us, crouching down beside Ama and taking her hands.

"Did you hear them?" Ama whispers. "They called me a monster."

"If you're a monster," Tera says slowly, "then I'll be a monster too."

This seems to break Ama out of her spell, because she smiles. "Did you see?" she teases. "We had the same memory."

Tera quirks a brow. "Was that on purpose?"

I remember the memory of the two girls looking through the window at each other.

"No, it's just a memory that we've both been thinking about recently."

They smile. Alex and I watch the girls, mesmerized. I don't know what the manifestation of love is in physical form, but this has to come close.

Ama turns to me. "That's a lovely thought."

Either it's the stress of the past hour or the psychic mental stress we just went through, but we're all exhausted. We lean against the wall in a row, Alex and I slumped over on one side, Ama leaning on Tera's shoulder.

That's how Dr. Koga finds us a half hour later. He coughs, and I open my eyes. He's standing over us, a curious expression on his face.

Alex takes Ama to her room, and I escort Tera to hers. She collapses onto her bed, immediately falling sleep. The lights are dimmed in her room, and I blame it on exhaustion, but I ache to crawl into bed with her. To find comfort in her and let the memories of the day wash away in dreams and forgetting. But that's not possible. She's a weapon, and I'm a soldier.

I lean down and brush my fingers against her cheek. "Sweet dreams, Tera."

On my out of the building, I run into Koga. "Jaewon-ssi," he says, bowing to me.

I bow back. "Dr. Koga."

I wait for him to say more, but he just waves and walks away. My mind is falling asleep, even if my body is still moving. I need to get home before I collapse altogether.

I call over a cab and head out of the city.

19

MISSING GIRLS

An incessant buzzing close to my ear wakes me Saturday morning. My phone displays the time in bold numbers: 06:45. I reach out to turn off it off, but it dips out of reach. It's my own fault. I've programmed it to persistently relay messages.

Blue light shines out from the screen, and a video message begins to play. I squint to see Alex's face and the upper half of his body. The light comes from an aquarium behind him, the dark figures of exotic fish swimming half a meter from his head. My eyes adjust, and I see that Alex wears a formal suit. At 6:45 in the morning.

"What is wrong with you?" I groan. He can't hear me. It's just a recorded message.

"The Director contacted me," his message begins.

"Your father," I mutter as I push off the bed.

Dim light peeks through the cracks in my window shade. I trip over a pile of stacked manhwa, wincing as the comic books topple to the floor. If my landlady wakes in the apartment below, she'll kill me.

"He wants us to meet him at his complex at the edge of the city. He's received Koga's reports on our progress and wants to discuss our future goals with each of us."

There's a lull in the message as Alex picks up a mug, probably coffee. I pause the video and move into the washroom.

After showering and brushing my teeth, I walk out of the washroom to where my phone hovers in wait. I resume the video.

Alex puts down the mug. "He wants to meet us around five tonight before he has dinner with his mistress."

His mistress. I wonder how Alex feels about that. The Director and Alex's mother, a diplomat residing in the American Neo States, are still legally married. The memory of the woman kneeling before the boy flashes through mind. *I'll come back for you,* she'd said. Had the boy been Alex?

"I'm thinking we should leave earlier from the Tower, maybe at 0800, have more time in the city before we have to report to him."

I reach for a pair of slacks, zip them up, and then look around the room for a shirt. One is flung across a chair, which I pull on as I move across the room to open the window. It's dark out, and the cold air that rushes into my apartment smells like rain.

Why does Alex want to "have time in the city"? It isn't

strange that Alex wants to hang out in the city—I'm sure it's fun for rich people—but it is strange that he wants me to join him.

My phone follows me across the room, determined to convey its message. "Oh, and one more thing," Alex drawls. "We're to bring Ama and Tera."

Abruptly, the message cuts off. The screen of my phone switches to the time. 0700. I stare blankly at the bright numbers before grabbing my phone out of the air and pocketing it.

I'm out the door in another ten minutes. Adrenaline pumps in my veins as I sprint down the stairs. On the second landing, an apartment ajumma leaves her door with a basket of laundry. She startles when she sees me, and I reach out to catch the basket as it falls. I place it in her hands with a smile, bow, and continue down the stairs.

My mind is racing. Is it just Alex, Tera, Ama, and me, or will there be a contingent of guards accompanying us? I wouldn't put it past Alex to find a way for it to just be the four of us, either through bribes or using his father's name as leverage. What would we even do in the city? Do I have any money?

I'm so caught up in my thoughts that when I hear the scream, it doesn't register for an entire block. I stop in the middle of the street, second-guessing myself. All night I'd had vivid dreams, replays of yesterday's memories, a carryover from the psychic link with Ama.

I turn and scan the street. Nothing out of the ordinary. There's the local mart. A bored girl unstacks plastic chairs and tables outside it for the early morning workers who want to catch breakfast before their shifts. If there *was* a scream, she'd have heard it. Then again, she's wearing headphones.

It's probably nothing. I turn and take several steps down the street. But what if it *is* something? Damn it. One sweep of the area, and I'll leave. At least it'll ease my conscience.

I start to walk back the way I came, this time focusing on the sounds around me, the squeak of windows opening in apartment buildings, the sound of a drill somewhere to the north. The girl finishes unstacking the table and chairs and heads inside. The streets are empty. Maybe I did imagine it, or the sound came from someone's early morning television program. There's no way to know unless I start knocking on doors.

Another scream. This time it's unmistakable.

I locate the origin of the sound in an alley across the street from the mart, a narrow one between two apartment buildings. I jog over.

At the edge of the alley, I stop and let my eyes adjust to the gloom. In the shadows at the back of the alley, three men have trapped a kid—a child—against a chain-link fence. One man keeps watch—poorly, considering he hasn't noticed my arrival—while two others tie up the kid and place a bag over his head.

"Hey," I say. "What's going on here?"

Of course I know what's going on here. They're kidnapping a kid. But I need to stall for time to think clearly. It's too early in the morning for this.

I don't have a weapon on me. I leave my electro-gun with the armory every time I check out of the Tower.

All three thugs turn to me at once. Each of them has a red circle pinned to their jackets. When did the syndicate resort to child abduction? Red Moon isn't a classy establishment, and eighty percent illegal, but kidnapping is a new low, even for Park Taesung.

I scan the thugs' faces. I don't recognize them from my time in the gang. They must be low-level grunts. I never made it past the fourth of the eight rings of my faction, but being best friends with the boss's son brought me into contact with members all over the syndicate.

Apparently I fail to impress them, because the largest of the three turns away. "None of your business." He continues to tie up the child.

A fight it is, then. Absurdly, the first thought that comes into my head is how messed up I'm going to look for my date. I make my way into the alley.

"Don't be a hero, kid." This from the one thug who's still watching me. He holds a long metal rod in his hand.

I'm not a hero. And I'm not a kid, not compared to that child they've got gagged and bagged at the back of the alley. I move in quick.

The thug with the rod takes a swing at my head. I dodge it, ducking at the last minute and keeping my head low. Using the momentum, I ram my shoulder into the guy behind him, slamming him into the wall. Another thug grabs me from behind, pinning my arms. I jerk my head backward, and it connects with his nose. There's a loud *crunch*, and he loosens his grip.

I'm fighting dirty. There's blood on my white shirt. The kid's cries through the gag egg me on. I fight like a dog, taking hits, shelling them out. One of the thugs tries to get me in the head with an iron rod, and I sidestep the blow, jabbing his nose with my elbow. Two broken noses. Not bad.

"That's enough," the last one says, presumably the leader.

There's the high-tone sound of a highTech weapon as it powers on, electricity crackling in the small chamber. I should have known. They're Red Moon gangsters. Park Taesung provides the best weapons for his men, grunts or no.

I turn to face the barrel of an electro-gun. Behind me, the child's cries turn to whimpers.

"Maybe we'll let you go," the thug says, "if you get on your knees and say you're sorry."

My pride has been beaten so many times that this request isn't that bad. It won't help the kid, though. I take a long breath. "I think you're making a mistake."

"I think *you're* the one who's made the mistake."

"I work for Park Taesung. My name is Lee Jaewon." If anything, this is even more of a blow to my pride, but it's worth it if I can get the kid and myself out of this.

The Red Moon gangsters tense up, exchange looks. "We've never heard of you."

"Call him."

"You think the *boss* of Red Moon would take a call from us?"

"Fine, I'll call him." I pull out my phone, which miraculously has stayed intact during the fight.

"No." He snatches my phone out of my hand. "You might call some of your friends over here. We're not falling for that trick."

"I don't have friends." At least not in the old city.

A whistle pierces the alley, sharp and shrill. From above. I squint at the low rooftop. There's a garden on one of them, two sad-looking potted plants sitting on the edge.

"What was that?" the leader growls. His gun moves from me to the roof.

A whir of rippling air sounds in the alley. Before the thug can look away, a sharp object slices the pocked skin along his cheek. It clatters to the ground at our feet.

A penknife. I pick it up while the gangster's attention is above. There's a rising tiger carved around the curve of the marble handle. I trail my thumb down the Hangeul engraved vertically down the side. *Lee Hyunwoo.*

An orb drops from above. I recognize it immediately—an EMP Tech Nullifier. It stops to hover a meter off the ground before spinning in place. I know from my Tech classes that it's releasing an electromagnetic pulse, destabilizing the gangsters' highTech guns. They will remain powered off for around three to four minutes—enough time for a quick change in the tide of a fight.

I back against the chain-link fence as the first of Young's crew enters the alley.

Jinwoon walks calmly out of the nearest doorway, a metal

bar against one shoulder, a backpack slung low over the other. Daeho careens through an open window, jumping feet first. "Ai—shhh," he curses. "I lost my—" The other half of a pair of shoes hits him in the back of his head, thrown from someone inside the building. "Ya!" Daeho yells, rubbing his head before beaming down at his sneaker. "There you are!" He leans against the wall, slipping it on.

Jinwoon breaks the nose of the lead thug with the edge of his metal rod, giving us three-for-three on broken noses. The man drops unconscious to the ground, his sprawled body causing the other two thugs to trip over him. Daeho backs them against the wall, lazily wielding a lowTech gun. Jinwoon opens his backpack and takes out a length of rope. He ties up the thugs as Daeho provides somewhat disparaging commentary from the sidelines.

With that settled, I turn to the kid, untie the ropes around his wrist, and pull back the canvas bag.

A girl looks up at me with tears in her eyes. She has ribbons in her hair. She can't be much older than six.

"Are you all right?" I check her for any injuries, but other than her reddened wrists, she appears unhurt. She doesn't respond, just looks at me, lips trembling, cheeks red and splotchy.

"Jaewon-ah," a familiar voice says from the doorway, "she's just scared."

Young emerges into the light of the alley. "Annyeong," he says, crouching by the girl so he's at eye level with her. "Can you tell oppa if you're hurt anywhere?" He's referring to himself as an older brother. Young was always good with kids.

She blinks at him, staring at his snapback. A patch of a golden crown is sewn onto the fabric.

"Do you like it?" He takes the hat off and places it on her head. "It's yours. A crown fit for a princess." He motions Jinwoon forward. "Jinwoon oppa will bring you home. He's very strong. He can carry you, if you'd like."

The girl nods again, raising her arms. Jinwoon easily lifts her from the ground. He doesn't speak to her, but she must feel safe with him, because she snuggles close against his neck.

I turn to see Jinwoon's and Daeho's work. They've gagged and blindfolded all the thugs.

"Here." Daeho hands me back my phone.

"Let's get out of here," Young says, and Daeho and I follow him out of the alley. We head over to the mart where the girl had been setting up tables earlier. Young and I take seats on the plastic chairs while Daeho heads inside. I groan and lean back. I should probably send Alex a text to let him know I'll be late.

"Haven't seen you in a while," Young begins.

"What were you doing around here?"

"We were following them."

Daeho emerges from the mart and pulls up a chair. He's purchased a roll of mediTape, which he hands over to me.

"Thanks." I unroll it and begin to wrap my bruises.

Apparently Daeho also purchased himself a rice ball, because he pulls one out of a plastic bag and eats it.

"If you're following members of Red Moon," I say, "then you know why they're abducting kids."

"Abducting girls."

I frown. "What do you mean?"

"They're only kidnapping girls, ages five to eight. Usually from single-parent families, and all from Old Seoul."

I lean forward. "Since when? Why?"

"For a long time now, but in more frequent numbers this past month. The girls disappear, but they don't show up in any prostitution rings, nor do they get transported overseas. They simply disappear. It's just like . . ." He hesitates, blinking too fast, nervous.

"What?"

"It's the same thing your father was investigating ten years ago. I think it might be happening again."

Young thinks it's the mention of my father that would upset me, and it does to a degree, but that's not what causes my heart to drop. The Amaterasu Project officially started around fifty years ago. Koga said they hadn't had a successful completion, not until Tera and Ama, and it's *their* success as prototypes which catapulted the project into a second stage: implementation. To put into use the weapons the project created. It's the reason the board invited Alex, Sela, and me into the Tower, a team to usher the project into a new era of Enhanced soldiers. But what if the first stage is an ongoing process—what if they're stealing girls from Old Seoul to create *more* soldiers like Ama and Tera?

Young watches me battle with my thoughts. "Do you know something? Does it have to do with your assignment in the Tower?"

He can read me so well. "Whatever's happening with Red Moon," I say, "don't get involved. Save the girls if you can. But don't go looking into this more than you have. You'll only get yourself killed."

I don't believe this, but it's something Young would expect me to say. After all, my father was investigating the disappearances before he died. And if Young can believe anything, he can believe that I do care for him. He betrayed me, but he was once my closest friend. We share so many memories that are good, like playing basketball in the yard, that remain untarnished by time or distance or betrayal.

"Jaewon-ah . . ."

"I have to go." I stand and head back in the direction of my apartment. I take out my phone to send a quick message to Alex.

"Hey, Lee Jaewon, wait up."

I turn to see Daeho running to catch up.

I remember that night I'd visited Young on his turf, and Jinwoon had given me *a talk*. I brace myself for another. Instead, Daeho hands me a rice ball.

"Thanks."

"I warmed it up in the microwave. I had two, but I gave you the one with more seasoning."

"Uh, thanks."

"Don't worry. Jinwoon and I will look after Young, since you can't right now."

I stare at him with suspicion. Daeho's so friendly, I can't tell if he's mocking me or not. "It's not about timing."

"No," he says, adamantly cheerful. "It's about forgiveness. You're not ready to forgive him, just like you're not ready to forgive your father or yourself."

"Forgive myself for what?"

"For not forgiving them."

"Jeon Daeho, please don't speak to me anymore."

He backs away with a grin. "See you later, hyeong!"

For some reason, I feel like I've just been given another talk. I shake my head. God, Young has a pair of meddling old ajummas for gang brothers. Still, I'm glad for them. Daeho's right; I can't be there for Young, and he needs people if he's involving himself in anything dangerous.

A ping on my phone signals a message. Alex. Meet us at Gangnam Station East Exit in an hour. We'll pick you up.

We? I hold back from asking if it'll just be Tera, Ama, Alex, and me, no guards. If Alex is baiting me on purpose, I'm going to murder him.

If this does end up being a date, I don't want to look like I've just been beaten up.

20

DOUBLE DATE

"You look like you've just been beaten up," Tera greets me when I climb into Alex's car outside the station.

I scowl at her, except she's not the one who can read minds.

"No, that's me!" Ama says. The girls are seated together on the stretch part of the car, while Alex sprawls on the two-seater. I move to the back and squeeze in next to Tera.

I went home and changed my clothing after the fight, and now I wear a gray sweater and black pants. Also a beanie and scarf, the latter of which I begin to unwrap around my neck.

"Jaewon," Tera says. I hold still as she drifts her cool fingers over my cut lip. "Who did this to you?"

"Just some thugs."

Her hand lowers. "Where?"

"Why? Are you going to go after them?"

"I could."

Her expression is serious as she waits for me to name the location of my attackers. Maybe I'm a sadist, because I find the idea of her avenging me really hot. "I'd like to see that, but it's all right. They got what they deserved." From Young and his crew more than from myself, but she doesn't need to know that.

"Why were you fighting?" Alex asks. He's tapping his finger against his knee, a nervous habit he usually shakes with a cigarette, but for some reason he isn't smoking.

"I don't know."

All three of them stare at me in disbelief.

"You don't *know* why you got into a fight?" Tera asks.

I consider telling them about the kidnappings, but I'm still unsure if it has anything to do with the project. I need to get more info, either from Park Taesung, or by investigating the project in the Tower myself.

I quickly change the subject. "How was this possible?" I gesture vaguely at everyone in the car, the fact that we're all together, alone, outside the Tower.

Alex leans forward and lightly taps Ama's ankle. She moves her legs, and he grabs four bottles of water from a cold-storage case beneath the seat. He hands one to each of us, then flips the cap on his bottle and takes a long pull of water.

"I could *live* in this car," Ama says. She leans over to shift through the case's contents. "Why is there so much alcohol in here?"

Now it's Alex's turn to change the subject. "Like I said in

my message," he says loudly, "my father wanted a report on the development of the project, and to see the girls in person. As it so happens, he's requested we go to him, since he refuses to step outside his property line as of late."

"Why not?" I twist open the bottle of water. It's in a recyclable container that'll be cleansed and resold at market value. Water this clean is costly.

"The UKL have made multiple threats against his life."

"Ah, sorry." I swallow a mouthful of water and wince as it slips into the wound on my lip. I look up to see Tera watching me. I attempt a reassuring smile, but it just pulls on the cut, and I wince again.

Tera clicks her tongue. "Don't smile if it hurts."

I raise a brow. "That sounds like a slogan."

She rolls her eyes. On her other side, Ama fiddles with the controls on the panel for the windows. She presses a button, and the windows switch from black to the vibrant colors of a variety show. Celebrities competing in some sort of singing competition. Ama and Tera are immediately enthralled.

"What kind of threats?" I ask Alex. "It's not like your father hasn't received them before. No offense."

"None taken." Alex reaches for his breast pocket, but finds it empty. His hand goes back to flicking his knee. "The moment he leaves his property, he receives messages in fifteen-minute intervals detailing his exact location, implying they could target him at any given moment. Although an overt threat hasn't been issued, his intelligence officers are advising him to stay out of sight. We think the UKL have some sort of satellite with a massive range of geo-spatial positioning."

I frown. "I thought the UKL was an underground movement. How do they have that kind of technology?"

"Underground. Aboveground." Alex shrugs. "They're just words. The movement is much larger than the media allows the public to believe. For ten years, the UKL has lain dormant, and the NSK has left them to simmer alone, too concerned with the war abroad to care about theoretical discontent at home. But the ideologies of that war have trickled through to the minds of many people over the years, not to mention the media blitzes by the Proselytizer. Many influential NSK citizens have defected to the rebellion, including Dr. Chung's predecessor, the Tower's most brilliant machinist and engineer. She was the woman who designed the initial blueprint of the Extension."

"Dr. Kim," Tera says, turning from the show to watch Alex. "She was around the first year I was brought to the Tower, and then she disappeared. No one spoke of her, and they wouldn't answer my questions when I asked where she went."

He nods. "She defected shortly after her brother died in the first battle of the Third Act. With technicians like her, the UKL will have weapons, advanced ones. And with overseas investors as well as the ones at home—whether the government believes they exist or not—the NSK has a real problem on its hands, should an uprising occur. And an uprising *will* occur, and soon, if the increase in UKL activities in the past months is any indication."

"What is the UKL's goal?" Tera asks. "Do they want a complete overthrow of the NSK?"

"I think their aim is higher. They believe in the abolishment of the Neo Council and the reinstitution of the sovereignty of nations."

I whistle. That's a tall order. Of course it's not news to me; most citizens know about the basis of the conflict for the war. But maybe it wasn't included in Ama's and Tera's education. After all, it's so ideologically circumspect. The Great War might have begun for a thousand different reasons, but at its core, it's a battle between two schools of thought on the theory of nations. The first school, those who created the Neo Council, believed in the creed issued after the First Act of the Great War, that war is a product of nationhood, that nationhood drives countries into conflict over land, wealth, power, and pride. The second school believes in the reinstitution of the ideology that nations are places of culture, and that the motherland is to be protected and cherished.

My father had much pride for his country. But if pride and love are finite, he gave all to his country and left none for his family.

Beliefs, in my experience, get you killed. And there are so many of them. How do you know which one is right, which one is good? Isn't it better not to believe in anything at all?

Ama clicks off the television, stopping the background noise of the show. She clicks the button again, and the windows and the ceiling of the car go clear, revealing the city.

We're passing through a busy intersection. Although the Grid prevents accidents, at peak hours, with more cars on the road, traffic *does* occur around intersections.

In all directions are massive skyscrapers made of vermilion, cobalt, and adamantine glass. Trailers for films and video games play short ads on giant holo-screens floating in the air. Overhead, the blue tracks of the skyway bloom yellow as a train sweeps by, the underbelly a blur of bright colors.

Our vehicle slows as the car in front of us releases passengers onto the busy side street.

"Do we have plans for the day?" I ask. We're still cruising along the streets of the Gangnam Station area where they picked me up.

"Not until we have to meet my father at 1700."

Ama gasps at something outside the car and then turns sheepishly around. "Sorry," she says. "I've just never been outside the Tower before."

If she was looking for the thing to say to make Alex give her anything she wants, that would have been it.

"We have all day," he announces. "What do you want to do?"

Tera and Ama exchange a glance. "Can we go shopping?"

■ ■ ■

The luxury mall at Jamsil doesn't open until 0900, but Alex arranges for workers to accommodate us an hour earlier.

Unlike mass-market retail stores that have automated services, the wealthy still like the personal touch of salespeople. We're greeted at the door by a host of uniformed men and women who bow and take our coats. They're trained enough not to react outwardly to the fact that the girls are wearing government-issued cotton shirts and pants and I have a black eye and a bruised lip.

The mall itself is a huge construct with more than three hundred stores across thirty floors. The interior walls are cream and peach with crystal chandeliers hanging from the ceilings. The floors are so polished that I feel bad walking on them with my shoes on.

We head to one of the upper floors with a bright arcade of shops selling clothing and other wearable items.

"Get whatever you like," Alex says grandly to the delight of the attendants working on commission. "The government is paying for it."

Ama's eyes widen. "They gave you an account?"

"They figured I would only use it for project-related expenses. They should know better. Nobody loves spending other people's money more than rich people."

"Tera and I are project-related expenses!" Ama says cheekily.

As the girls follow the female attendants toward the stores, I catch Alex's eye. "That was a lie, wasn't it?" The government wouldn't spend money on anything it would consider super-fluous, like the entertainment of its soldiers.

Alex nods. "I want Ama to feel at ease, purchase anything

she'd like without guilt. And it's only partly a lie. My father *is* the head of government. If it were a complete bluff, Ama would be able to tell."

Soon Alex gets hijacked by the male attendants, and I move away to explore the rest of the floor. It's impressive. The larger stores against the walls are for specific brands, while the middle of the space is sections based on products—gloves, hats, shoes, etc. There are even carved sculptures situated around the arcade.

One in particular catches my eye. It's of a woman, carved out of marble. The artist has put intricate details into her appearance—long, elegant eyes; round, smooth cheeks. She's naked, and her wings are folded against her back.

I read the plaque beneath the sculpture. *The Star Maiden* by Kim Heejong. The plaque describes the Star Maiden as a celestial being with supernatural powers who longs for the stars, but remains on earth due to humans' desires.

"Sir."

I turn. An attendant stands behind me. He holds a silver tray with grooming equipment. "Can I interest you in a shave or a haircut?"

I wonder if this is a hint at my general state of appearance. Still, I decline, although I take the comb from the tray. "Can I have this?"

He nods, looking skeptical.

I pocket the comb and wander back the way I came, catching sight of Ama and Tera moving into one of the brand stores, closely followed by their cloud of attendants.

At the front of the store is a couch, which I immediately sprawl over.

"Sir."

Another attendant has appeared. A different one, I think. He holds a silver tray with a coffee service. This one I'll take advantage of. I fix myself a cup and stick a biscuit in my mouth.

"I see you found the food," Alex says, sitting down beside me. He pours himself a black coffee and proceeds to down it.

I grimace. "Can't you drink it like a normal person?"

"No," he says. "Where'd the girls go?" He looks around the store and spots them heading into the changing rooms.

He puts the cup on the tray, and the attendant leaves. "I made reservations at a hotel restaurant. We can have an early dinner, and then head over to my father's."

"Which hotel?"

"Silla."

"Fancy." I look down at my gray sweater, unraveling at the sleeves. "They might not let me in."

"Ah," Alex says, "I forgot to tell you. We've got an appointment with the tailor to fit us for formal dress suits."

I frown. "Wait, why?"

"There's a sponsor event at the Tower later tonight. It isn't specific to the project, but the Tower wants all its representatives to be there, including us."

If it involves sponsors, then Park Taesung might be there. I can ask him about the kidnapped girls. "When were you going to tell me about this?"

He shrugs. "Right now?" The attendant appears with another pot of coffee. Alex begins to fix himself a second cup. "In any case, I figured we could pick up our suits early and wear them to dinner. I thought it'd be fun for Ama to dress up and go out."

I stare at Alex. He drinks his coffee at a slower, more human rate. "You care about her," I say.

He spins liquid in his cup. "We spend every day together."

It's not exactly an answer, but he doesn't say no.

"The young women are ready," an attendant interrupts. "If you would please follow."

Alex and I put down our cups. At the back of the room, the attendants are lined up like it's a gangsters' meeting, which goes to show the normative in my environment.

Ama and Tera stand outside the dressing room in front of a grand mirror. Ama twirls in a yellow dress. "How do I look?"

Tera raises her eyes to meet my gaze through the mirror. She wears a red jumpsuit. It clings to her shoulders and waist, flaring out at the legs to taper at her ankles.

Ama stops twirling, and Alex approaches her. "You look beautiful," I hear him say.

Through the mirror, Tera watches me. "You don't like it?"

"Do I look like I don't like it?"

She sighs. "What kind of answer is that?"

I scowl. "Of course I like it."

She whirls around from the mirror. "Why can't we have a normal interaction?"

"You look like a dream," I say, "one I never want to wake from." Some dreams are better than real life.

It's worth sounding like a fool when she blushes. "Do you dream in red, Lee Jaewon?"

I take a step toward her. "Now I will."

She matches my grin and moves forward to place a hand on my shoulder.

"Tera!" Ama yells, and we jump apart. "Alex says there's an *aquarium* here, and they have *whales*. Can we go, please?"

Alex pays for the clothing, and we head outside. It's already well past 1200, and the mall is filling up. We make our way into the crowd. There's a small line outside the aquarium.

"I can pay to have the aquarium to ourselves," Alex suggests, looking hopeful.

"That defeats the purpose!" Ama cries. "The animals won't be happy just seeing *us*."

"That," Alex says, "is not a thought I would ever have."

"Hey," I ask Ama, curious, "can you read animal minds?"

Ama laughs as if I'm joking, but I'm not joking. Tera shakes her head in our collective direction.

The aquarium fills up fast, but we take our time going from one attraction to another. At the end, there's a gift shop. Ama immediately rushes toward the display of whale-themed stuffed animals.

Tera joins her and stares at a blue penguin for a long time. She picks it up, stroking its soft plush.

"I'll buy it for you," I say from behind her. She jumps.

"No, it's okay," she says. "I don't want to spend your money. I don't need it."

She doesn't put the penguin back on the shelf.

"I have two jobs, Tera," I say, wresting it from her fingers, "not including the one that involves watching you, which I *am* getting paid for."

She laughs and follows me to the counter. "I should make your job harder for you, then."

"You could." I grin. "But then I'll stop buying you gifts."

After the aquarium, we look around the mall some more before heading outside to explore the outdoor shopping areas. Alex gets a call from Dr. Koga. We wait in silence as he listens before hanging up.

"Well?" Ama asks, exasperated when he doesn't immediately divulge the details.

"Dr. Koga's covering for us. We're good for now."

I blink, surprised. I wonder if that's a new development, or if Koga's been aware of today's events this whole time.

By the time Alex and I pick up our suits, it's already 1530, and we have to rush to make our dinner reservation.

■ ■ ■

The car pulls up outside the Silla Grand Hotel. We exit and hurry beneath the golden awning into the grand foyer. I've only been here once, when Bora called me to save her from a date. I'd shown up, and she'd proclaimed me her "kkangpae" boyfriend. We then left, called Minwoo, and hit up a noraebang for three hours straight, belting out songs until our throats were sore.

Tonight the hotel looks much the same, except for this time I'm the one on the date.

The restaurant is off the entrance hall. The host takes Alex's name and leads us to a private table at the back of the room. The restaurant, like the mall, is built in an unidentifiable Western style with mirrored ceilings and gilded tables. It's an open space. We receive curious stares, probably because Alex and I wear our tailor-made suits, and Tera and Ama look incredible in the outfits they picked out earlier. We're also the youngest customers in the restaurant. It's mostly upper-tier socialites and businesspeople. One man in a tux turns at the sight of Tera, a look of open admiration on his face.

"Jaewon-ah?" Tera says, noticing I've stepped closer to her.

"Ah." I scratch the back my head. "It's nothing."

"If you're afraid of all the bright lights, I'll protect you."

I laugh. "Yeah, you will." I lower my hand to her back. "Let's go."

We reach the table. I follow Alex's lead and pull out Tera's chair, then take the seat to her right.

Three servers converge upon us. Alex immediately orders a bottle of wine, which technically he and I are legal to drink at eighteen. The girls aren't, but the server doesn't ask any questions. Too classy to be legal? Another explains the menu, and the third fills our glasses with water.

"What are you getting?" Tera picks up the menu—a thin tablet—and scrolls through the contents. There's a feature to show descriptions of the food by tapping on their pictures.

"You order, and I'll eat off your plate."

She mock-glares at me. "If you eat my food, I will hurt you."

I tap a picture on her menu. "I'm having this."

"Lobster?"

I rub my stomach and grin at her.

On the other side of us, Alex is pouring wine into a glass for Ama. "Taste it first," Alex says. "You might not like it."

Ama presses the wine to her lips and then grimaces. "Yuck."

Alex chuckles, raising his glass to clink it against hers. "More for me."

"You do remember we're seeing your father after this."

He downs his glass. "Why do you think I ordered a bottle of wine?"

The rest of the dinner goes smoothly. I don't eat Tera's food, but we share two glasses of wine between us. Ama tells a story about the first time she met Tera, which we'd witnessed in the memory, but she elaborates. They'd been confined to separate rooms, but they'd shared a window. Although they couldn't hear each other through the glass, Ama's abilities allowed them to speak mind-to-mind.

"So," Alex asks, "at any point in time, you two could be talking without Jaewon and me knowing?"

Ama gives him a cheeky smile, her dimple showing. "Maybe."

I tell the story about the last time I'd been at this hotel, how Bora had called me, and I'd come into the lobby. Bora's performance as an aggrieved heiress with a wrong-side-of-the-river boyfriend was . . . dramatic, and I didn't think her date would buy it, but he did.

"Really?" Tera teases. "You? A gangster boyfriend?"

"And I didn't even have these on my face." I point to the wounds on my lips and eye, which don't hurt as much now that I've had some wine.

"I've been on blind dates," Alex says. "At this hotel, and other places. I should have called you."

I raise my glass. "Next time."

Ama glances curiously at Alex. "Did you date any of the girls?"

"Yes, on those blind dates."

Ama purses her lips. "You know what I mean."

Alex shakes his head. "Not seriously."

"What counts as a *serious* date?"

He looks at her. "When it matters."

A shadow falls across our table. I glance up to see a kid standing there. He's unshaven, hair hanging limp over his face, skin pale, and eyes bloodshot.

Alex is the first to recognize him. "No Seungri."

21

HOLLOW VICTORY

Seungri, No Seungpyo's twin. He'd been sent to study abroad in Japan after the test, and I'd mostly avoided thinking about him since then. An image flashes through my mind of the bridge in the simulation, of Seungpyo's laughing face as he volunteered to go first. *I got you, my cute little brother.*

Why is he back in the country? I wasn't close with Seungri, but I feel a flush of shame for not having gone to his brother's funeral.

"You look happy, Alex," Seungri says. The raw pain in his voice is palpable.

He stands at the corner of the square table between Ama and me with one hand deep in the pocket of his coat. Behind him, the servers have noticed Seungri. They start to make their way over. If I can somehow signal to them that we have a situation . . .

"Don't move!" Seungri growls.

He pulls a gun from his coat pocket. It's a fission gun, model SG-88. How the hell did he get one of those? One blast and it'll rip apart everything in its direct line of fire. The tension in the room ratchets up a notch. The servers stop approaching, and instead begin evacuating tables.

"No Seungri," Alex says calmly, "what are you doing?"

Seungri lifts the gun and points it at Alex. "It didn't have to be like this."

Does he blame Alex for what happened to Seungpyo in the test, for not having informed us beforehand about the change in the rules? How long has he been planning this revenge?

"Alex?" Ama whimpers.

Alex's gaze flickers to her before returning to Seungri. "Let's go outside. This is between us. We can talk outside."

It's a legitimate play by Alex. If he can get Seungri outside, then it'll lessen the chance of casualties as we stall for time. The hotel must have called security and notified them of the presence of a fission weapon.

"Alex?" Ama reaches across the table toward him.

"No," Seungri says, almost sadly, "you don't care about your life enough." He moves the gun until it points directly at Ama's head.

"Wait," Alex says, voice cracking, "just wait."

"A girlfriend you actually care about." Seungri sneers. "That's a first."

"She has nothing to do with this."

"Seungpyo had nothing to do with the test!" Seungri shouts. The gun trembles violently in his hand. "But where is he, Alex? Where is my brother? He should be here with me. We'd never been apart until— How am I supposed to go on?"

"Dammit, Seungri. I'm sorry. Shit, I'm so sorry. It's my fault."

"It is," Seungri says. His hands are shaking so hard he has to use both to hold the gun. It doesn't matter if his aim is off. A fission blast will wipe out anything in an eight-centimeter radius from the gun. "That's why I'm going to kill her. So you know what it's like to lose someone you love."

"Ama," Tera calls softly from across the table. The girls look at each other.

"Seungri-yah, please," Alex says, desperate now. "Take it out on me. Kill me."

Seungri's eyes go dull. "This is for Seungpyo."

It happens in a flash, literally. The fission gun goes off. A huge beam of concentrated nuclear energy aimed straight at Ama, and it . . . stops.

Midair, the beam stops.

It's being held back by an even greater force. Ama's eyes burn green.

Seungri stumbles back. "What the hell?"

Tera shouts, "Now, Jaewon!"

I have no idea what's going on. My mind is in a panic. Still, I don't hesitate, trusting Tera to know what she's doing. I rush for Ama and knock her to the floor. The beam explodes forward, flaring over me. I can feel the heat of it against my back. It burns a massive hole in the nearest wall, which fizzles out.

Turning, I see Tera snap Seungri's wrist. He drops the gun. She catches it, disables the mechanism, and throws it onto the table.

Ama's unconscious beneath me. Did she stop the beam with her *mind*?

"Ama!" Alex shouts, and I move aside to let him take her in his arms.

I wonder if Koga knows Ama has that kind of power. If he did, wouldn't he promote it to the sponsors? Tera knew—she'd called out to Ama right before Seungri released the blast.

Do the girls have powers they're keeping from the scientists?

Gasps and screams behind me. I turn see Tera punching Seungri in the face. Her eyes blaze blue.

Shit.

"Tera!" I shout. "Don't!"

But she either can't hear me, or she refuses to listen. Something has taken ahold of her. This must be what Koga and she herself had warned me about, an effect of the Enhancer manifesting in violence and an inability to think clearly.

I rush over and grab her by the shoulder. She backhands me across the chest. I fly backward and crash into a table.

I wipe blood from my mouth. Damn, she's strong. I haven't physically fought her, not in the Real. In the simulation, her

Enhanced strength must not have carried over, because it wasn't like this. If she's hitting Seungri at half the strength she just used on me, he's not going to make it. I stumble forward and grab her from behind again. She spins in my arms, raising her fist. I do the only thing I can think to do—I get in close and wrap my arms tighter around her. She struggles, but I hold tight. My hot breaths rake against her ear. "Stop," I say. "You're going to kill him."

Seungri lies on the floor, unconscious.

I can feel Tera's heart racing against my own. "He was going to kill Ama," she says, her voice cold, lethal.

"I know. It was wrong of him, but he's not himself right now."

She growls. "That's no excuse."

"You're right. It isn't. But he lost his brother, and he believes it was Alex's fault. There's nothing that makes what he did right. But he's subdued. What makes you want to hurt him now?"

She wants to hurt him—I can feel it. I want to hurt him too, for what he's done. But neither of us are killers. She needs to have the time to think.

While the staff rushes in to secure Seungri, I hold her until her heartbeat slows, until her breaths lengthen and deepen. One server is on the phone. Hotel security is approaching through the lobby in the distance, which means NSK forces aren't far behind. I lean back to see her eyes are no longer blue, but brown, warm and beautiful.

And then I notice her arm. "Shit." The beam must have

raked across it during the release. Her whole upper arm is bleeding and charred at the edges. "We need to get you to a medic."

I'm freaking out, but she remains calm. Her eyes sweep my face. I wince. She really did a number on me. The kidnapping thugs were nothing compared to one hit from Tera.

"Jaewon-ah?" Tera asks, anxious.

Alex hobbles toward us, having managed to get an unconscious Ama balanced on his back. "We need to get out of here," he says, "if we don't want to have to answer a million questions."

That's when we hear them, sirens approaching from outside the hotel.

22

DREAMS

Despite the restaurant manager's objections, Alex takes us out the back door of the restaurant and calls over his car. We pile in. Alex lays Ama down on the two-seater. She's small enough that with her knees curled, she fits comfortably. The rest of us collapse on the long end, Tera in the middle.

We head to Alex's house since we have to go there anyway, and he says he has a medical room.

We're quiet, lost in thought. I feel guilty, leaving Seungri unconscious on the floor, but the police will arrive soon, and they'll take him to a hospital. The Tower will cover up our involvement, no doubt, although I'm not looking forward to reaping the consequences of our actions, whatever they may be. If it's corporal, I can take it. If it's a dismissal . . .

I look over at Tera. Her eyes are closed, and she holds a

cloth napkin from the restaurant over her wound. If the consequence is a dismissal, I don't know what I'll do—just the thought of leaving her now gives me a sinking feeling in my chest.

The car takes us southwest out of the city and up into the mountains. I'm surprised that Alex lives outside the Dome—no one I know with Neo Seoul citizenship does. We drive up to a gate that scans Alex's car before opening.

The mansion itself is built into the side of the mountain, a mixture of modern and classical architecture, glass and wood and steel. The car self-parks in the driveway, and Tera and I put Ama, still unconscious, onto Alex's back. Technically Tera is the strongest of us, but Alex insists on carrying her, and Tera has a massive burn wound on her arm.

We enter the house through a side door. The lights are all off inside. If Alex has servants, they don't appear. It's likely all automated. And there's no sign of his father. To the left, orange and yellow light from the sunset seeps into the house through floor-to-ceiling windows.

Alex moves soundlessly across the wood-paneled floor before shouldering into a room off the kitchen. Automatic lights flicker on. It's a state-of-the-art medical facility. The cabinets appear well-stocked, and there's a low bed at the center of the room. This is where Alex heads, gently setting Ama down and tucking a throw blanket around her shoulders.

The room also has a fully stocked refrigerator and a large-screen television. There are several maid-and-butler bots in the corner, which, when powered on, are programmed to assist and clean. A person could survive an apocalypse in here.

"Do you get injured a lot?" I joke.

Alex tenses, his shoulders hunching slightly. Immediately I regret my words, reminded of the few times I've seen him with inexplicable injuries. "It's good to be prepared," he says evenly.

He motions Tera forward to check her upper arm. The napkin placed over the wound is soaked with blood. Slowly, Alex eases it back, revealing the clotted wound beneath. He picks up a bottle of saline on a side table and uses it to irrigate the wound. Blood washes away.

He frowns. "Does this hurt?"

Tera bites her lip, looking a bit sheepish. "No."

He pours water onto a towel and wipes the rest of the blood away to reveal her skin beneath. It's unblemished. Smooth. No sign of the burn from the fission gun.

She shrugs. "Regeneration."

"That's . . ." Alex searches for the right word. "Useful."

It's my turn next. I peel back my shirt, and Tera wraps my ribs with MediTape while Alex sticks me forcefully with remedy patches. Afterward, we gather around Ama and watch the slow rise and fall of her chest.

"Maybe we should take her back to the Tower," I say. This might be beyond our scope of understanding.

"No," Tera says. "This has happened before. Not this exactly, but where her powers have overwhelmed her into unconsciousness. It's a kickback from stopping the blast. She just needs rest."

We take Tera's lead on this. She grew up with Ama; she'd know what's best for her friend.

"I'll stay with Ama," Alex says. "You two should wash up. There's a bathroom next to this room. Tera, you can use that. And down the hall is my room." He nods at me. "Pick out a dress shirt from the closet. We still have to go to that party tonight."

"Ah." I'd forgotten about the party. So much for our tailor-made suits.

Alex walks over to one of the cabinets and pulls out a pair of sweats. He hands them to Tera. "They might be a little big, but they'll be more comfortable than what you're wearing."

She nods and takes the clothing.

Outside in the hall, I hesitate. I want to ask Tera if she's all right—beyond the burn wounds which she can apparently regenerate from. She almost killed a person today, which must be weighing on her, especially when what she fears most is her own history of violence. I want to tell her, *You stopped, and that's what matters*. But maybe she doesn't need to hear my thoughts—just needs space for her own.

Tera nods at me and heads into the bathroom. I find Alex's room at the end of the hall. A great fish tank dominates the middle of the room, casting everything in eerie shades of blue and green.

I step into Alex's closet—it's twice the size of my apartment—grab a shirt, and head into the bathroom. I take a slow shower, letting the heated water sluice over my cuts and bruises. My thoughts wander to the day, the morning with the gangsters, the day with Tera and Ama, the dinner, Seungri's face as he held the gun. I think of Tera, how she wanted to hurt Seungri, to kill him, but stopped herself. I think of her, showering only a few meters down the hall. I turn the knob from hot to cold, and finish up quick.

Towel-drying my hair, I put my clothes back on with Alex's borrowed shirt. In the hall, I notice the door to the guest bathroom is open.

"Tera?" I ask. When she doesn't answer, I peek in to see the bathroom's empty. The mirrors are fogged, indicating she finished not too long ago. In the medic room, Alex has fallen asleep on a chair next to Ama's bed, his head resting on the pallet beside her hand. I give the rest of the room a cursory glance, but Tera's not here.

I search the house, the rooms we walked through when we first entered, the kitchen. I'm moving through the back of the house when I see it. A sliding door is edged open, cool air whistling through the crack. I step through it onto a balcony. It overlooks the cities—Old Seoul and Neo Seoul.

The city. Seoul. For a moment, I just stare at it. My home. All those lights. All those people. Slowly I walk to the balustrade. My eyes are drawn to a gazebo a little way below, stone steps leading down the hill from the side of the balcony. A familiar figure sits on a bench inside the gazebo, knees pulled up to her chest.

Tera.

"You look comfy," I say, approaching her in the gazebo. She's wearing the sweats, rolled up at her elbows and knees.

She pats the bench beside her. "Have a seat."

It's already fast approaching 1800, and the sky has darkened. The blue of the Dome stretches over the city, like a ghostly planet fallen to the earth. I don't know where Alex's father is. He said the Director isn't leaving his home recently due to security concerns, so he must be around here somewhere. Still, I don't think about it too hard. Not when Tera sits beside me, peaceful. The wind catches her hair and flicks it against my shoulder.

"Jaewon-ah," she asks, "where do you live?"

I point a finger to the nearest district across the river. "Mapo-gu, Hapjeong-dong. In a small apartment."

"By yourself?"

"For the past two years."

"And before that?"

"I was in a gang. I lived with the other members."

She looks at me. "But not anymore?"

I shrug. "I left the gang." My hair, still wet from the shower, feels cold against my neck.

She's quiet for a moment. "Is it hard? To leave?"

"For me it was. But I had to do it. I thought—I thought I wanted something more."

Tera rests her chin on her knees. "Tsuko says that's the problem with humans. They want things. It drives them to do the unthinkable—to kill, to fight, to die."

I hate to agree with Tsuko, but he's right. The NSK is proof of the first. They kill to keep the power they've established. The rebels are proof of the second. They fight to gain back what they believe they have lost—their homeland, their country. My father is proof of the last.

An airship streaks a vapor trail across the skyline. The sun dips low behind the eastern mountains, until it disappears altogether, leaving only darkness. But not for long. All across the valley, lights flicker on until the city is a sky with multi-colored stars.

It's beautiful from far away.

It's beautiful from up close too, if you know where to look.

I know what I'd see if I were to zoom into the city. In Old Seoul, the bridge cart ajumma, brandishing her wooden spoon at the metalworkers who come to have a drink and a smoke after work. In Neo Seoul, Bora tugging Minwoo to some concert or shopping district, laughing as her wig slips from her head.

But from up here, it's like I can see them both at the same time, the distance between them so small as to be nonexistent.

Beside me, Tera drops her legs from the bench. She taps her feet lightly against the wooden slats. "In war, do you think people are born on a side?" A lantern in the gazebo flickers on. It must be on a timer, or maybe have a sun sensor.

"What do you mean?"

"I'm a government weapon. That means that I was made for war, a specific side of it. But for most people, you are born, you become someone, and *then* you choose. I just . . ." She leans forward. "I think—I think I'm becoming someone. Right now. Right at this moment."

There's pain her voice. I feel an echo of it in my chest.

"And what do you choose?"

She closes her eyes. "Freedom."

I'm reminded of the first time I met her, when she went to the roof not to jump, but to feel the wind.

"I once asked you why you went to the concert," I say, "when you could have escaped. You said I wouldn't understand."

She opens her eyes. "What is freedom to you, Lee Jaewon?"

I think of the definition of the word. "To have basic human rights."

She laughs, cocking an eyebrow. "That *would* be your definition."

"And what is freedom to you?"

"To me, freedom is a song that plays over in my mind, again and again." She stands and moves to the gazebo rail. "The night of the concert, I escaped my guard and rode the elevator all the way to the top of the Tower. I walked to the edge. It was so cold up there, and there was nothing but wind and darkness, and that perpetual searchlight. I felt so empty, that this was the highest place I could go in the city, and still it didn't seem high enough. But then I heard it—a song drifting through the night. I'd never heard anything like it, never *felt* such joy and sadness at the same time, bottled up inside me. It felt like a dream, but it was real, so real that if I reached out, I could take it."

She turns from the railing to look at me. "They tell me I'm a weapon, that I'm built for a great purpose, but I don't know how to be anything but myself."

I don't know what to say. She's opened her soul to me, and I'm left speechless by the beauty of it, the beauty of her. She steps forward until she stands before me. I close my eyes and raise my face. She brushes her fingers across my lips and cheekbones.

"I'm sorry," she says. "I'm sorry I hurt you."

"You said you would."

"I didn't mean it."

"This kind of hurt I can take."

"You shouldn't have to."

I open my eyes and curl my hand around her wrist. I pull her gently toward me until she's half on the bench, half on my lap, her leg draped over my knees. Wrapping an arm around her, I breathe into her hair, still somewhat damp from her shower.

We're quiet for a moment.

Strange, but I've never felt more safe, here in her arms. "I don't want to go back," I say.

"Inside the house?" she teases, willfully misunderstanding.

"To the Tower."

She laughs, her breath tickling my collarbone. "Where would we go?"

"My apartment."

"In Mapo-gu, Hapjeong-dong?"

"Yes."

"And what would we do there?" She snuggles closer. Her voice is barely a whisper.

She falls asleep in my arms. The lantern dims. I press my lips against her hair.

"We'd dream."

■ ■ ■

I'm startled awake—minutes, hours later—by a sound. Tera's also up, alert, her eyes on the house.

"What was—?" I begin to ask. Then I hear it again. Screaming, from inside.

"Ama!" Tera shouts. We're both off the bench in a flash. The lantern flares on, alerted to our movement.

"Go," I say. "I'll catch up."

Tera sprints up the stairs. In less than three seconds, she's inside the house.

I'm slower to follow. I run up the stone steps and through the sliding door. The house is shrouded in darkness without even the sunlight to illuminate the rooms. The screams have stopped.

I manage to make it to the medical room without tripping on anything. Tera sits on the bed with Ama, brushing hair back from the younger girl's tear-streaked face.

"What's wrong?" I ask from the doorway.

Ama's head whips in my direction. "It's Alex!" she yells. "He's hurting—he's hurting him!"

I pivot and sprint down the hall. I check Alex's room, but there's no sign of him.

"Alex!" I take out my phone and call him. It goes straight to his voice mail. I slide down another hall, my feet slipping on the wood. Dammit. This house is a maze, the rooms growing darker as I move deeper into the mountain. The lights must be voice-activated by the owners, because they don't turn on, and I don't see a control panel on the walls.

I turn a corner and see a light at the end of a hall. I rush down it and stumble out a back door into an outer courtyard. It's jarring after the catacombs of the house. I'm . . . outside, in what must be a recess in the mountain. Moonlight bathes an empty dirt courtyard, ringed on all four sides by wooden walkways. A bow and arrow set on a stand are situated on one side of the courtyard, a bull's-eye on the other. Across the courtyard, yellow light glows from a paper-paneled doorway.

I walk slowly toward the light. "Alex?"

A loud crash booms from within the room, and I flinch. Shadows move against the paper walls. A terrible smack reverberates through the courtyard as one figure brings his fist down, hard, upon another kneeling on the ground. It's Alex, and he's . . . with his father.

I shouldn't be surprised, and in a way I'm not. I'd lived the majority of my life in a gang. I understand violence. And I'd even seen the signs in Alex, the inexplicable wounds, the way he keeps mostly to himself and refuses to allow people close to him. But still, I'm surprised.

I step forward, and my shoe kicks a loose rock.

The Director's fist stops in the air. He looks up, but he can't see me through the cracked doorway, standing as he is in the light, with me in the darkness. He's wearing sleeping robes. Everything about him is clean and white, but for his bloody hands.

"Get out," he says, but whether he's addressing me or Alex I can't tell. Without another word, he exits the room on the other side, slamming the sliding door behind him.

Silence reigns once more.

"Alex," I say.

"Don't." He pushes himself slowly off the mat floor. The room is some sort of personal dojang, meant for martial arts training.

Alex limps toward me. I step back. He shuts the door quietly behind him, a contrast to his father's booming exit.

"The Director's in a bad mood," he says calmly. "We'll have to postpone the meeting."

"Shit."

He ignores me. "What are you doing out here?"

"Ama's awake."

He looks past my shoulder. "Is she all right?"

"She heard you."

I wonder how loud his thoughts are. He looks so quiet, so contained in this moment. A hint of emotion in the twitching of his cheek. "Let's go."

We're halfway through the courtyard when he stumbles. I catch him before he hits the ground, and then lower him gently the rest of the way.

"He's going to kill you," I say.

"I'm his son," Alex answers, defeated.

"Alex?" Ama appears in the doorway of the main house,

Tera close behind. "Alex!" Ama rushes into the courtyard and sinks to the ground beside him. Her small hands move to the back of his head, gently fluttering against his hair, wet with blood.

"His thoughts are chaotic," Ama says. "He's in so much pain." I don't have to read minds to know she's not just talking about the physical pain. Her brows knit in concentration. "No," she says, "it's not your fault." I think she's responding to thoughts of his father, but then she says, "You didn't know he would die."

Seungpyo.

Tears escape Alex's eyes. They trail down his face. Ama holds tight to him.

"Take it away," he whispers.

"I can't," she says. "I can't."

"You can. Please, take the pain away."

I look at Tera, who's come out from the doorway to stand in the moonlight. "She can do that?" I ask.

"She can take his memories away."

"No," Alex says, "not that."

"Or she can put him into a deep sleep, without dreams or thought."

Slowly Ama lifts her hand to brush it against Alex's temple. She closes her eyes. "Sleep," she says, "and when you wake, everything will be better. I promise."

I frown. How can she promise something like that?

"It's a promise to myself," Ama whispers. "That one day, he'll wake to a world better than the one he fell asleep in."

We wait as Alex's breaths change from short, frantic bursts to long, drawn-out sighs. Between us, Tera and I manage to get him back to the medical room. As we enter, one of the maid-and-butler bots in the corner immediately whirs on, coming to Alex's side. We let it administer to him, programmed as it is for moments just like this one.

A low, vibrating noise from his pocket alerts us to an incoming phone call. Ama pulls out the phone. It flashes blue with Dr. Koga's name.

Ama answers. "Hi, Dr. K," she says softly. "No, I'm okay. Alex is . . . asleep. Lee Jaewon? He's here. Okay, one sec."

She hands the phone over to me. I wonder if Koga had been kind to Ama on the phone because he bites out a quick order to me before hanging up. "Bring Ama and Tera back to the Tower immediately."

23

FAIRY TALE

Dr. Koga waits for us in the lobby of the Tower. He doesn't speak as he takes Ama and Tera to their rooms, ordering me to wait for him. I look down and see I have Alex's blood on the cuff of my sleeve.

When Koga returns, he motions me to follow. "I need to speak with you. Ride the elevator up with me? You don't have to stay for the party." It's not a request.

I step into the lift, and the doors close. Dr. Koga shifts the speed to its lowest setting before pressing the button for the Skyroom. The elevator car begins to ascend.

"I get nauseous if it moves too quickly," he explains.

"Ah," I say. It also gives him an extra few minutes to chastise me for failing to bring Ama and Tera back on time. I brace myself for the dressing-down.

"Rough day?" He nods, indicating the wounds on my

face. They're not as obvious after the patches I'd applied earlier, but to an astute observer like Koga, they'd be noticeable.

"I got into a fight." Well, two, but I don't have to bring his attention to the first.

"At the Silla hotel," Koga says. "News travels fast."

We're quiet for a moment. "How is he?" I ask.

"No Seungri? His father came for him. No charges are being pressed."

I'm relieved. Seungri shouldn't have threatened Ama, but his pain and grief were palpable.

"He's a good man," Koga says. "Seungri's father is. He served in the military for several years before receiving an honorable discharge. It was an injury, hit him right here." Koga presses the center of his chest. "Since then, he's devoted his life to manufacturing safe gear for combatants. A good man, and devoted to his sons."

A heat rises in my chest, unbidden. A good man. His sons, plural.

"You protected Seungri from Tera," Koga says. "You fought her, and yet here you are, alive and well."

I'd been nervous when I stepped into the elevator that he would berate me for not bringing Ama and Tera back to the Tower on time. But his demeanor is calm, pleasant. Koga takes off his glasses and wipes them on the cuff of his sleeve. Without the magnifying lenses, his eyes are smaller, kinder. Maybe I'm paranoid, too used to wolves disguised as people. From the moment I've met Koga, he's been honest. Maybe he's just that. Someone who is exactly as he appears.

He puts his glasses back on, and we both gaze out at the city, watching first the sides and then the rooftops of buildings as we leave the city behind and enter the sky.

Koga speaks again. "The board of the Tower voted on whether or not to bring you, specifically, into the project. After all, your records show little of your background and family history, only that you were a war orphan recruited into the Red Moon gang at the age of eight. Alex was already a candidate due to his father's backing, but you were a dark horse, and there were some who regarded your past as a gangster a detriment to your character. Of course, there were others who thought it could be an asset."

He smiles, amused at himself. "I voted in favor of you despite your many supposed faults, and would do so again. You tested above average in athletics and intelligence, and high in leadership and piloting, all of which would have made you a strong candidate as Tera's partner."

Koga taps the glass of the elevator. "But I voted in favor of you for one simple reason and one reason only, and that was because you tested high in empathy."

Empathy?

I must make a face, because Koga chuckles. "It's not an insult. You wouldn't kill Tera in the simulation."

"That's because I'd seen her before at the concert. I believed her to be a student at another academy."

"Yes, that matters, the connection you have with her. I am not one to take fate lightly. But it's more than that. You wouldn't kill her, because when you saw her, you saw a person, a life that needed to be saved. I had faith in the humanity you showed. Because of it, I took a chance on a kid from across the river. I swung the vote in your favor."

I don't know what he expects me to say. *Thank you?* I am thankful. Without his vote I would have never come to the Tower. I would have never met Tera.

"Some of my colleagues criticize me for being an emotional man, for seeing the girls as girls first, and weapons second. They think me a pathetic fool who believes Ama and Tera are my daughters. Of course I don't. But I have known them for almost their whole lives. I don't think they have memories without me. That's a responsibility I carry."

I lean my shoulder against the glass. "You *are* an emotional man."

Koga sighs. "Maybe."

It's a cloudless night. A great airship, likely a troop transport, flies in a southwesterly direction past the Tower. If it weren't for the searchlight, it might have even crashed into the structure. I realize the Tower is a lighthouse, warning ships in the night.

The airship hums as if it's alive, and in a way, it is. It carries the lives of thousands of people, a city in the sky.

Koga continues. "The creators of the Amaterasu Project forgot one thing in building the perfect soldier: that the ultimate weapon is not a machine, like the Marionette, but a human with the will to fight. Because they believe in something, because they want to protect someone. What makes Tsuko such a great soldier is that he believes in his endeavors, to the point where it is his reason for being. What is Tera's reason for being?"

I think of Tera's face as she looked out into the city. *I don't know how to be anything but myself.* "Does she need one?"

"Ah." Koga smiles brightly. "And *that* is exactly why I voted for you."

The elevator sounds our arrival. Level one hundred and forty-four. The Skyroom. The doors open to the sound of music.

Koga steps out. "Come, have some food before you head back out. I promise you don't have to speak with anyone if you don't wish to."

I get out because there are several people waiting for the elevator, and I don't feel like sharing a cramped space for the return trip. Koga's already left me to disappear into the crowd.

I've been here once before, the day I came to the Tower and met Tera on the roof. It had been set up as a restaurant then. Tonight the tables and chairs have been put away, leaving an open ballroom filled with well-dressed men and women. Music comes from the stage, where C'est La Vie is performing.

Sela's back with her band tonight. Her hair is long and starlit-gray. She's singing her new single. I've heard it at least five times since I lied to her about listening to it, playing at the mall and on the holos.

I scan the room for Park Taesung, but don't pick out his face in the crowd.

At the edge of the Skyroom there is a massive floor-to-ceiling window. I gaze outside at the bright lights of Neo Seoul far below. Every seventh second, the searchlight comes around to highlight the buildings surrounding the Tower. Even when I close my eyes, I can see the light, circling. I wonder when the people who live beneath the glaring light become accustomed to it—when it's no longer a nuisance but just part of the surroundings.

Sela's song ends, and a new one begins. "Please tell me. Please tell me why people hurt one another."

It's the song from the concert. The first time I'd heard it, I'd thought it depressing. But there's a subversive quality to the lyrics. I'm surprised it hasn't been censored. Then again, C'est La Vie isn't the Proselytizer, here to stir up a revolution.

"Please tell me. Why do people hurt one another? Why do people kill one another?"

I don't have an answer. I don't know if anyone does. All I know is, I'm ready to leave. It's been a long day.

I head back toward the elevator bank. Halfway there, I spot a figure in the crowd. My heart kicks in my chest. No. It can't be.

She stands with her profile to me, wearing a dress of deep blue.

It's beautiful on her. And even though I know I'll regret it, that I'll be disappointed, even devastated, that it's useless, I find myself moving toward her through the crowd until I'm standing behind her, and I know that she knows I'm there, that I'm *here* beside her, because her shoulders flinch as if taken by a chill.

She turns, slowly, and I say, "Mother."

It's strange the way you love the people that hurt you the most. For a second, I think she doesn't recognize me, but then she takes my hands in her own soft ones. "My son."

She looks the same. Maybe shorter. No, I've grown taller. The last I'd seen her, I'd been eight years old.

Her husband takes notice of her distraction. He turns and circles an arm around my mother's waist. She drops my hands.

"Ah, my wife's son," he says. He's a man in his late forties. He'd met and fallen in love with my mother when she'd worked as a lounge singer in one of the river bars in Neo Seoul. I can't blame him for loving her. Can I blame her for leaving me? She couldn't have brought me with her, not unless her husband had adopted me and put me on his family register, but he'd refused.

"The prodigy," he says, "a soldier in the Tower." He rests his hand on my shoulder. "We're very proud of you."

I ignore him and look at my mother. "How is my brother? How is Jaeshin?"

"He's well."

"You didn't bring him."

"It's a party, and he's so young."

"I want to meet him."

I can tell I'm making her nervous. She keeps shooting looks at her husband. "Jaeshin's at home," she says.

My hands curl into fists at my side. "Home. I don't think you've ever told me where you live." *In the letters you never send.*

She blanches. "It wouldn't be safe . . ."

"You know where I live."

Finally her husband interrupts. "Jaewon-ah, you know why we can't tell you. You only have yourself to look after, but there are four of us."

"You think I'm going to break into your house in the middle of the night?"

"No, of course not," my mother rushes to say. "It's not like that. It's just . . . the people you associate with. They're dangerous. Gangsters."

I blink rapidly. She forgets that she abandoned me to those gangsters. Is this how she sees me? Forever one of them, no matter how far I've come. The sounds in the room become muted. My mother opens her little pocket purse and fishes around inside, pulling out several hundred thousand won bank notes. "Please, take some . . ."

I feel numb as I watch her grapple with her purse. Noticing the curious stares we're attracting, her husband grabs her wrist and pulls her hand out. His face is reddening at the unwanted attention, and he whispers something into my mother's ear, causing her to flush in embarrassment.

A surge of anger rises in me, at him for being embarrassed at all for anything she could do, at her for believing I would take her money, but most of all at myself—for caring.

I swallow the thick lump in my throat and do the only thing I can in this moment. I smile, my most brilliant one— the one I share with my father.

My mother sucks in a breath.

"Mother," I say, "I'm a prodigy, remember? Someone worth something. I don't need your money."

I bow to her and leave, not caring that people are pointedly looking now.

The music has stopped, and Sela watches me from the stage. "Jaewon-ah!" she shouts, and her voice carries through the mike. She's coming down from the stage, but isn't making good progress through the crowd, and I walk on, pressing the button for the elevator. I groan in relief when the metal doors open. I back into the corner and sink to the floor as the doors close on Sela's face.

Ten years, and I still feel the same as when I was just a boy, eight years old and desperate for her love. Worthless, like I'm charity to her, the biggest mistake of her life.

■ ■ ■

By the time the elevator reaches the ground floor, I'm a mess. The doors open, and I step out. A man waits outside, a red moon stitched to the lapel of his black suit.

God, will this night never end?

"The boss wants to see you."

He leads me outside. It's raining now, which I hadn't known from my view above the clouds. The man holds an umbrella over me as we walk to a parked black town car. He opens the door, and I step inside. Leather seats face one another across a low table. Since the far side is occupied, I take the seat closest to the door.

The man shuts it. Across from me sits Park Taesung. The pebbled sounds of the rain are a melancholy backdrop to our meeting. Placed on the low table is a decanter filled with a golden liquid, two crystal glasses, and a bowl of ice.

Park Taesung leans forward, picks up a pair of silver tongs, and meticulously places three shards of ice into two separate glasses. He then fills each a quarter full from the decanter. He hands one to me, and I knock it back. The liquid tastes like smoke and wood.

"Lee Jaewon," Park Taesung says, "you've been busy."

I wonder what he's referring to. It's been a long day. Does he mean my run-in with Red Moon's low-level thugs, my date with Tera, my fight at the Silla hotel, my visit to the Director's home, my reunion with my mother?

I put the glass on the table.

"It's late," I say, and look out the window. The rain blurs the lights, making it look as if the city is melting. "What do you want?"

"You'll have heard about the arrest. Of the Proselytizer."

I grimace. "No." It must have happened sometime while I was at Alex's house, or I would have seen it on the billboards. Unless it wasn't broadcast.

"They killed the man this afternoon, without trial."

A feeling of loss hits me at this news. I might not have followed all the theories online about him, but there were many who took strength in his slogans, like the girl in the hot dog joint and the girl on the Skytrain. "That was quick."

"They got what they needed from him. They interrogated him, and he revealed a critical piece of information: the location of the leader of the UKL's base. Tsuko was called to the war front earlier today. They're going to send an alternate team, which will include Tera and you."

"You're a sponsor. You're not on the Board. How do you know all this?"

"Money. Spies. Threats. Power. They all go a long way in getting the information you want."

Want. The word makes me think. "What *do* you want? You're a gangster. You've profited in this war—dealing in illicit Enhancers, weapons, information. This project could end the war. It's a threat to everything you represent."

"An end to war," he repeats, holding his glass of whiskey in one hand, circling his finger along the rim with the other. "And how exactly do you end war?"

"When one side surrenders, or when the cost outweighs the gain."

"That might be how you end *one* war, the one we fight today, but how do you end war *entirely*? The First Act of this 'Great War' created the Neo Council. The Second Act cemented the Council's rule over both East and West. And now we're in the Third Act, in which resistance organizations like the Free Chinese Men and Women and the United Korean League fight for a return to the original order. It's a great circle. So tell me, how do you end war?"

"You can't."

He leans forward in his seat. "You *can,* by eliminating both sides through a third party."

"You're going to destroy the Neo Council *and* the UKL?" I ask in disbelief. "With what army?" Red Moon might be

East Asia's most powerful crime syndicate, it might have the resources and the manpower, but it's not a military organization with structure, trained soldiers, and God Machines. It's a bunch of gangsters with a bit of tech. He needs an army, and not just any army, but one more powerful than the combatants he hopes to overtake.

And then a thought strikes me. "The girls. That's why you're kidnapping them. For this purpose." He wants to create an army of soldiers like Tera. Maybe he's been *buying* weapons instead of selling them. And unlike Dr. Koga, who allows Tera and Ama small freedoms, Park Taesung would brainwash the girls, torture and mold them until they were true weapons in every sense of the word.

"Ah, I knew you'd figure it out quickly."

I lean forward. "It's wrong. What you're doing. They're children."

I expect Park Taesung to slap me for my disrespect. Instead, he laughs. "Weren't you a child once? Was it wrong what I did to you?"

I lurch back. "This has nothing to do with me. I knew what I was getting into."

"At eight years old? Because if taking these girls from their homes and forcing them into a life they didn't choose for their own is wrong, then was it wrong what I did to the son of the man who was once my closest friend?"

"Don't say it. Don't speak his name."

"Lee Hyunwoo trusted me to take care of you and your mother, and what did I do? I forced your mother into an impossible choice: leave you behind and live or stay with you and die. I forced you into my gang, where you were starved and beaten, where you were forced to fight for your life. I did all that, to the son of the man who was once like a brother to me."

And that's what I could never understand. My whole life, he's tortured me. My whole life, he's taken the people I love from me. My mother. Young. I don't understand it. How could someone my father loved so much bring me so much pain? I look at Park Taesung, his cruel, terrible face, etched with so much history of hatred. Was my father wrong to love him?

And then I ask a question that breaks my heart. "Did you always hate him?"

"I hate him as much as you hate him."

But I don't hate him. I almost say the words.

There's a glimmer of knowing in Park Taesung's cold eyes. What is he playing at? Was this a trick? I don't know if it's my injuries or the whiskey or the day, the night, my mother, my father, *him*, but I feel like I'm dying inside.

"It's almost over, Jaewon-ah. All our suffering. There's just one more thing to do. Bring Tera to me and let me show you a new world."

I look up. "Tera?"

"It's easier to harvest the Enhancer serum from her than create it ourselves. She holds the key in her blood, the only one to survive the physical Enhancer treatment."

"That's why you're telling me all this. You think I can get her for you."

"You were the best Runner in my gang. You could get anything. Even a beautiful girl locked in a Tower."

"This isn't a fairy tale."

"No, it's not," he says. He knocks on the window, and the door on my side opens. The powerful sound of the rain rushes into the car. "This is our reality, one we need to shape for the betterment of our future. Bring Tera to me, Jaewon, and you and the rest of this godforsaken city will have one."

24

THE MISSION

Park Taesung's tip about the UKL proves correct when I'm called to the Tower the following evening. I meet Tera in the upper floor of the GM hangar, which opens up to a docking bay. Powerful lights flood the open space. Two mid-size carriers are priming for departure, loading up basic ground and air GMs.

Less than twenty-four hours since finding out the location of the UKL hideout from the Proselytizer, these ships will take off in an attempt to capture a living legend: Oh Kangto, leader of the UKL and a veteran of all three Acts of the War.

The guards who had accompanied Tera bow and leave us. I was sent a brief overview of the mission on the way over here. It's a classic search-and-destroy. Root out the rebels and take hostages. The expedited nature of the mission is to prohibit the rebels' catching wind of it and either preparing a defense or fleeing farther north into the Neo State of North China. Their base is supposed to be located across the border.

Tera and I have orders to lend support but not engage in any direct combat unless specified. Technically, Tera is a weapon that hasn't passed inspection from the Neo Council and is therefore "unauthorized for combat."

"You're an illegal weapon," I joke. "How does that make you feel?"

Tera rolls her eyes. We move up the gangplank to board the first carrier. Tera and I are both dressed in the white-and-black uniforms of the NSK, identifying us as soldiers, if not our rank and purpose. Koga must have given notice that we're acting as free agents for the duration of this mission, because none of the officials we pass give us undue scrutiny.

I think of Koga's words to me last night—how he'd chosen me for the project because I'd tested high in "empathy." I'd recoiled at the word. It was instinctual. My father was once called a good man, a kind man. Men who are good and kind don't live very long. But maybe that's why I need someone like Tera to protect me.

I look up to see Tera eyeing me curiously over her shoulder. "Why do you look like that? What are you thinking?"

"Nothing."

Koga was right about one thing. Tera and I do make good partners. In the restaurant, when Seungri had aimed the gun at Ama, Tera had called out to me. After the fact, I realized she could have been killed in the blast of the gun. But in that moment, I trusted her to know what she was doing. And she trusted *me* enough to stop her attack on Seungri and fight against the Enhancer's powerful hold on her.

A low rumble sounds as the carrier's engine starts up. Overhead, the captain orders all personnel to stand by for takeoff.

We go from the outer boarding area to the interior halls of the ship, bypassing a camera crew dressed in civilian clothing. War correspondents. Their bright laughter cuts through the stale air. I wonder if they're war casters, reporters who specialize in documenting war in a stylized form for the consumption of the public. War casters were the reason that ace pilots even existed in the First and Second Acts of the War, presenting the pilots as celebrities, their statuses determined by their kill count and number of battles won.

They'd become less so in the Third Act, when the battlefield switched from pitched ground and aerial battles between government-sanctioned military forces to guerilla warfare, making it difficult to a) film and b) film in a way where the "right" side looks like heroes and not villains. It's hard to make a GM devastating forests in order to rout out rebels heroic, especially as often there are civilian casualties.

One of the reporters catches me watching them. I tap Tera on the shoulder and pivot through a doorway.

There's a brief feeling of weightlessness as the ship starts to ascend. It's a smooth takeoff, and Tera and I don't break stride as we make our way to the bridge.

We check in with the man heading the operation, a decorated Second Act war colonel named Go Woojin, currently in command of the NSK's auxiliary forces stationed outside Neo Seoul. Apparently he has a score to settle with Oh Kangto, hence his involvement. He's a powerfully built man in his late fifties, barrel-chested and tall. When he's introduced to Tera, his eyes widen. He gives her a not-so subtle once-over, obviously in disbelief that a girl of Tera's size and stature could be a dangerous weapon.

"They want to fight this war with children," he says beneath his breath. Louder, he shout-speaks, "I allowed you onto my ship because the NSK Board authorized your presence on this mission, but I won't be needing you." He gives me a cursory glance. "Either of you. If the Neo Council discovers we've put an unsanctioned weapon into combat without its express authorization, it will be considered a violation of the Neo Charter. I don't want to hear of either of you leaving this ship. We won't be resorting to Koga's . . . experiments to catch the old rebel leader. War is about honor, not politics and guerilla fighting and *tricks*." He sneers this last word for our benefit.

We're dismissed. One of the colonel's soldiers leads us to a room at the back of the carrier. It's small, with side-by-side beds that also function as escape capsules. The doors close behind the soldier, and Tera collapses onto the left bed.

"The Board wants me to have battle experience in order to pass inspection at the Neo Council, yet in order to have battle experience, I need to fight, but I can't because I haven't passed inspection." She sighs, reaching out to pull the blanket over her shoulder, cocooning herself. "Adults are confusing."

She turns to face the wall, adjusting the blankets over her face so all that I see are the wisps of her hair peeking out from the top like winter grass.

"Do you want to fight?" I'm genuinely curious. Her greatest fear is losing control of her powers and hurting others. But if she were given the choice, would she fight?

I always thought that if I were to fight, it would be because I was paid to do it—mercenary of me, perhaps, but in a military state, you don't need a reason to fight. You fight and kill because you're told to, because there's someone standing on the other side of the line that your government deems adverse to its establishment. It's no different from being in a gang, except it pays better.

"I don't know," Tera says, her voice muffled from beneath the blankets.

"What would you do if they sent you into battle?" If she were to go into battle, I'd have to follow as her partner. It would be the first for both of us, outside of a simulation.

"Who would I be fighting?" she asks.

"The rebels, I guess."

"I feel like," she says slowly, "if I was sent into battle, I'd just want to fight everyone."

That sounds dangerously close to Park Taesung's plan of a third party to destroy the main combatants. I briefly consider telling Tera about my meeting with my old gang boss, but she wiggles on the bed, distracting me.

"How is Alex?" she asks. "Ama's been worried sick."

"I called him this morning, but he didn't answer." I'd thought about taking a cab out to his place, but I figured if he wouldn't answer my calls, he wouldn't answer the door. He must be all right in the physical sense. Maid-and-butler bots are designed to assist in all medical situations and have a built-in alert to the nearest hospitals in case of emergencies.

"I told Ama to be careful. Even if others can't read her mind, her feelings for Alex are as clear as day in the way she looks at him."

"Careful?"

"I told her that it was impossible for her to be with him in that way."

I look down at my hands. "Is it?"

"However much"—Tera hesitates—"Ama might want to be close to him, it would be dangerous . . . for everyone."

Are we still speaking about Ama and Alex?

"Soldiers have families all the time," I say, "even if it's only for the purpose of having more soldiers."

"But I'm not a soldier. I'm a weapon."

"You can be more than one thing."

"I'm not even *human*. Ama and I can't *have* relationships. The Tower would never allow it. We're worth trillions in investments. We have a greater purpose."

"You have relationships. Ama's your friend."

"You're not listening."

"I am listening. I just don't like what you're saying. You said last night in the gazebo that you were more than a weapon, or *less* than a weapon if weapons are supposed to exist for a purpose. You're just . . . you. A girl with dreams and desires. If that's not human, I don't know what is. There's nothing special about you. Sorry."

Tera sweeps back the blankets to glare at me. "Words are so easy for you. After last night, you returned to your home in Mapo-gu, Hapjeong-dong. Where did I go? Back to my white room. You sound just like Ama, idealistic and unrealistic."

"You sound like Tsuko, cold and unfeeling." I don't really believe my words, but I'm pissed at the direction this conversation has taken.

She turns back to the wall. "Go away. I want to be alone."

"Alone in a prisonlike room," I say dryly. "How fitting."

She doesn't speak as I leave the room. In the halls of the ship, the soldiers I pass give me a wide berth. I don't have a destination, but it doesn't matter; I just need to walk off these feelings of frustration. How did we go from talking about Alex's health to prodding each other with insults?

The hall I'm walking down ends at a lift. To its side is the door to the stairs, which I take, moving up to the second level, then the third, fourth, fifth. I know the answer to my own question. If Ama and Alex can't have a relationship, then neither can Tera and I, for all the reasons she stated. The cage that surrounds her is more than the literal box of her room; it's the expectations of her "creators," as Koga said, the reason for her being. There are so many people who need her.

I'm just one person who wants her.

The door on this floor opens on a long, dark room, the far

wall a great window. This must be the observation deck, the highest point of the carrier. It's empty of people. We're still a distance from our destination, about three hundred kilometers out from the border of Manchuria, but soldiers will be on standby for deployment on the lower levels. I approach the window, my footsteps echoing across the open space.

It's dark outside. At some point in the night, we must have passed the old boundary line before the Great War, when the state was a country, and when that country was divided between North and South.

It's strange to think the world could be so different a hundred years ago from today as it will be a hundred years in the future. And yet not so different. The Proselytizer once said that he hated the past because it showed him the future, that humans are fated to repeat the mistakes of their forebears. It's instinctual, humanity's need to fight, to win, to kill, to live.

The ship must have been moving through a cloud drift, because the dark of the outside dissipates. Below the ship is a massive mountain range, the highest peaks cleaving the sky.

Mount Baekdu is here, in the great northern mountain range of Korea. It's like nothing I've ever seen before. The massiveness of it—mountains seeming to grow on top of mountains, dotted with snow-covered pines.

If we're here, we've traveled farther than I thought. Soon, we'll approach the border of Manchuria. Somewhere in the dark forests of that country hides a group of rebels, and with them, their defiant, charismatic leader, Oh Kangto. I wonder if he knows we're coming for him.

I'm turning away from the window when I catch sight of something—a pinpoint of light in the darkness. I squint, trying to figure out the source of the light. It seems to grow larger the longer I stare at it.

I realize what it is the moment the alarm sounds in the carrier.

We're under attack.

The first blast rocks the ship, and I stumble to the floor, covering the back of my neck with my hands as debris falls from overhead. I'm momentarily stunned, ears ringing. Then a high-pitched keening breaks me from my daze, and I look up to see cracks spiraling out from the glass window.

I scramble to my feet as the ship tilts, sliding and banging my shoulder against the far wall. Quickly I follow the signs on the wall to a panel. I bang it open, fumbling inside for a parachute, anything. There's nothing. Tera, as long as she stayed in the room, should be fine. The beds double as emergency capsules, but if I don't find a way out of here, I'll go down with this ship.

Through high whistling air that blasts into the carrier, I hear the screams of soldiers as they're whipped away into the sky.

Heads will roll for this, if we somehow make it back alive. The Proselytizer must have fed the colonel false information. Perhaps it was even *planned*—the Proselytizer's capture and this mission. How they didn't anticipate a preliminary assault is above my pay grade.

Another deafening rumble of the ship signals the engines

failing. My stomach drops. Gravity's taking hold of the carrier. I desperately stumble to the next wall panel, punching it open. Nothing. Flares and a medical kit.

The ship sputters, and then all is chaos—in the air, in my mind. The ship collides with the side of a mountain. The entire glass wall shatters, and I'm whipped through the opening into the night.

The last thing I feel is my body arcing through the air, the cold wind like stars piercing through my skin.

25

WANT

It's the pain that wakes me: a blistering heat that burns up my side. I move my hand downward and brush against a sharp piece of metal sticking out from beneath my ribs.

Shit.

I groan and sit up. Without giving too much thought to what I'm about to do, I grab the metal piece and yank it out. My head swirls, and I grit my teeth, fighting off the nausea. I drop the metal, coated with three centimeters of my blood. I take a minute to regain my breathing, then grab the edge of my shirt, rip away a strip of cloth, and wrap the wound tight, praying I don't black out. I fumble in my jacket pocket for some pain-killers, palming them into my mouth and grinding them between my teeth. The bitter taste helps to clear my mind.

Around me lies some of the wreckage of the crash. Broken

pieces of metal. Heat orbs, most of them shattered. There's no fire, which is a surprise. And no ship.

Tera.

I stand up quickly. It's a mistake. I stumble, catching myself against what's closest to me—a tree, its branches broken and scattered on the ground.

I have a fleeting thought: *I must have fallen through this tree.*

I stand up straight, wincing at the searing pain. I look desperately around for Tera. If she'd stayed in the room, she'd have escaped through a capsule. The air is cold and thin. My breaths puff out like chilled smoke.

I limp away from the tree and almost fall off a cliff.

Before me is a steep drop-off. A massive lake, several times the width of the Han River, lies below.

It's an eerie tableau. Pieces of the carrier sink slowly beneath the surface. All across the lake, bodies are caught in patches of ice, illuminated by burning debris. I spot several escape capsules floating in the middle of the lake. They're empty.

I step right to the edge of the drop, searching the waters. Can Tera swim? She's never left the Tower. Do they teach that in simulations? And if they do, would it be the same? To feel the water closing over your head for the first time, that instant chill, that lack of air. Can you mimic it?

Panic stirs within me, almost dispelling the pain at my side. *Use the panic.* My father's voice from long ago fills my mind. *Use your body's adrenaline—it's warning you. It's trying to help you.*

I turn and sprint down the mountain, following a clear path in the moonlight. The path is man-made and forks near the lake, the second path leading to a small temple nestled at the side of the mountain. I ignore it and take the path to the lake.

My blood seeps through the wrapped cloth. Every pound of my feet against the ground shoots a stab of agony into my side. By the time I reach the lakeshore, I'm gripping my side, and the blood has completely soaked through the bandage. I step into the water, the cold like frozen knives digging through my shoes.

For a moment, clouds cover the moon, throwing the world into darkness. I listen to the moans and cries and the creaking of the ice. If I live through tonight, this memory will haunt me.

The clouds pass. Moonlight leaps across the water, and I catch sight of Tera. She's several meters into the lake, her unconscious body sprawled across a thin slab of ice, a deep gash at the side of her head.

Hold on. I struggle out of my blazer. The weight of it will drag me under, and I'll need it for warmth, should we make it back. I rush into the lake, diving into the water when it's deep enough to swim.

I've almost reached her when she slips from the ice and disappears beneath the surface. Gathering breath, I submerge myself entirely in the lake. I'm blind beneath the water and can hardly make her out—just the shape of her, sinking farther and farther away.

It's cold. It's so cold. And I'm tired. I have no breath. But I have to reach her.

You can always have what you want, Jaewon, because you know the value of commitment. When you've committed yourself to something, you can never fail, because you know there's only one path you can take: to see it through to the end.

More words from my dead father.

You can always have what you want, you just have to want *it.*

I want it.

There are so many things that I want.

I want the light on my face in the morning to be just that—light, not a cold reminder that I'm awake.

I want this ache inside me to leave, the one that says I'm alone, and that I always will be.

I want to believe in the world I live in, to see it in the light of day and in the darkest of night and realize it's a world worth fighting for. It's a world worth living for.

What do you want, Jaewon? What the hell do you want?

I want her.

I reach out, unseeing, and find her hand in the darkness.

I circle my good arm around her, pulling her toward me, and use the other to push us to the surface and into the light.

26
THE TEMPLE

The first thing I see when I wake is the low glow of a hundred heat orbs, staggered in the air like fireflies. The first thing I feel is the soft pressure of fingers, gently brushing against my wrist.

"Jaewon-ah," Tera asks, her voice groggy, hoarse, "are you awake?"

"Mnh," I mumble, rubbing my eyes. The memory of where we are, and how we got here, returns in fragments.

The lake. I'd had to drag Tera onto the shore, still unconscious from her head wound.

The path. The path away from the lake was scattered with debris from the crash. I'd found a bag of heat orbs, a thermal blanket, and a spare uniform.

The temple. It was halfway up the path, a crack in the

mountains. Abandoned, a one-story edifice with faded green-and-red-paneled doors and a shrine, robbed of its idols. Inside, I'd laid Tera down on the wooden floorboards, using the last of my energy to release the heat orbs from the bag, strip us of our wet clothing, and wrap Tera in the thermal blanket. I'd just finished rewrapping my wound and throwing on the dead soldier's spare when I'd blacked out.

I didn't feel a thing until the gentle brush of Tera's fingers against my wrist.

Beside me, letting out a low breath, Tera sits up. The heat orbs mirror her movements, rising lazily in the air to form a disjointed halo around her head.

"You look warm," I say.

She watches me, her brows knitting together. "You look cold. Your lips are blue."

I lift my fingers to my lips. They don't feel cold. Or they don't feel colder than the rest of me. I grab a heat orb out of the air and bring it to my mouth, pressing it to my lips. I glance at Tera, grinning. "How's that?"

She looks away, a blush brightening her cheeks.

I release the orb and roll out the tick in my shoulder. It's a mistake; the pain in my side wakes with a burn.

"Jaewon-ah," Tera asks, anxious, "are you all right?"

I count to twenty in my head. There's a fogginess at the periphery of my vision, and when I look at Tera, her features are blurred. "It's just the altitude," I manage to get out. "I'm not used to it yet."

"I don't believe you," she says. "Ama gets that look

sometimes when she's saying something but it's not the truth."

"When she's lying?" I ask, dryly.

Tera huffs in annoyance, and I laugh, shaking my head. It's silent for a bit before I say, "It's good that you had—*have* Ama. As a friend, I mean. It must have been hard, growing up in the Tower alone."

Even if I've been alone for the past two years, before that I was always surrounded by friends—Young, Jinwoon, Daeho, all the boys in our gang. I don't think a day went by when I didn't see at least one of them.

Tera shakes her head. "It wasn't always just us two."

"What do you mean?"

"The project is on its third trial. There were many Teras who came before me. Amas as well. Of course I didn't know all of them. Some of us were kept in different facilities. But I knew enough of them to know they were just like Ama and me. Some were war orphans like us, while others were brought to the Tower because they were sick, and their parents thought the Enhancers would help them. But they didn't help them. Not in the end."

Tera pulls her legs to her chest. "What makes Ama and me so special?" she says. "Why do we get to live while they all died? In a way, I want to *be* the goddess the experiment wants me to be, if only for all those girls who couldn't, but at the same time, I'm so . . . I'm so angry. For what they did to those girls, my friends, to me, and to Ama. Tsuko thinks I'm ungrateful, and he's right. I am *not* grateful for what they've done. But Tsuko also said I was made with a purpose, and others have sacrificed for that purpose, and isn't it my responsibility to pick up the burden that was too heavy for them to carry?"

I don't have an answer for her. Tsuko said something similar in the elevator, about the responsibility of war. Does Tera carry the responsibility of the project? It seems like a heavy weight, even for someone as strong as she is.

Tera reaches out to brush the hair back from my face. "But you're right. I do have Ama. I am grateful to the project for bringing her to me. She's everything to me, the one person I cherish most in the world."

"One person?" I ask, hopeful.

She laughs. "Well," she teases, "one of two."

I close my eyes and smile. Maybe she feels pity for me because I'm wounded and feverish and slightly delirious, but I'll take it.

Her hand moves over mine. For once, hers is warm. Or maybe it's my hand that's cold. "Jaewon-ah," she says, "while you were sleeping, you must have been dreaming, because you kept saying someone's name. You sounded so sad."

I'm tired of being sad.

"Who is Young?"

"He was my friend," I say. "My best friend."

"Tell me," she says.

And even though I've never spoken to *anyone* about Young, I tell her.

"We grew up together. He lived in the apartment next to mine, and only a thin wall separated our rooms. I always knew when he had a bad dream, because I could hear him. His mother died when he was five, and his father was absent most of the time, so my parents looked after him. When they were gone, all I had was Young. He was my brother in everything but blood. Together we joined a gang. Old Seoul gangs have a difficult initiation process, but Young and I saw each other through it. And for five years we were Runners in Red Moon.

"We also managed to go to school, even while in the gang. I always wanted to skip, thinking it was a waste of time, but Young kept me going. He'd say, 'You're smart, Jaewon. You can make something of yourself.' He used to get terrible grades in school, but he'd go anyway, because he knew if he didn't, then I wouldn't.

"When we weren't at school or running for the gang, we'd bum whole nights in simTech rooms. They're rooms you can pay a standard fee for and use the simTech to do whatever. I'd play games. Sometimes I'd make money playing the games. I was always good at them, even when I was a kid. We got by. It was a way to live."

"Jaewon-ah," Tera asks softly, "what did Young do to you?"

I close my eyes. "So the initiation process into gangs is pretty harsh. It involves a beating to show your determination and strength. To get out, it's even worse. I was accepted into the military academy at Apgujeong with a full scholarship. Young sent in my application without me knowing. I promised to go if he'd leave the gang with me."

"How old were you?"

"Sixteen."

"Then what happened?"

"When we arrived at the headquarters of Red Moon, the rest of the gang had gathered. To . . . see us off. The boss asked me if I was set on leaving. I said I was. Then he asked Young if he was sure of the choice he had made. I should have suspected something was wrong, with the way the boss was looking at Young, a smug smile on his cruel face, with the way he was looking at me, as if he'd won a game I didn't know we'd been playing.

"But I didn't suspect. Not even then." I close my eyes, and the memory comes back to me. "I didn't see it coming. Not that first punch."

I was on the ground, surrounded by them, my hands grasping the back of my neck, my elbows blocking my ears. And even though I knew I should keep my head down, protect myself, I looked up, searching.

I needed to make sure.

Daeho wasn't in the circle of gang brothers who were beating me. He and Jinwoon stood a little back, their faces turned away. But they weren't the ones I needed to see.

"Young-ah," I croaked, looking up at the circle—one face after another. None of them were him. But then the circle opened, and he stepped through with his father.

"He's calling for you," Park Taesung said to him, not smiling.

Young looked down at me.

I searched his face for something, anything to make it

possible for me to understand, for me to forgive what he'd done to me. But he didn't say anything. He just stared at me, his face empty of emotion.

This is what I thought in that moment. What I wanted more than anything.

I want him to say, "Forgive me," so I can forgive him.

I want him to say, "I didn't mean this," so I can believe him.

He said nothing. He lifted his foot and brought it down hard on the center of my chest. I wondered if he could hear the bones breaking through my screams.

Back in the present, I open my eyes. Tera's hand comes up to wipe her warm fingers against my cold skin. "I'm sorry for your pain."

"It's all right," I say. "I got better." It only took a month of mediTape wrapped around my ribs to heal the bones. Sleep and painkillers got rid of the rest of the pain.

"No," Tera says. "You didn't. You're not better. Not yet."

"The thing is, I'd have forgiven Young if he'd asked, even after he'd betrayed me. Because I knew if I couldn't forgive him, then I'd have to leave him. What do you think of that?"

"I think you would have rather stayed in the gang and been with him then go to the academy and lose him. He made the choice for you. You stay mad at him because he was the one who abandoned you."

"Is that it? I didn't know I was so pathetic."

"He left you alone. There's nothing pathetic about feeling like you're all alone."

I nod slowly. She's right. But what can I do? I feel all alone because I *am* all alone. I forget what it feels like to belong to someone.

There's a whirring sound in my head, and there are rocks in my throat, and there's a snowstorm in my skin, and then there's Tera holding me.

And I think of Ama telling Alex that it will be better when he wakes, and now I get it, because I believe Tera when she promises me, over and over again, that things will be better.

I just have to wake.

■ ■ ■

"Jaewon-ah! Jaewon-ah!"

Tera screams my name. Or at least I think she's screaming my name. She sounds far away.

But when I open my eyes, she's gone.

I drag my body off the floor, my movements slow and uncoordinated. I feel as if I'm carrying a heavy weight across my shoulders. There's a thickness in my chest that makes it hard to breathe. A gust of wind breezes through the open doorway, rustling the dead leaves scattered across the temple.

Outside, a half meter of snow covers what was once the temple's graveled pathway. Early morning light tints the snow purple and pink. It looks like a painting. I blink back a wave of dizziness, my hands going out to hold the temple's doorframe.

I focus on the evidence of Tera's movements. Her footsteps are spread far apart in the snow, spaced as if she'd been running away from me toward the lake. Why?

I take a step into the snow.

I hear the knife before I see it, whistling through the air. I stumble out of the way, the blade nicking my ear. The knife embeds itself to the hilt in the wooden wall behind me.

A body drops from above, landing in the snow to my right. A fist connects with the wound in my side, and I see red. I drop to my knees. When I look up, I'm met with a gun pointed at my face.

"Filthy traitor," says a thickset man, his hard eyes narrowed. "You underestimated us. Didn't think we'd put up a fight? Arrogant bastards."

I bat his gun to the side. It fires into the snow, the sound of it somehow stifled even with the close proximity. "What did you do with her?" I grind out. "If you've hurt her, I'll kill you."

The man pushes his gun into my cheek. "You're just a kid. What could you do?"

His words chill my blood. I back away, trying to get back on my feet. "Tera!" I shout weakly. "Tera!"

The man pushes me into the snow again. This time his nozzle rests on my collarbone. When I try to stand again, he brings the gun down hard on the side of my head. The pain is almost unbearable. He raises it again, striking my shoulder. I hold my hands up to protect myself, but he's relentless. There are other men beside him, watching. Where they've come from, I don't know. At least they don't join in. It's just the first man, hitting me, again and again.

"Stop this," commands a new voice, somehow clear even through the haze of my mind.

I feel the first man moving away, giving me space. "Sir, he came down with one of the ships. And he's wearing a soldier's uniform."

"The boy survived a brutal crash, and you beat him for it. You have disappointed me." The second man comes to stand beside the first. My vision is so blurry, I can't make out the features of his face, only that something about him seems to calm the group of rebels. My attacker begins to lower the hand that holds the gun.

"Jaewon-ah!" Tera calls out.

My attacker twirls around. This time, when he lifts his gun, he's the one who's not quick enough. Tera knocks his hand to the side, and he screams as it breaks. The others move to intercept her, but she's too quick. I can't make out the details, but I can hear a chorus of painful cries.

The man who stopped my attacker, the leader, crouches down in the snow beside me, watching the faint breaths issuing from my lips. "Forgive me," he says. "I did not want this."

I close my eyes, too weak to keep them open.

The fight is over quickly. I hear one last cry, and then Tera's beside me. Her hands smooth back the hair from my face. "Jaewon-ah! Please wake up. Please, please open your eyes."

Tera. She's here. I want to see her. I want to see that she's okay, but I can't.

My eyes won't open.

"Good work, Tera," a new voice says.

"Colonel, please, you need to help him! He's burning up. There's a wound in his side. He's lost so much blood—"

"I'm afraid the medic died in the crash," Colonel Woojin says. "A ship will be here soon to pick us up."

"It'll be too late!" Tera screams. "He needs help now. *Please*. He's dying."

"Let me help him." The calm voice of the crouched man. "It's the least I can do." I feel a new pair of hands on my forehead, my neck. Cool, roughened hands. Then, a short intake of breath. "It can't be," the old rebel whispers. "Lee Hyunwoo?"

I stop breathing.

"Jaewon-ah?" Tera's voice, panicked. "Jaewon-ah!" she screams.

I hear the colonel's voice, muffled in the background. "Stop filming," he orders someone. "Hurry and tie up the traitors."

Tera's gone from my side, and suddenly I hear the sounds of fighting.

The colonel shouts, "Have you gone out of your mind? What do you think you're doing? That's Oh Kangto you're protecting!"

"I don't care who he is," Tera shouts. "As long as he saves Jaewon."

I feel the pressure of hands, Oh Kangto's hands, at the center of my chest. He presses down, counting a rhythm, like heartbeats. One . . . two . . . three . . .

I black out.

■ ■ ■

I come to with a jerk, air whipping through my lungs. I cough, my eyes cracking open.

"Jaewon-ah." Tera's beside me again. Behind her, Oh Kangto's being dragged away by NSK soldiers. "I'm so sorry I left you. You had a fever, and I didn't know what to do. I thought I could find some medicine for you. How badly did they hurt you? I saw them hitting you, and I—"

Behind her, the colonel orders two men forward. One holds a tranquilizing gun. But she's so focused on me she doesn't notice.

"Tera," I croak. At the same time, the soldier shoots her in the back.

She collapses onto me, unconscious, and I'm no better.

■ ■ ■

My father used to say there's a fine line between death and sleep, and that both are ways to escape an unendurable pain.

But he never spoke of the choice you'd have to make to wake.

27

MY FATHER

The dream, when it comes, isn't a surprise. It seems almost natural to dream about my father now, when I'm so close to seeing him again.

Or maybe it's not a dream, but a memory—a memory I've failed to forget.

■ ■ ■

I am eight years old, and my father has his hands on my shoulders. He's crouching down in front of me so that I can see the steadiness in his eyes. Unlike Young's father, my father never stands over me.

"Jaewon-ah," he says, "listen to your mother. When she tells you to stay, stay. And when she tells you to run . . ."

"Run."

He smiles, his eyes crinkling at the corners. "Good boy."

I poke the lines branching from his eyes. They spider out from the corners, and I lose them in the darkness of his hair.

The old CD player is crooning out a melody I've heard before. The lilting notes distract me. My eyelids flutter—I'd been sleeping before my father woke me.

"Look, Jaewon-ah," my father says, and I open my eyes wide. He holds something in his hands now, pulled from the pocket of his long coat. My father always keeps surprises in his pockets—pieces of chewing gum, a deck of cards, a photo of my mother.

"A sparkler," I say as I take one of the two thin metal wires from the palm of his hand. When we light the ends, they will burst with colored sparks, a mini fireworks display right in front of our eyes.

My father takes my hand, the one without the sparkler, and together we climb to the rooftop of our apartment. I feel giddy with excitement. It's past midnight, and even though my legs shake with tiredness, I push past it, blinking rapidly.

The windows in the apartment building across from ours are open, lines of thick string bridging the gap between the buildings, articles of clothing stretched and drying in the cool air. I see a pair of Young's boxers dangling from one of its short legs, and I grin.

"Appa, look," I say, pointing to the penguin-print boxers and laughing. Young is going to be embarrassed when I show

272

him the boxers tomorrow. I'm so excited, thinking about Young's reaction, that I don't see the last step.

I trip, my hands out before me to stop the fall.

But I don't fall.

My father catches me.

And even though he hasn't picked me up for many years, he holds me in his arms like I'm a baby again. I pretend to struggle, pretend that I don't like it because I'm a big kid, and Young would laugh if he saw. But it's chilly outside, the middle of winter, and my father's arms are so warm cradled around me, like a blanket of leaves.

We reach the top of the roof. My father takes me near the edge, placing me on top of a cinder block so I can see over the railing. Together we light our sparklers. They burst into color, slowly burning to the quick. Before they go out, my father writes his name in the air, and I write mine beside his.

Lee Hyunwoo.

Lee Jaewon.

I don't understand that he's giving me a good memory of him, so that tomorrow, when he does the unforgivable, I'll remember that I once thought the sun rose and set on his smile.

■ ■ ■

My father blew up a government facility, killing every single person inside, including himself.

28

OH KANGTO

My fever lasts a week. I'm transported to the NSK's military hospital in Gangnam immediately upon arrival in Neo Seoul, excused from school due to "injuries sustained in combat." I don't know this until after the fact. I'm mostly delirious until the fever breaks, kept on sleep-inducing drugs.

Alex visits when I'm more lucid. "You look awful," he says, walking around my bare hospital room.

I don't respond, too relieved that he's healthy enough to insult me. The last I'd seen him, he'd been broken on the floor.

He grimaces. "I've been cleaning up the colonel's mess. Luckily, the mission ended up a success even if it began as a disaster. Oh Kangto is in custody, on his third round of interrogations. The old bastard won't give anything up." He walks over and crosses his arms. "Actually, that's why I'm here. To see if you've recovered enough." He glances away. "I have a favor to ask."

When he doesn't elaborate, I say, "What?"

"Oh Kangto won't respond to any of the standard methods of torture. They want to use the Helm on Ama, but you saw how that went last time." He hesitates, obviously not used to asking favors. "She doesn't want to do it. She's afraid. I thought maybe you . . ."

"I'll do it," I say, "but just so you know, I scored poorly in interrogative methods." It was one of the few classes at the academy that I almost failed in. Apparently I'm bad at dissembling, which is ironic, because my whole identity is a lie.

"I think out of all of us—you, me, Koga, Tsuko, whatever—you'll be the one the rebel talks to."

"Really?" I ask, genuinely surprised. "What makes you think that?"

Alex looks at me hesitantly, as if anticipating a negative reaction. Immediately, I know why he's asked me. I scowl. "Alex, just because I'm from Old Seoul doesn't mean I speak a different language than you."

"Whatever," Alex says, cracking his knuckles. "The rebel won't talk to anyone. He hasn't spoken a word since we brought him in. He just sits there and takes it all, the beatings, the hot iron, the fast-acting poisons, the electrocution. The old man's a stone wall. I need you to breach it. I'll be back to pick you up at 2000 tonight." Alex walks to the door. "Get dressed. Take a shower. You may look better than Oh Kangto, but that's nothing to be proud of."

■ ■ ■

Alex isn't late to pick me up. He brings us straight from the hospital to the Tower. My fever might have broken, but I'm not fully recovered yet. I keep my movements slow, close to my body, careful not to open up any sealed wounds.

I follow Alex to a basement room of the Tower guarded by two soldiers. The guard on the right nods at Alex and scans his wrist across a panel to open the doors, revealing a small viewing room that looks through a glass window into another—an interrogation room.

I'm not surprised to see Tsuko by the window, watching Oh Kangto through the glass. Beside him stands Colonel Go Woojin. The third person in the room I *am* surprised to see.

"Are you feeling better?" Sela walks over to me with a look of concern in her violet eyes. She blinks, and her irises turn sky blue.

"I am."

"Congratulations on your capture of Oh Kangto. I saw the footage. You were very brave."

I grimace. I saw the footage as well, when I'd been lucid enough to work the tablet attached to the hospital bed. The footage aired to the public included a clip of me getting beaten into the ground by the UKL rebel, complete with a voiceover explaining my existence as a "young, brave soldier of the NSK." It then proceeded to show my rescue by Tera, another "soldier of the NSK." It hadn't released her association with the project.

The footage cut off right at the moment when Tera turned on the NSK soldiers, protecting Oh Kangto so that he could save my life.

I look past Sela and through the window. The old rebel sits in a metal chair behind the glass, a black bag over his head. His wrists are cuffed to the metal table in front of him with silver bands.

"How long has he been sitting like that?" Alex asks.

"Two hours," Sela answers. "He hasn't moved."

I frown. "Who was the last person to speak with him?"

"I was," Colonel Go says.

"The colonel asked questions"—Sela nods at the older soldier—"but the rebel didn't respond to any of them."

"Which is why we should use the weapon," Colonel Go demands, "Bring it in and use the Helm."

Alex grits his teeth. "*Her* name is Ama, and she wouldn't be able to read him after the torture you put him through. Ama's a mind reader, and you've ensured the rebel hasn't a mind to read."

The colonel growls. "You insolent bastard. I don't care if you're the Director's son. You can't speak to me like that. We'll bring in this *Ama* and put it to actual use."

He signals for the guards, but before they can approach, Tsuko raises a hand, stopping them. Slowly, he turns his head to stare at the colonel. He doesn't say a word. After a drawn-out pause, the colonel lowers his eyes—a strange sight, considering the colonel's advanced age compared to Tsuko's youth.

"My apologies, General," the colonel says.

I'm surprised at Tsuko's reaction. Either he's angry at the colonel for his massive blunder in the north, resulting in the casualties of hundreds of soldiers, or he's protecting Ama. Maybe both.

There's an undeniable connection between Ama, Tera, and Tsuko, a shared history. But what, I don't know. Or when. It's common knowledge that Tsuko was "found" by the Director at a military orphanage in Taipei. When could he have come into contact with Ama and Tera? Unless it's true that the "common knowledge" is actually fabricated knowledge, and there's more to Tsuko's murky past than what the public was given.

I surface from my thoughts to find Tsuko watching me.

"I was informed that you would conduct this interrogation," he says. "Is it true you've earned high marks in interrogative procedures?"

"It's true," I lie.

Tsuko nods. "Good. Interrogate Oh Kangto with any means possible. This man is responsible for the deaths of thousands of NSK soldiers. I will not be denied his full confession and the names and whereabouts of every single traitor beneath his command." He reaches to pick up his medaled cap lying on a table, then turns to Alex. "After Soldier Lee conducts the interrogation, send the traitor to my facility." Placing the cap atop his head, he exits the room, trailed by the colonel.

Left alone in silence with Alex and Sela, I sigh. "Let's not interrogate him and say we did."

Sela giggles.

Alex frowns. "We're being monitored," he says, his eyes moving to the camera in the corner of the room. "And Sela's here to write up an account of the interrogation. Try not to do anything to get kicked out of the Tower." He hands me an earpiece, which I plug into my left ear. "I'll relay to you the questions you're to ask him."

I move to the door separating the viewing room from the interrogation room and stop before the threshold, turning to Sela. "Can you release his cuffs?"

Sela widens her eyes, then nods. "I will."

The door opens, and I walk inside.

The interrogation room is significantly colder than the viewing room. One lone camera at the back tracks my movements. The silver cuffs release with a *click*.

I wait a minute, but when the old rebel doesn't make a move to take the black bag from his head, I pull it off him and toss it to the floor. Then I circle the table and sit in the chair opposite him.

Face-to-face, I can see the damage wrought by the days leading up to this meeting. There's a long, charred scar that runs across his face from his left temple, across one sealed-shut eye, through his flat, reddened nose, and down to his gray-stubbled chin. The other wounds, although fierce in their own right, seem insubstantial compared to this blatant marring.

I swallow and look down, feeling strangely ill at ease.

"Talk to him," Alex orders in my ear. "Make him feel comfortable with you."

I take a breath, then blurt, "Tell me the names of the leaders of the UKL."

Alex groans in my earpiece. "You weren't kidding when you said you sucked at interrogations."

The old man stares at me blankly from out of his one working eye.

"Are you thirsty?" I ask, and then say loudly, "Maybe he can't speak. His mouth is too dry." I turn my head to look directly at Alex and Sela behind the one-way mirror, going against the idea that you're not supposed to talk about the criminal while he sits in front of you.

Oh Kangto and I wait in silence for several minutes before Sela enters the room and puts a steaming mug of barley tea in front of the man.

He doesn't even glance at her. Just stares at me. He doesn't pick up the mug of tea.

"Nice," Alex drawls into my earpiece as Sela shuts the door behind her.

Another couple of minutes of silence pass before I work up the will to speak.

"You look more like a harabeoji than an ajeossi." These are the brilliant words that come out of my mouth—he looks more like a grandfather than a middle-aged man. According to our records, Oh Kangto is a little older than the colonel, somewhere in his mid-sixties. The mountains of the north have not been kind to this man. He looks like he's much older, his hair completely gray, with drooping bags beneath his eyes. His face is a mask of wrinkles. I'm surprised he endured even one beating, let alone the countless beatings I know he's suffered.

"My harabeoji was a lot like you," I continue. "You two would have gotten along. You'd have sat there and said nothing to each other for hours straight, and after you had left our home, my harabeoji would have turned to me and said, 'He is a good man.' Of course, my harabeoji died when I was very young, so I didn't know him too well. Maybe he would have said, 'He is a boring man.'" I shrug. "I guess we'll never know, will we?"

When the old man doesn't answer, I answer for him, my voice quiet in the still room. "We won't ever know."

I'm getting tired of this. The old man isn't going to speak. He's just going to stare and stare and step on me with the force of his gaze.

"Are you going to tell me where the rest of your rebels are? Are you going to name the agents in your organization who've infiltrated this city? The traitors hiding amongst us? Are you going to confess your plans, the ones you have to destroy the NSK?"

The old man doesn't even blink.

I turn away from him, looking pointedly at the one-way mirror of the interrogation room, and shrug. This was obviously a bad plan.

I'm about to stand when the old man creaks forward in his chair. "Ah," he breathes huskily, his voice thick with age and pain. "Hyunwoo-yah. I've missed you, my comrade."

I freeze where I sit. My heartbeat doubles in my chest,

and my numb hands slide against the metal arms of the chair.

"Hyunwoo-yah, where have you been? We scoured the land for you. We looked everywhere for you. I felt your ghost at my bedside at night, asking me, *Why? Why?* Oh, Lee Hyunwoo, where have you been? And your lovely wife. And your son. Forgive me. Forgive me."

The old man begins to cry, tears seeping through both his working right eye and his broken left. "Hyunwoo-yah, forgive me. I did wrong. I made you stay with me when you should have gone with her. She would have kept you warm. She would have healed all your sorrows. She had scarless hands. It meant she was safe."

He turns from me, looking off into the distance, looking at something only he can see. "The winds are frigid in the north, and the wolves howl for my blood."

I shake my head. "There aren't any wolves in the north."

"Yes, there are. Hungry, cruel predators. They're nothing like the tigers that used to roam Mount Baekdu in the old days. Those noble creatures protected us from our enemies. We were never afraid, because we *knew*, we knew we were beloved.

"Hyunwoo-yah, isn't it strange? I've reached this old age, older than my halmeoni was before she died. She was so wise, my halmeoni. I don't feel wise, Hyunwoo-yah. I feel tired and bitter and cold. I miss the days of my youth, when I was a boy in the city. All my friends and I cared about was how sweet the watermelon was in the spring, and in the summer, how much fun it was to play muk-jji-ppa in the park. And all we shared was everything. They're all gone now."

The old man wipes tears from his face, the wetness of them mixing with the dried blood of his wounds. "I never could beat my halmeoni at muk-jji-ppa. She had quicker hands than me."

He looks down at his hands, gnarled with age and weathered after many winters in the north.

Something snaps inside me, watching him watch his hands. Maybe it's that he's mentioned his halmeoni, and I have a weakness for halmeonis. Maybe it's that he knew my father before my father left, before my father met my mother. Maybe it's because he's old, and he's suffered, and no man deserves such cruelty dealt upon his body and his mind. There's an anger bottled up inside me, and I don't know where it's come from, or why it's even come at all. Why it won't leave.

I stand and place my palms on the metal table, feel the bite of the cold steel. "Why are you doing this?" My voice comes out harsh, cracking. "What makes you hold your tongue, old man?"

Oh Kangto looks up at me, his one eye finding mine. I read pity in his gaze, pity for me. It goes straight to my soul. I pound my fist on the table. "Speak!" I scream. "Just tell them what they need to know, and they won't hurt you anymore!"

In my ear, Alex finally speaks, his voice muffled. "Ask him where his comrades are."

"Where are your comrades, Oh Kangto? Where are they hiding?"

Oh Kangto lifts his head, his tears getting caught in the lines of his face. He presses his hands against his heart. "Right here," he says, his lucid voice now sure and strong. He reaches his gnarled grandfather hands across the wooden table, placing their scarred palms over mine. "Right here."

He smiles at me, a sad smile. "Who guards the mountain in the north, Lee Hyunwoo?"

"I don't know," I whisper, my voice foreign to my ears, weak and tired.

"You know, my son."

The door of the interrogation room opens. "We've got what we need," Alex says, stepping through. I nod, shakily getting to my feet. I don't know what they got out of that, but I'm done.

In a moment of suicidal adrenaline, I turn to Oh Kangto and bow at the waist, showing him a deference I actually feel for once.

"Did I mention the whole thing was recorded?" Alex asks once the door closes behind us.

I look away from him and through the interrogation window. The old rebel has his face in his hands. He's weeping.

"Jaewon, I'm serious. This won't look good."

"Why not?" Sela chimes in, patting me on the back. "Lee Jaewon was *acting*." She laughs. "Jaewon-ssi, I want you to be in the next drama I star in. You were amazing. And you even got Oh Kangto to talk. No one else has. And he's revealed something *huge*. The name of a potential rebel. This Lee Hyunwoo person. True, Lee Hyunwoo is probably dead, seeing as Oh Kangto thought you were his ghost at first. But we know that both he and Lee Hyunwoo used to live in the city, the *old city*. He's confirmed there *are* rebels in the city, or at least, they began there. We thought the UKL had most of its operatives situated abroad, backed by foreign powers, but if they're across the river, they've been working right beneath our noses. We can root them out quick and bring an end to this rebellion once and for all!"

Alex and I both stare at Sela, stupefied expressions on our faces. This is the most I've heard her speak.

She laughs. "I can go on and on about subjects I'm passionate about. Do you think they'd let me participate in Oh Kangto's transport to General Tsuko's facility?"

I blink, surprised she wants any further part in all of this. Apparently, she's more bloodthirsty than I thought. Or more ambitious than I thought.

"I don't see why not," Alex answers slowly.

"Oh, good," she sings. "I'll escort him, then."

Alex must have signaled to the guards that we'd finished the interrogation, because five of them march through the doors. They remove Oh Kangto from his chair, shackling him with electro-braces.

The old rebel doesn't make a move to stop them. He doesn't even look at them. Or me. He passes right by me, unseeing. It's like his mind has fled, his one eye roving without focus.

Something in me knows he won't speak again. He had only spoken to me because he had mistaken me for my father.

He'll go to Tsuko's facility, and they'll torture him until he's dead, never learning a thing beyond what he revealed in his strange confession to me, of a cherished boyhood long ago.

"Are you all right?" Alex asks, watching me. "Maybe you should go back to the hospital."

I shake my head, turning to head out of the room and out of the Tower. Alex's advice is good, but I have a different idea of what will make me feel better.

29

FORGIVENESS

I'm wasted by the time Young finds me sitting at one of the rickety plastic tables set up in a hazardous maze next to the bridge ajumma's food cart. Two bowls, emptied of ramyeon, and a half dozen soju bottles litter the table, one or two tipped over and dripping over the side.

I'm pouring myself another shot when Young takes the glass from between my fingers and swigs it back. He swallows and squints at the taste.

"Jaewon-ah," Young says, pouring himself the last of the bottle, "what are you doing out here? Drinking all by yourself like an old, buggered ajeossi?"

I flinch at his choice of words, remembering Oh Kangto's hands atop my hands. I swipe the glass from Young, bringing it up to my lips and tipping in the liquid. I can't even taste it anymore.

"Jaewon-ah, did something happen at the Tower?"

"No." I push hair out of my face and rub my eyes.

"You look terrible."

I grimace, reaching into the pocket of my coat for some painkillers. Like before, Young's hand comes out to stop me. This time, I push it away. "Don't," I growl.

"You have to stop this," Young says, his voice laced with frustration. "This isn't like you. Where's the Lee Jaewon I know? Who's calm and collected all the time, who'd never be found drinking by himself in the dead of night?"

I shrug. "Not here."

Young holds my gaze for a moment and then leans back in his chair, his hands crooked behind his head. "Jaewon-ah," he says, his voice light, "remember the old days, back when we were kids . . ."

I start in my chair. Young's words closely mirror Oh Kangto's. *When I was a boy in the city.*

"Remember when you used to listen at the walls between our apartment buildings? They were thin walls. We could have a conversation between them, if we screamed loud enough and the windows were open. And remember how you used to listen through the walls, every night, just in case . . . in case you heard the yelling. And then you'd come, as quick as lightning, jumping off your balcony and onto mine, rushing in to save me, like a goddamn hero in a book. When my old man used to bring out that damn police baton, you'd be there with me, getting hit as well. You'd share the bruises with me. And they'd be less."

"And all we shared was everything."

I close my eyes.

"Jaewon-ah, what's the matter?"

I can tell Young anything. I can tell him about the rebel in the Tower, and how none of what he said makes sense, his love for my father, his devotion to his cause—even if it means he'll die for it all in the end. I can tell him about Tera and how she makes me feel—helpless and full to the brink of something, longing, maybe—and even though I don't know what it means, I could tell him anyway. Because he's Young.

But I'm so drunk. If I open my mouth, I might fall to weeping, and I haven't cried since I was eight.

"God, you're wasted." Young walks over to crook my arm around his shoulder. "I should be happy, I guess. I never get to see you like this." When my full weight crashes into him, he stumbles to the side.

The food cart ajumma clicks her tongue as we pass, muttering about "boys" and "troublemakers."

Neither of us speaks until we're beneath the flickering bulb of the streetlight a block away from my apartment.

"I need to take a break." Young leans me against the wall of a building.

The position I'm left in has my face angled to the ground, watching the dust motes in the slivers of light that filter over the nearest doorway.

"Jaewon-ah . . . ," Young says, and I turn to see him

standing beneath the streetlamp. He sounds tired, and not from carrying me eight blocks down roads riddled with pot-holes. What has he been doing with his time? I used to know everything about him. Just six months ago, he left Red Moon and joined the Seven Kings. It was an unprecedented move to many, as with time, he would have been his father's second-in-command, and eventually the boss of Red Moon. But truth-fully, I wasn't surprised. Bitter maybe, but not surprised. Young had never been ambitious. Growing up, he cared more about helping kids get off the street than wealth or power.

"Are we going to talk about this?" Young says quietly.

"There's nothing to talk about."

He sighs. "Is it nothing that you were almost killed? Is it nothing that the brutal beating you took in the north was tele-vised to the whole city?"

"It doesn't . . . ," I say, placing my hand against my aching throat. "It doesn't matter."

"Stop lying to yourself!" Young shouts. "If it didn't matter, it wouldn't be killing you inside."

"Why do you even care?" I shout back. "None of this has anything to do with you!"

"It has to do with me because it has to do with you," Young says, his voice dropping. "Jaewon-ah, we've been friends longer than we've been—"

"Enemies?" I suggest weakly.

"Than we've been lost."

I close my eyes, knowing exactly what he means—it kills me to know what he means. "You were the only one," I say, hoping my voice won't break on my words. "You were my only family after my father left, and then my mother. I needed you, and you left me."

"Jaewon-ah," Young says, taking a step closer, "I did it for you! You think my father would just let me leave? You think he'd just let me go? If I'd left with you, we'd have never been able to stay together in that school. My father would have done *something*, and both of us would have been kicked out. I knew that if I could let you go, if I could only let you go, you could be free of everything—the gang, the streets, my father . . ."

Young trails off, looking away. "Even me," he whispers. "I thought you'd be better off without me."

I stare at him, the shock of his words making it hard to speak.

"Bastard," I say finally, "why didn't you say anything?"

"Because you're my friend. And I knew that you'd never have left me if you knew I wanted to go with you but couldn't. I couldn't go. I threw you away, and it hurt, like nothing I'd ever felt before." He has tears in his eyes, and his nose is red, and it has nothing to do with the cold.

I'm no better.

I can't speak. I don't know what to do, now that we've reached this point. There's so much lost between us, I don't know if our old friendship can be what it once was—when we'd been dependent on each other, when a day didn't go by when we didn't see each other.

Maybe it doesn't have to be that way, maybe it can be another way, but I don't know anything.

I sink to the ground. "Shit, I'm so drunk."

"Yeah," Young says, laughing—the sound strange but familiar. He holds his hand out to me. "Let's get you to bed. You need to sleep it off." He looks over to the stairs leading up to my apartment. "We're almost there."

I take his hand. I let him help me up from the ground, and I let him help me up the stairs, and I let him find the key to my apartment he knows is hidden in my mailbox. I let him shove a tonic down my throat to help with my inevitable hangover, and I let him throw me onto my bed at the back of the apartment.

That's where I am when I finally fall into sleep, sinking into the warmth of the sheets—a little more whole than I'd been when I'd first woken.

MUGUNGHWA

I don't surface until noon the next morning, greeted by the worst hangover headache of all time. It's worth it.

I lost my phone during the crash, so I search my apartment for an old model, finding one behind a stack of manhwa in my bookshelf. I log onto my server. I have more than fifty messages, most of which are from Bora. They range from: Are you okay? I heard about the crash! to If you don't answer this message, I'm going to assume you are dead and steal all your clothing from your locker. Minwoo's one message is: Man, I'm so jealous you get to miss school.

I text Bora back: I'm fine. Lost my phone. How are you?

My phone pings with her immediate response. I miss you. Coming to school?

I text back, Not today.

This phone doesn't have a floating option, so I throw it onto the bed, take a quick shower, and get dressed. By the time I return, I have a response from Bora. It's a picture of her in class with her eyes closed as she pretends to sleep.

I send back a laughing sticker and head outside, checking the rest of my messages. The last one is from Young, one simple line: It's time to put old ghosts to rest.

A picture of my father as a young man accompanies it with the date of his death, ten years ago today. A sharp pain stings my chest, and the old anger resurfaces. *We only just made up, and Young's already pushing me.*

But that's what friends are for. Young would always call me on my crap. And he's right. It *is* time to let go of the ghosts that haunt me. If that means finally visiting the grave of my father, so be it.

I make a quick trip into the mart to purchase a hangover drink. I step outside and down it. It tastes sticky and medicinal, but I already feel the fogginess in my head receding. Another ping from my phone. I take it out, expecting to see another message from Young, but it's from Alex.

Check the news, he says. I'll meet you in the lobby of the hospital. Cryptic.

I open my browser and scroll through the recent headlines. They're all the same. I click on one, and a short video begins to play, the bright lights of the Grid flashing behind the news anchor.

"During the transport of the United Korean League's

leader, Oh Kangto, from the Neo State of Korea's Tower of Defense in Gangnam to an undisclosed prison facility for war criminals, a band of suspected United Korean League operatives opened fire on the Grid. In the ensuing crossfire, four NSK soldiers were injured. This video footage, taken from Grid surveillance, shows the successful transfer of Oh Kangto from the NSK prison car to a black off-Grid van, which shortly disappeared after these events, presumably to a location outside the Dome. The escape of Oh Kangto follows on the heels of an assassination attempt on the Director only three weeks prior to this event. The Tower has not issued a response to the perceived threat from the UKL."

I scroll through several more articles while grabbing my coat.

Oh Kangto *escaped*. By now he'll be recuperating in some safe unknown location.

My eyes catch on more headlines.

A DEVASTATING EXPLOSION IN THE NSK'S SOUTH CHINA WEAPON MANUFACTURING FACILITIES LEAVES HUNDREDS DEAD, A LIST OF CASUALTIES

MEMORIAL SERVICES FOR FALLEN SOLDIERS WILL BE HELD AT THE FOLLOWING LOCATIONS

Still, Alex's message mentioned meeting outside the hospital. But which hospital, and why?

A sputtering of news articles appear across my screen in quick succession, ones newly posted.

C'EST LA VIE'S SELA HOSPITALIZED FOR GUNSHOT WOUNDS

C'EST LA VIE'S SELA SUFFERS SEVERE GUNSHOT WOUNDS AFTER UKL ABDUCTION

C'EST LA VIE'S SELA SURVIVES UKL TERRORIST ATTACK, HOSPITALIZED AT CITY HALL'S MERCY HOSPITAL

I pocket my phone and catch the first cab I can find heading across the bridge.

■ ■ ■

Alex waits outside the hospital, which is already teeming with reporters alerted to the fact of Sela's hospitalization.

In the lobby, I buy a branch of flowers in a basket.

"Mugunghwa," the store owner tells me as I take them, the five petals of the flowers colored a light pink. "They were cut this morning. They only live for a day."

I nod, paying him, and catch up with Alex by the lifts.

Outside Sela's door on the eighth floor stands an armed guard unaffiliated with the NSK, judging by his civilian clothes. "She's not taking visitors," he states after Alex and I stop outside Sela's door.

"We need to get a report from her," Alex counters.

"She's not taking visitors," he repeats.

Alex scowls. "We're not visiting, we're here to get her statement. She's a witness to a crime."

The guard steps forward, his face centimeters from Alex's. "She's not taking visitors."

"Maybe it's the only sentence he knows," I say.

"Jaewon-ssi?" Sela's voice drifts from behind the door. "Is that you? Won't you come inside? Alex, stop bothering Isao."

The guard turns to face me.

"I'm Jaewon-ssi," I say, raising my hand.

"You should have said." He clicks the button to release the doors.

Alex raises an eyebrow. "When did you get friendly with the pop star?"

"She's a pop rocker." I enter the room first. Sela sits propped up in the hospital bed. It's like a garden in here. Or a toy store. She's surrounded by flowers and gift baskets filled with toys, food, and stuffed animals.

I hold out the flowers I bought in the gift shop. "I got these for you, though it looks like—"

"Mugunghwa!" she shouts happily, reaching for them. "These are my favorite," she says, beaming at the flowers and then at me. "Thank you very much, Jaewon-ssi."

She turns and pushes aside a vase of flowers to place the basket of mugunghwa by her bedside.

For a girl who's been shot, she's pretty upbeat. I check her for bandages, evidencing a gunshot wound, but half of her body is covered beneath a pile of blankets.

There's one thing different about her, though.

"Your lenses are out," Alex says. "You look better without them. Brown eyes suit you."

She ignores him. "Jaewon-ssi, I apologize for letting your prisoner escape."

"He wasn't my prisoner," I say. "If anything, I'm glad he escaped. I liked the old man."

Alex scowls, scanning the corners of the room for cameras or hidden microphones.

"There aren't any," Sela says. "Isao already checked. I like my privacy in the moments when it's mine."

Alex nods, and then turns to me. "What the hell, Jaewon? Are you trying to get yourself killed?" He starts pacing. "Sela, what can you tell us about what happened yesterday? Did you see who the rebels were, any glimpses of faces?"

"No, I didn't, and there isn't much to tell. I was shot shortly after we were initially fired upon." She points a finger at her leg, covered beneath the sheets. "After I was shot, I fell backward into Oh Kangto, and he caught me. He said, 'You'll be all right,' and then he gently covered me with the body of another soldier who'd already fallen. Then I fainted."

Alex scowls. "Well, we'll leave out his heroics in the report. It won't do to piss off Tsuko any more than he already is." He moves to the window and notices a bouquet of yellow roses. "Can I take these?"

"Yes," Sela says, cocking her head to the side.

Alex scoops up the flowers and marches through the door. It slides open at his approach.

I watch the door, scratching the back of my head. "Eh, I guess I'll leave too." I turn to Sela and bow. "I hope you feel better soon."

Sela doesn't blink as she stares at me. I turn to leave. "I wonder if Ama's favorite flowers are roses," she says.

My gaze flits to the door Alex just passed through.

"Jaewon-ah," Sela whispers, "are you like Alex? Did you bring me mugunghwa because you thought they might make me happy? Because you cared enough to want to make me happy?"

"I thought they'd make you feel better."

"Jaewon-ah. Are you like Alex?"

The fact that she's dropped the honorifics, switching from jondaenmal to banmal, isn't lost on me.

"No," I say, turning back to meet her gaze. "I am not like Alex."

"I want to ask you something, but once I do, it can't be taken back. It'll be up in the air, and I'll be at your mercy. I've never been at another person's mercy before. Not, at least, of my own free will."

My heart beats painfully in my chest. "Then don't ask."

In the ensuing silence, I hold my breath, not wanting to hurt her feelings by leaving, yet wishing I were anywhere but here. I'll hear her out if that's what she needs. As a friend, I owe her that, at least.

"Okay," she says.

I blink, not expecting her reaction. "What?"

"I won't ask. Good-bye, Jaewon-ssi." She smiles at me, a sad, lovely smile. "Maybe some other time."

I nod, taking her dismissal for what it is.

■ ■ ■

The lobby of the hospital is jammed with reporters and Sela's fans. Sela's PR people team up with the hospital security to create a human barrier between the crowd and the lifts, but I can see some determined fans making a break for the less-guarded stairwells.

I opt out of navigating the crowd, doubling back toward the gift shop. Next to the shop is the opening of the hospital's funeral services area—there's bound to be an alternate exit off it.

I've always thought it morbid to attach a funeral parlor to a hospital, but I guess it's convenient for the families of the deceased. Anything anyone would need for a service is provided by the hospital—clothing to dress the body, food to feed the mourning.

I round a corner, coming upon a dark hallway lined with mahogany sliding doors. It's quiet here, especially after the loud tumult of voices in the lobby.

It smells like incense. Subtle wisps of fragrant smoke creep beneath the doorways, coating the floor in a pillow of smog.

A blue EXIT sign glows at the end of the hall, like a light at the end of a tunnel—an ironic thought. I walk to it, passing closed door after closed door. The door to the last room is open. I reach for the control to open the exit, inadvertently glancing into the room.

A woman around my mother's age kneels before a small raised platform. A photograph sits atop the platform, a rare nondigital framed photograph. A young man smiles out of the photograph, and from the way she looks at him, I know he is her son. An array of uncovered dishes is spread out before the photograph—a fish painstakingly deboned; a teapot beside a cup, half full of barley tea; a tin bowl of rice; a stone pot of thick, clear soup. The woman lifts trembling hands to slowly push the cup closer to the photo, as if she believes that the reason her son can't reach the cup is because it's placed too far away.

I look closer at the picture and see that the boy wears a uniform.

"Lee Jaewon."

I freeze, turning around slowly to find Tsuko standing behind me in the hall. A shiver runs up my spine. I hadn't heard his approach. The light from the exit sign casts an eerie glow on his face. One white chrysanthemum dangles by the stem from his long fingers.

"What are you doing here?" he asks, his eyes narrowed in suspicion. I notice that for once, he isn't wearing his uniform, but a black suit.

"Visiting Sela," I say. "I was just leaving."

The grim line of Tsuko's lips seems to get even straighter. His brows furrow in contempt. "You shouldn't be here."

And what about you? What are you doing here?

The woman appears in the open doorway, her hair falling messily from her bun. "My son," she whispers, coming toward Tsuko and falling against him. His hands go up quickly to steady her.

Surprised, I glance between them, seeing if there's a resemblance, but then she continues, "What have you done with my son?"

Tsuko's hands tighten on her shoulders, the stem of the chrysanthemum crushed between them. "Madame Siu . . ."

"You were supposed to protect him," she shouts. "He wasn't supposed to die!"

He releases her, and she stumbles backward into the room. She goes back to the altar, where she moves every one of the dishes closer to the photograph until they're all crowded around the young soldier's face, obscuring his soft smile.

Tsuko doesn't look at me again. Gripping his damaged flower, he steps into the room after the mother. He shuts the door quietly behind him, leaving me in the dark. My eyes adjust enough to see the trail of chrysanthemums he's left beside every door.

31

MEMORIAL

I take a cab back across the river into Old Seoul and pick up my motorcycle from the food cart ajumma. Seeing Tsuko honor and grieve his fallen soldiers reminds me of my own resolution to visit the grave of my father. I can't cut through Neo Seoul on my lowTech bike, so I take the western highway that curves around the Dome, the route Old Seoul workers take into the northwestern city of Incheon. Most of the metalworkers that stop by the bridge ajumma's cart in the late evenings are men and women who work in the huge shipbuilding factories out in Incheon, massive platforms that produce ships meant for sea and sky travel.

As I move off the highway and head into Incheon, huge swaths of reclaimed land pass by in the distance—thousands of square kilometers of land that were created out of the ocean—where conglomerates have built God Machine factories. The machinists might develop prototypes in the Tower, but GMs are mass-produced in these factories, tested on the open space of the reclaimed, backfilled land and over the ocean. Moving lights on the fields against the twilit sky indicate that a test might be in process at this very moment.

It takes me another fifteen minutes to reach my destination. The ashen fields of Incheon's old weapons base are several kilometers out from the main part of the city. I'm not surprised to find Young waiting for me when I arrive. Small dust devils flit across a field littered with broken debris. The site was never cleaned up after the initial fallout from the explosion. Crumbled buildings lay in ruins, as do old God Machines, stripped of their parts, the bones of giants.

I ride up to Young, who is standing beneath the shadow of one of the bigger ruins, then turn off the engine and drop the kickstand. Pulling down my antipollution mask, I take off my goggles. "How long have you been here?"

"Not long." He glances at my face. "Rough night?"

I shake my head and look around. My stomach falls at the sight. All around the ruins are little shrines made of stacked stones, lovingly covered with wilted flowers. My father wasn't the only person who died that day ten years ago, who was loved, who is missed and then remembered. None of the shrines look recent, which I'm thankful for. The idea of meeting someone whose loved one my father killed is enough to make me want to leave this place and never look back.

Young reaches into his coat and pulls out a bottle of rice wine. "I figured you wouldn't have time to prepare anything."

"Thanks," I say, and take the bottle.

"Don't drink it," he warns with a grin. "Not until after you've bowed, at least."

I haven't conducted a memorial before, but I know what to do, I think.

There's a soft noise to my left, a scuffing of feet against the ground. I look over to see Jinwoon and Daeho circling the ruins.

"You brought the kids?" I ask, jokingly referring to when Jinwoon and Daeho would call Young and me "mother" and "father." We were a year older, and our dynamic was that they would do something idiotic, I would clean up their mess, and Young would scold them.

Young chuckles. "What can I say? They're my ducklings." He cracks his knuckles. "But jokes aside, we have business to take care of after this."

"Gang business?"

Young shrugs. "Something like that."

I raise a brow. It's not like him to be close-lipped.

He changes the subject. "We figured out why Red Moon is taking the girls."

I grimace. "Because Park Taesung wants to create an army."

Young blinks, surprised. "How'd you find out?"

"He told me."

Speaking of Park Taesung reminds me of the memory I

witnessed in the Tower. "He was here that day. The day my father died." I look around, trying to spot a landmark, something to tie that memory of the past to this moment in the present, but nothing stands out.

"That's the thing that I can't understand," Young says. "My father *loved* your father. How could he ever hurt you? How could he separate you from your mother, *use* you now that you're in the Tower? It's shameful of him, and I'm so, so sorry."

"You don't have to apologize for him."

"But I do. After all, he *is* my father."

His words are a sharp blade in my gut. I realize with a sudden guilt what I've done to Young every time I said, "I am not like my father." For even when I'd denied being like him, Young would never believe me. To him, it could only be a good thing to be like Lee Hyunwoo, who was kind and would entertain the local boys with stories and games. To a kid neglected by his father like Young, Lee Hyunwoo was a hero.

But if Young believes I am like my father, then he might also believe he is like *his*.

I grab his shoulder. "Park Young, trust me when I say this. You are nothing like Park Taesung."

Young laughs softly. "It's okay. True, I don't love and respect my father the way you love and respect yours . . ."

I open my mouth to interrupt, but he shakes his head. "But I *am* like him. I'm stubborn like he is. I'm selfish like he is. There are a lot of other ways I am like him, but the difference is that I fight it. I don't want to be like him, so I fight the part of me that is." Young takes a step forward, and I drop my hand from his shoulder. "I don't think you fight it, Jaewon. I think you *want* to be like your father, and it comes naturally to you. You're brave like your father. You're good like he was. It makes people want to stand by you. Even if they themselves aren't inherently good, they know they can only do better by helping you."

"Is that why you stand by me?"

"Ay," Young says, chuckling, "you're a habit for me. I'm so used to following you around."

"Young-ah," I say, swallowing the lump in my throat, "I'm sorry. For everything."

"I know. Me too. That's why we're going to be okay. That's why, although we are like our fathers, in the end, we are not them. We are our own men."

I let out a short breath. "Ay, jasik. When do you come up with lines like that?"

"What can I say?" Young shrugs. "I'm wise."

I shake my head.

Before he takes off, he says, "I had a tip that something's going down over at the reclamation fields, where the GM factories are. It might get hectic, so you should head back to Old Seoul when you're done here."

"Something?"

Young shrugs. "Something, something."

Again, it must be gang related. "All right. Thanks for the warning."

Young signals to Jinwoon and Daeho. "I'll leave you to it, then."

I nod. "See you around, Park Young."

"Yeah," he says, holding his hand in the air as he walks off. "You will."

■ ■ ■

Left alone, I realize I have no idea what the hell I'm doing. I lift the bottle of rice wine, pop the cap, and place it on the ground. How does one speak to the dead?

There's nothing to focus on, no memorial plaque or urn of ashes or photograph of my father. There's just the dust and the smoke and the memory of him.

Lee Hyunwoo. Lee Jaewon.

I wonder if I would have missed you less, had I loved you less.

Even now, it hurts. "Why does it still hurt?" I ask aloud. The question doesn't last in the air, swallowed up by the dust. And yet there's something right about the fleeting sound of the words—it makes them feel safe, secret.

After all, they're for my father.

I clear my throat, gaining strength in knowing that although I don't believe in ghosts or spirits, there's power in this moment, ten years and a day from the last time my father looked upon me and smiled.

"I know why you did what you did," I say, my voice loud in the still air. "I know why you woke up that morning and came here and destroyed the Tower. You believed that the creation of weapons could not end the war, that it could only prolong the war. In order to stop the Tower from creating more weapons, you made an impossible decision—you murdered thousands in order to save millions."

I take a shallow breath before continuing. "And I cannot forgive you for that. I know this war has claimed millions of lives, that it has torn apart our country and hurt our people, and still I cannot forgive you . . . and maybe that makes me the fool. I can't differentiate how one life is worth less than a thousand. Or how a thousand lives are worth less than a million. All I know is what your life was worth to me, and to me, your life was worth the world."

These last words come out in a rush.

"You left me," I gasp, putting all the selfish accusation and pain I've felt for years into that short phrase, words I'll never say again. I let the truth spill out for the first and last time. That my anger of ten years was not because he chose to kill, but because he chose to die. That while others might have hated him for his act of terrorism against the state or respected him for his act of bravery to end the war, I had resented him for leaving me. It was selfish of me, and maybe even bitter, to confine his actions to how they hurt me, and only me. But I had loved him. He was—he was my father.

Blinking hard, I realize I've fallen to my knees, my hands digging into the dry dirt. I pick myself up. The charcoal shards swirl in the air, rising with me. They stick to my damp face, and I wonder: if someone saw me now, would they think I was the ghost of my father? I wipe my forearm across my eyes, smearing the dirt.

My confession has left me clear-headed. The guilt I've

carried, of hating the one person I'd once loved the most, has disappeared, and I feel weightless.

"Father," I say, "although I can't forgive you for the choice you made that morning ten years ago, I can forgive your desire to protect the people you loved in the only way you knew how. Maybe it's because I didn't know what it was to love someone so much that you would die for them. Because you went all the way, didn't you? You died for what you love. For your country. For the UKL. For Mother. For me. You died for all of us."

Swallowing, I open my eyes. "But I don't want anyone I love to die, not anymore. And . . . I don't want to die. Father, tell me, how do I protect the people I love? How do I give them a world where the path of sacrifice doesn't need to be taken, doesn't need to *exist*? Where they can live without fear or suffering or pain?"

I lower my voice to a whisper. "Is this idealistic world of mine even possible? Am I a fool for even wanting it?"

My father doesn't answer. His ghost doesn't appear beside me, telling me which pathway I need to take to get what I want.

But he doesn't have to.

I know what I want.

And I know what I have to do to get it.

32

THE DEMONSTRATION

I'm on my way to my bike when I get a call from Dr. Koga. "Where are you?" he asks without preamble.

Immediately I'm on edge. "Incheon. Why? Is something wrong? Is Tera all right?"

I might have been discharged from the hospital yesterday, but a week has gone by since we crashed in the north. I regret not having gone to see Tera after my interrogation of Oh Kangto, to at least assure her that I'm okay, that we're okay. I had planned to. But I wasn't prepared for the effect my meeting with Oh Kangto would have on me, him calling me by my father's name, his hands on my hands.

"Incheon?" Koga asks, puzzled. "Why are you—? Never mind. We're holding a GM demonstration to counteract the negative publicity surrounding Oh Kangto's escape."

I'm not surprised when he tells me the location of the demonstration.

"It'll take place on the testing grounds over by the GM factories. Tera will pilot the Extension. I need you there to support her."

"I'll be there," I say.

When I get off the phone, I immediately dial Young. He'd warned me to stay away from the factories, and I need to know why. What could Young's gang, the Seven Kings, want with GMs? He doesn't pick up. Neither does Jinwoon or Daeho. Dammit.

I jump on my bike and head over to the reclamation fields.

They lie at the edge of the Yellow Sea, over hundreds of square kilometers of reclaimed land created by dumping cement, dirt and clay over the tidal flats. The GM factories are built on the mainland, but the testing grounds for the GMs extend over the land and sea.

A metal maze is set up on the field. Vid-droids surround the maze to record the GMs as they run the course. During the demonstration, the droids will project the feed onto large screens over the viewing area. I've gone through courses like this before in simulations. The pilots maneuver their GMs through obstacles, shooting down targets and avoiding being shot down themselves. It's a way to test new GMs before piloting them in a more difficult simulation map.

I pass by security, scanning my name and ID number with my wrist chip, and park my bike at the edge of the grounds behind a barricade of elevated stands that comprise the viewing area. They're boosted several hundred meters off the ground and far enough away from the testing site so as not to be caught in stray gunfire. Reporters and city officials arrive in transport ships, docking directly on the metal levels of the stands. Men and women in dark clothing emerge, taking seats.

Across the field, massive trucks rumble onto the field, each pulling a GM on a giant flatbed.

The first truck reaches the middle of the field. Its transport pilot maneuvers the massive machine into a sitting position. When its legs hit the ground, the impact causes the dirt to shake, kicking up a cloud of dust.

The GM straightens, reaching its full standing height with its legs apart for balance. The part of me that's always loved GMs takes a moment to admire the impressive make of this one. It's an upgraded version of the main offensive GM utilized on the battlefields in South China, the M-19. The color of gunmetal, the GM stands at above twenty meters. Its right arm is equipped with a built-in blade extending above its fist. The left arm is equipped with a jagged shield. On its back, it holds an arsenal of secondary weapons, including a steel sword and a power rifle.

The designer of this specific GM added a head with narrow black eyes that reflect the low light—more for aesthetic effect than utility. The thickest, most impenetrable part of the GM is its torso, built to protect the pilot sitting within.

A small earthquake signals the standing of the second GM, a rare destroyer type, the DX-100. The bulky, barrel-chested GM, known for its central weapon—a long beam cannon—was infamous at the end of the Second Act of the War. The DX-100 burned holes through cities, often wiping out whole platoons in one blast of its beam cannon.

The last GM, still concealed beneath the black tarp, is smaller than the others. The Extension. Which means Tera must be . . .

"Jaewon-ah!"

Tera exits out of a side building and sprints across the distance. She's fast. I blink, and she's in my arms. Her grip is strong but gentle.

"You're all right," she says into my neck. "I was so worried."

"I'm sorry," I say. "I should have come to you sooner."

She leans back, and I look at her. She wears a piloting suit. It covers her from wrists to ankles. There's no evidence that she'd had a head wound only a week before; her temple is clear of scars.

She scrutinizes me with the same attention. "There's something different about you." She trails her fingers across my cheekbones. "The shadows beneath your eyes are gone."

Can she see it? The weight that's lifted from my shoulders? "Tera," I say, "there's something I need to tell you—"

"What's this?" a voice snaps. We turn to see Tsuko standing behind us, wearing his uniform, which is dry and ironed. His cap is placed firmly on his head. He gives no evidence that a few hours ago, he'd been holding the mother of one of his fallen soldiers as she'd soaked his black mourning suit with tears. Except for his eyes. They're red-rimmed.

Tera releases me, stepping back.

Tsuko's eyes follow the movement. "It all makes sense now why you've been so defiant." His gaze moves from Tera to me. "Do you remember what I said I'd do to you if you ever did *anything* to destroy this project?"

He used stronger language in the elevator. I remember. He said he'd kill me.

"This has nothing to do with Jaewon," Tera says. "I've been feeling trapped for a long time."

"You don't think *I* feel trapped? You don't think I wish every day to leave the war behind?"

"Su—" Tera says, her voice cracking.

"When the war ends, *then*, and only then, will we be free."

A loud sounding of the horn signals the demonstration's about to start. A woman, wearing a uniform of the corporation that owns these GM factories, approaches us.

"Excuse me, General Tsuko," she says, bowing, oblivious to the tense atmosphere. "If you and the soldiers could proceed to the testing ground, we will begin the demonstration shortly."

Tsuko swallows back any further words and nods, ever the obedient soldier. Tera walks behind Tsuko, who follows the official. Tera watches the back of his head with a look of open concern. Their connection, their friendship, however much I might dislike it, is undeniable. She worries for him. She must be mulling over what he said.

We board a small truck and are driven out to the fields. The official gives us an overview of the demonstration. Each of us will maneuver through the large metal maze set up on the field. Tsuko and I will demonstrate using the upgraded versions of the M-19 and DX-100, but it's Tera in the Extension who will be the real star of the demonstration.

The official drops me off first. The M-19 stands like a sentient fortress on the muddy fields. I glance at Tera before exiting the truck, but her attention is on Tsuko.

An engineer and machinist are making last-minute checks on the GM. They nod, acknowledging me as I step onto the GM lift. It begins to ascend. Twenty meters off the ground, the lift jerks to a stop outside the M-19's open chest. The transport pilot, a sharp-featured woman with a shaved head, steps out from the cockpit. "You know how to pilot this model?" she asks.

"In a simulation."

"Simulations are different from real life." She leans into the cockpit, pointing out various features. "Split screens for viewing. Control panel for adjustments. Thrusters for liftoff. Orb for piloting. You can flip the switch here to open the hatch for an emergency ejection."

It's nothing I don't already know, but I thank her anyway, bowing.

"Good luck, kid."

She takes the GM lift down as I step into the cockpit and settle into the piloting seat. Across the field, there's a low rumbling sound. The third GM, the one on the flatbed of the truck, rises into a standing position. The black tarp that had been covering it falls away from its shoulders, pooling around the GM's feet. The last time I'd seen the Extension, it had been incomplete.

It's finished now. Its hands are six-fingered claws, each claw a thin, straight knife. Long, distended legs culminate in large, pointed blades. Its four metal wings double as shields; its horned head has slanted slits for eyes.

I can imagine the reactions of the sponsors in the viewing stands. *This* is what they'll invest in. An Enhanced GM with faster reaction times, unbeatable speed, and an arsenal of deadly weapons. I've no doubt that the Extension has the potential to be the deciding factor in the war. It's also a pretty badass-looking GM.

I press the button to close the cockpit shield. It's cold inside. I rub my palms on my legs, gathering warmth, then move them to the control panel, adjusting the outside cameras to ensure a view in all directions.

Behind me are the sponsors. My rearview camera automatically zooms in on their faces, scanning them for weapons and dismissing them as non-threats. My front camera goes haywire as it scans the Extension, having difficulty identifying the make and model of the suit. It blinks the red word [UNIDENTIFIABLE].

Because it can't identify its opponent, the suit can't offer strategies to combat it.

Weaknesses [UNKNOWN].

Strengths [UNKNOWN].

If I didn't know the pilot, I'd have reason to be afraid.

Tera lifts off first in the Extension, the boosters behind its shoulders igniting to blast her upward into the sky. The GM gracefully twists through the air, its wings spreading out like a fan. Its golden-red finish flashes in the sunlight. If the Extension were to descend on some backward village, I wouldn't be surprised if they'd mistake it, and Tera, for a goddess—one that deals in destruction.

It's my turn to take off. I slide my left hand across the display screen, unlock the M-19's clutch, and ignite the thrusters. With my other hand, I shift the GM into piloting mode, and the seat automatically moves backward, giving me a broad view through my split screens.

Like most modern GMs, the M-19 comes with a piloting orb—an egg-shaped device that acts as the main control for the GM. Sliding my hand against the smooth surface triggers the GM into jetting forward. Its feet drag huge channels in the ground, and then I lift off, propelling myself into the sky.

When my GM calculates that I've reached an altitude of one hundred and fifty meters, I slow its ascent, maneuvering forward and backward through the air to get used to the feeling of weightlessness.

There's no lag between my use of the controls and the GM's performance of them. I sweep my hand diagonally across the orb and the GM cuts through the air in a diagonal motion. I twist the orb, and the GM spins around, its arms automatically ready as if to block an attack from behind. With a GM like this, I'll be able to counter attacks from all sides. Whether or not I'm quick enough will be on me, not the GM.

I spend the rest of the prep time getting used to the controls, keeping an eye on my surroundings.

Tsuko shoots a warning shot from the ground, signaling the start of the demonstration, before taking off himself. The DX-100 has double jet packs due to its substantial heft.

I turn on the vid-link between the GMs, and Tera pops up on my screen. Tsuko must have disabled his connector, because I don't receive a visual of him.

"Nice wings," I say.

Her gaze flits downward to the image of me appearing on her screen. She smiles. "Watch this." The Extension spins in the air, flaring out its wings.

"Show-off."

The official from before appears on screen to inform us that "the demonstration will commence shortly. Please follow the agenda." On my right screen, a docket for the demonstration materializes. It's a simple evade-and-destroy, in which we'll fly through a maze, avoiding gunfire from shuttle bots and destroying targets. The purpose is to demonstrate the abilities of the GMs in a controlled environment.

I'm up first. "See you on the flipside," I say, and then accelerate into the maze.

Immediately panels open up in the steel walls, releasing mini bots that begin to pummel me with lasers. I dodge about eighty-five percent of their shots, picking off the red flags that stick out of the maze with my power rifle. It's actually pretty fun. GMs, in general, are fun to pilot. They're just purposed to kill people, which makes them terrible toys.

I'm almost through the last turn when something clips me in the side, close to the chest. My whole GM shakes in the aftermath. Whatever hit me, it's too powerful to be a bot. I look through my rearview cameras to see Tsuko in the DX-100, advancing like a tank, the barrel of his huge beam cannon aimed at me.

Tera's coming up behind him, fast. "Tsuko!" she screams.

He releases the beam, and I manage to dodge out of the way, but not without taking a hit in the shoulder. My bot sparks, but I'm still airborne, my jet pack intact.

Tera rams into Tsuko from behind, shoving him against the wall of the maze. "Dammit, Tsuko," she says. "Don't do this."

He might have turned off his visual link, but not his audio. I can hear his crackling response. "If he's gone, maybe you'll come to your senses. You must know that you can have no future with him, so why are you giving into such a false hope? A hope like his is cruel. Can't you see that? The more you care for him, the more it will hurt you when he leaves. And it is inevitable that he will leave when his time in the Tower is through. Let go of your dreams, Tera. They're not *real*."

I'm about to interject my own thoughts—that he's wrong, that her hope in me isn't false, that I won't let it be— but she answers first. "I'm not dreaming," she says. "I'm awake." She grabs his GM's arm, the one that holds the beam cannon, and rips it off at the shoulder. She then grabs his boosters at the back of the DX-100, rips them off as well, and drops him. As his GM falls, Tsuko ejects out the back with a parachute.

Damn.

I wonder what the sponsors make of this. We've definitely gone off the agenda. I zoom into the stands only to see the majority aren't paying attention to us. Their eyes are on the sky.

33

SECOND PROMISE

Heat signatures from above. Three of them. A beam, like the one from the DX-100, shoots downward to explode one of the three GM hangars surrounding the factories. The viewing stands erupt into chaos as sponsors rush to their transport ships.

Tera flies her GM beside mine. "We're under attack," she says. "Should we engage?"

"Well, technically, *we're* not under attack. The facilities are." Another beam from the sky, this one directed at Tera and me. We break apart, and it slides between us to hit the maze. Pieces of the maze crumble off. "Ah, never mind."

"Engaging." Tera accelerates into the sky. "Back me up."

Beneath us, Tsuko reaches the ground, where he clips off his parachute and sprints toward the GM hangars. Soon he'll be in the air again, more prepared—and furious—than before.

I lift my rifle to my shoulder, sighting one of the enemy GMs and trailing it with my scope. All three of the attacking GMs are MK-19s, but without the upgrades and with mismatched weapon sets, which explains how one carries a beam cannon. I almost feel bad for these guys. I don't know what their agenda is here today, but I'm sure they didn't imagine they'd battle an Enhanced soldier. I figure I'll just clip one in the wing, bring it down to decrease the chance of causalities. We've still got civilians on the ground, and it'd be better to capture the pilots alive.

I get a clean shot on one of the GMs, but I stop before firing. Something niggles at the back of my mind, Young's earlier warning to stay away from the reclamation fields. He might have known about this attack and didn't want me involved. But why would he care? What could the Kings, a small upstart gang, gain by taking out the GM hangars? It's more of an operation suited for UKL operatives.

I lift the rifle and once more sight one of the GMs through my crosshairs. Tera runs circles around them, not engaging in a direct assault. I lower my rifle.

"What's wrong?" she asks, appearing at the bottom of my screen.

"I need to check something. Can you distract them for a few seconds?"

"Distract three GMs by myself?"

"Yes."

She grins. "Easy."

I pull out my phone and dial Young. Again, he doesn't answer.

I was an amateur hacker for my gang when I was thirteen. I exercise those unused brain muscles now, trying to hack into the communications link between the enemy GMs. I try different codes until finally I get static.

"Ay, boss," says a familiar voice. I groan. "What's with this guy and his skinny bot?"

"Jeon Daeho," Young responds. "Focus. Stick to the plan."

"You mean, the plan of not dying?"

"We only took out one of the hangars. There are two more."

"Ah, right."

I close the link. "Tera."

"Jaewon?" she answers, looking concerned. "What's wrong?"

"It's Young."

"Young?" She frowns. "As in your estranged best friend?"

"Not estranged anymore, but yes. It's him and two of our friends."

"That's not good," she says, the understatement of the year.

I can't risk bringing them down. They'd be arrested in a flash. But soon Tsuko will arrive with reinforcements. I rack my brain on how to get out of this with the best outcome—Young and his boys free, and Tera and I not facing charges of treason.

"Can you reach him?" Tera asks.

They're shooting at Tera as she talks to me. She easily dodges the bullets.

"Yeah, one sec."

I open up the communications to Young. "Ya, jasik-ah!" I shout. "What are you doing here?"

There's a pause. "Jaewon-ah? Lee Jaewon? Didn't I expressly tell *you* not to be here?"

"I was called in to do a demonstration for the GM corps' latest models."

"Ay," Young groans. "Just my luck. If I'd known there would be a demonstration, I obviously would not be doing this right now. Who is that guy, by the way? I've never seen a GM like it. I didn't think they could move that fast."

"Long story," I say. "Just know that you're fighting an Enhanced soldier."

"Shit."

"Why did he stop attacking?" Daeho interjects, having listened in on our conversation. "Whose side is he on?"

"He's a she," I answer. "Her name is Tera, and she's on my side."

"Tera?" Young asks. "Is she your girlfriend?"

"Jaewon-hyeong's gotta girl?" Daeho smirks.

"We're in the middle of a GM battle," I growl. "Is this really the time?"

"It's always the time to talk about girls," Jinwoon adds in his low baritone. It's possibly one of the few times I've ever heard him tell a joke.

"Jaewon-ah," Tera says. She must have heard the exchange,

now that all communications are open between the GMs. My face heats in embarrassment, and the snickers of Young and his crew fill the M-19's cockpit. "The factories are deploying troops."

The laughter stops. "Oh, shit."

"Our objective was to destroy the factories," Young says, "but one is good enough. Do you think we can get out of here?"

There are at least thirty GMs on their way, and I'd bet my entire savings that Tsuko is inside one of them. "I don't know."

"Jaewon-ah," Tera says. There's a steely look in her eyes. "Take your friends and go."

"What? No. I'm not leaving you."

"You have to," she says. "If you fight them now, and I know you will, you're so loyal you'll eventually be caught and arrested. Unlike me, you'd be immediately killed." She leans forward into the camera. "Let me do this for you. Let me protect you and your friends."

I hold her gaze. We have to leave now if we want to get away. "I'll come back for you," I say. I don't care that Young and the others are listening. "I promise."

"Okay." She smiles, and it's the most beautiful smile I think I've ever seen.

This isn't a good-bye, and I won't jinx it with one. "Let's go," I tell Young.

The four of us fly away from the fields while Tera heads toward the squad of GMs. As I escape, I watch her through my rearview cameras. She flies straight into the cloud of GMs, and seconds later, a storm of light appears. She's magnificent. Fierce in her desire to protect me.

And now, officially, I'm a traitor and enemy of the state. Tera as well. If I'm captured, I'll be executed. Still, I don't regret the steps that have led me to this moment. I'll return for Tera. I'll do whatever it takes to get her back. After all, like my father used to say, when you want something, when you love someone, no one and nothing can keep you away.

■ ■ ■

We land our GMs in an empty lot in downtown Incheon, several meters from the old weapons base. I bring my GM to its knee to assist my dismount since I don't have a lift, then climb down the emergency rungs and land on the dirt. I wait for Young to stumble out of his GM before approaching. He raises his hands in a placating gesture. "Wait a minute. Remember, I was the one who told you not to go over there."

I frown, curious. "What are you doing?"

He lowers his hands. "You're not going to punch me?"

"Why would I punch you?"

"Because we just left your girl back there to cover our tracks."

"I mean, I'm pissed about that, but we'll get her back. Also, she can take care of herself. Now tell me—what the hell were you even doing blowing up the GM factories?"

Young sighs. "A couple months ago, Oh Kangto reached out to me. I didn't want to tell you. Your father died carrying out a mission given by Oh Kangto; I didn't think you'd react well."

"You're right. I probably wouldn't have." I need answers right now more than I need to get mad at him. "Go on."

Young glances at Daeho and Jinwoon. "You know us, Jaewon. We're all orphans. I mean, yes, I have a father, but I haven't spoken to him since I left the gang six months ago, and even before that we didn't speak, and he never was a real parent to me. We live in a world where orphans like us struggle to survive in gangs like Red Moon. Even the Kings isn't a great organization. When Oh Kangto reached out to me, I remembered your father, all his many sayings, that conviction he used to show every day. He wanted to change the world for the better. And I do too. I *believe* in Oh Kangto and the UKL. I want to make the world better for the kids we were, for the kids running those same streets now. But in order to do that, it all has to go—the Tower, the Dome, all the things that divide us, the symbols that oppress us."

Young places a hand on my shoulder. "What do you think? Are you in?"

"Ay, jasik. Being a gang boss has made you a talker."

"I've always been a talker. Now I just have people who are required to listen to me."

"I don't know if I'm in," I say, wondering what I've gotten myself into. There's no going back, though. "But I'm here. What's next?"

"Well, after blowing up the factories, we were supposed to meet up with Oh Kangto. He has this battleship. It's amazing, designed by the world's premier machinist, a woman named Kim Woori . . ."

My phone pings in my pocket. Damn it. Have they tracked it already? I pull it out, expecting a message from Koga about my defection. It's from Bora: "The Director came to the school. The entire student body was called out to the courtyard. I think it has something to do with Alex. Come quick."

"What is it?" Young asks, seeing my expression.

I grimace. "I have to go."

Young shakes his head. "You're an enemy of the state. If you're caught, you'll be imprisoned and probably killed without trial."

"It's Alex," I say. "He might be an asshole, but he's . . . a friend. From the sound of it, he's probably in as much trouble as we are. I'll be right back. Where's the meeting point?"

"Old Seoul."

Searching for a cab, I start to jog over to a side street.

Young follows. "You're cheating on me with Alex, aren't you?"

I wave him away with a laugh.

■ ■ ■

I'm in the cab, heading toward Apgujeong, when the billboards in the sky go static, replaced by a video feed. In the video, Oh Kangto, his wounds cleaned and bandaged, sits at a large mahogany desk. He wears a white hanbok. His empty hands are placed one on top of the other. Behind him on the wall hangs a massive flag, its most significant feature a taegeuk, a red-and-blue yin-yang.

Every screen—from the billboards to all personal devices, my phone included—has been taken over by the feed.

Oh Kangto's deep, arresting voice reverberates through the holos' speakers, echoing across every nearby audible device.

"This is a message to the Tower and the Neo State of Korea. My name is Oh Kangto. I am the leader of the United Korean League. We are a group of nationalists divorced from the NSK and the Neo Council. The purpose of our League is the eradication of the current military dictatorship and the restoration of the nation of Korea. We have an undying love for this country. We long to have it returned to all of us. To this end, we will engage in acts of violence against the NSK, starting with the Tower, a symbol of oppression. We will attack the Tower early tomorrow morning at 0400 hours. You have twelve hours to evacuate all people in a three-point-five-kilometer radius. This is not a threat. This is a forewarning."

34

PUNISHMENT

Dozens of camera crews wait outside the gates of Apgujeong Military Academy. A floating camera droid swivels in my direction as I approach. The red light of its lens hones in on my face and begins to emit a clicking sound as it takes a photo every millisecond. My face will grace the Internet in about .33 seconds. If soldiers aren't already on their way to arrest me, they will be soon.

I shoulder through the crowd, pushing droids away with the back of my hand whenever they get too close. The school must have activated its sound barrier, because once I step through the gates—my student ID granting me access—the noise of the outside disappears. I haven't been back in school for over a week, and it's jarring to see the sea of uniformed students spread out before me in the courtyard, eerily silent.

They all face the front of the school, their backs to me. I realize, stepping farther into the crowd, they're waiting for something.

As students recognize me, many of them move aside. Briefly I wonder if it's because they know I'm technically a fugitive. I break through the final line of students and come to a halt.

There's a large space at the bottom of the stairs at the academy's main entrance, the crowd forming a half-moon around the area.

I grab a boy to the right of me. "Why is everyone standing out here?"

"You don't know?" he asks, genuinely baffled.

"No, I—" I look past him up the stairs to the main entrance of the academy. Two NSK soldiers drag a limp, battered body down the stairs, holding it up by the arms. The prisoner's face is covered with bleeding lacerations as well as purple and green bruises. Lank hair sticks to his forehead, wet with his own blood. His hands are shackled in front of him with blue-metal braces.

At first I don't recognize him, my mind not registering what my eyes see, but then the soldiers reach the bottom steps, and the prisoner turns his face to the side, shooting a heated glare at his captors. He spits blood, and it hits the skirt of a girl standing too close. She lets out a loud yelp, and the crowd moves back to give them space.

"Ai—shhh," I curse, trying to press forward. I'm stopped by a hand on my shoulder. I turn to see Minwoo and Bora.

Minwoo drops his hand. "Don't," he warns. "You'll get yourself in trouble."

I'm already in trouble, but neither of them seems to know that. News of the demonstration must not have been broadcast to the general public.

"Jaewon-ah," Bora asks, always perceptive, "did something happen?"

I shake my head and look back at Alex.

"There's nothing you can do," Minwoo says. "You'll only make it worse. They say Alex disobeyed a direct order from his father—"

"What do you mean?"

Minwoo hesitates before answering. "I don't know. His father arrived at the school with soldiers and they searched the place. They found Alex with a girl. Apparently his father had warned him not to meet with her. I don't know why. Maybe she's an heiress or—"

A high voice, full of anguish, screams from behind the guards. "Alex!"

I watch as Ama sprints from the school building.

Hearing Ama's voice, Alex tenses, his eyes darting back and forth in panic. He braces his feet and jams his shoulder into the right guard, throwing him to the ground. The left guard grabs him around the waist, pinning his arms. Alex struggles, trying to shake the guard off, but his shackled wrists make it difficult.

I curse under my breath and rush forward. I pull the left guard off Alex, punching him in the neck before throwing him into the crowd of students. He doesn't reappear, and I'm guessing I either knocked him out, or Minwoo finished the job.

I turn to see Ama rush over to Alex, placing her hands over his shackled fists. I'm relieved to see that she hasn't suffered as Alex has—her face, arms, and legs are clear of cuts and bruises. Something's off, though, when I look closer at her. Even though she isn't showing signs of a physical fight, her hair is a tangled nest, as if she's just woken up from a fitful sleep, and her yellow dress—the one she purchased at the mall that day—is inside out.

"Why are they doing this? Why did they hurt you? I'll—I'll hurt them!" She looks wildly at the crowd and then up at the double doors of the school building.

The Director has appeared at the entrance, flanked by six NSK guards. Alex's father's shadowed eyes watch the couple.

Alex doesn't even spare his father a glance. Slowly he lowers his fists, forcing Ama to drop her hands.

"Alex . . . ," she whispers, confused.

"Ama." His voice is muffled by the bruising on his mouth. I can only make out what he's saying because of how close I stand. "We—*I* broke protocol."

"What do you mean? No, you didn't." She takes a step toward him, reaching out, but he takes half a step back. "You've taken care of me," she says, her voice faltering. "You've protected me. You're—you're everything to me."

He shakes his head.

"You loved me."

At these last words, Alex looks away, as if in pain, as if these last words hurt him more than the bruises and broken bones.

I can see the warring expressions playing across his features—confusion, frustration, and anger. I can tell the exact moment when his resolve takes over. He straightens his back, a shadow briefly falling across his face, and I know he's shut his emotions down under an unyielding shield.

He's made a decision, and he won't stray from it.

I get ready to take Ama away from him.

"I have . . . loved you," he says. "It wasn't right of me. I took advantage of you. It shouldn't have happened. I won't ask you for your forgiveness because I don't deserve it. Just know I regret everything."

"What are you saying?" she whispers. She doesn't believe him. I can see her eyes reading his, her mind seeking his. Whatever she sees in the dark depths of his thoughts causes her to break away from him in shock. She stumbles backward into my arms. She's so much smaller than me, smaller than Tera. I can feel her tears through my shirt as she turns, bunching her fists into my coat.

Alex meets my eyes over her head, his expression remote, giving away nothing of his thoughts. "Take her away."

I nod, ignorant of the specifics of the situation, but knowing that anywhere is a better place for Ama than here. She looks shell-shocked, unable to process what's happening. I think of safe places I could take her, but it's a useless endeavor. NSK soldiers are already approaching us.

I raise my hands in surrender. No use fighting when we've already lost.

Four guards break away from the group to lead us over to the school's main building. I pass the Director, keeping my eyes down. I swallow a curse when I see the blood on his knuckles from the beating Alex took inside the building.

We've made it up the stairs and through the sliding doors of the school before we hear the first bone-splitting punch, metal against flesh. Ama stumbles into me with a cry, as if she herself has taken the hit.

And maybe she has, if she's reading his mind.

Accompanied by our guards, we leave the main lobby of the academy and enter an elevator. I wonder how public the events of the demonstration are, or if news of Oh Kangto's impending attack on the Tower have taken over any and all feeds. Minwoo and Bora didn't seem to have known about the demonstration. The guards, although sticking close by, haven't arrested me.

At the roof of the school, we wait for a military transport carrier to arrive. I board it behind Ama, taking the seat by the window to block her from the view below. As we fly over the school's courtyard toward the Tower, the public punishment continues. Even through the noise-barred windows, it's as if I can hear the thick, wet *thud* of every punch. If Alex stopped picking his wretched body off the ground, I wonder if his father would end this. He takes each hit on his knees with a bitter solemnity. With every punch, his head pitches to the side, only for him to doggedly bring it back to its original position, his eyes meeting his father's as the Director's fist comes down again and again. It's a public punishment to show the city that disobeying the Director cannot go unpunished, not even for the Director's own flesh and blood.

"Is it finished?" Ama asks softly. She's looking down at her hands, curled in her lap. She means the public punishment.

I hesitate before answering. It's impossible to lie to a girl who can read my thoughts.

"It's finished," I say.

She nods, accepting the lie.

I could ask her how she got out of the Tower and met up with Alex—the last I'd seen him, he'd been leaving the hospital after we visited Sela—but it feels wrong to question Ama, especially when tears begin streaming down her face.

Is she crying because of what the Director has done, *is doing*, to Alex, or is she crying because of what Alex has done to her? The extent of his punishment suggests he probably slept with her, which was somehow made known to the Director. Why Alex and Ama were on school property, I have no idea. I'm guessing whoever discovered them identified Alex and informed the Director. To someone like the Director, Ama wouldn't be a girl but a weapon. An object created for him to command.

Maybe he'd forbidden Alex to meet with her. Whatever the case may be, it made him angry, and I don't think the Director even needs anger to justify beating Alex.

Ama stares down at her lap. Her curled hands unfold, revealing the open bud of a yellow rose at the center of her left palm. It's wilted, broken by the weight of her hand crushing it.

She brushes a petal with her thumb. "Roses shouldn't smell like smoke," she says.

I'm reminded of Alex's words back in the Tower. *I don't see the use of flowers.* And yet I recognize the rose she holds.

"Roses are your favorite flower," I say softly. "Yellow is your favorite color."

She nods, her lips trembling. She's quiet for a moment before she speaks. "When nothing is mine, why is it that I have to keep this feeling inside me? Why is this the only thing I'm left with?"

Her words are thoughts spoken aloud, and they're not for me. Even so, I wish I were someone who could offer her comfort, lessen some of the pain she must be feeling. Because even if we're not an intimate part of each other's lives, we share someone who always will be.

Ama's breath catches. "You're right," she says, raising her eyes to meet mine. "I have something more. I have someone more."

I don't have to read minds to know we're both thinking of the same person.

Tera.

Ama nods.

I remember my promise to Tera that I'd come back for her. I look at Ama and hold her gaze. *I'm going to help Tera escape the Tower. We're going to flee the city together.*

Ama lets out a small gasp. She brings her fist to her mouth, coughing to cover her surprise. Her gaze darts to the guards sitting directly across from us. She reaches out and takes my wrist, and for a second I think she's trying to seek comfort from me or give comfort to me, but then she squeezes, gently, and a series of images flash through my mind.

An aerial view of the Tower. The Skybridge. The inside of the hangar. And lastly, the image of Tera handcuffed in the room where the Extension had been held, glaring defiantly up at her captors.

Ama's voice is a light my mind. *When you find her, tell her I love her, that I will always love her.*

I'm dropped abruptly out of the visions and blink back a throbbing headache. The transport ship docks at the Tower. Ama still holds my wrist. As the doors open, she squeezes, putting pressure against my skin. *They're always watching you. Be careful.* She lets go.

I walk out and stand on the docking platform, where guards are waiting for me. They must know who I am and what I've done, because they roughly take me by the arm. Behind me, the transport doors shut before Ama can alight. The ship then glides away from the platform in a westward direction. There's nothing more I can do for her now. Where they're taking her, I have no idea.

But I do know this: even though she's breaking, she's not broken.

35

LAST GOOD-BYE

I'm escorted by a different pair of guards to a holding room right off the docking port. A guard spits the word "traitor" as they leave. I hear the familiar *click* of a lock engaging, and when I press my wrist to the scanner, the doors fail to open.

Dead-ended before I've even begun.

I pace the room, opening and closing my hands in frustration. At least Ama's left me with an image of where they're keeping Tera in the hangar. If I could just reach Tera and release her from the cuffs, then we could figure out a way to escape together. But first I have to get out of this room.

I sit on the bench and wait. Hours pass. What time is it? Oh Kangto plans to destroy the Tower at 0400 hours. I take out my phone, but it's nothing but static. The UKL must have shut down communications in the city.

The suffocating silence of the room is interrupted by voices in the hall. I press my ear against the door. When the voices grow louder, I step to the side, curling my hand into a fist.

The doors open. Alex stumbles in, falling to the floor. He's torn up, wrecked. The doors close behind him—my one chance of getting out—but it doesn't matter. I can't leave Alex, not like this. I crouch beside him.

"Don't. Let me be." His hands come up, aggravating his inflamed, open wounds. He sucks in a sharp breath at each prod of his fingers, as if purposefully prolonging his pain. I reach out to stop him. Like a whip, he grabs my wrist, forcing it to the floor. He opens his eyes to slits. "I said, let me be."

He lets go, and I don't move, frowning at the way his hand has left white pressure points on my skin.

The marks are already fading, but I'm reminded of Ama, the way she'd deliberately put pressure on my wrist so I'd take notice. Her words: *They're always watching you. Be careful.* I brush my fingers against the bump in my wrist. "Our scanners are tracked," I say, thinking aloud.

Alex squints. "I wouldn't be surprised."

I stand, looking around the room for something sharp.

My gaze falls on a plant in the corner and the bench, the only two objects in the room. This would be funny if it weren't so damn frustrating.

Alex curses, rolls to his stomach, and pushes himself up off the floor. Reaching into his coat pocket, he pulls out a short knife.

I must look surprised, because Alex laughs. "You're probably wondering how I managed to keep a weapon on me. They did search me back at the academy, before the beating. The mistake they made was not searching me after." Alex chuckles, clearly amused. "My father keeps knives in his boots. One fell out and I grabbed it. It wasn't strategic. I just happened to see the knife. My father always says to think on your feet. Or on your knees, in my case." Alex spits blood onto the floor.

I grimace. "You shouldn't talk. Your jaw might be broken."

"Whatever."

He holds the knife out to me, and I take it.

Gritting my teeth, I make a clean slit along the inside of my wrist, then reach into the flesh to extract the scanner. I drop the bloody device onto the floor, kicking it to the corner. I cut a piece of cloth from the bottom of my undershirt and begin winding it around the wound. I'll need someone to stich it up later, but for now, this will have to hold. Hopefully I didn't open any veins.

Other than the sound of my awkward movements, silence fills the space.

Alex closes his eyes, resting his head against the wall behind him. His face appears calm, relaxed. It's the opposite of the look on Ama's face right after she left Alex—it held an unmistakable grief, a terrible loneliness.

I tighten and knot the makeshift bandage. "Was it worth it?"

He opens his eyes. "What do you mean?"

"Was what you did worth it?"

"You mean," Alex says slowly, his eyes narrowing, "was sleeping with her worth it?"

I hold his stare. He knows what I mean. With one mistake—one choice—he's abandoned all his goals. I wouldn't call them dreams. Alex doesn't hope for things, live or die for things. But they were endeavors—to be at the top of his class, to be one of the few who'd earned a placement at the Tower. His next goal was probably as ambitious and as unattainable for anyone but him. Now they're all moot. By sleeping with Ama, he's lost the respect of his father and likely the admiration of the public.

Alex looks down at his hands, stretching his fingers. "I don't know what's worth anything anymore. All my life, my path seemed straightforward. One step leads to another. If I want something, I can have it. Nothing is out of my reach. My life is so structured. I wake up, I do what I have to do. What I want to do. I go to bed. I have no enemies. Not even Tsuko counts as an enemy, even if he is an asshole. Not even my father."

"You have no one you love." The words come out before I can stop them.

He closes his eyes, but not before I see his expression, of pain, of aching loss. "I wish I had someone who I'd be forced to love—a sibling, a parent. Someone who loves me. Ama, she's so innocent. I didn't mean to do it. God, I'm the worst kind of person."

He groans, curling over, his torn-up face in his bruised hands.

What must it be like for him to *know* the people who are supposed to love him couldn't care less that he was born? Even at my lowest, I knew my father loved me. Even at his bitterest, Young knows his father would rather he were alive than dead.

Alex can't say the same of his father. *Love is absent in a prideful father.*

Abruptly, Alex lifts his head. "Give me the knife."

There's a beat of silence.

"I'm not going to kill you," he drawls.

When I don't give him the knife, he scowls. "I'm not going to kill myself, either." He snatches the knife from me, turning it and pressing it to his wrist. He makes a deep cut.

"Shit, Alex!" He didn't have to go that far.

He pulls his tracking chip out of his wrist, shouting, "Ha, that was easy! You made it look painful." He pockets the bloody chip, then walks over to the corner, picking up the one I dropped. "They're readying me a transport ship heading to the war front," he says. "I'm to be stationed there as a foot soldier. A new beginning, as my father likes to think of it. Even if it is a death trap." He turns to face me. "If I get on the transport ship with your tracking chip, they might think you're with me. Hopefully this will steal you some time. If you leave now, you can still get to her."

I blink, startled. "How did you know?"

"I'm not a fool," he says dryly.

I get to my feet. "Alex—"

He shakes his head. "If you're waiting for a poignant good-bye, you're not going to get it."

"I was going to tell you to take care of yourself."

Alex sighs. "That's the same thing." He raises his fist against the door. "I'll cause a distraction. When they come in, make a break for it."

"That's not going to work. They're—"

Alex bangs his fist hard against the metal. The switch on the panel turns from red to blue, and the doors open.

I don't realize until it's too late that Alex still holds the knife. He raises it high, then brings it down to stab himself in the gut, crumpling to the floor.

In the panic that ensues—guards rushing toward Alex to stop the flow of blood, others rushing away to find a medic—none of them notice one more body fleeing the scene.

I'd worry more about Alex, but I have feeling he'd resent that. He's given me a chance, one I'd be a fool not to take.

Hurrying down a crowded, chaotic hall minutes later—the Tower in full evacuation mode for the UKL attack—a realization hits me: on this day, both Ama and Alex have helped me, each risking their lives to secure Tera's and mine. Theirs is a debt I hope to repay one day.

36

PARK TAESUNG

I'm running across the Skybridge when there's an explosion in the Tower. I'm thrown to the floor. Beneath me, I feel the reverberations of metal bending as the Skybridge gives an ominous groan. A screaming wind whips through the corridor in a howl. Above me, small fractures appear in the glass ceiling. There's another explosion, this one from up ahead. A wall of smoke plummets down the walkway, and instinctively I raise my arm. The storm sweeps around me, particles of the dust sticking to the sweat on my skin.

What's going on? The attack was planned for 0400 hours. I couldn't have been in that room that long. Outside the glass walls of the bridge, the sky is dark. It must be some time around midnight. I'd only met Oh Kangto briefly, but he didn't strike me as someone who'd go back on his word. If he says he'll destroy the Tower at 0400 hours, then that's when he'll do it. But if he's not triggering explosions in the Tower, then who is?

I push myself up and sprint into the smoke.

The loud thump of my feet gives way to a resounding echo as I enter the hangar. The smoke from the explosion is thick, and I can't see beyond my hands. I listen for the sounds of voices, gunfire, to suggest the Tower's under attack, but there's only silence. The floor transitions into a metal industrial walkway. I've been in the hangar once before and remember the design, an open space with upper floor industrial walkways level with the chests of GMs.

I take a step and catch myself on a railing, then shimmy to the right until my foot hits the edge of the escalator, powered off. I creep down the steps, listening ahead of me. Halfway down, I leave the smoke behind. Bodies are strewn about the hangar, dead or dying from gunshot wounds. I duck low, an open target on the escalator, but I don't see any signs of the enemy.

Then again, who is the enemy?

At the back of the hangar, the Extension lies on a flatbed. In Ama's vision, Tera had been cuffed on the floor of the back room where the machinist had been working with her on sims the first week I met her. Keeping low, I hurry the rest of the way down the escalator. I can hear the groans of the dying soldiers around me—except, they're not soldiers. They're engineers and machinists. They're civilians. I don't want to believe this of Oh Kangto.

I run across the floor of the hangar. Outside the back room, though, a figure slumps against the door. I recognize the stooped shoulders and thick glasses.

"Dr. Koga!" I crouch beside him. He has a bullet wound in his upper chest. I reach out for his wrist. Relief sweeps through me at the hint of a pulse. I need to find a medical kit, or he'll bleed to death.

He grabs my arm. "Lee Jaewon."

I tug gently. "Dr. Koga. Let me get you some help."

He shakes his head. His glasses are foggy with tears. "No." His breaths are shallow. "There's no time."

"What happened here?"

"We were under attack."

"By who?"

"I don't know. I couldn't see." He doesn't speak for a while, his breathing labored, but then he gathers his strength. "I wasn't lying when I said I didn't think of Tera and Ama as my daughters." He coughs, a low, wracking sound. "I'm too old to have daughters that young."

"You're not too old, Dr. K."

"I think—I think grandfathers have a special love for their granddaughters, don't you?"

I lower my head, unable to speak. He reaches for my hand and places a small metal object at the center of my palm, closing my fingers over it.

"The key to Tera's cuffs," he says. "I should have given it to her a long time ago. Will you give it to her for me?"

I nod and get to my feet. Koga closes his eyes. He's not gone yet, but . . .

"Go," he says.

And so I go.

The doors to the back room are slightly open, and I slip through. Immediately I see Tera, spotlighted at the end of the room, hands cuffed. She still wears the flight suit from earlier. None of this makes any sense. Why is she sitting there alone? My instinct tells me something's wrong. I pause on the threshold, still crouching.

Tera's eyes widen as she sees me. "No, Jaewon," she says, panicked. "What are you doing? You can't be here. You have to leave. It's a trap."

The lights in the room power on. I flinch and the door snaps shut behind me.

I'm met with a circle of guns held by a group of men and women, all dressed in black with masks concealing their noses and mouths. I stand slowly, skimming faces, recognizing none.

The circle breaks apart, and a man steps forward, pulling his mask down with a gloved hand.

"Welcome, Lee Jaewon," Park Taesung says. "We've been waiting for you."

I take a breath before responding. "Strange. I hadn't been expecting you."

Although I should have been. The bodies. Park Taesung doesn't care about hurting civilians to get what he wants.

Park Taesung takes a cigarette from his pocket and lights it.

A woman behind me snatches the key from my hand. "I'll take that." She walks toward Tera.

If they think thirty thugs with guns will stop Tera, they're in for a surprise.

Park Taesung watches me with a cold expression. He drops his cigarette, crushing it beneath his steel-tipped shoes.

"Why are you here?" I ask. "What do you want?" Is he here for Tera? Did he realize I never had any intention of bringing her to him?

"What do you think I want?"

I grasp for the obvious reasons. "Power. Money. Respect."

He shakes his head. "I have all those things."

"Then what?"

The smile drops from Park Taesung's lips, and for once, he looks deadly serious. "I want revenge. The Director and his little lapdog of a general are already amassing their troops. Soon they'll be here to try to take back the Tower."

"You won't win. NSK soldiers are trained in GM combat. Your thugs aren't."

"Yes, but I have the Extension, and I have Tera."

I frown. "She won't fight for you."

Park Taesung watches me, a curious expression on his face. "I know," he says simply.

He raises his voice to address the Red Moon members. "It's about to begin. Pick a GM and wait for my signal." They bow, disappearing silently through the door, leaving only two behind with their guns still trained on me.

What is Park Taesung's goal? He said he wanted to destroy the Neo Council and the UKL. But his actions suggest this is a coup d'état. Was this always his goal? Not to "end war" like some enlightened leader, but to instate *himself* in the seat of power?

Park Taesung closes his eyes. "It's almost time," he says. "Before I go, there's something I'd like to share with you. A story, if you will."

I shake my head, frustrated. "General Tsuko's main target will be this hangar. He'll want to take out the weapons before you can use them. If any of us hope to survive, we need to get out of here. Now." I calculate the time elapsed since the first bomb. We've got minutes before Tsuko arrives with a GM aerial battalion.

Park Taesung ignores me, his mind rooted in the past.

"The story begins with two friends. They grew up together on the streets of Old Seoul. They were nothing alike. While one believed he could take what he wanted with force, the other believed in earning the right to the things he wanted. One believed in forgiveness, the other in revenge. Yet that didn't stop them from knowing beyond a doubt that they'd do anything for each other. They treasured each other, because in a world as cruel as theirs, finding a true friend to trust was the only kindness afforded them.

"When the time came for them to serve their military quotas, they left for the war front. It was in their platoon where they met a man unlike any other they'd met before. He had thoughts they never thought to think. He had dreams they'd never hope to have. He was charismatic, brilliant. He was a revolutionary. He believed in a unified Korea. He believed in a nation. One boy got caught up in the fervor of that dream. The other didn't.

"Four years later, when they returned from the war, they

came back to find that a girl in their neighborhood, a girl who had followed them around when they were boys, had grown up. Kim Sunhee was a very beautiful girl." Park Taesung stops speaking, as if lost in his memories.

"To this day, I still think she's the most beautiful girl in the world. Even though one boy could only offer her heartbreak, she chose him anyway. It's a simple story, really. The girl chose one boy. That one boy chose revolution. And the other boy was left with nothing."

I hold his gaze. "You want revenge on my mother for choosing my father. You want revenge on my father for choosing the revolution."

"No," Park Taesung says. "I want revenge on a world that destroys more than it gives. I want revenge on a world that allows these choices to be made. I want this city, this *nation*, to burn and suffer and *feel* what it is to give up on its people."

"It's not the world's fault. It's the fault of the people. If they can destroy it, then they can fix it."

A strange look passes over Park Taesung's face, a look of loss and confusion. "You sound just like your father."

"Jaewon-ah?" I turn to see that Tera now stands uncuffed. A rush of relief sweeps through me. Together we can get out of here. But she doesn't move. What is she waiting for?

There's a *click*. Park Taesung holds a gun to my head. "I'm sorry," he says, "but this story doesn't have a happy ending."

"Jaewon-ah!" Tera screams.

"Don't move. I *will* shoot him."

Tera's fast, but there's a chance she won't get to me before he or the other two Red Moon members get a shot out.

And she won't risk my life. Park Taesung *knows* this. He's using our feelings for each other against us, as he always has. He walks around me and kicks the back of my legs. I fall to my knees, then look up into his face. I realize that I'm more familiar with his face than I am with my father's. The scar. The cold eyes. The small frown on his face that sometimes makes me think maybe, maybe he'll change his mind, that although this is the path he's chosen, that he'll step off or turn back. It's never too late.

There's a sharp pain in my shoulder from behind. An empty tranquilizer clatters to the floor.

"Lead Tera to the Extension," Park Taesung says to the other Red Moon members in the room. "She won't resist."

My blurred vision only catches the shadow of Tera as she leaves the room.

"That's the trouble when you love someone," Park Taesung says. "It gives even someone with inhuman powers the most human of weaknesses."

We all have this weakness, I want to say. *Except for you.*

"Sleep, Jaewon-ah," Park Taesung says, his words sounding muffled. "This world isn't safe for kind-hearted people like you and your father."

My hands are on the floor, my cheek pressed against the stone. I'm falling into the deep abyss of oblivion. My last thoughts are of Tera and how if love is a weakness, then how it is that I—even with the world darkening around me—have strength in the hope that Tera and I will find a way back to each other?

Everything goes black.

37

C'EST LA VIE

I'm jolted awake, thrown from a bed onto an ice-cold floor. My stomach drops, and I feel the familiar pull of gravity as the floor and ceiling dip and rise. I'm on an airship. I scan the room, taking in the details. Beside the bed is a low metal table with one chair. I get to my feet, and the door to the room slides open.

"You're awake."

For a moment I'm speechless. The newcomer wears a flight suit, her pink-tinged hair pulled back in a fierce ponytail.

"Sela? What are you—?" A sinking suspicion grips me. "How should I feel right now, gratified or betrayed?"

Sela raises an eyebrow. "I'm not in Red Moon, if that's what you're implying."

"Then this is an NSK ship." What the hell did I sleep through? Has Park Taesung's coup ended? Did Tsuko arrive to take back the Tower?

Where is Tera?

I start to panic, my heart hammering in my chest.

"Lee Jaewon, focus," Sela says. "Remember when you visited me in the hospital. I told you I wanted to ask you something."

I think back to that morning, only yesterday. I'm reminded of why Sela had been in the hospital in the first place. She'd been shot. Looking at her now, she stands with one hip cocked, no evidence of a gunshot wound.

"What did you think I was going to ask you?"

"I thought you were going to ask me if I liked you." It sounds ridiculous now, but it's what I thought at the time. My mind had been on Alex and Ama, and on how Ama's favorite flowers were roses.

"Do you like me?" Sela asks the question without emotion, her expression giving away nothing.

I answer with the truth. "I don't know you."

The starry-eyed singer is gone, replaced by an intelligent, enigmatic girl. Sela's lips quirk in a small, barely there smile. "Let me tell you who I am. My name is Gu Saera. Eighteen years ago I was born in the Neo State of Japan, to parents of Korean descent. My parents were nationalists who fled the NSK when accused of having UKL sympathies. When I was eight, they were assassinated in our home. I was spared only because the assassins didn't know I was there. My mother told me to be quiet, and so I was. I didn't make a sound. It's ironic, considering who I am now, the NSK's representative vocalist. Most everyone in Asia has heard my voice."

"C'est La Vie's a cover," I say, not hiding my amazement. The most famous band in the Neo State is a *cover*.

"Yes."

I shake my head, replaying all our conversations in my head, everything I know about her. "You're one hell of an actress."

"I know. I've won awards for it." She smiles, a confident, knowing smile.

The ship tilts, and we brace ourselves, reaching out to hold the walls. "I was wrong, wasn't I? About the question you were going to ask me back in the hospital?"

"I was going to ask you to join the UKL," she says. Before I can respond, she shakes her head. "I wasn't going to ask you because I think you are a great soldier or because I think you'd add anything to the revolution." She pauses. "No offense."

I grimace. "None taken."

"I was going to ask you because I thought it was what Oh Kangto would have wanted. Oh Kangto is like a father to me. He adopted me after I was abandoned by the neighbors who found me crying beside the bodies of my parents. When I had nothing, he gave me everything. He gave me my brothers, my family. He's given me an unconditional love that is—that is . . ." She searches for a word. "Unrepayable. He's given me the means to fight for what I believe in. He has never asked anything of me in return." She takes a breath. "Not until today. Today he asked me if I would save the son of a friend he had loved."

To think, one man had loved my father enough to hurt me, and another had loved him enough to save me.

I open my mouth—to say something, to thank Sela—but suddenly the ship takes a sharp turn. We both stumble, missing the walls and falling to the floor.

Sela's the first to jump to her feet. "What is he *doing?*" she asks cryptically before rushing from the doorway. I'm quick to follow.

She runs down a short hall, passing through a set of double doors that slide open at her approach to reveal the ship's bridge. My stare passes over the crew, situated around the bridge in various concentrated roles, and focuses on the clear shield of glass separating the bridge and the sky. Now I understand the reason behind the erratic movements of the ship.

We're in the middle of a battle raging over Neo Seoul.

The ship's pilot, C'est La Vie's friggin' drummer, expertly directs the ship through a melee of battling GMs, fighter planes, and bombers. Her two guitarists act as gunners for the ship, shooting down any GM or aircraft that gets too close.

"Nunim." A tall boy with a shock of dyed white hair swivels in his chair to face Sela. "We just received a message from the commander. They've begun the countdown for the Ko Cannon." Which means it's nearly 0400. Oh Kangto's final threat is imminent.

I look up past the battle raging beneath the Dome to the

higher sky above it. A massive battleship looms overhead, an island in the sky. The triangle of light that signifies the Ko Cannon glows a bright red, aimed directly at the Tower. When the cannon is fully charged, it'll let out a powerful beam of energy, a concentrated nuclear explosion that'll break through the Dome and destroy the Tower and everything in a three-and-a-half-kilometer radius. The outcome is undeniable, and yet the battle still rages on.

C'est La Vie's drummer swerves the ship out of the way of a falling GM, its metal chest incinerated through.

"That's going to fall on the city," I say. My gaze flits across the battlefield, from burning aircraft to burning aircraft, all crashing-falling toward the city.

The boy with the white hair pulls up a live video feed of Neo Seoul. It's lit with the blue light of explosions.

There's no sound, but I don't need to hear the screaming to know what it sounds like. The bridges from Neo Seoul into Old Seoul are packed with civilians attempting to flee, but it's after midnight, and the Dome has solidified. They surge against the barrier that traps them inside. It's chaos, anarchy. In order to prevent enemy aircraft from entering the city, the government must have refused to lower the barrier for fleeing civilians.

"This is what Park Taesung wanted. Not the Tower, but total destruction of the city."

Sela nods, her expression grim.

"Tsuko should have realized Park Taesung's intent. Why didn't he recall his troops?"

Sela grimaces. "Tsuko's been . . . preoccupied."

The white-haired keyboardist pulls up another live video feed. In it, two GMs clash in a ferocious battle: the Extension and Tsuko's famous God Machine, the Shi.

The Shi, an entirely black GM with red eyes, blends almost seamlessly with the dark sky. It's a stark contrast to the bright red and orange of the Extension. They light up the night with every clash of their swords, causing reverberations in the sky, only to fly backward, releasing a barrage of bullets with stunning accuracy. The other battling GMs give their ruthless leaders a wide berth.

I grit my teeth. "How long have they been fighting?"

"Since the battle began," Sela says. "Three hours ago."

They show no sign of lagging.

Tsuko's Shi swivels out of the way of the downward arc of the Extension's blade, an impossibly quick movement.

One of the gunners whistles. "How is he so fast? He's gotta be Enhanced."

"He is," Sela says.

I turn sharply to Sela. "He's on Enhancers?" I'd easily believe it, except for the fact that, even at his angriest, he's still completely in control. If he were on Enhancers, he wouldn't be so composed.

"No," Sela says. "Tsuko's not on Enhancers. He's Enhanced." Sela holds up three fingers and puts one down with each name. "Ama. Tera. Su. Tsuko was the only subject of the Amaterasu Project to survive the Su variant."

I frown. "How?"

"An anomaly. They've been conducting studies, but so far have had no results."

"What can he do?" the left gunner asks. We watch as the Shi brings its sword down. Tera blocks the attack, sparks flying. With the way they're angled, they appear locked in an embrace, neither one of them moving.

Is he speaking to her as they fight? What is he saying to her?

You must know that you can have no future with him, so why are you giving into such a false hope? Is he repeating those words to Tera?

"He has a combination of the skillsets that both the Tera and Ama variant have, but to a lesser degree. He's Enhanced physically and mentally."

I stare at Sela. "He can read minds?"

"I don't know the full extent of his abilities. I stole into the Tower's archives and read his file, but it's not conclusive. His doctor died before his trial was completed, and he was immediately recruited into the military."

A loud *crack* outside the Dome eclipses Sela's last words. Oh Kangto's battleship has released a powerful blast that hits the Dome, sending shock waves across its curved surface. It's not the battleship's main Ko Cannon, but a lead-in, a warning of what's to come.

"Ai—shhh," the pilot curses. "We need to get out of here before the commander looses the cannon. Once the Dome breaks, we'll need to outfly the aftershocks."

"Right," Sela says. "Let's move out. We just need—" She cuts herself off, gasping. A lone shock of plasma pierces through a crack in the Dome. Like lightning splintering through the sky, it hits the very tip of the Tower. The searchlight, which had been blaring red throughout the chaos, goes dark. We collectively hold our breaths, watching as the searchlight of the Tower plummets a kilometer. It lands directly on top of the GM hangar, crushing it.

"Shit," says the right gunner into the silence. "Good thing we got you out in time."

The pilot leans forward, squinting. "What's that?"

There's a light streaking through the sky.

The screen zooms in on the Extension flying through the night at a breakneck speed. It hurtles to the ground, landing by the collapsed hanger. The red beam of its scanner sweeps the debris.

The chest of the Extension begins to open—Tera, trying to get out—but suddenly the Shi is there, slamming it to the ground. The Extension twists, shooting a missile straight into the Shi, throwing it back a league. It returns to the hangar, falling to its knees. Again Tsuko stops Tera from opening the chest of her GM, this time grabbing the Extension from behind. He alights into the air, taking her with him.

The hangar explodes again. If I'd still been alive in the hangar after the impact with the searchlight, I'd have been dead now.

Tera's GM struggles out of Tsuko's grip, treading air.

Their battle recommences, but something's off. Tera's movements, once quick and sharp, are erratic, reckless. Every move she makes is filled with desperation.

362

It's as if . . .

"It's as if she's given up the fight," the ship's pilot says, voicing my thoughts. "What wrong with her?"

There's silence on the bridge.

I turn to see Sela staring, not at the screen, but at me. "She has nothing to fight for. Jaewon was supposed to be in that hangar."

My hands curl into fists. "Is there a GM on board?"

One of the gunners answers before Sela can stop him. "Just the standard one for scouting. It's in the hold."

I sprint out of the bridge.

"It's damaged though," he shouts after me. It doesn't matter. I just have to reach Tera.

I find a hatch in the ship's hull, opening it to reveal the open chest of a GM directly beneath, cramped in the small cargo area of the airship. I swing my legs onto the seat.

"Jaewon!" Sela shouts, catching my bandaged wrist. "What are you doing?"

"I'm leaving."

"What do you mean, you're leaving? The whole point of Oh Kangto sending me here was to get you. I can't let you leave."

"I have to."

"Shit, Jaewon. Oh Kangto's going to release the cannon any minute. He's going to shatter the Dome. We need to get out of here. Now."

I flinch at the pressure of her hand on my wrist, and she lets go. "Sela," I say, looking up at her, seeing the way the hallway silhouettes her hair in a golden light, "back in the hospital, you asked me if I knew whether mugunghwa were your favorite flowers, the way Alex knew that roses were Ama's."

"Are we seriously talking about this right now?" she shouts, exasperated. "Who cares? It doesn't matter."

"It matters because I don't know Tera's favorite flower. I don't know what her favorite color is, or what food she likes to eat when she's sick, or what she thinks of first when she wakes. But I want to. I *want* to know everything about her. If she doesn't have a favorite flower, I want to show her all the kinds in the world until she finds one. I want to show her that life isn't made of battles to be won. That life isn't about winning or losing, and that her existence doesn't need to be something she needs to deserve. That the fact that she exists is enough, always."

Sela swallows, watching me. "I'm not a sentimental person, Jaewon."

"How could you not be?" I grin. "Your songs are so depressing."

I sit down in the seat of the GM's cockpit, adjusting the controls, powering on the screen, and checking through the inventory of weapons. This scouting GM only comes with a common sword and a power rifle.

Sela still stands in the hall, watching me from above. "We're going to release the Ko Cannon whether you're in the vicinity or not."

"Good." I nod. "If the Tower's gone, Red Moon and the NSK won't have anything left to fight over."

I feel the underbelly of the ship opening beneath me. The sounds of the screaming wind and the booming of heavy gunfire meet my ears, deafening. Soon the GM will drop from out of the airship's hold and straight into the middle of the battle.

Sela reaches out, keeping the chest of my GM from closing. "Jaewon," she shouts over the wind, "what do I tell Oh Kangto? What do I say to him when I stand before him without you, and I have to tell him I've failed?"

Her voice cracks on the word "failed," and I realize how much Oh Kangto means to her.

I look up at Sela, meeting her worried gaze. "Tell him . . ." I hesitate. "Tell him to do what he needs to do. Tell him that I'll see him soon, and that"—I give Sela a smile that's full of everything I'm feeling: determination, anticipation, and a burgeoning, unbreakable hope—"I won't be alone."

38

TSUKO

I fly through a battlefield in the sky.

God Machines burn and fall around me. Hundreds. Thousands of them. They light up the night with a dizzying array of colors—deep blue and blood red. You'd think something as colorful as this would be beautiful. In simulations, a battle is just a game, but in real life, battles are full of endless sorrow.

What are they fighting for? Who are they fighting for?

In the distance, Tera and Tsuko continue their isolated struggle, swerving in and around the Tower, blind to the chaos around them, to the battleship looming above us all, its main cannon primed to obliterate.

Several kilometers from the Tower, my transmission picks up the audiolink between Tsuko's and Tera's GMs. I try to respond, but the communicator in my GM is damaged.

"I won't let you do this," Tsuko is saying. "You can't exist with a false purpose."

The sound of Tera's voice answering fills me with longing. "Please," she whispers. "Why are you making this harder than it already is? Why can't you just leave me be?"

Tsuko takes another powerful swipe at Tera with his GM's bladed hand. "You're an abomination, a weapon without a purpose. If you won't fight for the Neo State, then you won't fight at all."

She raises her shield, blocking his attack. "Leave now," she pleads. "If you stay, I'll end up killing you."

Tsuko laughs harshly. "You can try." He takes another downward swipe. Tera breaks to the left, narrowly avoiding the slash of his blade. "I'm doing you a favor, Tera. You've wanted to die all along, haven't you? Come. *Here.*" He makes a grab for her. A sharp thrust of his blade pierces the side of her GM's chest, leaving an ugly gash. "Why won't you die?" Tsuko shouts. "If you love him so much, then you should join him!" He strikes again with his blade, gouging a piece of metal from her plated armor.

Inside my GM, I look at the distance marker on the screen. I'm still thirteen kilometers out from her.

Tera's voice is so soft I can hardly hear it. Turning up the speakers to their top volume barely brings her voice through. "I do love him," she says, and I catch my breath. "Is that so hard to believe?"

"No," Tsuko says. "I believe it of you. Just like I believe Ama was fooled into thinking she was in love with Alex. Both of you are weak and pathetic, thinking you're more than you are, humans instead of weapons. After I kill you, I'll find Ama, and I'll kill her. You're both defective. The project has failed in you."

"The project may have failed in us," Tera says, her voice hard, "but it has failed you if you believe you are no less human than we are."

"Be quiet! I am not like you." He plunges his bladed arm toward her. But this time, he's too focused on the attack—acting on his emotions. He makes the critical mistake of leaving himself defenseless. Tsuko's blade embeds itself to the hilt into Tera's shoulder, but she uses the momentum of his attack to wrap one clawed hand around his head, jamming the other into the Shi's gut and ripping out a portion of its most central gears.

She releases him. The Shi sputters, the gaping hole in its abdomen sparking. Tsuko attempts to lift its arm, causing a small internal explosion and pushing it back through the air.

The fight between them is over. The battle has its final victor.

Left unharmed in the Shi's chest, Tsuko's options are few. He can surrender. He can self-detonate. Neither of them seem like viable options for the general of the NSK.

The Extension and the Shi float in the air, motionless, the crystal apex of the Tower spiraling behind them toward the broken sky.

Tsuko's voice, when it comes, is quiet. "What are you waiting for, Tera? Finish this. Kill me."

A pause. "I can't."

"If you don't kill me now," Tsuko growls, "I will come after you. I will never rest until you are dead."

"I don't believe you."

"Then you're an even bigger fool than I thought."

Tera lowers her weapons. "Su," she calls, and Tsuko gasps at the sound of his name spoken softly from her lips. "If you had asked me to fight for you, I would have. Because even at your cruelest, you were always mine, in the way Ama will always be mine. In the way—in the way Jaewon should have been mine." She takes a heavy breath. "You say that I cannot love because I am a weapon, but it's strange; I cannot kill you now. I don't think I could kill you ever."

"I don't . . ." Tsuko chokes.

I'm almost there, just a hundred more meters.

Above, there's a terrible booming sound, the crackling, deafening static of electric fire.

The sky is lit entirely red.

This is no preliminary shot. This is no warning. This is it.

"Tsuko, listen to me!" Tera shouts. "This doesn't have to be the end. It's never too late to choose a different path. Ama, you, and me, we can start over. The world is changing, day by day. We can be part of a new future, a future of our own making."

Fierce pride and joy courses through me at her words. Even after everything—the captivity, the experiments, the loss of so many of her friends and loved ones, she has the determination to live. She has the hope of a future.

"Help me, Su! Help me build a better tomorrow."

"Tera," Tsuko says, and strange, but for the first time, he sounds almost . . . content. "I never told you this, but before I came to the Tower, every day of my life I spent alone. Afraid. Nobody understood what it was like to be me. You and Ama were my first friends, my only friends. I'm sorry for all the pain I've caused you both.

"I'm sorry for everything, but I'm not sorry for you." The Shi's red eyes flicker and turn black. Its engine finally gives out.

"From time to time," he says, and though I can't see him, I can hear the smile in his voice, "won't you think of me?"

The Shi drops from the sky.

"Tsuko, no!" Tera shouts.

Everything happens within a breath of a moment.

The Ko Cannon shatters the Dome.

My GM reaches Tera, slamming into her. The force carries us a distance away, but not far enough. Behind us, I feel the massive heat of the plasma cannon as it shoots out of the sky, piercing the Tower clean through. There's a roar of sound, the surge of the explosion fanning out, a wall of energy sweeping toward us.

We're caught in the heart of the blast.

I watch through my melting cams as the paint on the Extension's face peels off, the advanced armor beneath withstanding the heat.

My GM is made of a weaker metal.

I don't even know when the bar meter goes from red to

broken. It's completely black inside the cockpit, black and burning. This GM will explode in a matter of seconds.

I jam the soles of my boots against the metal of the GM's chest until it gives. It opens to a shattered sky, one without a Dome.

I only have time to think one thought, one name, before I jump.

EPILOGUE: NEW WORLD

Neo Seoul is a city that dreams of a better tomorrow.

At the NSK's Apgujeong academy, a girl and boy stand gazing out a window, their faces turned toward the sky of the greater Gangnam area.

"Bora-yah," the boy asks, pointing, "what's that? It looks like pieces of stars falling."

"Ay, Chang Minwoo." The girl laughs. "When did you get so romantic?"

"Just now, I think. I mean, look at it. Isn't it beautiful?"

The Dome that was once a part of the sky is gone, blown to rose-colored fragments of light. The fragments float down like crystallized snow. Or as the boy likes to think, like stars.

The girl wonders if this is the beginning of a new world.

■ ■ ■

On an airship fleeing Neo Seoul, a cold-eyed man looks out at the destruction he's brought upon the city he'd once promised to protect. He feels no regret. He knows that there will come a day when he'll return to this city—once beloved, now hated—to finish what he's started.

■ ■ ■

In a warehouse in Old Seoul, a young boss rescues a group of girls, kidnapped by the now-disbanded Red Moon gang. He's joined by another boy with a silver crown pinned to his shirt. "I think we got them all, boss," the boy says, panting. "They're a little traumatized, but I think they'll be all right."

"Good job, Daeho-yah," the boss says. "We'll bring them back to their families."

Daeho frowns. "What about the ones who don't have families?"

"We'll be their family," a third boy says, taller than the other two. "We won't abandon them."

After his friends leave, the boss looks up at the sky. A moment of deep sadness hits him—he wonders if he'll ever see his father and his best friend again—but then the sadness passes. The future is bright and new, and he has hope in what tomorrow might bring.

■ ■ ■

At the center of the bridge in a crowd of refugees fleeing across the broken Dome's barrier, a woman calls her young son from the railing. "Jaeshin-ah. Don't stand so close."

He doesn't answer. His eyes are riveted to the sky.

"Lee Jaeshin!" she calls. "Come here right this minute!"

"Eomma!" he cries, pointing. "It's a shooting star."

She thinks of scolding him. She even opens her mouth to follow through with the thought, but then he turns from the railing. For a second, she can't breathe—he looks just like his father and brother.

"Eomma," he says, "I made a wish!"

She smiles. "What did you wish for?"

"That hyeong will like me, that he'll want to play with me when I finally meet him."

The mother holds back the tears that rise unbidden to her eyes. "Of course," she says. "I know Jaewon will love you."

■ ■ ■

In the sky above Neo Seoul, there's a boy, falling.

And there's a girl reaching for him with the extended arms of a God Machine.

She catches him gently in the palms of her GM's hands, bringing the cradled hands of the machine near to its chest so that when it opens, he's right there, waiting for her. She jumps through the air, landing beside him. "Jaewon-ah!" she shouts, taking the boy into her arms. "You're alive! What were you thinking? How could you just jump like that? When you were the one who tried to stop me from jumping off the Tower!"

"It's a little different," he says, feeling a little dazed from the fall, and from the way he feels in her arms—safe.

She scowls. "How so?"

"I knew you would catch me." The boy grins a lopsided grin.

The girl can't tell if it makes her more furious or more overjoyed; all she knows is that it makes her heart race.

His grin grows wider. "I heard what you said, you know."

The girl frowns to hide the sudden blush in her cheeks. "It's easier to speak of love when you think the person you love is lost to you forever."

He thinks of making a joke about leaving, but her lips are trembling, and he thinks maybe he can save the jokes for a different time.

"I'm sorry I took so long to get to you," he says softly.

She nods. "But you did get to me."

"Yes. I tried really hard."

"Did you?"

"I needed to get to my girl."

"Is that all I am? A girl?"

"Yes," he teases. "That's all you are."

She frowns again and he laughs at her annoyance. He likes this vulnerable side of her.

His body hurts all over, but it doesn't stop him from sitting up. He takes her face in his hands. "You're just a girl. A girl I think I'm falling in love with."

"You think?"

He brings her face closer to his. "How do I show you how I feel?" he whispers against her lips. "How do I show you how much you mean to me?" Softly, he kisses her. He thinks, with growing wonder, that it's a different feeling to kiss someone you love.

He hurts everywhere, his wrists, his stomach, his legs. But it's like the pain leaves with her kiss, replaced by something stronger, something that burns within him. He moves one hand to the back of her head, drawing her closer. He's so desperate to show her how he feels that when he finally ends the kiss, they're both breathless.

She stares at him, at his boyish, dazed smile and bruised lips. She feels a little stunned. She doesn't think anything could make this moment better than it already is.

"I love you," he says.

■ ■ ■

My father used to say that the way he loved me was the same way he loved his country, a fierce pride that couldn't be contained, and for a long time I couldn't understand that, and maybe I still don't understand.

All I know is that I love Tera. It's a knowing that in one person I have peace and home and family. If this is how my father felt about his country, then it must be something to fight for.

Tera squeezes my hand. Together we'll fly to Oh Kangto's battleship in the sky, and maybe for a little while, we'll be safe.

■ ■ ■

Love is a country. It's vast and endless and full of an unbreakable hope.

Maybe this love is a love that's worth dying for, I don't know. All I know is that it's worth living for, again and again.

REBEL SEOUL

annyeong: hello

appa: father (informal)

ajumma/ajumeoni: a middle-aged woman/formal address

ajeossi: a middle-aged man

Apgujeong: an area of Gangnam, Neo Seoul; location of Jaewon's military academy

banmal: informal language used when speaking to close friends or children, denotes familiarity; when addressing another person, the informal ending is: -ah/-yah

Banpo Bridge or Banpodaegyo: a major bridge over the Han River

Busan: a city located on the southeastern tip of the Korean peninsula

chaebol: a business conglomerate

daebak: jackpot (informal)

dojang: a formal training hall for martial arts

Gangnam: a district of Neo Seoul; location of the Tower

geojinmal: a lie, a "false word"

geonbae: "cheers"

Incheon: a city located on the northwestern part of the Korean peninsula

jasik: rascal

jondaenmal: formal language used when speaking to elders or strangers, denotes respect; when addressing another person, the formal ending is: -ssi

jjajeungna: annoyed, irritated

halmeoni: grandmother

Han River or Hangang: a major river that flows through current-day Seoul, South Korea

hanbok: a traditional Korean article of clothing

hangeul: Korean alphabet

Hapjeong: a neighborhood of Mapo, Old Seoul; location of Jaewon's apartment

harabeoji: grandfather

Hongdae: a region of Old Seoul, near Hongik University; gang turf for the Seven Kings

hyeong/hyeongnim: older brother; males use to address older males/formal

kkangpae: a gangster

manhwa: comic books

Mapo: a district of Old Seoul

Mount Baekdu or Baekdusan: a mountain on the Korean peninsula, shares a border with China

mugunghwa: Hibiscus syriacus; the national flower of current-day South Korea

muk-jji-ppa: a variation of the rock-paper-scissors game

Neo Seoul: the capital of the Neo State of Korea, south of the Han River

nuna/nunim: older sister; males use to address older females/ formal

noraebang: a song room, a private room for karaoke

Old Seoul: north of the Han River, northern half of present-day Seoul

odeng: a fish cake

oppa: older brother; females use to address older males

ramyeon: instant noodles

saekki: curse word

saturi: dialect; for example, "Busan saturi" means "Busan dialect"

seonbae: upperclassman

sinsegye: new world

soju: an alcoholic beverage

taegeuk: symbol on the present-day South Korean flag

eomma: mother (informal)

won: the currency of present-day South Korea

ACKNOWLEDGMENTS

To my editor, Stacy Whitman: I could have not asked for a more perfect editor for *Rebel Seoul*. Thank you so much for your enthusiasm for this story and its characters. Because of you, this book is the best possible version of itself. 고마워요. Thank you to marketing geniuses, Hannah Ehrlich and Jalissa Corrie, as well as to my brilliant copyeditors, Shveta Thakrar and Yeojoo Lim. To Lee & Low and the rest of the Tu Books team: it was an honor to receive the New Visions Award and have this opportunity to work with all of you.

To Elizabeth Casal for the fabulous book design and to Sebastien Hue for the coolest cover ever!

To my agent, Patricia Nelson: thank you for your belief in me and your enthusiasm for my books. Because of you, I have confidence in my writing and have never been more excited for what the future might bring!

To all my friends throughout the years who have encouraged me in my writing, and who have helped me become the person I am today. Special thanks to: Gabby Sutjiawan, Stephanie Huang, Diana Fox, Lucy Cheng, Michelle Thinh Santiago, Megan Hurtz, and Jennifer Kwong.

To my Las Vegas and SCBWI-Nevada friends, so great to have found my people in the desert! Special thanks to Cynthia Mun, love you 언니, you inspire me every day with your hard work, boundless enthusiasm, and generous heart.

This book began as a draft in 2013, and has been shaped by the loving hands of many wonderful critique partners over the years. To my CPs who help me every day to grow as a writer, this is for you:

To the Speculators: I look forward to many more years of friendship and laughter! Special thanks to David R. Slayton, Liz Mallory, and David Myer for early encouragement and feedback on Rebel.

To the Sailor Scouts/Oh My Dramas crew: Nafiza Azad: in you, I found a friend who loves books the way I do, and Karuna Riazi (a.k.a. Kaye): you are the CP I have known the longest, and the writer whose beautiful words always remind me why I love reading in the first place. So proud of you, friend.

To the Magick Six: Candice Iloh, Devon Van Essen, Stephanie Willing, Michelle Calero, and Gaby Brabazon: couldn't be more proud to be a part of this talented group of women!

To Thudsters/Writer's Block Party: This year has been the best because of all of you! Shout-outs to: Mara Fitzgerald, Katy Rose Pool, Erin Bay, Amanda Haas, Meg RK, Maddy Colis, Melody Simpson, Christine Lynn Herman, Amanda Foody, Ashley Burdin, and Ella Dyson. Special thanks to early readers of Rebel Seoul—Akshaya Raman, friend and confidante, your enthusiasm and generosity of spirit is a constant strength to me—and Janella Angeles, the Jessie to my James! I'm grateful every day for having you in my life! *loud Stitch noises* *insert a million emojis*

To Michelle Kim: for your advice about "saturi," and also for always shaming me for not reading the books I recommend you, and to Judy Lin: thanks for being an awesome Pitch Wars mentee, but an even greater friend!

To the many teachers and mentors in my life, thank you for your encouragement and generosity: Ellen Oh, Professor Jin-Kyung Lee, Jeremy B. Gregersen, Susan Goodman, Tracey Baptiste, David Elliott, Jason Reynolds, and Michelle Knudsen.

To all the booksellers, bloggers, and librarians: Thank you, thank you! I knew I was a reader the first time a librarian gave me Ella Enchanted in elementary school. I knew I wanted to be a writer at the first book signing I ever went to in college at my local bookstore. The community that loves books is the community I belong to.

To my family: 친할아버지, 친할머니, 외할아버지, 외할머니, 사랑해요, to all my aunts and uncles, Como Helen for always supporting me in my writing and feeding me yummy foods, Uncle Doosang for always asking, "What are you reading?", to Como Katie for all the happy memories visiting you in Florida and going to Disney World, to Como Sara for introducing me to Robin McKinley when I was eleven, to Como Mary for your enthusiasm and love, and to 외삼촌 and 외숙모 for giving me my first K-pop album—Finkl's Blue Rain; to all my cousins: Bokyung 언니, Adam (the original Stinky), Xander, Saqi, Jennifer, for introducing me to H.O.T., Jim, Wyatt (my favorite cousin), Bosung & Wusung, for tolerating my extreme love of K-pop, Busung, Sandy, Susie, Christine, we need to have another *Escaflowne* marathon, Kevin, Bryan, Josh, and Scott. I love you all so much!

To my cousin Sara: Words cannot express how much you mean to me. You are my older sister, friend, and confidante. Thank you for reading everything I've ever written, and for the long, late-night convos, and the laughter. I love you!

To my cousin, Katherine: If I had included you in all the groups above, I would have thanked you three times already! CP #1, jaeger copilot, K-pop and K-drama fangirling buddy, Song Joong Ki, Trowa and T.O.P.'s wife, BFF and 언니. Thank you for your belief in me, and for the sweet jokes. Love you!

To my puppy, Toro. Mong mong!

To my brother, Jason. 보고싶어.

To my sister, Camille. Favorite sister ever! Love you, love you!

To Dad, I've never gone a day without laughing because of you. I love you!

And lastly, to Mom, I am a writer because of you. You are my first reader, my strongest supporter, the person who gives me the most confidence and who has always believed in me. I love you with all of my heart. Thank you.

AUTHOR'S NOTE

Neo Seoul is a fictionalized city based on the geography of current-day Seoul with many authorial liberties of the imagination. My love of the sci-fi technology of Japanese anime and my interest in Korean culture, past and present, all influenced my creation of this brutal, but often beautiful fictive future that I hope brings enjoyment to readers.